PHANTOM PACT
THE BEARER'S BURDEN

CHAD QUEEN

ENCODED PRESS

*To my mother, who taught me to push the limits of
imagination.
And to my father, who taught me to push the limits of
perseverance.*

ACKNOWLEDGMENTS

I could not have created this book on my own, especially being a first-time novelist. So many talented individuals helped me shape this book into what it is today, and I would like to take time now to thank each one.

I would like to thank my first editor, Andy Meisenheimer of NY Book Editors, who took my early manuscript and helped me understand how I could transform it and keep the vision of the world I had built.

A special thank-you goes to my developmental editor, Erin Young, who was instrumental in helping me craft the version of the story as it exists today. And thank you to the talented Allister Thompson, who provided the copy editing for the book.

Thank you to Katherine Stephen for proofreading and thank you to Alyssa Queen for the final proofreading and editing.

The cover illustration was created by the exceptional James Ma, and Jake Clark provided the masterful typography and formatting of the print and ebook versions of the novel. The map illustration was created by Robert Altbauer of fantasy-map.net.

Special thanks go to my early beta readers, Allison Queen and Brian Bander. And a thank-you to Adam Poe, Amanda, Lee, and Rachel of Frostbite Publishing for their help and feedback on the book.

The unique constructed language for the world of Phantom Pact was built by language expert Joseph Windsor.

Of course, the deepest and most heartfelt thanks go to my family: Alyssa, Wyatt, and Naomi. I spent years building the details of this story, and I am so very thankful that they put up with a dad whose head is constantly jumping between worlds.

And thank you. It takes a leap of faith to pick up a book by a new author. I have done everything I can to make sure your trust is not misplaced.

No more stalling. Let the adventure unfold.

PHANTOM PACT
THE BEARER'S BURDEN

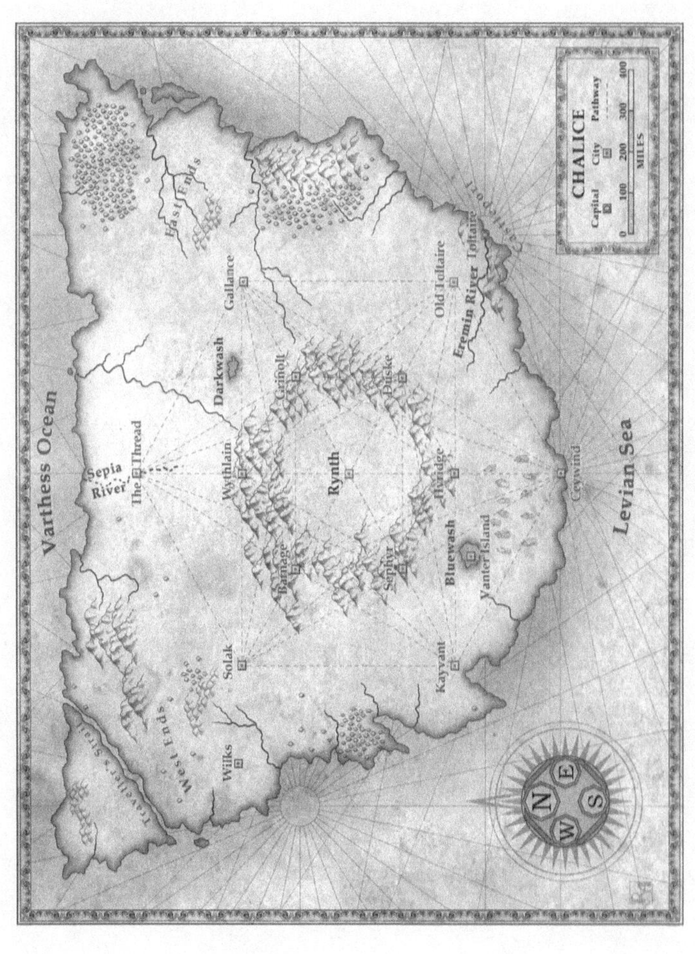

Varthess Ocean
Levian Sea
Sepia River
The Thread
East Ends
West Ends
Traveller's Strait
Gallance
Darkwash
Wythlaim
Barnage
Grinolt
Rynth
Solak
Wilks
Sapphor
Kayyant
Bluewash
Yanter Island
Huidge
Pluske
Old Toltaire
Eremin River
Toltaire
Ilodestone
Ceywind
CHALICE
Capital
City
Pathway
MILES
0 100 200 300 400
N
E
S
W

PROLOGUE

HOME

*Pity the Bearer of Phantoms. While the powers he possesses
are vast, he labors with a burden far beyond measure.*
—*Excerpt from* The Book of the Traveler

ONE MORE DAY, Cade Elegy thought as the hills before
him screamed of battle. One more day to keep the dream of
hope alive, or one more day until the dream vanished
for good.

They assembled the last of their remaining army to bear
upon Gigan's Hill. Just beyond lay a great structure known
as the Thread—the bastion in which the mysterious enemy
known as the Wraiths had taken refuge.

Hulking soldiers of the Wraiths, humanoid yet
possessing an exoskeleton like a great mantis, swarmed the
battlefield. While they looked like giant insects, they also
bore a striking resemblance to humans—walking on two
feet, and articulating finger-like appendages on their hands.
Within seconds, the enemy surrounded their entire legion.

There were thousands more than reported. Their intelligence was wrong.

"What are you waiting around for? *Move!*" Commander Jord Black of the 12th Bearer Corps led the mission. Cade didn't need to be told twice. The unit advanced, rushing toward the enemy line.

They were the tip of the spear for the assault. The mission was simple in order, but not in execution: kill the Wraith scouted in the area—a message to the world the Wraiths were mortal.

Cade fought, taking down one creature after another, as the rest of his dwindling unit fought alongside him. The smell of gunpowder and smoke hung thick in the air. The clash of weapons and the cries of agony bled together into a nightmarish cacophony. "Get down!" A voice pierced through the chaos. Jord's voice. Cade felled another creature as he turned to find a Bearer-class grenade hurtling toward their position.

Time slowed to a crawl. Jord snatched the grenade with both hands and threw himself down on the ground.

Cade reached out—a futile attempt to halt the inevitable. A dark, metallic color spread across Jord's body as the man attempted to harden his body against the blast. As the grenade detonated, the concussive force tore into Jord's body. Cade looked away.

Selfless to the end, Cade thought. A wave of grief swelled within him, outmatched only by the rage following in its wake. There wasn't time to mourn; he had to keep moving. He knew Jord, and Jord's determination to finish the mission. "You will, my friend, you will."

Cade afforded himself a moment to close his eyes, searching for the phantom Jord left behind in death. It was there, faint but recognizable to Cade amongst the discordant sounds of combat. Cade spoke the words, the ones sealing a pact with his former commander.

Cade, bolstered by Jord's phantom, fought with renewed vigor. They needed to cut straight through to the camp with their dwindling force. It would be suicide, but it was the only option left.

"Incoming!" a corporal wailed as the body of a soldier hurtled past him.

"Hells," Cade spat.

A gigantic creature, one Cade had never seen, lumbered toward him and the remaining men. Exposed sinewy muscle and dark metallic plating covered its body in overlapping segments, like the scales of a reptilian beast.

He continued to fight—fight for Jord, fight for the phantoms he bore, fight to live to sing the songs of those who had passed.

His zeal got the best of him. As he struck at the massive creature, he felt the last of the power granted by his phantoms drain from him. The creature lunged at Cade. His vision went dark as excruciating pain enveloped him.

When he came to, Cade found himself hoisted on the shoulders of the soldiers from his unit. He felt his sidearm against him, hot as if discharged, though he had no recollection of firing it.

But it did not matter. They had won the battle. They had defeated the Wraiths.

They could go home.

COUNTLESS BLACK MOTES swirled from Cade's sight as the waking vision ended and he returned to reality.

It's over. It's over, he thought again to calm himself, his heart still pounding. The war was over.

The drug the military issued to members of the Bearer Corps still brought him these unbidden visions. They called the side-effect "veiling". Cade was glad he no longer needed the vile stuff.

Protector of the Realm, they now called him. Cade tried on the honorific as the vibrations from the railbus he rode rattled his tired mind. The title didn't fit. He shut his eyes as he sat in the seat of the passenger car and tried to control his breathing.

He was almost home. His mind raced, still trying to process the end of the war. The king himself had heralded Cade a hero. And his prize, the only one that mattered, lay at the end of this track.

The old metal railbus slowed, and his heart beat faster. The car was near bursting with passengers eager to return home. He was thankful they left him be. The newfound celebrity he gained in Toltaire, the capital of Chalice, was unnerving. He preferred the quiet comfort of his simple home, and above all else the company of his wife and children.

The thought conjured up memories of them, waiting at the table for him. His youngest, Jessa, unable to sit still, bounding from the table and running circles around the kitchen, wooden spoon in hand. Etan, just shy of ten years old, leafing through an archaic tome from the library, one he had already read at least six times before. Cade smiled.

And his wife, Serafina. Her smooth brown hair falling just past her shoulders, her soft green eyes melting him with a simple glance, and her smile. He could see it with perfect clarity, the same smile she would give him when he saw her again. His heart skipped a beat. It still did, even after all these years. She would busy herself with some trivial chore, awaiting his arrival. When she was nervous, she had to keep herself occupied with some task, no matter how menial it might be. She would look out the window, trying to glimpse him walking up the worn red-brick path that led to the house.

The once boisterous passengers settled down as the railbus slowed. Soon, the entire car was silent. *Something is wrong*, Cade thought. His eyes snapped open, and he rubbed the sleeve of his worn duster jacket on the dirty window. He could just make out the village coming into view. There were many long, colorful banners pulled taut from building to building, congratulating the returning soldiers. But something felt off. He looked at the houses and storefronts surrounding the humble train station.

"Where is everybody?" an old man said, clutching his hat to his chest as if it might fly away from inside the car. Cade continued to scan the village, but not a single person was in sight. It was not a large village, but there were always people roaming the streets, and there should have been a crowd gathered to welcome them home.

The railbus was coming to a stop, and while most of the passengers stayed frozen in shock and confusion, Cade leapt from his seat—not bothering to grab his rucksack—and threw open the door to the still moving railbus. He jumped, tumbling across the gravel ditch running alongside the tracks. He stood up, ignoring the rising pain from his fall, and cut a path through the center of town.

His head whipped from side to side, trying to glimpse someone, anyone who might have answers as he sprinted down the brick road.

"Was the city evacuated?" he panted to himself as he stopped to catch his breath. The sun was at its highest point, and his heart raced as sweat beaded upon his forehead. It didn't make sense. The war was over. They wouldn't have evacuated, not anymore.

The pit that had formed in his stomach grew like a rooted weed. *Stay focused, Cade,* he told himself. *Don't panic. There must be an explanation for this.*

He turned the corner from the main road, down the street to his house. He could see the house now. The faintest bit of smoke trickled from the cobblestone chimney. *There, you see?* he thought. *They must be there.* But he did not slow his pace. Cade ran up the steps, trying to peer into the front window. He expected to see his wife poking her head out and then calling to the children, but there was no sign of her. The door was already ajar, and he could see the brass hinges of the front door had been ripped from the frame. He popped the leather strap securing his caster, a rare handgun of ancient origin, and drew the firearm from its sheath.

"No. No, no," he said as he threw the door aside. "Sera? Etan? Jess?" he called out, going from room to room. No reply. He entered the kitchen, where all he found was a single white plate shattered upon the floor in front of the sink.

Cade wheeled around, frantic, his heart pounding. His right arm, still clutching his weapon, fell to his side. He closed his eyes and tried to control his breathing.

He listened, not for signs of life, but for the absence. His body trembled, not prepared for the answer. As the heartbeat in his eardrums subsided, he heard the music he did not want to hear. It was like the song of a music box, its notes spilling out one by one as the cylinder turned. It was the song of a phantom; of one who had passed on but remained with one ethereal foot planted within the world of the living.

It was the song of his family—gone.

Cade's knees gave out. He collapsed to the floor, fighting back tears. His family...taken from him—murdered. The entire town, taken. The war was over. Who, or what, could have done this? He pushed his grief down deep within himself, and his face grew hot with anger. He had fought to protect his family, and now he was alone.

No. Not alone. He was a Bearer. One who could ally with phantoms.

He spoke the words his father had taught him long ago. "Song that lingers unfinished," he said, his voice a hoarse whisper. "The one whose sigh has escaped to the stars..." He could feel the energy of the phantom grow as he spoke. "Allow me to sing your final verse."

The song—notes drifting from an unfathomable instrument played as if hidden behind a divine curtain—became clear, grew louder, and swallowed him whole. He held his breath as the notes played within him, becoming a part of his own song.

A maelstrom of memories and emotions that were not his own crashed and roiled inside him. He clutched his head with his hands as if to contain the deluge. His mind shifted and transformed as the phantom became part of him, already adapting to survive within the shared space. The storm retreated, and Cade lowered his hands, breathing heavily.

A faint voice echoed within him. "Pact accepted."

1

THE TAKEN

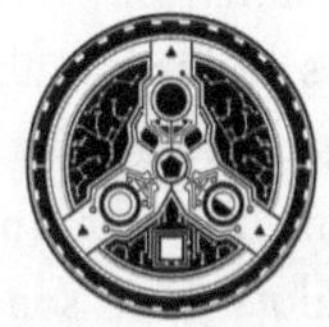

Through encoding, a Bearer can use a phantom to absorb the properties of the world around him. With careful practice, he can make himself lighter, heavier, or even stronger.
—*Excerpt from* The Book of the Traveler

ONE YEAR LATER

ONE MORE DAY, Cade thought as he fell upon the broken stones of the road. It was a promise he made to himself far too often. He rolled to the side as a rusted blade swept down where he fell, cutting into the road, sending bright orange sparks scattering into the night. The weapon —clumsy and slow—a relic of the war—wasn't meant for a human adversary, but the man hadn't much of a choice after Cade stole his sidearm.

His opponent, overcommitting on his swing, was off-balance. Cade encoded tungsten into his left hand. Even under the meager scraps of light the night afforded, he saw his hand turn a dark silver, the color moving across his skin like a shadow. He brought his fist square into his attacker's jaw, shattering it. The man crumpled to the ground, unconscious.

Cade crouched low to get a good look at the man's face. He didn't recognize him, but he did recognize the red robe of an Acolyte. The upstart rose from the ashes of the war and campaigned tirelessly for members while denouncing Bearers and anyone associated with them. Their presence confirmed his suspicions from the information he had gathered. These robed zealots were somehow wrapped up in systematic genocide. But why?

He sniffed at the air as he ran through the street, the tail of his duster jacket rustling behind him. The air was thick with an acrid smell, like wood smoke, only sharper. It was not unlike the smoke in the air at Gigan's Hill, one year earlier. *Am I too late?* Every lead followed in the last year had left him empty-handed. Thousands of people taken, one town after another, and not a trace left behind.

Cade looked up to get his bearings but was met with a starless night—the habit still hadn't died. There had been stars before the war—a reminder of infinite possibility. Now the night only brought the claustrophobic reminder of failure.

The sole source of light came from the Thread—the Wraith-controlled facility over five hundred miles to the east. Visible even in the far reaches of Chalice, the thin thread of white light projected straight up, piercing the sky itself. As he hurried through the town, arcs of energy from the Thread radiated through the night sky, like a cage of sinister energy.

Cade sprinted past building after building on the main street. All were quiet. *I'm too late,* he realized. Faint wisps of smoke rose from the chimneys of houses, where not a single person stirred within. It was if all the residents had just vanished. Almost no sign of resistance or struggle. Just...gone.

He ran, hope dwindling, until he came to an abrupt stop at the edge of town and looked across the hill at a group of buildings just outside the city.

In one of them, a candle burned to life.

Cade approached, taking careful steps and keeping outside the sight lines of the building's windows. As he drew closer, he recognized the structure of a Bearer training camp. Bearer camps had been common in the Ends. It was critical to keep them far from the front lines to prevent the Wraiths from finding them.

He surveyed the area and found the camp to be almost identical to the one he trained in as a recruit: barracks, combat dummies, encoding obelisks, and a target range used for decoding practice. He made note of the layout. The locations of the stations here might be of use to him.

He crept his way up toward the lit building—a mess hall —careful not to alert the occupants. He noticed a small metal sphere, no larger than a piece of fruit, perched upon one of the window sills of the building. It hummed to life as he neared it. Cade froze and cursed under his breath. This was not the first time this had happened. Every time he neared one of these ancient machines, this would happen.

Careful. It's a trap.

That voice again, Cade thought to himself.

Sometimes Cade heard a phantom he bore like a quiet voice in a storm. But this voice was strong and clear, as if there was someone talking right next to him.

You need to listen to me.

"Sure, whatever," Cade muttered and thought better of

it. He shook his head. *Don't acknowledge the voice*, he thought. He was losing his mind. Hearing voices was a sure sign of it. But it didn't matter to him if he could tell what was real and what wasn't.

It is difficult for me to contact you. Every time I do, I risk detection.

Cade rounded a corner and saw that the flickering light was within the mess hall.

A familiar voice, thick and raspy, cut through the night. "I know you're out there, Cade. Come on inside and let's have a chat."

Cade sighed and entered the hall, letting the double doors swing shut behind him. Dusty old tables and broken benches littered the room. Abandoned packs were tossed into the corner, and a lit stove warmed a battered copper pot. At the end of the hall, leaning back on two legs of a chair, sat a short and stocky man. He bore a wiry gray beard, making him look far older than his years would have suggested. He wore the deep red robes of the Acolytes.

"Rast? You're an Acolyte now?" Cade asked.

"Cade! Thought you were dead, I did. At least that's what everyone told me. Come on over and have a drink with me."

Cade stepped forward and paused as he caught the faint glimmer of a tripwire. He halted and raised an eyebrow.

Rast shrugged.

"You always fought dirtier than most," Cade said.

"And you never fought dirty enough." A wide smile spread across Rast's face, revealing worn teeth. "It's been over a year since I last saw you on the battlefield."

Cade shook his head. "We don't have time for small talk. I don't know what you're mixed up in, but you can still help me. It's not too late. All the people taken from the villages...you and I both know it's not the work of raiders. What are the Wraiths up to?"

Rast looked down, a chuckle escaping his travel-chapped lips. He rocked back and forth, ever so slightly, his jaw tight, as if biting down upon an imaginary bridle. He relaxed and spoke.

"Dammit, Cade. You don't know what *you're* mixed up in." He looked up and shook his head. "We can't stop them. You don't understand the Wraiths...what they are capable of. The things they have taught me make the encoding techniques we learned look like cheap party tricks. As an Acolyte, I have a chance. *You* still have a chance."

"No. You were on the battlefield, same as me. We're nothing to them."

Rast snorted. "Maybe so. But I like my odds better on this side. The Wraiths left me behind for you. You're lucky it's me and not one of those other putty-brained Acolytes. They don't even remember their own *names*." Rast gestured to the door. "Take your leave and stop looking. It's the least I can do for a fellow soldier."

Two approaching from the back of the room. The voice again.

Cade would never stop, and it seemed Rast knew it. He looked down at the tripwire and closed his eyes. He readied the phantom within him.

Almost in range—now.

Cade kicked the tripwire and encoded with tungsten, the dark silver color eclipsing his arm as it hardened. The tripwire triggered an axe secured to a long pole from the ceiling. It swung out like a pendulum to greet him. Cade used his hardened hand to deflect it and sent it into the man on his right.

The other man took aim with his sidearm and fired off three rounds. The man-made firearm wasn't powerful enough to hurt him while he encoded, but it might leave a mark.

This is what happens when you don't listen to me.

Cade ignored the comment and encoded with aluminum, becoming lighter. He swung hard to his left and lunged toward his opponent, also adorned in the red robes of the Acolytes. He switched his encoding to lead and slammed his elbow into the man's chest. The man groaned and collapsed.

Cade looked to Rast—or at least where Rast had been. The old soldier had always detested a fair fight. "Fair fights make for fair corpses," he'd once said during his time in the Bearer Corps. Cade had half-expected the man to defect to the Wraiths.

Cade left the hall and scanned the camp in the dim light. No movement.

I can sense him.

Cade made his way to the looming obelisks in the training gauntlet. With them, Bearers learned to shift their body composition from flesh to a different material using encoding.

Each obelisk possessed a core element. Tungsten, aluminum, and even wood was utilized. It was much easier to encode when more of the material was available. The slabs towered over Cade and were large enough for even a neophyte Bearer to encode with the material.

There.

With so many places to hide, Rast had to be there. He made his way to the encoding area, staying low, careful not to give Rast any more of an advantage. Cade rounded the corner of the first obelisk—steel—when the obelisk slid forward and slammed him hard against another obelisk of solid stone. He encoded with steel to keep from being crushed between the two obelisks, but the pressure built until both obelisks came free and fell to the ground with Cade caught in the middle. He strained against the weight, but the steel obelisk on top of him wouldn't budge.

The old soldier shook his head as he looked down on Cade. "You should have just died back on Gigan's Hill."

Cade grimaced under the tremendous weight as he tried to catch his breath. "I was never any good at dying."

The man laughed. "I like you, Cade." Rast, kneeling beside him, pressed his weathered hand down on the steel obelisk with phantom-assisted strength. "It's a damn shame they want you dead so bad." The man winced, his jaw tightening once more. He took a deep breath and refocused on Cade.

"Either your phantom will tire out and you'll be crushed, or you'll encode too far and become a permanent statue." Rast shook his head. "But that's just cruel, and I wouldn't do that to an old friend." He unbuttoned the holster strap on his right hip, pulled out his sidearm, and pointed it at Cade's head. "You deserve a soldier's death."

Rast was right. Cade could die either of those ways. But as he had hoped, the man had underestimated him. Cade encoded to diamond and felt a rush of strength course through him.

He heaved the giant chunk of steel forward, flipping it onto Rast and pinning him to the ground.

Cade stood up and looked down at him. The man's eyes were wide with surprise, and blood started to pool underneath him.

The soldier's face paled, his breathing labored. He looked up. "You have more than one phantom kicking around in that thick skull of yours? Hells, I should have guessed."

Cade kneeled next to him. "You don't have much time. Tell me what the Wraiths are doing with them. And why are you and the other Acolytes helping them?"

The light in the man's eyes grew dim as he coughed and shook his head. "Not much time...what a relief that is. I'm doing you a favor by not telling you a damn thing."

Cade took a breath, trying to quell the anger rising within him. "We fought together once. Help me one last time."

The man chuckled.

Cade's eyes narrowed as he grabbed Rast by the collar, eliciting a bloodied cough from the wounded man. *"You will give me answers."* He took his free hand and pressed the palm hard against the fallen obelisk, but a dull grunt was all Rast could afford.

"War's over, Cade. We lost. But you're still on the battlefield." Rast snorted as a cruel smile stretched across pained features. "Don't worry...I'll say hello to your wife for you." Rast's breathing slowed, and he was no more.

As the old man's body grew cold, so did the trail Cade had followed for the last year. He stood up over where Rast's body lay, his head bowed low under the starless night.

2

RESOLVE

A song plays within each of us; it vibrates through everything we do, telling our story and entwining with those around us. This is the essence of the phantom.
    —*Excerpt from* The Book of the Traveler

ASHLYN WINSHIRE HURRIED down the grand hallway of the castle as fast as her court attire, a light blue dress with far too many skirts for her liking, would allow. Her uncle, Rolan, had sent for her.

She was already grinning, though it was not becoming of royalty, or at least that's what her etiquette teacher would have her believe. Ashlyn did not care. Her uncle just had that effect on her. She remembered how he would, without fail, bring her back some trinket or oddity from his travels when she was a child. One time he brought her back a chocolate filled with delicious crème made from the petals of a yalis flower. They soon learned the flower possessed a mild amatory effect when young Ashlyn ran around the castle, trying to kiss all the boys. That had been a fun day.

She smiled to herself. Of course, the incident had not endeared Rolan much to her father.

Ashlyn kept up her pace through the winding hallways of the castle. She hoped Rolan's new contact from Rynth had secured the information they needed regarding the disappearances around Chalice. Her father had refused to let her pursue the matter, insisting it was the work of raiders and the Chalician Navy would handle the incursions. But Ashlyn and Rolan suspected more. Ashlyn would prove to her father she was every bit as capable as her younger brother, Elon.

As she neared her receiving room, she slowed, raised her head, and smoothed out her dress. She was already beaming in anticipation of seeing Rolan. Her uncle always had a way of making her happy. With her mother no longer around and her father busy with the rule of Chalice, she was closer to Rolan than to anyone else in her life. She turned the corner to greet him and froze.

Lying on the white marble floor of the small room was Rolan. She rushed over to him and fell to her knees. "Rolan? Rolan?" she said, trying to rouse the man. She placed her hand over his chest and could only make out the faintest of heartbeats.

"Help! Someone please help!" Ashlyn yelled.

A guard rushed in the room. "Princess? What is the..." The man fell silent when he saw the body on the floor.

She looked up at the guard. "Fetch a doctor and my father straight away." The guard nodded and sprinted down the hallway.

"Rolan, don't you leave me. You can't leave me." His eyes opened partway upon hearing her voice. He lifted his hand and rested it on his chest. She took his hand and held it. "That's it. You stay with me." He smiled at her one last time, and his face went slack.

Ashlyn bowed her head as the tears came, one by one, soaking Rolan's navy blue vest.

A man wearing a crisp white button-up shirt with rolled sleeves entered the room. He carried a brown leather medicine bag, which he set down beside him. He knelt next to Rolan and checked his wrist for a pulse. Ashlyn made no acknowledgment of the man's presence. She just sat beside her uncle as her heart went numb. She blocked out the sounds and the swirl of activity as she stared at the face of the man who had loved her like he would his own daughter.

"Ashlyn? What is the meaning of this? You must clear the grand hallway at once." Her father, King Liam Winshire, followed by his long train of advisers and sycophants, swept into the room.

Ashlyn only looked up at her father, expression blank and unable to speak.

The man cast a brief glance toward Rolan. "A shame," he said as he turned to one of his advisers. "It is not surprising, with him running off like a man half his age would do. It was just a matter of time. See to it he has a proper burial."

Her father had never liked Rolan. The king blamed Rolan for allowing the assassination of his wife, Queen Sashion, after the end of the Wraith War. Ashlyn had been in court the day Rolan pledged himself to the king's service after her mother's death. Her father's reply: "I'll ask for your help when I'm ready to meet my wife again."

Rolan blamed himself for Sashion's death, and he felt honor-bound to do what he could to atone for his failure. That was when he swore an oath of fealty to Ashlyn.

Despite everything that had happened, Ashlyn didn't

understand how her father could treat him so coldly, even in death. "Father," she called out, her cheeks growing hot.

He turned to her, his expression stern. He opened his mouth to reply when a breathless messenger ran up to the king. "Your Highness. The, ah, Wraith. It's here. It seeks an audience." The king muttered something under his breath and strode from the room.

Ashlyn sighed and looked once more upon Rolan.

"Ashlyn..." Ashlyn looked up to see her brother, Elon, had entered the room. He sat upon an ornate wheelchair, crafted by the king's chief artisan. Complications in childbirth had rendered Elon lame, but the king was nonetheless overjoyed to have a son and heir to the kingdom.

Ashlyn didn't bother to look up. She hardly knew her brother outside of the handful of awkward exchanges they shared at official events. To Ashlyn, Elon was just a younger version of her father. "Don't. Just...don't," was all she could say.

She heard Elon heave a sigh as he wheeled himself out of the room, following her father's entourage.

A symphony of odd, clacking sounds echoed down the hallway, as if a hundred walking canes were making their way down the hall. Ashlyn looked up to see a procession of Skex marching past the room, their striated tan exoskeleton appendages scraping across the marble. Though she had seen them run on four legs—which was a terrifying sight— these were upright on their two hind legs. Their hands, if you could call them that, possessed long, finger-like appendages that gripped the energy rifles they were known to carry into battle. Their heads appeared to be encased within metal helmets, which had no opening through which they could see. She still did not know how they could navigate without eyes.

Ashlyn knew little about the creatures other than they were the hands of the mysterious Wraiths. They were both soldiers and beasts of burden, guarding key Wraith outposts or carrying supplies back to the Thread.

Marching in front, astride the beasts, were a pair of Acolytes in their flowing red robes. Though they wore no expression, their faces appeared strained, as under some unseen duress. Ashlyn knew little about them, other than they were connected to the Wraiths, though she could not fathom why.

Within the center of the procession walked a solitary Wraith. Ashlyn caught herself holding her breath. It was rare to see a Wraith in person since they rarely visited the cities of men. They were rumored to dwell within a vast ship among the stars, looming above Chalice. The Wraith had the same basic features as a human, but everything about it felt wrong. The way it walked, the way its eyes moved within its head, and above all, the haunting voice with which it spoke. It wore simple black robes, and its skin was a shiny dark gray, almost like polished coal.

It turned its head toward her as it passed and fixed its unnatural eyes on her. It smiled, and the sight of it sent a cold shiver reverberating through her.

She regained her composure and pushed aside her anguish. She looked up at the adviser who was now talking to the doctor. "Leave me," she said.

"I'm sorry?" the adviser asked.

"I wish for a moment alone."

"Yes, yes. Of course," the man said, and he and the doctor exited the room. Ashlyn stood, closed the doors, and locked them.

Ashlyn surveyed the room. Her uncle was not young, sure, but he was hale and hearty for his age. She refused to believe he died of something as mundane as a heart attack.

She spied a broken teacup on the floor. That wasn't surprising. Her uncle loved tea. "The blacker the better," he would always say. He was not a morning person and would generally drink five cups of the earthy stuff before starting his day.

Ashlyn furrowed her brow. What was upsetting her now was less what she saw than what she didn't see. Where was the teapot? They always served his tea with a full pot. Unless someone had already taken it from the room? She knelt and sniffed at the rug where the teacup had fallen. She could smell an almost floral note in the spilled tea. "My uncle would never have taken more than a sip of tea like that," she said aloud.

Continuing to explore the room, she found that his folio, the one in which he kept all his notes and correspondences, was nowhere to be found. Her uncle was never without it.

She knelt next to him again. "Somebody did this to you, Uncle. What did you discover?" She looked at his vest, where his hand rested, and could see a faint black spot that had seeped through his vest. Her eyes grew wide. She reached inside the lapel of the vest, her hands still shaking, and broke the stitches of the secret pocket Rolan had sewn into its lining.

When she was a little girl, she would steal away with his coat and run around the palace pretending to be a world-famous spy, just like her uncle. Rolan started hiding candy in secret pockets he had sewn into his jackets to see if she would catch on. She had nearly forgotten.

Whatever is in this pocket cost him his life, she thought as she pulled a sealed letter from the vest. She stood up, her eyes filled with determination. "I'm going to finish this, Uncle. And I'm going to find whoever did this to you."

Ashlyn thought she could hear strange music playing somewhere in the distance, perhaps down the hall. It was unlike any music she had heard before, yet it bore a sense of familiarity. She shook her head.

Ashlyn opened the letter and scanned its contents. "But where do I start?" she found herself saying out loud. "Who can I trust? If only I could just ask you—" She snapped her fingers.

"I know who can help us."

3

NOCTURNE'S CALL

Beware the Bearer of many phantoms. Their minds twist and fracture, losing all sense of self.
—*Excerpt from* The Book of the Traveler

AT TIMES LIKE THIS, Cade wondered how he ended up in the only town that had a drug dealer with a conscience.

"You've been cleaning me out of Nocturne lately," Tic said. "It's not the easiest thing to get, you know? Plus, the rate you are gulping these down, it can't be good for you. I'm pretty sure your dose is too high. Have you heard of veiling? That's a thing, you know? One minute everything is normal, the next everything goes—"

Cade held up his hand. Tic was a good kid, which some might think strange to say, considering his line of work. He wasn't cut out to be a dealer. Tic just cared too much about his clients. But life hadn't given him the opportunities he needed. He easily could have been a healer in Toltaire, had he the means.

Cade, hand still raised, cast a furtive glance over his

shoulder. Tic was in his usual spot, standing in the alleyway adjacent to a small pharmacy where he worked during the day. A few overflowing cans of trash lined the wall but did not provide suitable cover for Cade's tastes. He would have preferred to be somewhere more private. But he had no choice. The voices were getting louder.

"You told me I could count on you when I needed it. Has that changed?"

Tic looked down and sighed. "I know, I can't help it —I've read—"

Cade didn't hear the rest. He grabbed his head, wincing. It was getting harder to think clearly. He shouldn't have been away for so long.

"You okay? You don't look so good."

Cade looked at the mouth of the alley and saw a small group of children running by. He shoved his hands into his pockets even though he had already taken off his rings.

"Listen, it's not good for business if I lose one of my best customers to my own product. I can't synthesize this in my lab, you know? I have to import it from black market military surplus, and no one even knows what's in it. This is as nasty as it gets."

Cade's hands shook, and he felt as if he were being pulled in many directions at once. He had shared his mind with his phantoms for too long. Cade tried closing his eyes, but it only made the sensation worse. He forced them open and took a deep breath to steady himself.

Cade glared at Tic. "Either you give me the Nocturne *right now* or I'll let your parents know how you've been helping pay the rent."

The young man paled. Even in his state, Cade still felt a pang of remorse; Tic was just trying to help. Tic reminded Cade of himself when he was a young man. A mess of brown hair, a lean but strong build, and a quiet disposition. That youthful image of himself came back for a moment before he remembered what he looked like now, too many scars to count, hair cut short, and his eyes had turned almost silver. Tic thrust the bag into Cade's hand, stuffed the money into his pocket, and stalked off without a word.

The phantoms within him pulled at his mind. He needed to get home, and fast. The town itself was nice but woefully small. Most towns on the Ends were, with more and more people being taken. If you had the means, you got out. This made Cade's presence all the more difficult to hide. Thankfully, his house was off the beaten path.

Cade crossed through the main street of the town and overheard two local men talking outside of the saloon.

"Looks like the raiders took Wilks," the first man said.

"It's only a matter of time until they come for us, too," the second man said, expression grave.

The first man spat. "We'll have to move. It's not like the king will help the likes of us. And we don't want no Bearers coming here. Not after what they did in the war."

Cade took his hands out of his pockets as he hurried by them. It would be too conspicuous if he concealed his hands while walking. Bearers weren't looked upon too kindly these days, and encoding rings were a dead giveaway. Most Bearers had been processed through the government's poor excuse of a training system, and they had not been selective in their recruitment. This had led to a glut of postwar Bearers who abused their power within the smaller towns of the Ends.

His head felt like a too-crowded room, thoughts tripping over each other while others disappeared completely. Twice he had to stop to remember where the house was, even though he had been there many times in the last few months. With some backtracking, he was able to find the familiar faded dirt road that led home. It was a simple house, long abandoned by a family that didn't want to take any chances with all the recent disappearances. Luckily for Cade, it was far enough away from the town center to deter any unwanted guests.

As he walked toward the front door, his vision began to fail. Thin black tendrils encroached from the periphery and grew until he could see nothing but darkness.

"No. Not now. Not outside."

His legs became heavy, as if cast in stone. He considered encoding to diamond but had enough sense remaining to know it would have no effect. The darkness around him shattered into countless pieces, and the vestiges of reality disappeared. New pieces flew back into view. He was no longer in the Ends but was on a great grassy hill. The sun had almost set, but a sliver of golden light still peered over the horizon as the shadow of night lumbered across the countryside.

He knew this hill. Gigan's Hill, the doorstep to the Thread, which lay less than a mile away. In front of him he could just make out the great structures of the Ancients, an advanced civilization that had once inhabited Chalice. "The Thread," he found himself saying in wonder. But something was different. The great beam of light, which lit the land through night and day, was extinguished.

"Impossible," said Cade, his voice hardly a whisper. The Wraiths had never turned off the Thread over the past year. Cade had almost forgotten the city of small structures that surrounded the Thread. Unfathomable buildings of silver alloy ringed the tower of the Thread, and an incredible concave dome the size of a castle courtyard sunk into the plain just past the hill.

It was just like it had been before the Wraiths had come to their planet. "That would mean..." Cade turned around and could make out the distant skyline of Wythlain, the city due south of the Thread. Wythlain fell just short of the great mountains that ringed the center of Chalice. He had forgotten what the city looked like before the Wraiths destroyed it. But here it was, brought back to life. The sight almost brought him to tears. He admired the great city, a crucial mining hub of Chalice, as the sun slipped away and the night took its watch.

Cade looked up, expecting to see the stars laid out before him. Instead, they began to disappear, as if a great blanket had started unfolding from the heavens.

"No," Cade said, reaching skyward. A feeling of dread crept over him as he brought his gaze once again to Wythlain. A great flash of light illuminated the entire countryside, and an odd thunder cracked overhead, so loud Cade could feel his teeth rattle. He ducked down, trying to shield himself from the event, but it was already over. When he leveled his gaze toward Wythlain, all he could see was smoke and ash. This was how the Wraiths had greeted them, one year ago.

Something immense whirred to life behind him. At first it felt like a low thumping sound, but it picked up speed until it was an almost imperceptible buzz. The immense disc of silver behind him flickered with broken chains of white energy, as if it had swallowed a thunder cloud whole. In moments, the great beam of the Thread shot straight up through the sky, and the aftershock of its awakening knocked Cade to the ground.

Cade shook his head, standing up, and found he was now somehow mere inches from the Thread, the beam pulsing only inches from where he stood. It was a pillar of pure light—he could feel the energy and heat emanating from it as it flowed upward.

"This is not real, this is not real," he murmured, frozen in place. It was impossible to be this close to the Thread; the Wraiths wouldn't allow it. Wythlain was a testament to that.

It was beautiful. He hated the Thread, yet he could not pull himself away. It was the symbol of Chalice's enslavement to the Wraiths, disguised by the gift of free energy.

He reached out his hand to touch it, and the energy surged while it pulsed rhythmically through him. He pulled his hand back, but the light *stretched*, sticking to his hand like luminescent tar. His heart beat faster as he pulled harder against the encroaching light. Undeterred, the light enveloped his arm and pulled him into the beam itself. He tried to encode, but his phantoms remained silent. His scream was cut short as the light continued to consume him, until he was engulfed within the beam.

He saw faces in the light, shifting with mouths open, calling out in some alien tongue. "Eos..." the voices seemed to chant. Almost as quickly as it had taken him, the light receded. He found himself curled upon the ground in front of his house, heart pounding in his chest. His wits crashed back down on him, and he stood up, looking around to see if anyone had witnessed his hallucination.

He made his way into the house, careful not to trigger the alarms. Once inside, he leaned against the heavy door, taking long and slow breaths to calm himself. At that moment, a reflex beckoned to him from a saner recess of his mind. The questions. He wasn't sure how far gone he was, but the questions would give him a good idea. They were what grounded him; a simple tool he had devised to help him maintain his identity among the phantoms with which he shared himself.

What is my name? The baseline. If he couldn't answer this, he would be close to forgetting himself entirely. "Cade Elegy," he replied, voice less sure than he would have liked.

He could still hear the voices getting louder. *Forever my song will play,* a soft voice chanted from the back of his mind.

Where was I born? A more difficult question, but simple enough. "Kayvant," he said aloud. Except that was wrong. He checked the tattoo underneath his forearm. "Hells," he said, shaking his head. "Gallance."

And with you my heart will stay, the soft voice continued.

It was worse than he thought. He decided not to ask any more. *Must keep moving,* he told himself.

The house was sparsely furnished, the living area appointed only with a broad oak table and a few worn chairs. Next to it sat a pile of splintered wood and an old crate. Whoever had lived here before him had taken care not to leave much behind.

He knelt next to the worn crate by the table and sifted through the array of broken leather straps and belts that lay within. He pulled out a length, which still had its buckle in decent shape, only a few spots of rust. Tucking it under his arm, he also grabbed a short piece of leather and set it on the table.

Cade pulled out a chair, worn but solid. With luck, it would hold. He sat down in the chair and secured his legs to the makeshift iron bracers he had attached to the front. He ratcheted them as tight as the straps would allow. The rough metal edges cut through his clothes and bit into his skin, drawing blood.

He took out the vials of Nocturne and fought the urge to drink. *Stay focused*, he told himself. He set them on the table.

Hands trembling, he looped the belt and with some difficulty slid both hands into it. He grabbed the tail of the belt with his teeth and pulled it taut against his wrists until the buckle's catch found its notch.

Forever my Song will play. A different voice this time.

What was I doing again? he thought. Cade sat looking around the room, forehead beaded with sweat, until his eye caught the black vials he had set down on the table.

He snatched at a vial with his bound hands and used his teeth to draw out the stopper. Its bitter smell hit him straight away, a cross between freshly tempered metal and charred wood. Cade poured the contents into his mouth. A single vial had once been a month's supply. The liquid coated the inside of his mouth, becoming viscous and bringing a soft warmth. It felt like he was trying to swallow a wet sponge. It hung there for a moment, as if reluctant to plummet to its fate, and then seemed to relax, allowing him to swallow.

He felt a cold chill envelop him, covering both inside and out. He fought the urge to shiver, but his body ignored him as it shuddered under the overwhelming sensation.

A sound, or rather sounds, crawled and scratched at the edges of his mind, growing ever louder. His arms and legs jerked as he convulsed under the harsh prelude of Nocturne. He felt his gut wrench as wisps of dark light materialized and swirled around him, a maelstrom of black energy. The sounds divided, the waves of notes crashing upon each other, with neither garnering purchase on the other's shore. The sensations were too much for Cade. His eyes snapped open, feral and desperate, as he focused on the light that continued to pour out of him. His jaw nearly unhinged as he let out a primal scream, every muscle in his body protesting their restraints.

The cacophony of sounds assembled, like tumblers of a lock falling into place. A song began to emerge. It was altogether beautiful and moving, yet alien, as if played with instruments far greater than any of this world could offer.

He had heard the song before, and he hated it.

The remaining light pooled into two entities before him. But there was also someone else in the room. A version of himself, sitting in a chair that didn't exist, reading a paper. As if sensing Cade's gaze, the doppelgänger lowered the paper and studied him, expression somber. He shook his head and resumed reading.

As the beat of the music slowed, so did Cade's heartbeat. Barely a whisper now, the music stopped. The room, and Cade's mind, fell silent.

CADE AWOKE to the sound of a bell. He opened heavy eyelids and found himself on the floor with broken pieces of the chair scattered around him. Blood trickled out of his mouth and onto the battered wooden floorboards. He spat out the blood-soaked restraint, wiped his mouth, and stood up.

Cade turned and looked in the mirror that hung in the hallway. He hadn't looked at himself in a long time. To him, mirrors only reflected the time he had wasted. His hair had gray streaks along the sides—when had that set in?

Out of the corner of his eye, Etan, his son, bounded in from the front door and into the bedroom. But it was only a hallucination. Sometimes, while on Nocturne, when he left the house, he would look toward the door and see his wife smile and wave at him. The visions were strongest right after taking the drug, though there was no way of knowing when they would manifest. The voices were quieted, though, and that's all that mattered.

Or did it? For the first time in a year, he had no more leads. He had opened every door, turned over every rock, and had found nothing. Why did he continue to torture himself? He would never pay the debts he bore.

Cade eyed the other vial of Nocturne, which still rested, unopened, on the table. He had heard of soldiers who had overdosed on Nocturne, an easy way to escape the horrors of the war. If he drank another vial... Carefully taking it in his hand, he pulled the stopper.

A knock came at the door. At first Cade ignored it, thinking it another hallucination from the Nocturne. He raised the vial to his lips. The knock came again.

He remembered the bell he had thought he heard earlier. He cursed under his breath that he was caught unaware. Someone must have seen his episode outside the house, and now they had come for him. He stoppered the vial, grabbed the rings out of his pocket, and hastily put them on. He holstered his guns, though he hadn't had any real ammunition for them since the war. Still, he felt better having them.

He heard them try to open the door. *Good luck with that*, he thought. Cade had set up an alarm perimeter around the house in case he ever had uninvited guests. The tripwire was the first line of defense. He had also built a special front door, reinforced with lead. One couldn't be too careful in the Ends.

He encoded to diamond, giving himself the strength to move the weighted door just enough to see out.

As his eyes adjusted to the daylight, he saw the form of a beautiful young woman with long auburn hair and piercing green eyes. Squinting, he realized he knew this woman.

On his doorstep stood Ashlyn Winshire, Princess of the Realm.

Okay, maybe my dose is *a little too high,* he thought.

4

HERO OF THE REALM

Bearers must only become such to help those who remain behind. Those whose songs continue to play can only find peace through the careful help of those who bear them.
—*Excerpt from* The Book of the Traveler

BEING face down in the dirt, thousands of miles away from home, and running on suspect information from local youths who would make up anything for a chipcoin had Ashlyn second-guessing her entire plan. *This was a mistake.*

She freed her foot from the strange rope that ran across the garden, brushed off what she could, and smoothed out her traveling skirt. She took another look at the house, if you could even call it that. Ashlyn had grown accustomed to the opulence of Toltaire, but this house had seen much, much better days. The roof was a disjointed patchwork of rotting thatch, the path to the front door was overgrown with wild, twisted weeds that went up to her waist, and most of the windows were boarded over. There was little chance the resident of this place was any more than a simple squatter, let alone a hero.

But she couldn't turn away—not yet. Bearers were almost nonexistent in Toltaire, and good riddance, for most were more monsters than men—wicked necromancers who preyed upon captive spirits. But a Bearer was what she needed if she were to get to the bottom of this. And who better than the most famous Bearer in all of Chalice? No one else would do. Plus, she was sure escaping the castle would vex her father, which was a convenient bonus.

Battling through the dense tangle of overgrowth, Ashlyn made her way to the front door. She knocked and waited. No response. She tried once more. Putting her ear to the door, she thought she could hear movement inside. Her heart beat faster in anticipation. But still no one answered.

This was a mistake. She knew it was dangerous to sneak out of the castle, but what choice did she have? Toltaire had become so engulfed in politics and espionage after the war that if you had even the slightest bit of influence, you had to assume everyone from the housemaid to the postman was in on the game. She recalled a day when a florist brought in tulips to decorate the castle. She had mentioned to him how much she loved the yellow ones, and from then on, every caller to the castle had brought her yellow tulips. Information was a prized commodity, bought and sold like groceries at the market.

She didn't trust her father, who would no longer acknowledge her, and she didn't trust her brother Elon, who had been sequestered at birth to be groomed for kingship. How could you trust your own family if the extent of your interaction was a handful of simple pleasantries exchanged during royal galas? The only person Ashlyn had ever fully trusted was Rolan, and he had been taken from her.

Someone would pay for that.

Ashlyn needed someone she could trust, but in absence of that, perhaps Elegy would do. She tried the doorknob—it was unlocked. She tried to push the door open, but it wouldn't budge. Undeterred, she put her shoulder into the door and pushed again. Nothing.

She sighed and turned to leave.

The old door groaned as it opened a few inches. The interior was dark, but she caught a glimpse of the man she had met once, long ago. A look of recognition flashed in his eyes; he remembered her. She opened her mouth to greet him, and the door slammed in her face.

Finding herself at a complete loss as to appropriate etiquette in such a situation, Ashlyn felt her face flush and caught herself feeling indignant. She was a princess, after all. Who was he to treat her like this? She took a deep breath to regain her composure and knocked on the door again.

A faint but commanding voice sounded from inside the house. "Go away." She could hear him making quite a commotion inside.

Ashlyn would not be put off. "I will not. You are Protector of the Realm, and you are bound to serve and assist in any capacity requested of you by a member of the royal court. Besides, you will be rewarded handsomely for your service."

"Oh, of course, I had forgotten. Come right in." The door did not budge.

She sniffed, growing even more irritated. "You know I can't move this door."

He opened the door a crack. She could see an open pack lying behind him. "Listen, I don't have time for this. Every time a nobleman's dog dies, one of you comes knocking at my door. You are in danger, and you'd best take your leave." The door slammed shut once more.

"*Danger?* Are you threatening me?" She pounded on the heavy door with both fists. The sound of rummaging continued from behind the door.

She had heard rumors Elegy had killed a man in Wilks, and that brought her a good measure of unease. She chose not to believe the rumors—yet he was a Bearer... If he were no longer the man she believed him to be, she would have no choice but to investigate Rolan's murder on her own. It was not a heartening prospect. Being a princess had its advantages, but there were places where not being recognized was important. No one wanted to get mixed up with a princess. Royalty attracted too much attention, and too much attention attracted spies. And spies were bad for business.

I'm going to need to try a different tack, she thought. She knocked on the door again. "It's not raiders."

The commotion from inside ceased. A moment later, the door opened wide enough that she could see his face. It had been a year since she last saw him, but she did not remember him having eyes of silver. They were like the color of smoke from a dying campfire. He did not look much older than she remembered, but the years were reflected in those eyes. She had seen the same look in soldiers who had survived the war, the ones who had seen real battle. Ashlyn stepped closer and took the opportunity to speak. "So, it is true. You have been searching for the taken?"

His eyes searched her own, as if trying to decide whether she could be trusted.

"My uncle was as well...and now he is dead." He opened the door farther at this. Ashlyn continued, "If you are still a true Bearer, defender of the dead, you will help me."

The man looked at her, eyes narrowed. "Hells," he said finally. He disappeared from the doorway. She took it as an invitation.

When she entered the house, Elegy slammed the heavy door shut with inhuman ease. He brushed past her and took a dusty lamp off the hearth.

The boarded windows did not afford much light. As her eyes adjusted, she did not see the comfortable home of a decorated soldier; rather, the home was stripped bare, with the occasional practical item: a chipped plate, a rusted cup, a threadbare blanket. But what caught her eye was the open pack near the threshold. An old tome, covered in white dust save for the fresh fingerprints around the spine, sat aside it.

"Is that...?" she started.

He looked over to her and nodded. "An original translation."

"I thought they had all been—" She stopped herself, embarrassed.

"Destroyed. Yes, we have the royal decree to thank for that, don't we?" He carefully picked up the book and wrapped it in a worn tatter of tanned leather.

"You are a follower of the Traveler?"

He paused, and she noticed him touch the intricate silver band on his right hand. "My wife is—was—a scholar. It was her most prized possession." He stood up. "What information do you have about the taken? Be quick about it."

"I will tell you once you agree to help me."

He laughed, shaking his head. "I don't have time for games. More precisely, *we* don't have time for games. You came to me. If you won't show me what you have, you're free to go." He gestured to the door, eyes fixed on her.

She bit her lip. What did she have to lose? She sighed and produced a small note from within her sleeve, which she held out to him.

Elegy took the note and turned it over in his hands. The daub of wax that sealed it had already been broken, but you could still make out the lettering of the initials "OP". Cade furrowed his brow, studying the symbol.

"Order of the Phantom," Ashlyn cut in. "That's what the seal represents. It's the name of the intelligence network my uncle runs...or, used to run."

Cade nodded, unfolded the letter and began to read. It didn't say much, and she had committed it to memory already, just in case:

Rolan—Rynth no longer safe. Leaving first railbus out. We have proof the disappearances are not by the hand of raiders. We know Liam is involved. Seek out Karessa in Solak. She will guide you to the Foundation. Be always vigilant.

—Faye

"It's not much, but if we can track down this contact in Solak..." Ashlyn said hopefully.

"Why me? You have your own spies. Why not have them track down this person?"

Ashlyn bit her lip.

He sighed. "You want me to form a pact with your uncle."

Ashlyn nodded. "He could help us. And..."

"You want revenge."

She fell silent.

"I know someone who might help find the contact in Solak," Cade said, breaking the silence.

Ashlyn brightened. "Let's go talk to them!"

He shook his head. "Can't."

Ashlyn frowned. "What? Why not?"

"You don't get it, do you? This isn't some scrap of intrigue to busy yourself with when your head has grown weary of its tiara. Go back home to your father."

Her eyes narrowed. "My father couldn't care less about me. I'm here of my own volition." She was quiet for a moment, then sighed. "Many years ago, I passed a servant as he carried the royal seal to my father's court. The man—Gilliam was his name—tripped, and the seal tumbled out of its box, splitting it into two. The look on his face...I've never seen anyone so terrified." She shook her head, cleared her throat, and continued. "I had seen people put to death for far less. When the head of the guard asked what happened, I told him I was the one responsible."

Elegy's eyes followed her as she spoke, steady yet impassive.

"I was imprisoned in a cell for a month's time, with no clean water and little food. But I would do it all the same if I had to. The look on Gilliam's face when I stepped forward is one I'll never forget. The incredulity...he *expected* me not to save him."

She faced the Bearer. "I realize what it means, me coming here. And it's my responsibility to do what I can for Rolan, and for my kingdom."

He nodded as she fell silent. His eyes seemed able to peer into her thoughts. Not an uncommon feeling when dealing with Bearers, she remembered. Many gamblers refused to play cards with them for the same reason. "Great story. Still can't help you."

Ashlyn's face fell. "You don't believe me?"

"I believe you, but I've been following this for too long, and you'll only get in the way."

Before she could reply, he picked the lamp back up and crossed into the adjoining room. She followed, annoyed but determined, and gasped at what greeted her. A tall pile of twisted and broken furniture lay next to the kitchen. Elegy pulled the top off the lamp and poured its fuel over the display.

"What is that?" was all she could manage.

"Kerosene."

"Yes, but what is all this for?" She felt her face grow hot. She was growing tired of being treated in this manner.

"You were followed," he said matter-of-factly.

She looked at him evenly. As a princess, she was used to being underestimated and discounted. It had its uses, this tendency to underestimate her, but it caused her no end of grief.

"Correct. Two agents. One agent is my father's. He is assigned to me whenever I go out, though I'm not supposed to know. I imagine he is quite excited to have some adventure in his otherwise dull routine." She continued, "The other I'm not so sure about. Likely a freelancer looking for a big score."

He looked impressed. "Not bad."

She couldn't help but let a small grin escape.

"Too bad it's wrong," he said as he continued to spread the kerosene around the pile.

"What?"

"You've probably picked up a lot more than that, traveling by yourself like this. And I assume you've been asking people around here about me?"

"Yes. Why?"

She heard a bell ring.

"Time's up," Elegy said.

Another bell rang. She heard him curse.

"What is..." was all she could get out before he lunged at her, scooping her up in his arms. He turned as she heard the window next to her shatter. His arms felt cold and rigid, and she felt his body jerk, as if something had hit him with tremendous force. She tried to wrest herself free, but she found his grasp unyielding, as if trapped in a statue's embrace.

"Time to go." She felt his arms relax, and he set her down upon the wooden planks of the small house. He reached into a small indentation in one of the boards and threw open a hatch that appeared to lead underneath the kitchen. He ushered her through the hatch, but not before she saw his hand turn a dark brown. She almost thought it a trick of the light until she saw him strike a match on his palm and toss it onto the pile of broken furniture. *He's encoding*, she thought. Encoding was all but illegal in Toltaire, so his casual use of it caught her off-guard. The color retreated, and he followed her down.

The darkness below fell away as Elegy fired another match and lit a large candle next to him. She gasped as she made out a small, winding passageway under the house. He pointed to the tunnel. "This way."

She struggled to keep up with him, her shoulders brushing the sides of the cramped passage. She wanted to ask him the thousand different questions racing through her mind, but she feared their pursuers might overhear. Despite her shock, she marveled at the time required to craft such an escape. She might have been impressed if she wasn't so scared.

The passage widened as they made their way through. The air was thin and smelled of rust and stale ash. She reached out in the dim light and touched the wall.

"Stone?" She frowned, confused. How did he make this tunnel? Cade's quick pace left her farther in the darkness, so she turned back to catch up with him. "Ouch!" she exclaimed, tripping over a metal object. Cade backtracked to her. With the glow of the candlelight, she could see a pickax at her feet.

"A mine?"

Cade nodded. "Most of the towns in the Ends only exist because of the mining industry around here. Come, we must hurry."

She rubbed her foot and stood up. "Where are we going?"

"The rail station. I will take you as far as Solak. There you can catch a Pathway railbus back to Toltaire."

She frowned. "You are a Coda master. Aren't you supposed to *want* to help people?"

He stopped and turned to face her. "What do you know about Coda? Please, regale me." His tone was mocking, but he remained expressionless.

Ashlyn set her jaw and tried to match his stoic gaze. "I know it is a religion about fighting, based on the teachings of the Traveler. And that you are honor-bound to defend others."

He winced at her description and shook his head. "It's not a religion. What do they teach you in Toltaire?"

She felt her face flush and was angry with herself for letting him get to her, which made her face flush even more. Why did she care what this man thought?

Cade regarded her for a moment and seemed to take pity on her embarrassment. He sighed. "It's a belief. A belief it is the duty of the living to guide the phantoms, which cannot rest. The 'fighting,' as you put it, is a martial art based around the use of the phantoms."

"Right. So, you *do* help people," she said plainly.

"Yes, but thankfully the dead talk less. Let's keep going."

They came to the end of the winding mine shaft, where a large wooden hatch was set above them. Cade threw the hatch and disappeared through the opening. She waited for a hand that did not come. Ashlyn struggled to pull herself out of the makeshift exit, but instead of standing at the top, she tripped and fell face-first onto the hard earth.

She heard a loud noise and could see in the distance Cade's house crackle and collapse. She looked at Cade, who just waved at the shell of a house, a ghost of a smile on his lips and sadness in his eyes. Peculiar.

Being face down in dirt, thousands of miles away from home, and traveling with a Bearer she was no closer to trusting, had Ashlyn again second-guessing her entire plan.

Mistake or no, I will see this through to the end.

5

FOLLOWED

The art of Coda revolves around developing a deep connection to the realms beyond our sight. One must embrace the philosophy of Coda if they are to become true Bearers. Without this, madness will consume.

—Excerpt from The Book of the Traveler

"YOU'RE GOING THE WRONG WAY," Cade said to Ashlyn as the crush of people from the railbuses weaved past them at the Solak station. She looked at him without saying a word. He pointed to the platform on the opposite end of the station. A sleek, contoured railbus engine, its brushed metal still looking brand new despite it being centuries old, was boarding passengers. "This is a Pathway station, so that train there is the fastest route back to Toltaire." The Ancients built the Pathways, a rail network, to connect their major cities. Now that the Pathway trains had been activated by the Wraiths with the signing of the Accord, every citizen of Chalice had easy and reliable passage to any city connected to the Pathways.

He continued walking. The Nocturne dose he had taken was in full effect, providing him the quietness of mind he needed to think about his next move.

He sniffed the air and wrinkled his nose as he emerged from the exit. Solak had an unpleasant odor, one Cade could never quite place. It was an engine that fueled itself on equal parts depravity and opulence. *Perhaps this is the exhaust*, he thought.

"What's that smell?" Ashlyn asked, holding her nose.

"Stop following me. I only agreed to take you as far as Solak."

"Last time I checked, I was the princess. I don't take orders." She pulled her hair back, securing it with a light blue ribbon.

Cade turned and started down the street.

Ashlyn followed a step behind. "Is it always this busy here? I thought a city near the outer edge of the Pathways would be a little more...quiet."

It was, in fact, a lot busier than normal. Cade knew why, and he hoped it wouldn't stop him from getting out of the city.

"It's the Orange Festival."

"Really, the Orange Festival? That's today? How exciting, I've always wanted to see a festival in Solak!"

He grimaced. There was *always* a festival in Solak. It was a tourist destination. Next week it would be the blue festival, or the flower festival, or the beer festival. It didn't matter what week you came.

"For a girl investigating a murder, you sure have a lot of time on your hands."

She fell silent. It was more proof to Cade that she was not prepared for what she set out to accomplish.

"Where are we off to?" she said, looking around.

Cade shook his head as he put his encoding rings back on. Thankfully, Solak did not have the same distaste for Bearers as the towns of the Ends.

A carriage sped across the busy street, despite the throng of people crossing, and nearly hit an unwitting pedestrian—likely some too-important merchant. Cade walked close as it was about to pass him, encoded to the ring of pure diamond on his right hand, and grabbed the back of the carriage, whisking him down the street.

The main street off the station relayed the many splendors available to the affluent. There were restaurants specializing in exotic foreign cuisine, with lines of people trailing out of their doors. Bespoke fashion designers for hire demonstrated the latest trends to enraptured onlookers with live models. Theater buskers pitched the promise of the new show from the capital. But what stood out the most were the vibrant and garish gambling dens where the fools rich enough to play parted with their ill-earned money. At one time he had thought it all a wonder, but now he knew better.

He didn't have far to go. He leapt off the back of the carriage when he saw the bright red letters of The Seer Tavern.

Cade entered the tavern through the thick wooden door. He found an empty table and sat down. A slender bar maiden, not even old enough to drink but with the clever face of someone who grew up quick, came to take his order. "What'll you have?"

Cade placed a small pin on the table. It was military issue and consisted of four interlocking rings of dull brass. Her eyes flickered and she nodded, retreating into the back room.

Cade looked around the tavern. There were only a

handful of patrons, and most seemed content gazing into their oversized steins. They might not be spies, but they *were* likely the type to sell information to the right buyer, and Solak was near bursting with buyers. Men who frequented bars this early in the day were seldom upstanding citizens.

As Cade sat back in the sturdy chair, the large door in the front of the bar slammed open, catching the attention of Cade and the rest of the inebriated patrons. There stood the princess, panting and furious, scanning the room.

Hells.

Seeing Cade, her eyes narrowed to slits and she marched to the table and sat down.

He rubbed his temples. "Subtle."

"How *dare*—" she began, but Cade raised his hand and leaned in close.

"Listen, the bigger the scene you make here, the more difficult you're going to make it to get out of here. You think the lowlifes here wouldn't turn you in for a few chip-coins if they recognized you?" Her eyes darted to a man who was watching them. Cade shook his head. "A princess without her guard? What a price that information would fetch."

She closed her mouth and just glared at him.

The door behind the bar opened, and a tall, wiry man who looked about ten years Cade's senior, walked up to them. Cade stood and held out his hand. "Seek, old friend, I figured I would find you here."

The man, smiling, took the offered hand, and Cade felt the force of diamond-assisted strength bear down on him. He was already encoding tungsten, preventing the man from crushing his bones. Cade could sense Ashlyn's alarm, her eyes wide and transfixed on their color-shifting hands.

"No surprise, since I own the place," the man said, smile fading.

The man's arm shimmered from the increased encoding. "You've got some nerve showing up here." Cade bolstered his own encoding to match.

"You wanted me to get the job done. I got the job done."

"Yes. And you destroyed an entire warehouse," the man said, face showing signs of strain.

"It wasn't that nice of a warehouse."

"It was *my* warehouse!"

"I thought we were past this. I did the job for free."

That just seemed to make him angrier, and Cade could see the man's face shimmer as his skin became more translucent.

Cade pushed diamond through his own arm and broke the grasp. "I have come here for your help. After I am through with what I must do, I will return and you can do with me what you wish. But right now I need my friend."

The man snorted and took a seat. He regarded the princess with a nod. "Apologies for meeting under such circumstances, Princess."

Cade's heart sank. "Word has already spread?"

"She's not exactly disguised."

Cade frowned. "It couldn't be helped. I need help finding someone."

Seek laughed. "You came to the right place. This city is crawling with washed-out spies. Who are you looking for?" He motioned for the barmaid to bring them drinks.

"Her name is Karessa. She is with an organization called the Foundation."

Seek rubbed his chin. He sighed and motioned to a somber-looking man at a nearby table. The man leaned forward and Seek whispered into his ear. The man nodded and left.

"Never heard of her, but I have heard of the Foundation."

Cade raised an eyebrow. "What have you heard?"

"I heard they are working with a certain Coda Grandmaster you may know."

Cade's heart sank. "Dol's in town?"

The man nodded and grinned wide, relishing Cade's discomfort.

The barmaid set the drinks on their table. It had a light citrus scent, not the usual overpowering yeasty smell of most brews in Solak.

Two large men, silent, entered the bar and took seats at a corner table.

"He arrived a few days ago. My sources tell me he will enter Taction as the champion for Coda."

Cade sat in silence for a moment. This would complicate things. "You're kidding."

Seek shook his head, took a long drink from his mug, and set it gingerly upon the coaster in front of him.

A man and two short-haired women, well-armed, entered laughing and sat at the corner table at the opposite end of the room.

"Do you know why?"

"Can't say. I'm not Dol's favorite person. He's not a fan of my ilk."

Cade had his own suspicion. Had Coda fallen so far?

Another four men, wearing dark colors and long coats, entered the bar and took seats near them. All the tables now were quiet, with the newcomers casting furtive glances toward their table.

Seek grinned. "You two are quite popular. It's probably best you take your leave."

Cade nodded. "I owe you one, Seek."

"You owe me a great deal more than that. Just don't get yourself killed before the debt is paid."

"Deal." Cade stood up to shake the man's hand when the bar exploded.

6

———

CODA

Not much is known about the complex structures and underground passageways left behind by the race known as Ancients. The majority of discovered sites seem to indicate that Chalice was once home to a highly advanced mining operation. The true purpose of other structures, such as the Thread, are still a mystery.

    —*From* Chalician Archaeologist's Quarterly, *Vol. 3*

THE SMOKE HUNG thick in the air, and his ears rang from the blast. Even though it was only an elaborate firework reserved for festival celebrations, firing it indoors made for a more than suitable distraction. Cade couldn't help but think for a spy, Seek was a bit flamboyant when orchestrating an exit. Seek ushered him and the bewildered Ashlyn into the trapdoor under the table.

The dark passageway led to a set of storm doors with a few fingers of light reaching through. Cade boosted Ashlyn up to the doors and then pulled himself out. They found themselves in a vacant alley behind the Seer Tavern.

The distraction would help throw the spies off their trail for a while, though you could never disappear for long, not in Solak.

Cade dusted himself off as best he could so he wouldn't stand out. He looked up at Ashlyn and noticed she was staring at him pointedly. "Was that necessary?"

Cade shrugged. "To be honest, I wasn't sure *how* he would get us out of there. Sometimes he has to improvise."

She scowled. "I'm not sure if passing this off as a normal part of your routine is encouraging or unsettling."

"I don't remember inviting you along in the first place."

"The sooner you accept it, the easier this will be. Partners?" She held out her hand.

"You are nothing if not persistent."

"It's not the first time I've been told that," she said, smiling.

"One condition. You do as I say, without question."

She hesitated and sighed. "Fine, Mr. Elegy."

He shook her hand. "Cade. We must keep moving. Put the hood of your cloak up—a ponytail does not count as a disguise."

She opened her mouth as if to protest but seemed to think better of it and did as he instructed.

They weaved their way through the back streets and alleyways of Solak, careful not to draw any unwanted attention. Splashes of bright red, yellow, and blue lavished the elaborate architecture of countless monolithic casinos, but they soon gave way to more pedestrian structures. As they continued to the outskirts of the city, all the color seemed to bleed out from the buildings. Soon all that remained were ramshackle hovels, sun-washed with decayed brick spilling from their walls, and roofs bowed from overgrown moss. Crude buildings—patchworks of sticks, clay bricks, and the occasional sheet of rusted metal —sprawled outward, overlapping and supporting one another like a house of playing cards. The deeper they penetrated, the more the inhabitants took notice of them. Cade realized he and Ashlyn were dressed too well; their clothes didn't have the telltale signs of wear that only hard labor could show.

He turned to Ashlyn, brow furrowed. "Can you stop walking like that?"

"That's rude. This is how I walk," she shot back.

Her posture was impeccable, and her slender arms swept gracefully from side to side as she moved. Her head was held high, and an air of confidence exuded from bright green eyes and proud chin.

"Yes, but, can you act less...royal? I need you to blend in. Look around you."

She regarded the people who dotted the dirty road. Men shuffled by, heads down, trying to avoid eye contact. An old woman bustled about, hunched over the burden she carried. "I...oh." She pulled her cloak closer and tried to keep her head down.

Ashlyn clung closer to Cade as they made their way. "They don't mean us any harm," he told her. "When they see people that have means, they are more scared than anything."

"Scared? Of us?"

Cade nodded. "This city built itself on the backs of these people. Lots of money flows through Solak. Being close to the Ends allows the upper class to bend the law to their liking. The people here are nothing more than glorified slaves."

"I will have to speak with Father—"

Cade snorted. "Don't fool yourself. Your father knows

what happens here. And even if it didn't happen here, it would happen somewhere else. That's how it works."

They happened upon a boy pulling up a bucket from a well, the old pulley creaking in protest. The bucket soon arrived, filled only with thick black mud.

"It's terrible."

"My mother used to call Solak 'a toilet you can live in,' though I never knew why until I visited the outer city and learned how it all worked. And I keep finding a reason to come back here somehow. I should just rent an apartment."

"*That* would make your mother proud," Ashlyn said.

Cade laughed. It was the first genuine laugh he'd had in a long while.

They stopped at a building surrounded by an ornate carved stone wall. The wall, like the rest of the outer city, was in bad shape. Different parts of the relief had crumbled, and some depictions were altogether indecipherable.

"We're here."

Ashlyn touched one the images chiseled into the wall. "This is amazing. What is this?"

Cade cocked an eyebrow. "It's the story of the Great Betrayal from the *Book of the Traveler*. What are you paying those tutors of yours?"

Ashlyn flushed. "I've heard of it. I just hadn't seen it like this before."

Cade saw through the lie but let it go. "It's a shame the book was banned after the war. Without it we would never have been able to Pact. Come, let's go."

They passed under the archway that led to the court-yard surrounding the temple. He was pleased to see the gardens within were just as beautiful as when he last visited. He glanced at Ashlyn, who looked equally impressed.

"I've never seen anything like this!"

On the right half of the garden there were trees of different varieties, some that looked as if they were wrapped with freshly cut paper and others with tightly bundled branches that shot upward like a fountain of green leaves. There were also bushes surrounding the bases of the larger trees that looked almost impossibly full and bright, given the season. On the left half of the garden it was a veritable sea of color, with flowers in the peak of their bloom, yellow ones with fat heart-shaped petals, flowers with spindles of fine blue petals, and countless clusters of flowers arrayed in rainbow-colored sequence. There was a forced juxtaposition between the two sides; not a single flower was allowed purchase on the right side, and not a single pinecone lay on the left side.

"First time at a Coda temple?" he asked.

She nodded, transfixed.

"Not all have gardens like this. The curator, Jalek, fancies himself a gardener."

"What does it mean?"

Cade sighed. There used to be a time when everyone at least knew the foundation of Coda, but he struggled that this was a different time. "The core of Coda is the Song and the Sigh, the two forces that make life possible." He gestured to the flowers. "The Song is the essence that defines who you are and who you will become—the music that plays within yourself. Like the flowers, there are moments of vibrancy and abundance, the seasons its verses. The Sigh—" he pointed to the trees, "—is what gives us life. And like the deep, intertwining roots that tie the trees to the earth, the Sigh is the breath that ties us to this world."

Faint music spilled into the gardens.

"What's that?" asked Ashlyn.

"This way," Cade said, pointing to the temple.

Ashlyn gasped. "This is a structure of the Ancients!"

Cade nodded. The temple that sat just beyond the gardens was a temple in name only, since it was not a construction made by any hands of this age. Its brushed metal exterior, wrought from an alloy that refused to rust or scratch, shone in the midday sunlight.

"It's huge!" she said excitedly. The temple was very large and reminded him of a hangar, a place where you might build train cars or carriages.

"I forgot—there are no Ancient structures like this in Toltaire, are there?"

Ashlyn shook her head. "What do you suppose they used this for?"

He shrugged. "Not sure. Let's keep moving."

Cade, with Ashlyn following behind, entered through the main doors into the temple, and the music became louder. The doors themselves were of modern origin, secured into the ground because there were no tools that could penetrate the unique metal of the structure. The main entrance led to an auditorium-style room with rich, dark hardwood floorboards running the entire length—also a post-Ancient modification. On the far wall hung a banner of the symbol of Coda. It somewhat resembled a trident, with each prong punctuated by a thick dot. But what was most intriguing was that inside the temple the walls were transparent, and you could see the two sides of each garden bisect the center of temple. This was another reason these structures were preferred by the masters of Coda. One could meditate and experience nature from within the temple. The temple itself eschewed any other adornment so as to not remove focus from the gardens outside.

The auditorium was filled with over a hundred people;

Cade recognized a few of them as the civilians they had seen on their way to the temple.

The music was played by an eclectic mix of young and old people. It was disjointed, they missed notes, and the song would stutter as different performers fell out of harmony. Cade winced. Soon the song came to a merciful end. Ushers dimmed the lights and drew massive curtains over the walls as a small boy stepped forward to play. The instrument he held looked like nothing more than a hollowed tin box, strings pulled taut across an opening in its center. Not a classic instrument, but the notes that tumbled from it possessed a stark beauty.

More kids shuffled on stage, each holding a single candle, surrounding the performing boy. Ashlyn leaned over to Cade and whispered, "What's going on?"

"It's a play of sorts. The boy is playing a Constellation Song from the *Book of the Traveler*. The ones holding the candles represent the constellation of stars that represent that particular Song."

Ashlyn looked thoughtful, eyes now glued to the stage. "Like the Song you mentioned in the gardens?"

A young girl with dark hair spilling playfully past her shoulders stepped forward, nervously gripping an old recorder as the boy fell silent. Its reed was too long from its river, but the song held its shape. Even with the most worthless of instruments, the right song could make it great once more.

Cade nodded. "The same. One of these Songs plays through you, too, though we all have our own variations that make us unique."

He could see her smile as she continued to listen. He marveled at the size of the audience. Maybe there was still hope for Coda. There were no performers representing the martial art of Coda, but it didn't surprise him.

He closed his eyes and breathed in the air of the great room; the familiar mixed floral scent washed over him. He could hear his father's voice. "Just as the sword becomes an extension of your arm," his father sliced the air as the blade he held came to an abrupt halt, "the phantom is an extension of your Song." Bright silver enveloped his father's arm as he used the phantom he bore to encode with the metal of the blade. "Forging a bond between two worlds where they may play together as one."

The last of the musicians played their final note, and the room fell dark as the candles were extinguished. Ashlyn reached out and found his elbow. "What's happening?"

"They are preparing for the final act. The Lament of the Progenitor."

Ashlyn, no longer embarrassed by her ignorance, asked, "Who was the Progenitor?"

"It is believed the Progenitor was the Traveler himself. He gave the Ancients the key to the afterlife so they could protect themselves from the Betrayers."

"The key...you mean the phantoms?"

"Yes. Watch."

A single light emerged from the center of the stage, illuminating a man kneeling on a large woven mat. "Ironheart," excited whispers called out from the crowd. Upon his head was a large mask, with hair of wild straw painted myriad colors. The face of the mask sparkled like stars, bespeckled with polished gemstones inlaid within the lines of its somber expression. The man lifted the mask and placed it on the floor next to him. He drew a long silver flute from the sleeve of his robes, held it to lips, and began to play.

A haunting melody poured forth, the notes smooth and

precise. A familiar chill ran down Cade's spine. The long, rolling notes pierced him with sorrow but at the same time reinvigorated him, awakening hope. The Lament was not an altogether sad piece but rather a blending of emotions. There was a steep price for beauty, however: only those who had experienced true loss could ever capture the ethereal spirit of the Lament. As the final note hung in the air, Cade observed a handful of people in the audience weeping. He knew how they felt.

The lights came up and the room broke out into applause. The man bowed deeply with the rest of the artists and retreated backstage.

"Let's go," Cade said, leading Ashlyn through the departing crowd.

They came to an unmarked door behind the stage, and Cade knocked. No answer.

Cade entered the room anyway. It was unadorned, with no furniture or decoration in sight. The far wall, part of the original building, showed the full view of the gardens, giving the illusion that no wall existed at all. The man the audience had called Ironheart knelt in the center, placing the silver instrument into an ornate ebony case. He had always been slight of frame, but his exposed arms showed he had not neglected his training. He was focused on his task; if he had noticed them, he made no acknowledgment.

Cade knelt across from him and waited. Ashlyn glanced at him before folding her traveling skirt and following suit.

"Hello, Dol."

Dol closed the lid and fastened the clasps on the ends of the case. "People have forgotten the music. Once, every great musician on Chalice was trained by Coda masters. Now we are closing more and more temples with every passing day. I am a relic of an age that is coming to an end."

"But look at all the people here. Surely there is hope for us," said Cade.

The man's eyes narrowed as he met Cade's gaze. "*Us?*" He let the word hang in the air. "Do you see these people? Slaves, clinging to survival. We are more shelter than school."

Dol was right; Cade did have some responsibility to bear. "The war wasn't going to fight itself. I could not stand by while we did nothing and had our world taken from us."

"It was not our business to interfere," Dol fired back. "Our charge has been to fight for the phantoms so that they may pass to the Transcent. Using them for your own selfish ends is abuse. Bearers have no right to wield the Songs of others as they see fit."

"Without the Bearers, there would be no one left right now. The Wraiths would have wiped us out."

Dol laughed, shaking his head. "Do you really believe that? Strange things have been happening, Cade, more and more disappearances every month. The truce was just an easier way for them to get what they wanted."

Cade knew better than to argue. Besides, Dol was right.

"I heard a rumor," Cade said. Dol raised an eyebrow. "You aren't planning on participating in the Taction, are you?"

Dol stood up and turned to look upon the temple grounds. "Our Order will be gone before too long unless we recruit new members. The Taction is the best-known tournament in the entire world. If we can win that, perhaps we can start to grow our numbers again."

Cade shook his head. "This is not what Coda is supposed to be about."

"Coda stopped being about a lot of things after the war twisted everything around. You of all people know that,"

Dol sneered. "Instead of being respected as selfless heroes, we now walk in fear amongst those we once protected."

After the military disbanded the Bearer Corps, Chalice was flooded with soldiers who did not know how to wield their new power. Most of these soldiers had no training in the guiding principles of Coda and could not cope with their newfound power. Bearer-related crime, even a year after the war, was still a problem.

After his comment, Dol clutched his chest and gritted his teeth. Cade could see him encode, and Dol regained his composure.

"But Dol, what about your..."

Dol cut him off. "Don't. Don't you dare. I do *not* need you to protect me."

Cade knew there was no reaching Dol once he set his mind to a task. It was what made him someone you could always count on, but also what made him a real pain in the ass.

After a moment, Dol spoke again. "You wouldn't be here unless you needed something. What did you come for?"

"I'm trying to find someone from the Foundation. Her name is Karessa."

Dol smirked. "They are not to be trusted. She's one of *them* now."

Cade looked at Dol, confused. "Them?"

"She's an Acolyte. She was trying to solicit us to help join the Foundation's cause a mere week ago, but now I find out she's an Acolyte."

"Where is she?"

Dol shrugged. "I'd imagine she'll be with the rest of them at the Taction. You've overstayed your welcome. I'd like you to leave."

Cade stood up and turned to leave. "Let's go, Ashlyn."

She ran after him as he exited the temple. "How could that man talk to you like that? You are the Protector of the Realm, Hero of the Wraith War. Who does he think he is?"

"My brother."

7

THE TACTION

The Taction began its life as a sacred tournament allowing fighters from all martial arts the opportunity to compete on the world stage. Once revered and respected, the influence and pressure of organized crime lords has devolved it into nothing more than a brutal blood sport for those of considerable means to spectate.

—From The Toltaire Times

"SOLD OUT," the gruff woman said from behind the counter, not even bothering to look at him. She had the world-weary face of someone who had seen it all and was not interested in seeing it again. The dimly lit bar was quiet, or at least quieter than it should have been. Groups of men huddled at the small tables, voices hushed as they exchanged documents. This particular bar was nothing more than a lazy front for gamblers to place bets on the upcoming fights. But Cade had not come to place a bet.

"Even for the Protector of the Realm?"

The woman sighed, putting down her quill and looking

up at him. "And I'm Princess Ashlyn, nice to meet you. We're still sold out," she said as she looked back down on the ledger before her.

Ashlyn stepped up from behind Cade, pulled a diamond earring from her lobe, and set it on top of the counter.

The woman paused, and her eyes grew wide, admiring the sparkling gem before snatching it from the table and pocketing it. "I suppose we can make room for the Protector of the Realm."

She handed him two entrance tokens and a folded slip of paper with directions to the arena.

Ashlyn looked at Cade. "Do we really have to do this?"

Cade brushed past her as he read the slip. "Karessa is the only lead we have, and if she's at the Taction, we don't have much choice." That was only part of the reason for Cade, though. He was worried about Dol.

"I suppose you're right. Where are we going?" she asked wearily.

He folded the paper and put it in his pocket. "Underground."

Solak, like many of the abandoned cities of the Ancients, was home to massive tunnels and caverns that ran underneath the entire city.

"If the Taction is so popular, why all the secrecy?" Ashlyn asked as they wound through the streets.

"Most of the fighters are Bearers. Even in here, of all places, Bearers could be hunted."

The Taction was once the most prestigious tournament in the world, held within the capital and attended by royalty. Now, after the war, it was an echo of its former self.

They came upon a dead-end in an alleyway. A large man with fists like hammers stood next to an access portal on the ground, which had been sealed with a huge metal cover. A large sign was bolted on to the building nearby, depicting the letters "SSF" overlaid with a large red "X."

Ashlyn, puzzled, looked at the sign.

"SSF is the Solak Security Force. The underground is off-limits to all citizens. The sign indicates the SSF does not patrol the area." Not to mention they were paid well to stay away.

"You sure know how to treat a lady." She shook her head.

They walked up to the wall of a man. "Token," was all he said, face expressionless.

Cade handed the man the small token. The man lumbered over to the seal and squatted, grasping the handles on each side. His arms began to shimmer like diamond as he lifted the heavy seal from the portal, which revealed a ladder descending into darkness.

Cade gestured toward the opening. "Ladies first."

Once underground, Cade paused to let his eyes adjust to the darkness. There were thin strips of light running along the tunnel, but they only offered a soft glow. They did not need the map anymore; they followed the clamor of people gathering from a distance. The tunnel was as large as a railbus, and they travelled unencumbered.

They followed the commotion down the access tunnel until they came to a clearing that would rival any open-air stadium in Chalice. It was a massive dome, ringed with hundreds of people who were finding seats and excitedly placing last-minute bets with the bookies working the crowds. Closest to the front of the arena gathered Solak's wealthy and beautiful, resplendent in custom finery with obscenely large gemstones dangling from their necks and ears. Corruption radiated outward from the arena, with the most pedestrian of criminals being farthest from the action.

The dome afforded them much more light than the tunnel. Cade looked up and saw why.

"Stars!" Ashlyn exclaimed.

Cade was awestruck. It was exactly as he remembered. For a moment, he allowed himself to be fooled.

"Cade?" Ashlyn said, waving a hand in front of his eyes.

He caught himself with his mouth open and promptly shut it.

"This is the Stardome! I've read about this in my studies. Have you never been here?"

Cade shook his head.

Ashlyn continued, "It's one of the great Ancient wonders of Chalice. You see those colored stars there? Scholars believe it could be a map. I read that even before the Wraiths activated the Thread, the stars were fully lit."

They did not have much time to appreciate the Ancient-made wonder as a tall, well-muscled man wearing flowing red robes addressed the audience. On the other side of the arena stood Dol. Cade and Ashlyn pushed their way through the crush.

"What you are about to witness is proof of the power of the Mancando church," the man bellowed, silencing the crowd. "We do not take joy from what we must do, but know this: we will not tolerate the perverse way of the Bearers and the so-called Coda 'masters.' Our strength comes from within, not from the continued torment of the deceased."

That's the real reason Dol is here, Cade thought. Dol said it was about recruitment, and in a way that was true. The reason recruitment had been difficult was due to the stream of propaganda being pushed by the Acolytes. *Dol has come here for revenge.*

Ashlyn stood on her toes to try to get a better view. "Is that an Acolyte? I've never seen one in person. Is your brother in danger?"

Cade remembered back to his fight with Rast in Wilks. Was this Acolyte a former soldier of the war too? "Yes," he replied.

The Acolyte continued, "Man is imperfect and cannot help but to use powers he does not understand for his own selfish ends." He turned and pointed at Dol. "Coda is an affront to everyone here, a fabrication based on a book of profane magic tricks and no more credible than a child's fairy tale." The man raised his hands and faced the crowd. "If you wish for true power, I beseech you to look no further than the Church and its Acolytes." Cade noticed the lines in the man's face ran deep and dark, like they had been etched with a hot iron. He caught a glimpse of what he thought were eyes of dark gray.

Cade stood up, trying to get a better vantage point. "I don't like this." He was the reason Dol had taken the burden of the Coda Order upon himself, when it should have been Cade's to bear. And now his choice had put his only brother in danger.

A giant bronze bell rang, signifying the beginning of the match.

Dol raised his hands and took an offensive stance. His opponent, however, made no movement. The man's hands were clasped together and his eyes were closed. Cade could sense Dol's unease and could see his face turn red, flushed with anger at the man's boasting.

Impatient, Dol went on the attack, launching a flurry of strikes at the stationary man. The Acolyte moved, but only just, turning away each strike as though he were a cat batting away a mouse.

"He's playing with him. Something is not right," Cade muttered under his breath. Each strike Dol threw was encoded; it would have been impossible to block strikes like that if the defender was not encoding himself. The continued ease with which the man turned away the attacks was unsettling. "Wait here," Cade whispered to Ashlyn.

He made to enter the arena to stop the fight, even though he knew it meant disqualification for Dol. He had grabbed the cord that ringed the edge of the arena when a slender hand fell upon his shoulder. He turned to find a petite woman draped in red robes, glaring at him. She looked familiar. "Karessa?"

She responded by punching him square in the chest, sending him away from the ring and sailing into the crowd. The strike dazed him. *Dodge left*, a voice sounded in his mind. He dodged to his left, narrowly avoiding another strike from his attacker.

So you can *hear me. I was beginning to think there was a malfunction.*

He shook his head, as if to shake out the voice. It was the same voice, a man's, he had heard when he fought Rast back in Wilks.

He stood up and turned to see Karessa approaching him, expression cold and unmoving. *The Acolytes got to her before I could, dammit. Another soldier turned against me. Just like Rast.*

The lights above the Stardome blinked out, eliciting gasps from the crowd as the entire arena was plunged into darkness. The star lights above them began to turn on, one-by-one, revealing a single constellation. Cade knew this pattern of stars: *Hunter's Way*.

I think someone is trying to tell you something.

Cade recalled the Constellation Songs, the series of Coda martial arts forms he learned long ago. The sequences outlined the optimal combat techniques to utilize if you could discern an opponent's Song—the one that played within them—based on the 128 constellations.

The woman was upon him again, this time delivering an encoded roundhouse kick. Cade caught her off-guard by twisting into the line of the kick and using her momentum to throw her sprawling to the ground. It was a risky maneuver, but that was the point of using the Constellation Songs; you took bigger risks when you tried to anticipate your opponent's moves.

He blocked her next attack, a testing strike, and countered with a strike of his own. Karessa stumbled backward but recovered. As her head snapped back up, he noticed a marked change in her demeanor. She glared at him with burning eyes and leapt back into the battle with unnatural alacrity. As she continued her assault, he followed the techniques of the Constellation Song, trying to anticipate the next move. He intentionally exposed his left side to press forward with a takedown throw. Instead of locking her wrist as he expected, however, Cade took a devastating hit to his ribs. It was an encoded punch, most likely with lead. He encoded tungsten to try to dissipate the force of the attack.

He stole a glance up at the Stardome and noticed the constellation had changed to *Infinite Waterfall*. He hadn't seen the change, but it explained why she had taken advantage of his opening. Whoever, or whatever, was helping him had made a mistake. Or were they misleading him? He had to make a choice. Cade started humming *Infinite Waterfall*. Karessa went straight for his throat. Cade, anticipating, locked Karessa's arm, encoded his fist to lead, and struck her shoulder. His fist made a sharp "clink" as it connected; she had encoded to protect herself from the blow.

After he connected his strike, the Stardome flickered and showed the constellation *Vision Seeker*. Cade looked at Karessa, and her gray eyes changed from a look of rage to a measured expression, one that seemed more calculating and thoughtful.

Gray eyes. The realization struck him immediately. He *had* seen her before. She had been a Bearer squad leader during the Wraith War. It was rumored she was one of the few Bearers who had carried more than one phantom.

Sensing his hesitation, Karessa pushed her advantage and carried Cade's momentum forward. *Pay attention*, he heard the voice inside him say. Off balance, he was flung onto his back. The crowd roared at this and began shouting and hollering. Smiling, Karessa encoded her hand and closed it around Cade's throat. Cade encoded his neck to prevent it from being crushed and used his other phantom to encode his fist with lead. This was one of the key advantages of having multiple phantoms. Each phantom you bore allowed you to hold another encoding to a material.

He didn't have much leverage, but he punched as hard as he could. It connected, but all he heard was a dull "clunk." He noticed that Karessa had a silver hue about her; she had encoded her whole body. She couldn't keep that up for very long, but if she had more phantoms than he did, she would outlast him.

The world around him began the fade, and the dark tendrils that foretold of a Nocturne dream swirled at the edges of his vision. "Not now," he croaked as his vision faded away to nothing.

He found himself looking over Gigan's Hill but facing the destroyed remains of Wythlain in the distance. The bodies of soldiers lay twisted and broken across the landscape.

A lone survivor, a woman, plunged a sword as big as herself into the last Skex, which shrieked as it collapsed. The woman fell to her knees, tore off her helmet, and gasped for air. Long blond hair matted with sweat tumbled out, and her blue eyes, tired and bloodshot from exhaustion, welled with tears.

The woman collected herself, taking slow, controlled breaths as she surveyed the aftermath. She stood and made her way to a fallen soldier only a few steps away. She said the words, sealing the Pact. She got up, walked to the next soldier, and said the words once more.

Cade ran over to her, urging her to stop, but she could not hear him. He tried to grab her arm, but his hand just passed through her as she sealed Pact after Pact. Cade could only watch, helpless.

The woman formed the final Pact with the last of her unit. She grabbed her head, wincing under the collective burden, and fell to the ground, unconscious.

She awoke moments later with gray eyes cold and purposeful, no longer the person she once was. She retrieved her sword from the carapace of the Skex and headed back into battle.

Cade snapped back to reality, tendrils of pitch retreating to the edges of his vision. Karessa's expression was wild with battle-lust, a soldier long forgotten, still fighting on a battlefield she still remained a part of, unable to break free. Cade could see himself in those eyes. He understood.

Her mind was nothing more than splinters, each vying for control of its host. Without Nocturne to quiet the phantoms in her mind, they would eventually erode her identity until there was nothing left.

Desperate, his mind raced to think of a way to bring Karessa—the real one—back. His windpipe constricted, he picked the first thing that came to him. He fumbled for the vial of Nocturne in his coat and flipped the stopper out with his thumb. Cade managed to put the vial up and drain its contents into his mouth. He encoded his arms with diamond, continuing to encode his neck to keep it from being crushed. He felt the familiar surge of strength course through him. He used it to pull Karessa's face close to his own. Cade noticed her expression change, her eyes growing wide with alarm. Cade looked into her eyes for a moment and put her lips against his as he pushed the Nocturne into her mouth.

The torrent of force that had threatened to crush on him abated. Karessa's arms fell to her sides. She looked at Cade and then brought her hands up to look at them, as if seeing them for the first time.

"Master," a familiar voice sounded next to him. Jalek, the gardener from the Coda temple, stood next to him. "I will tend to her. You must help Master Dol."

He looked up to see his brother, still battling the large Acolyte. The Acolyte looked at Cade as he pulled up the sleeve of his tunic. Cade saw the man's hand shimmer as it began to shift and change. *He's overencoding*. The forearm transformed into a translucent, shining piece of diamond. Overencoding was permanent. The man's hand would forever be a piece of diamond.

Dol dove in with volley of quick strikes, but the man dodged each one. Finding an opening, the man struck Dol square in the chest with his overencoded fist, sending Dol sprawling backward. *Stay down, you idiot*, thought Cade.

Dol struggled to get up on one knee when he grimaced and clutched his chest.

A memory grabbed a hold of Cade. Not a Nocturne's veil, but it was every bit as vivid. He recalled his combat training with his father and Dol. "Dol, you must strive for efficiency in your movements," his father would say. Dol would have to take breaks during their sessions because his heart could not keep up with the effort. But he was stubborn. He refused to give up. Afterward, his father pulled Cade aside. "Cade, your brother...there will be times he will need you. Times when I cannot be there. Can you promise me you will look after him?"

The Acolyte approached Dol and hovered over him as he raised his overencoded hand to strike. He brought his fist down, but not before Cade's own fist connected with the man's chest, sending him stumbling backward.

I promise.

Dol's voice was hoarse, but Cade could hear it through the raucous din of the crowd's blood lust. "I don't need your help."

Cade said nothing and continued to face the robed man. The Acolyte's eyes showed mild surprise, but for some odd reason, he was smiling.

An official for the Taction entered the arena to end the match by disqualification, but the Acolyte backhanded him, crushing his jaw. The official collapsed to the floor like a rag doll. The frenzied crowd cheered.

The Acolyte lunged at Cade, much faster than Cade would have anticipated given the man's large size. Cade tried to dodge but still took a hard hit to his shoulder. By then Dol had stood up and kicked the Acolyte in the back with an encoded leg.

The Acolyte didn't even budge. He had rooted himself

and hardened his entire body. Cade and Dol exchanged a quick glance, unsure of what the Acolyte was doing. They paced around the man, searching for an opening.

Cade heard the familiar cracking sound as the Acolyte's other hand overencoded.

The Acolyte spun around and threw a hook full force into Dol's chest. Dol crumpled to the ground. Cade roared and threw himself at the man. The man was grinning, his eyes wild with glee. No matter what attack Cade threw at him, the man was faster and stronger.

Cade was astonished when he noticed the man's forearms had changed back to normal. Cade was convinced his eyes were playing a trick on him. Overencoding was permanent.

More officials rushed into the arena. Cade caught a glimpse of Dol and saw that blood had pooled around his mouth. *Get out.* Cade cursed under his breath. The voice in his head was right. Whoever this man was, Cade was no match for him; they had to leave. Cade ducked behind one of the officials and scooped up Dol. He dodged through the crowd, which ignored them, distracted by the new melee that had taken center stage.

On the edge of Stardome, Cade laid Dol down upon the ground. "Dol?" he said, searching for a reaction.

He noticed Dol's chest rising and falling fast. Too fast. The breaths were short and labored. He took Dol's right arm, the one adorned with an aged iron bracer. The bracer had accumulated a greenish patina over the years, but you could still see the intricate filigree etched upon its surface. Cade rested the right hand upon Dol's chest. "Deep breaths, Ironheart. Deep breaths."

He could see the color of the iron seep into Dol's skin as Dol encoded to it. His breathing began to slow and settle.

Dol opened his eyes and focused on Cade. "Hey...I got him right where I want him," he managed to say with some effort. "Just...point me in the right direction, will you?"

Cade faked a smile. "Yeah, you really did a number on him. It's a sure thing."

Dol smiled back. "I'm pretty sure you would have never done anything stupid like this. That's why Dad wanted you to become the Grandmaster and not me. 'Dol, you're too impulsive.'"

Dol coughed as he tried to laugh and instead winced in pain. Blood had already soaked through his uniform. Not good. Cade was amazed he could even speak.

"It's okay, I never really wanted the job anyway. Too many meetings...here, it's your turn now."

Dol took Cade's hand and placed a necklace in it. It was threaded by a simple ring. The ring of the Traveler, it was called. It was a symbol of the Coda Grandmaster, passed from one Grandmaster to the next. Cade closed one hand around the necklace and held tight to his brother's hand.

Dol smiled one last time and closed his eyes.

8

REQUIEM

Not all phantoms stay behind, clinging to the Firmere. The call to return to the Transcent, where all things are born, is tremendous. Do not take Pacts lightly, for a phantom's denial of ascension exacts a great toll.

—*Excerpt from* The Book of the Traveler

THE FAMILIAR SEED of despair grew like a weed within him, and blood pounded in his ears. A failed husband. A failed father. And now a failed brother. "Protector of the Realm." A joke that continued to haunt him. Cade watched as they lowered Dol's body into the ground. They chose to bury him in the gardens of the temple, just as the sun had begun to set. It was a beautiful service, but Cade didn't notice. Such a massive crowd had come to pay their respects, you would have thought they were burying royalty. The truth was Dol had touched the lives of so many in this disadvantaged community. In an attempt to keep the dying art of Coda alive, and in turn give communities like this a chance to grow and learn, Dol had given his life.

Cade could not take any more. He turned and brushed past the hushed crowd and into the temple, to the room where his brother had stayed. It was simply appointed with a dresser and bed. The room was clean, and the bed was made. Dol was never much for material possessions. His only true possession was his silver flute, a gift from their mother.

He took off the black formal uniform Jalek had provided him. He felt like an impostor in the robes meant for a grand-master. He folded the traditional clothes and walked to the dresser in the corner of the room. As he placed the uniform in the drawer, a scrap of paper caught his eye. It was in a worn envelope that was still sealed and addressed to Cade. A postman had written upon it, "Returned to sender." The postmark indicated it had been sent over a year ago. Cade took a breath and broke the envelope's seal.

Cade, I wish I could understand why you insist on joining this war. What could men do against an alien force that has the power to level an entire city? Using the phantoms you bear in a war that they have nothing to do with goes against everything we have been taught. What you are doing could destroy everything we've built. I hope you will understand and return from this futile quest. Father is getting worse. I don't know how much longer he will be with us. At least return for his sake. You are his successor, and it means everything to him for you to take his place.

Dol

Cade sighed and put the letter back in the drawer. He sat on the bed and buried his face in his hands. A knock sounded at the door.

"Cade? May I come in?" It was Ashlyn's voice. Cade did not respond. The door cracked open and Ashlyn stepped inside. "I...I saw you leave and I thought... Of course, I'm sorry. I'll leave you alone." She turned around and grabbed the door handle.

"Was it worth it?" Cade said, looking at the floor.

Ashlyn turned. "I'm sorry?"

"The war. Was it worth it?"

Ashlyn shook her head. "I don't know what you mean."

"The Wraiths leveled Wythlain without even trying to talk to us. We weren't anything to them. But our hubris...our gift to Pact led us to declare war on them. Was using that power worth what it bought us? We lost so many. My brother is dead. And now the Coda Order is on the brink of collapse."

Ashlyn was quiet for a moment before speaking. "I don't know. But the war allowed us to sign the Accord."

Cade scoffed. "And what has the Accord bought us that we didn't have before the Wraiths came? Free energy to power some railbuses? We've become slaves to that power, and we're not any closer to understanding the Wraiths and what they are after. What has our dear king been doing?"

Ashlyn winced. "My father...he meets with the Wraiths on occasion, but I do not know of what they speak. He is not a good man, to that I can attest. But he has this intensity... this fierce belief that he is doing what is best for the people of Chalice."

"What is best. I wish I knew what that was."

Ashlyn sat on the bed next to him and put her arm around him. "Your brother...this is not your fault."

"Whose fault is it? The Acolytes? There is something... unnatural about them. I can't help but think they are another piece in the game the Wraiths are playing."

She continued to hold him, saying nothing.

Cade sighed, frustrated. He met her eyes. She had kind green eyes, just like Sera. His gaze lingered for a moment, and he stood up. "I need to be alone."

She nodded, stood up, and left the room. He was disgusted with himself. His wife had only been gone a year.

Cade walked over to the translucent outer wall of the room and placed his hand on the structure of the Ancients. "Why did you leave us here to fend for ourselves? What did you leave behind that brought the Wraiths to our door?" He encoded tungsten and punched the wall, eliciting a loud clang. "Bastards. Even with all your technology, you ran, too. And now we are trapped here with your mistake. And soon we will be gone, too."

He grabbed his head as the voices in his head began to rise, faster and louder than normal. He felt his heart rate increase. *Stay calm*, he told himself. The occasional hallucination was much better than the alternative. Cade started his ritual with the questions. *What is my name?* "Cade Elegy." *Baseline is good*, he thought. *Where was I born?* "Gallance," he said aloud. He checked the tattoo under his forearm. It matched. *What color are my eyes?* "Blue," he stated. He checked the tattoo once more. "Dammit," he cursed. *I need Nocturne.* He hated his constant reliance on Nocturne, but a dose of it was the only thing keeping him from madness, like he had seen with Karessa. He had been able to buy more from Seek, at least enough to keep him going for a bit longer. He reached into the dresser and pulled out a black leather belt from the top drawer. He threaded his hands through it and pulled it taut with his teeth until the catch slid into place. He grabbed a vial and swallowed the pungent and viscous liquid within. He eyed the other vial he had bought. "And soon...we will be gone, too." He bit off the stopper and swallowed just as the first dose hit him. His muscles began to seize with the Nocturne onslaught. The seizure was stronger than any he had experienced before, his muscles straining and locking so tight that his screams could not escape him.

This is it, he thought. *I'm going home.*

Forever my song will play.
And with you my heart will stay.

CADE WOKE to find himself at home, in his bed. He smelled the familiar hint of lavender perfume on the pillow next to him. He looked over to the other side of the bed, but his wife was not there. As he sat up, he heard the faint clinking of dishes coming from the kitchen. Serafina must be letting him sleep in, since he planned to take some time off after his tour of duty. He had considered trying to patch things up with his brother, but he knew the wounds there were still too raw. His brother was a good man, but he was also the only person he knew who was more stubborn than himself.

Cade pulled on a shirt and stretched, reaching high into the air. It felt good to be home. No, it felt *wonderful* to be home. He had replayed the moment he would return over and over again in his mind. It was what spurred him on, kept him sane during his mission. Every soldier needed to have something to look forward to, something to cling to that was greater than themselves. He did not fight out of a sense of duty to his country. He fought to protect. Protecting his family was his greatest responsibility and was what drove him through the final assault on Gigan's Hill.

He smiled. "Protector of the Realm," they called him. Truthfully, he didn't feel he deserved the title; he wasn't sure what had transpired to end the war. It was a detail no one else seemed concerned with, but it continued to haunt him. To everyone else, the events that had unfolded by his hand were the catalyst for peace; that was all that mattered.

Cade pushed those thoughts away. He was home, and he could hear oil popping on a hot pan as the smell of breakfast wafted through the room. He made his way to the kitchen and saw Serafina dancing around the kitchen with his son Etan while eggs and bacon cooled next to the wood stove. Etan was a quick study, and you wouldn't have imagined a boy so young could dance like he'd been doing it for decades. Jessa, his youngest, ran around with Cade's battalion flag wrapped around her like a cape, exclaiming she was "Protectress of the Realm."

The sight brought tears to his eyes. It was exactly how he had imagined it would be when he needed a thought to hold on to. He hung in the doorway, not wanting the moment to end. Maybe if he held his breath and didn't move, it would do just that.

His wife glanced over and saw him. "It's about time you woke up. Getting Jessa to leave you alone is no small feat, you know. She's been asking about you all morning."

She looked at him again when he didn't respond and noticed the tears that had welled up in his eyes. "Sweetheart, what's the matter? Are you okay?"

Cade shook his head. "It's nothing. Let's eat."

Serafina leaned in and kissed him on the cheek. "I'm afraid my cooking has not improved while you were away.

It's a bit hard to master the culinary arts while trying to watch after these wild beasts."

She was being modest, of course. Her cooking was fantastic. She always excelled at whatever she did. Not because of innate talent but because she always worked so hard at everything she tried. In many ways, Serafina was stronger than Cade. She could always be counted on for advice, she would always take on more work to get something done, and she always found time to spend with the children, no matter how hectic things got. Cade liked to think that he was an independent person, but the fact was he relied on her far more than he wanted to admit.

He sat down at the table, and Etan, having finished his dance, bowed to Serafina and joined Cade at the table. Jessa had come in, and seeing Cade, she hopped up on his lap to eat, rather than taking her own seat at the table. Serafina laughed. He had missed that laugh so much.

Serafina sat down at the table, but to Cade's horror, the room began to dissolve. Every part of the room turned into tiny points of light that began to swirl and take off at great speed until everything was gone.

In what felt like an instant, all that remained was the table, the chair Cade was sitting in, and another chair opposite Cade. The floor had become nothingness, lined with opposing white lines in an odd grid-like pattern.

Opposite him in the chair sat a man who resembled Cade looking back at him.

The man spoke. "Hello, Cade."

It was the voice that he had been hearing. It sounded a bit like Cade's own voice, if a bit distorted.

"What happened to my family? Where did they go?" Cade was having trouble thinking clearly. It felt like his mind was a ship casting about, searching for harbor.

"Your mind has constructed a false reality, the world as you want it to be. You need to wake up."

Cade shook his head. "No. I know who I am. It's you that needs to go."

A grave expression descended upon the doppelgänger's face. "Your family is gone. They were taken by the Wraiths. But you can stop them."

Cade believed the man was telling the truth, but he did not want to accept it.

"What's wrong with living in this reality? I have my family here. I don't care much for a world without them."

"Have you forgotten your Promise?"

In the blink of an eye, a flurry of tiny dots flew around Cade, painting a picture in all three dimensions. He recognized his surroundings. It was Grinolt Pass, near the city where he had grown up. It was the middle of spring, and the forest leading up to the path was so dense that only narrow scraps of light could filter through. He knew where he was and when he was.

"Bearer, are you sure this path is safe?" A young woman's voice.

Cade turned to her. "No, I'm not sure."

"What does my husband say?" she asked.

Cade bit his cheek. "It...it doesn't work quite like that." It was his first Pact. Her husband had passed away the week before in a tragic hunting accident. "But I said I would get you there. It's what he would have wanted, right?"

The woman nodded, tears welling in her eyes as she continued to follow him.

As they began their ascent through the path, the sun had begun to set, casting a long shadow over the pass.

"Well, what do we have here?" a deep voice bellowed from above. A large, bearded man, armed with a long rifle, came into view. More men began to appear through the trees; Cade counted twenty. He guided the young mother behind him.

"Your purses," the gruff man said.

Cade nodded to the woman, who pulled out her purse and handed it to him. Cade took his own coin pouch and threw both on the ground.

"Smart man. And...lady?" The man jumped in front of Cade, who took a step back, arm still barring the woman. "Now, now, traveler. I just wish to see this maiden's face."

Cade hesitated then stepped aside as he made note of the formation of the bandits. *Steady*, he thought. *Remember your training.*

"My, my, what a beautiful woman. Not like those beasts we are used to in Wythlain. What do you men think?" The men all shouted and laughed, hoisting their weapons high in the air. "Leave her, and you may pass."

Cade remained silent.

"I'm not going to ask again, boy. I suggest you take my offer."

Cade closed his eyes and took a deep breath, visualizing the phantom within him. The phantom felt different than it had earlier. Something in it, something powerful, began to stir. There were too many, he thought. But if he was careful, there was a chance. Win or lose, there was only one choice. He opened his eyes to see the man had taken aim at Cade's head with an old rifle.

"The hard way it is," was all the man said as he pulled the trigger. The bullet bounced off of Cade's encoded skull. He leapt forward, encoded diamond, and wrenched the rifle from the man's hands. He flipped the barrel and fired. One down.

The action had bought him precious seconds as the

shocked men began to understand that they were up against a Bearer. And one trained in Coda martial arts, no less. Cade dashed over to a group of men fumbling for their weapons and punched the first one with an encoded fist, knocking him unconscious. He twisted the man's arm behind his back and used him as a shield as the other men tried to run him through with their spears. He sent the human shield into the group, knocking them down. Behind him, he heard the woman scream. Cade turned to see the other men, rifles loaded, taking aim at him.

Every phantom has a purpose. For the husband, the protection of his wife was his. The sensation that had stirred within him became greater as the sound of gunshots echoed in the pass that evening. Cade looked to see the bullets from those guns had frozen mere inches from his body. When the purpose of a phantom is threatened, the Bearer reaches affinity with the phantom. The Bearer and phantom become one, their Songs harmonizing in time. Time stands still. Affinity lasted only seconds, but the Bearer could move freely, and for a master of Coda, seconds were all that were needed. Every movement had meaning, a distinct purpose, like a choreographed dance. Each second was a gift from this man's spirit. He felt the emotions of the phantom flow through him. It was purity, it was truth, it was love.

As the affinity wore off, twenty men lay defeated before him. Cade knew then what his Promise would be.

He returned home after fulfilling the Pact and made his Promise:

> I will be a bridge for those who cannot cross
> I will be hope for those who have none

> I will be the shield for those who have fallen
> And I will sing their Song so they will not
> > be forgotten

> I am Elegy.

He committed it to memory and threw the paper into the fire, sealing the Promise. As he watched the paper burn, he remembered feeling better than he ever had before. As the ashes fell away, so did the imagery around him, and he found himself before the doppelgänger once more.

"I remember."

The man remained silent.

He looked up. "What's happening to me?"

"Nocturne pushes the phantoms you bear deeper into the Firmere, quieting them. If you take too much, you risk pushing your own phantom into the Firmere as well."

"So you exist in the Firmere and were able to find me? Who are you?"

"That's a story for another time."

Cade shook his head. He was getting nowhere. "What are the Wraiths doing with the taken?"

The image grew dimmer. "Find Eos, if she still exists, and we may still have hope. For now, you must wake."

Eos—that name again. He had heard it during his last hallucination. Cade pleaded to the fading light before him. "But how?"

"Choose."

The points of light faded, and the man was gone. Thousands of new tiny lights flew in, and Cade was back in his home, standing next to the table.

His wife looked up at him with an eyebrow raised.

"Honey, are you going to join us? It's getting cold. You know I hate it when you don't eat it while it's hot!"

Cade looked at her, fighting back tears.

She looked at him, concerned. "What's the matter?"

"There are people...that need me."

"Then you should go help them."

"I want to stay here," said Cade, shaking his head.

She smiled. "Do you know why I married you?"

"What do you mean?"

"Well, there are many reasons. But one of the biggest is that you have always put others ahead of yourself. It's downright infuriating sometimes, but I wouldn't have it any other way." She walked over to him and took his hand into hers. "I will be here for you when the time comes."

Cade found himself shaking, his hand gripping hers tight, unable to let go.

Choose.

He took a deep breath and closed his eyes.

I am the bridge. I am hope. I am the shield. I am the singer of Songs.

The tiny lights shattered and faded into darkness. Cade also began to dematerialize, and he watched as particles of himself broke free until he was gone.

His eyes opened, and he found himself looking up at the ceiling of his brother's room. The buckle that bound his wrists had snapped, and his throat was dry. *How long have I been out?*

A knock sounded at the door. "Grandmaster. Karessa has awakened," he heard Jalek, the temple's caretaker, say from beyond the door.

Cade sat up and rubbed the bruises on his wrists. He nodded to himself.

Time to get some answers.

9

OLD SOLDIERS

Casters and their origin are still shrouded in mystery. They are one of the few artifacts left behind by the Ancients that we can utilize. Their design is simplistic, yet the creation of casters eludes weapons craftsmen. Through the art of cast-forging, detailed in the Book of the Traveler, the creation of bullets imprinted with those who have passed is possible, but we are limited by the number of casters in existence.
—From Chalician Archaeologist's Quarterly, *Vol. 11*

CADE ARRIVED to see Karessa sitting up in the bed, a gray wool blanket pulled around her. They had taken her to a room within the interior of the temple. Jalek wanted to make sure they could protect her if the Acolytes decided to come for her. Her gray eyes, which had burned brightly only days before, appeared sunken and scared. He glanced at the table next to the bed and saw an empty vial of Nocturne. They must have used it to keep her mind under control until she woke. With her permission, they could help her rite of Pact closure. It was a frowned-upon but sometimes necessary ritual.

Jalek and Ashlyn were in the room with her. When Cade entered, she looked at him. "I believe I have you to, uh, thank for saving me." Cade blushed, remembering his last-ditch effort to get her mind to resurface amongst the phantoms of the soldiers she bore.

"Yes. You're...welcome."

Jalek broke in, "You had recently come here, asking us to join in helping the Foundation. From what you told us, the Foundation is a rebel force working against the Wraiths."

She nodded. "Yes, that is true. But my memory is fragmented somehow. I think I was an agent of some sort. I don't quite remember."

Cade frowned. "What do you remember?"

"I remember running into an old friend, a soldier from the war that I had met before. They weren't wearing the robes of an Acolyte, so I didn't think much of it at the time. We went to get a drink at a tavern. I only have brief glimpses of memories after that." She shivered and pulled the blanket tighter around her.

Ashlyn took a step forward. "It's okay, you don't—"

"No. It's fine. I remember being in a room, like a laboratory of some sort. I was lying on a metal table. I couldn't move, but I wasn't restrained. It was like I was just an observer in my own body. I would lose consciousness before I could remember any more." She shook her head. "Conditioning, they called it later, after I was out. Though I don't remember much, I just knew that I never wanted to go through it again. If you ask too many questions, you have to be reconditioned."

Cade spoke again. "Why are the Acolytes attacking Bearers and the Coda Order?"

Karessa looked at him again. "They want to eliminate any possibility of resistance. They see Bearers as a substantial threat to the success of the Ascension Drive."

Cade raised an eyebrow. "The Ascension Drive? What is that?"

Karessa shook her head. "I don't know. I only know that is why the Acolytes exist. To ensure the success of the Ascension Drive." She grabbed her head, and he could see her grinding her teeth, much like Rast had done back in Wilks. "Even now, they try to speak inside my mind. But the Nocturne helps. The voice is hardly a whisper now."

"Do you remember where the Foundation is?"

"No," she said, her face full of regret. "They took things from my memory, chunks of memories, leaving only pieces here and there. All I remember is that before I was abducted, I was heading to Rynth to meet a man, an archaeologist."

Cade cocked his head to the side. "Do you remember his name?"

"It started with a J...Jace...something. I'm sorry, I can't remember the rest."

"Jace Exile?" Cade said, trying to hide his astonishment.

Her face lit up. "Yes! That's it. I'm sure of it."

Cade rubbed his chin. How did Jace figure into all of this?

Jalek rested his hand on her shoulder. "Thank you. That is enough. Please rest now. Tomorrow we will perform the rite so that you may find some peace."

Karessa, grateful, lay back down on the bed as they left the room and closed the door.

Cade turned to Jalek. "We have to get to Rynth right away."

Jalek nodded. He motioned to a student, who ran up to him with a small rucksack. From it he pulled out a worn brown leather bandoleer, each small pocket containing a different caster shell with unique, intricate markings etched into them. Cade knew each one by heart. Even though it had been over a year, every name and every story those shells carried was still ingrained within him, chiseled into the bedrock of his mind.

Cade pulled out one of his casters—the one he called Justice—and broke open the barrel to load it. Casters weren't ordinary guns; they were artifacts of the Ancients, discovered long ago by archaeologists on Chalice. From a distance, they looked very much like a typical pistol. Up close, however, you could see finely etched patterns of lines decorating the body of the weapon. Casters also possessed a vertically inset cylinder which would spin up before firing. Aside from these unique details, they were seemingly simple constructions, consisting of a wide barrel, grip, and trigger. But much to the consternation of the land's finest blacksmiths, no man-made caster had ever demonstrated the abilities of the Ancient-made ones. As such, each was worth a fortune.

Caster shells were equally a mystery. While they could be forged, they could only be usable if imprinted with the Song of one who has chosen to pass on to the Ascent. Once imprinted, the shells could do impossible things beyond explanation. The shells could alter their path after firing to track their intended target and they could even make their target completely vanish.

Followers of Coda had discovered passages in the Traveler's writings that hinted at the use of casters in the war against the Betrayers. The passages spoke of how the Ancients had used weapons as the sole means to fight back against the nigh-invincible Betrayers. The discovery, along with learning how to forge the shells needed to use them, was the breakthrough that gave the people of Chalice a fighting chance during the Wraith War.

Ashlyn watched as he loaded the weapon. "Is that...the caster that killed the Wraith?"

Cade nodded.

Jalek handed him one more shell. The shell had been newly cast and gleamed brightly. Cade took the shell into his hands and closed his eyes. He opened them a moment later and tucked the shell into his belt.

Cade holstered his caster and finished fastening the bandoleer across his chest. "Time to go."

10

ENCROACHING DANGER

Rynth still holds too many secrets to count. As a result, many legends exist and continue to circulate. Some speak of an infinite source of power, hidden deep within the Nexus. It is believed the Ancients are buried there, frozen in time, and will one day awaken to lead us.

—From The Labyrinth of Rynth

CADE WAS JOLTED awake aboard the Malix Express as it clambered topside from the underground railways. The conductor, Malix, was a long-time friend of Seek's, and by association, Cade. Use of the underground railways was forbidden by law, but much like the underground battle arena, the authorities turned a blind eye to it. For a small fee, of course. It was the best way to get out of Solak and not be seen.

He hadn't slept much over the past week, but somehow the vibrations of the railbus had managed to coax him to sleep. Ashlyn sat in the seat across from him, looking out the small window as the Pathway route to Rynth spread out before them.

Malix didn't say much, and his face, beset with the deep lines of age, seemed locked into a perpetual frown. Cade wasn't sure how Seek came to know Malix, but Seek assured Cade that he could be trusted. He remembered Seek describing him as "One of the friendliest guys you'll ever meet who hates everyone." In Seek's experience, grumpiness was roughly proportional to trustworthiness. Cade hoped he was right.

Ashlyn, seeing him sit up, looked at him and smiled. "Good morning. I'm glad you finally got some rest." Cade averted his eyes from hers, gazed out the window, and nodded. He called to Malix, "Where are we now?"

The man who was helming the front of the railbus did not appear to hear him. Or he was ignoring him. Cade left it.

Ashlyn cast a glance toward Malix and grinned at Cade. "I've never been to Rynth. At least not since I was very young. Father believed it safest for me to remain in Toltaire, so I've never really seen the City of the Ancients."

Rynth, the massive city built by the Ancients, was an archaeological paradise. The inhabitants continued to discover new artifacts and hidden passages there, despite the city being discovered over a hundred years ago. But they weren't going there for that. Jace was there, and he might have the answer they needed. If they could find him, it might give them enough of a clue to piece together the mystery of the taken.

As they rolled over the hillside, a small village appeared on the horizon. Malix yelled, in a loud and grating voice, "Next stop, Barnage! Gotta top up!"

As they approached the village, it became apparent

something was not right. The familiar pit in Cade's stomach began to grow.

Ashlyn noticed it, too. "Where are all the people?"

The railbus rumbled to a halt and the doors opened. As they stepped out, they were greeted by nothing but eerie silence.

Malix's grin had given way to a solemn expression. He took off his hat, holding it close to his chest. "Another town joins the taken. May they find their way back home."

Cade held gritted teeth behind his scowl. "Killed. Not taken."

Malix's brow furrowed as he cocked his head toward Cade, but the old man remained silent.

There were those who still clung to the possibility that their family and friends were still out there, but Bearers knew better. Bearers could sense the presence of phantoms. All they had to do was listen for the gentle notes of music being played across the Firmere, as if not to disturb those who still lived. It was faint, but the Song was there, playing for those who chose to hear it.

Cade closed his eyes and quieted his thoughts. Notes began to tumble out all around him, quiet yet constant and flowing from all directions. Many Songs, too many, now held concert over Barnage.

There was no way for the government to explain this. Barnage wasn't some small mining town in the Ends. It was a Pathway town in the interior of Chalice. There would be no way for an invading army to get this far inland without alerting the military. The Wraiths were becoming bolder. But to what end?

Malix grumbled something and headed to the station to charge the batteries on the railbus. It wasn't as advanced as most of the trains in Chalice, which ran without batteries now that the Thread supplied them with power. Cade was surprised a railbus as old as Malix's was still in service. Archaeologists in the area loved dissecting older relics of Ancient technology, hoping for the stepping stone that would allow them to start creating more advanced technologies. Cade wished they'd hurry up and find a breakthrough. He despised being dependent on the Wraiths.

A loud, cracking noise sounded in the distance. Cade looked up and saw the faint telltale plume of dark gray smoke waft into the air. "Caster fire."

Ashlyn looked incredulous. "What? There's somebody still here?"

"Ashlyn, I'm going to need you and Malix to stay in the railbus. Malix, how much time do you need?"

Malix cursed under his breath. "Five minutes, tops."

Cade exited the silver metal railbus and ran into a nearby alley off the main road toward the smoke. Barnage wasn't as large as Solak, and there were only man-made buildings here. It served as a critical waystation between Solak and Rynth, so it had a variety of trading posts and a large central marketplace. The silence unnerved him. Even the birds and insects were quiet, as if out of respect for the dead. As with the other towns that had been taken, there was little sign of struggle. However they did it, they did it with brutal efficiency.

As he snaked down the back alleyways of the buildings, he heard voices. He made his way toward the voices, careful to remain hidden until he could hear them clearly.

A deep voice sounded around the corner. "This is where I saw the smoke. Look at this."

Cade heard a yelp, followed by a soft clink. "What happened?" a new voice said.

"That coin is burning hot! Here, give me your jacket so I can pick it up," said the first voice.

"Oh, hells no, get away. Use your own jacket," the second voice said.

"Leave it. Hells, is that...a caster? Looks legit," said a third voice.

"Jackpot. Come on, let's go. We have to catch that railbus we heard before it charges," said the first voice.

Cade heard them run off. He figured there were at least three of them, going by the voices. He couldn't see their faces from his vantage point, but he didn't need to; they were bandits. Every time a town was hit, some were bound to show up. They made their living by looting from those taken. Robbing people that weren't coming back was a lucrative business, so these incidents tended to attract thieves from all walks of life. Competition was stiff amongst them, which meant they carried a considerable amount of firepower to defend their claim if other bandit groups happened upon them. It was a venture that favored the quick, the bold, and the unstable.

As the voices grew fainter, Cade slipped around the corner of a building and saw some effects scattered upon the ground, still steaming with heat. No body, but that was expected. A caster shot completely evaporated its target. Cade noticed a large coin. He took a handkerchief from the pocket of his duster and picked up the coin, still hot. It bore the insignia of the Wraithbreakers, an elite Bearer fighting unit. *A challenge coin.* Every unit in the military had their own. Another soldier turned Acolyte. Why were they brainwashing soldiers?

Cade retreated the way he had come, taking care not to make a sound. As he neared the railbus, he heard another voice call out. "Please help us! We just want a ride back to the city!" said a short man with a flat nose and sunken eyes. *No points for originality*, Cade thought. The good news was that common criminals only knew common tactics.

Cade stepped out into the open, encoding lead. "Hey!" he hollered to the man. A split second later, Cade heard gunshots from two separate locations. One hit him in his right arm, the other on his left shoulder. He turned to the right and saw a man hunkered down behind the railing on the second floor of an old storehouse. Cade felt he couldn't get a clean shot, so he took cover behind the building he had stepped away from. He released his encoding and pulled out his caster, the one he called Justice, from its holster. He sighed, not wanting to use a caster shell.

While casters could fire bullets made of metal and gunpowder, what made them special was that they could fire shells that had been imprinted. These special shells were what allowed the caster otherworldly abilities. The imprinting process, pieced together using translations from the Book of the Traveler, allowed castforgers to imprint Songs of those who had departed to the Ascent upon the shells. These shells needed no gunpowder, yet could fly distances far greater than any normal bullet.

He ran his index finger along the bullets in the bandoleer. Tenth from the top. Tolita Par. Mother of two, died at the age of sixty-five defending her children from a Skex attack in her village. Cade memorized the story behind every shell he carried, per the precepts of Coda. Everyone had a story. Those that chose to remain behind to imprint caster bullets shells were no different. It was important to Cade that he try to match the shell with his target; it was his way to honor those who had passed.

His caster, anticipating intent, began to throw blue sparks as the barrel spun up, whistling softly.

Cade stepped out and fired his caster at the man hiding behind the railing. A loud crack sounded, and a thin tracer raced behind the bullet as it fired and then *curved* to hit the man while he was in cover. The man evaporated, a burst of smoke taking his place. One down.

By then the man at the railbus had given up the charade and put his hands up in the air. Not surprising, since the man was in plain view with no cover. "Please, don't shoot!" Cade spun the chamber to a gunpowder bullet; no need to waste priceless ammunition on an easy target. He fired and found his mark. The man fell. One to go.

He turned to his left and scanned the area, encoding tungsten as a precaution. He figured the last man was probably on the balcony of the old hotel, since that would give him the best vantage point, along with no shortage of places to hide. Cade was weighing his options when he heard another loud crack coming from the hotel itself.

He felt a moment of panic, since his encoding meant very little to a caster bullet. Once the moment had passed, he realized he was not the target. *That must mean...*Cade took the risk of exhausting one of his phantoms and encoded to the wood of the hotel balcony to boost himself up. Sure enough, just near the doorway, lay the gun of the bandit, white-hot, but the stolen caster was nowhere to be found. He looked up to see the tail of a red robe disappear from the doorway. An Acolyte. Cade raised his caster as he gave chase. When he turned the corner, the Acolyte was gone.

Cade continued to explore the small hotel but could find no trace of the mysterious gunman. Cade returned to the room and noticed a small silver shell casing on the ground. Its markings were unfamiliar, but Cade noticed a translucent inlaid square, similar to those found in chipcoins. It was a caster shell but unlike any Cade had ever seen.

He snapped back to the task at hand. The shooter was likely nearby, and it was best to leave quickly. Cade did not want to test his protective encoding against a caster bullet, let alone a new type. He made his way to the railbus, careful not to expose himself too much.

When he returned, he saw Ashlyn staring at him, wide-eyed, as if horrified. When he met her eyes, she turned away and moved to the back of the railbus, eyes locked to the floor. Cade sighed and sat down. "Let's get out of here," he said to Malix.

"Oh sure, ol' Malix will get moving," the old man said. "Let's just pretend that there wasn't just a shootout...with *casters*. Nope. All fine here. Next stop: Rynth."

Cade sat on the railbus, turning the unusual casing over in his hands, unable to shake the feeling that things were about to get a whole lot worse.

11

RYNTH

For the safety of the people of Chalice: All invocations of a phantom, including encoding of any kind, is forbidden within the cities of Chalice. This war has brought to light a grave error in our judgment as a young nation. Man should hold no sway over the dead. The Book of the Traveler is to be outlawed without royal authorization, and any copies publicly available must be put to the torch.

—From King Liam Winshire's Royal Decree following the disbandment of the Bearer Corps

THE TRIP to Rynth had left Ashlyn's mind reeling. What she had watched Cade do in Barnage had shaken her so much she didn't even remember their arrival. Cade seemed to know where he was going. He had known who Jace Exile was, but she didn't know any more than that.

The man's house was not far from the Rynth station, a sprawling Ancient-built structure that served as a hub for thousands of people coming and going at all hours. After they managed to free themselves from the crush of people hurrying to their trains, Ashlyn followed behind Cade until they arrived at a cozy house of brick and wood. The house was dark, so Cade took the liberty of opening the back door with an encoded push. If she hadn't been so tired, she would have protested.

Cade led her up the stairs to a small room in the loft of the house. "Sleep," he said. "Jace will likely return soon."

Still speechless, she obliged, hoping rest would give her some clarity.

It felt as if she had just closed her eyes when she awoke to hushed voices downstairs.

"You're still carrying them? It's been over a year, Cade."

"Yeah."

"You have to let them go. They wouldn't have wanted this. It's not worth your sanity."

"We're close this time, Jace. It won't be much longer now. I owe it to them."

The man sighed. "You look like you just emerged from the ninth door of the Forgotten Hells, Cade. Are you sure you can make it?"

"I'll be fine. Do you happen to have any...connections here?"

"Do I look like the type of person that would have connections? I heard they stopped manufacturing it after the war. After that supply runs out...well, I don't need to tell you what could happen."

"It'll be fine. I'll be back soon. Can you please watch over her?"

"Of course, of course. Just hurry back, we've got a lot to catch up on."

She heard a door close and let sleep take her once more.

SHE AWOKE JUST as the sun began to fill the loft with a warm glow. The sunlight had never been quite the same since the arrival of the Wraiths. She couldn't quite explain it, but it now felt less vibrant to her, like it was being filtered. Ashlyn glanced around the small room. It was cluttered with all manner of books and scraps of paper, but it had a comfortable feel, like the cabins she visited back when her mother was still alive. On the walls were maps. All kinds of maps: maps of Chalice, maps of circuitous roads winding into each other, and maps diagramming...trade routes, perhaps?

Her attention moved to the large window. It offered a breathtaking view of the city, if only a small portion. Rynth, City of the Ancients, was gigantic, second only to Toltaire. Seeing the city now, she wished she had disobeyed her father's orders to remain in Toltaire whenever he traveled to Rynth. The skyline was breathtaking; she could see a fantastic golden spire, referred to as the Nexus, towering over the city, its peak stretching into the clouds.

Looking down, she could see streams of people bustling about upon every street. It was the city of opportunity; there was adventure to be had and untold riches yet to be discovered. The opportunity brought with it characters from every part of the world. The true purpose of the city remained a mystery to researchers who tried to decipher the artifacts the Ancients had left behind.

Her gaze traveled skyward, and she was again awed by the size of the Nexus, the great obelisk that rose so high, she could barely see its peak. No clouds drifted near it, or the rest of the city skyline for that matter. It was perfect, except for the occasional bolt of electricity arcing from the Thread, which stood hundreds of miles away. The weather was no coincidence; the Ancients had designed it that way. The temperate climate made the city suitable for all, including those too poor to survive anywhere else. Many of Chalice's destitute population called the endless spiraling corridors and alleys of Rynth home.

The bulk of the city appeared to be wrought from a brushed silver metal with no visible seams or joints, as though it were cast from an impossibly large mold. Ashlyn could see lights inset in buildings, casting a bright but inviting glow onto the streets. She remembered reading about how much of Rynth had power even before the Wraiths reactivated the Thread, just like the Stardome in Solak. Scientists and archaeologists were still no closer to understanding what inexhaustible power source Rynth was using to control the climate and keep the lights glowing bright all these years. She imagined the Nexus, the fabled undiscovered core of Rynth, must hold the answers.

Mixed in with the city's structures, she could see the man-made houses built on top of the metal streets, a patch-work quilt of old and new. The stark contrast between the two architectures underscored how far behind their own technology was.

Despite the breathtaking view, the memory of Barnage pulled her back to reality. She lamented that Chalice had needed the help of Bearers to secure the Accord with the Wraiths. From what she had witnessed, Bearers had little regard for the lives of others. The man near the railbus, surrendering. Cade had killed him...with no hesitation. She had thought he was different, but she was wrong. She looked at the window latch and placed her hand on it. If she escaped, she would be no closer to finding Rolan's killer. But staying meant trusting a monster.

She sighed, taking her hand off the latch, and turned to face the room. On the desk sat a candelabra, inset with a small lit candle, casting light on some curious items. Upon closer inspection, she realized they were chipcoins, though they were not of any denomination with which she was familiar. She was about to pick one up when up when she heard a loud yell from downstairs.

Ashlyn burst out of her room to see what was the matter. In hindsight, she thought herself foolish—what advantage could she lend if they were under attack? But her instincts were always to help when she could.

The great room of the house was overwhelming. Books lined every shelf and ledge, spilling from bookcases as if they were multiplying on their own. Large burlap sacks, like the ones she'd seen within the castle's pantries, filled the spaces in between. She was surprised to even see some machines, Ancient artifacts, in crates near the room's long table.

"You're awake! My doing, I'm afraid. I hope you'll accept my apologies. I've had quite a breakthrough and couldn't contain my excitement."

A slender, bookish man with short, messy blond hair and an ornate pair of reading spectacles stood before her. She didn't see Cade anywhere. Where had he gone?

"Look at these two maps! They align perfectly. How did I not see it before? Now, if I also take this one," he said, grabbing another map off the table, "...and overlay it with these..." He rubbed his chin, contemplating. "Wait, no. That's not right."

As if breaking from a trance, he stood upright and looked at Ashlyn. "Where are my manners? It is an honor to meet you, Princess Winshire. I apologize that the accommodations are a bit...austere, but I was not expecting royal company today. A shame, as I would have prepared a more suitable arrangement for such a distinguished guest as yourself."

Ashlyn's alarm subsided. "I'm sorry, you've caught me at a bit of a disadvantage, Mr...?"

The man grinned broadly, eyes shining like a lit prism. "I am Jace...Jace Exile. Cade is an old and good friend of mine. I assure you that you are quite safe here; it would appear Cade went to great lengths to make sure you were not followed. He had to leave for a bit, but he will return shortly. Please, have a seat, and I'll fetch you a cup of tea."

Ashlyn sat down in the solid wood chair Jace offered. "Pleased to make your acquaintance, Mr. Exile. Your name, 'Exile,' I've never heard a family name like that before."

"I will admit it is rather unique, but that is because it is my Promised name."

Ashlyn's brow furrowed. "Promise? You were promised that name?"

The man chuckled. "In a sense, that's true. My family is originally from Gallance, as is Cade's, if you're curious. That's how we met each other, once upon a time. Now, you see there is a standing tradition in the city that when you turn fifteen years old, you must make a Promise to yourself. It's a rite of passage of sorts, only more personal. You don't have to share your Promise with anyone else if you don't want to, but you do get to change your name to something that you feel represents your Promise. It's a reminder that you always keep with you." He smiled. "In Gallance, they like to say that your first name is your given name, and your last name is your taken name."

"And the Promise...is a secret?"

Jace made a dismissive gesture with his hands. "Oh, goodness, no. I'm an open book. My Promise is simple. I had lived in Gallance for my whole life when I became of age, and I never quite fit in there. It was an old city, and its economy, like most outer towns in Chalice, was based on mining within the mountains that surrounded it. As you might deduce on your own, scholarship was not a highly valued trait, nor was it easy to find any knowledge outside of basic geology. I came to the realization I had to exile myself from my own homeland to follow my dream of becoming an archaeologist. And here I am in the Ancient city of Rynth, an archaeologist's dream city if ever there was one."

Ashlyn couldn't help but be envious of the man's story. She had always longed to escape the routine of the palace but felt duty-bound to remain and make sure she was available to assist in royal matters, even if they did seem pointless and superficial.

"Are there still things to find in Rynth? I thought most artifacts had been discovered by now."

"Yes! There is much, much more to find. We are literally just scratching the surface. The entire city extends underground. Once we find out how to gain access to more of its depths, imagine the treasures we will find! And we are still far from discovering the secrets of the artifacts we have already found. The Ancients have left us so many unanswered questions. If we can answer even a few of them, imagine what we could do!"

Ashlyn remembered the maps in the bedroom. She felt stupid for not considering it before. "You're trying to find the entrance to the Nexus!"

He grinned and nodded. "It is the key to everything. The underground passages we have discovered host a labyrinth of buildings with no entrance. The outer rings we can easily navigate, but once we start going deeper, we end up right back where we started. They had to have left us a way inside."

Ashlyn was fascinated. Despite being the princess, she had never learned much about Rynth. Most archaeologists in Rynth were cautious and private about their work, so much of it remained unpublished. Rynth was crawling with corporate spies. If any headway was gained, chances were good a corporation would muscle its way in and seize control. Chalice was no country for true scholars. She did know that the Nexus had no discernible entrance, and access to it had eluded everyone who sought its secrets.

"I've always wondered, can't you just drill inside?"

Jace shook his head. "We tried that. Like most things the Ancients built, we can't seem to penetrate the metal. We located a first-generation drill from one of the quarries the Ancients used to mine, but we can't seem to get it running. It uses a fuel source we are not familiar with, but there is a team of scientists working out how to retrofit it with a different power source." Jace rose and paced around the room, lost in the discussion. "I will find a way inside one day. And within it, the ultimate treasure," he said, looking up and nodding.

Ashlyn found the man's enthusiasm infectious. She leaned in closer. "The ultimate treasure?"

He opened a thick leather book on the table and pointed to a faded sketch.

She furrowed her brow. "A railbus?"

He leaned in close, eyes sparkling like a child's. "A starship."

"A starship...?" She heard the front door creak open, and Cade walked in. He seemed off-balance and almost tripped on his own feet when he crossed the threshold. He looked at her and then at Jace. "Uh-oh, what stories are you telling her? You've got that look you get when you tell stories."

Jace frowned. "I have no such face."

Ashlyn saw Cade smile. *How can this man smile after all he's done?* she thought, keeping her expression even. Cade continued, "I'm looking at it right now. You're talking about the Nexus again, aren't you? You still haven't given that up?"

"Every riddle has a solution, my friend, and the challenge makes the discovery all the sweeter."

Cade snorted and sat down in the chair next to Ashlyn.

The machines in a crate next to him began to whir softly and light up, as if reacting to his presence.

Jace raised an eyebrow. "Wait. How did you do that? I've never managed to get these artifacts running."

Cade shook his head. "I don't know. It's been happening to me a lot lately." He pushed the crate away with his foot, and the machines deactivated. "As much as I'd like to speculate on the mysteries of Rynth, there is a matter that I'd like to discuss with you, but we have to keep the conversation just between us."

Jace nodded, the expression of child-like wonder fading. "This is a big city, but I'll help you as much as I can."

"There is a woman, Karessa, from an organization known as the Foundation. She said she was coming here to see you. Do you know why?"

Jace's face paled. "So Rolan is dead."

Cade raised an eyebrow. "How do you...?"

Jace sighed. "I'm with the Foundation."

THE TRAVELER'S LEGACY

Chipcoins are by far the most ubiquitous artifact left behind by the Ancients. The small discs were so prevalent during the settlement of Chalice that archaeologists began using them as a form of currency. Though the makeshift currency has been officially displaced by the Chalician dollar, the coins are still used as a recognized currency in most Pathway towns.

—*From* Chalician Archaeologist's Quarterly, *Vol.* 2

"YOU'RE A *SPY?*" Cade was incredulous. He would never have imagined his most trusted friend could hide something like that from him, and he realized the secret hurt a bit more than he wanted to admit. He was having a hard time collecting his thoughts; it felt like his mind was a cooking pot that had boiled over. He had just taken a good dose of Nocturne, so it couldn't be his phantoms.

"Allow me a moment to explain." Jace sat next to Cade and Ashlyn and took a deep breath. "As I'm sure you are aware, it's been harder and harder for archaeologists in

Rynth to lay claim to any artifacts. As soon as a discovery is made, one of the corporations in Toltaire would find out and steal the artifact for themselves. In order to continue our research, a group of us banded together and formed a secret society of sorts to act as counterintelligence against these corporation-controlled spies."

Forever my song will play, a distant voice chanted, as if lost in a storm. *Why can I still hear them?* he thought. Perhaps the Nocturne was diluted or had been cut with something else. He shook his head to shake out the voices and turned his attention back to Jace.

"The thing is, we got really good at it. Mostly because we could employ spectacularly good agents. You see, when spies in Toltaire come to know too much about their employers, their lives become expendable. The best ones see the writing on the wall and take up residence in Rynth, since there is a rather healthy demand for their skill-set. Our counterintelligence gave us all the protection we needed to find and retain our artifacts so we could continue researching. From there we took the next logical step: we started collecting our own intelligence."

Cade had already heard about corporations stealing from the scientific community, even though they performed all these actions covertly. Anyone who could read between the lines knew what was really happening. "Who did you spy on?"

"We're a community of scholars, and we couldn't help but have...theories about what is happening in Chalice. If we were going to protect our interests going forward, we decided we had to dig deeper." Jace leaned in closer, smiling. "This is where it gets interesting. One of our theories is centered on the Thread. It acts as a power plant for us, as you already know, but I do not believe that is its primary purpose. I have reason to believe it is, in fact, a transmitter to the Wraith ship parked in orbit around our planet."

Cade was incredulous, but he couldn't help but recall the dreams he'd been having about the Thread. "If they are giving power to us, then what are they transmitting back to the ship?"

Jace ignored Cade's visible disbelief. "We had one of our team monitor the Thread and record any abnormal activity. We also had agents throughout Chalice record approximate timings of the last few villages that have disappeared over the last year. We discovered that shortly after those disappearances, the Thread's energy would reverse course. It was only for a few minutes, but we are almost certain there is a correlation."

"They're sending...the people they take?" Cade asked.

"That's the, uh, prevailing theory." Jace did not meet Cade's gaze as he spoke.

Ashlyn interjected. "How are they sending them? Are they taking bodies through the Thread itself?"

Jace shook his head. "We believe they somehow are able to capture the phantom from someone who has recently passed. There is just too much we don't understand about the Wraiths and their technology."

"But the phantoms are left behind. You know that."

"Yes, but what if the phantoms that are taken are the ones that chose to ascend? Not the ones that chose to remain in the Firmere."

Cade paced the room, lost in thought. According to the Book of the Traveler, there are three known planes of existence: the Veris, the Firmere, and the Transcent. The Sigh represents the life force of a person and exists within our bodies inside the Veris, the physical plane. The Song, more commonly known as a phantom, exists in the Firmere, the ethereal plane in between the Veris and the Transcent. When a person dies, their Sigh travels to the Transcent, the highest of the three planes. At that point, their Song can choose to persist in the Firmere or rejoin with the Sigh in the Transcent.

Ashlyn looked confused. "But to what end?"

"We don't know. This is all just speculation. From what we have translated of the Ancients' language, there are clear mentions of the Sigh and its connection to the Betrayers in the first war. Partner that with the fact that villages are being systematically taken, with not a single clue left behind. That in itself should tell us something." Jace had stood up and was pacing around the room. "I don't believe what we are seeing with the taken is a simple genocide by the Wraiths or some other unknown enemy. The collection of the taken has a distinct purpose."

Ashlyn turned to Cade. "What did Karessa mention earlier—the Ascension Drive? It has to be related."

Cade rubbed his chin, considering. "But where does this really get us, Jace? I've known, along with everyone with two wits to rub together, that the Wraiths are somehow behind the disappearances. Even with intelligence like this, it doesn't change the fact that we're powerless to move against them."

Jace held up a finger. "Ah, but I haven't got to the best part yet. The Ancients' technology on Chalice, as you know, shows three generations of distinct evolution. Now, the architecture of the Thread has always stood out, because it doesn't match any of the three generations of technology. Some archaeologists refer to this as fourth-generation technology, but others, like me, don't agree. You see, I believe the Thread isn't Ancient technology at all."

Cade raised an eyebrow; he had not heard this theory before.

"Part of the Accord was to allow the Wraiths use of the Thread, which they would in turn use to provide us with power. Why do you suppose they wanted to use the Thread, of all places?"

Cade shrugged. "So they could steal the technology for themselves."

"Perhaps. But perhaps the Thread was the original forward operating base for the Wraiths during the Battle of the Betrayer." Jace paused, looking at them expectantly. "Don't you see? The technology was their own. After they were driven out so long ago, they regrouped and came back to claim it. By signing the Accord, we gave them the very thing they had come for."

And with you my heart will stay.

Cade rubbed his temples—his headache would not subside. "The Betrayers...you're saying that they are the Wraiths? Let's say for a moment that you're right. There's still no way we can get anywhere near the Thread to find out what they are up to."

Jace had a devilish look on his face, the one he got whenever he had a wild idea, which also meant it was probably something dangerous. "I think it is time for us to visit the Foundation itself," he said.

Cade looked at Ashlyn. She had been through a lot in Solak, and there was no telling where they would end up next. "Ashlyn..."

Ashlyn shook her head. "Not that again. Rolan was the closest thing to family I had after my mother died. He died for this information, and I *will* find out who killed him. I *will* continue his work."

Cade looked at Jace, who grinned. "Aren't archaeologists supposed to be reading dusty old tomes and studying artifacts?"

Jace's grin faded. "It's no longer safe here. More of my friends, Rolan included, have either been mysteriously killed or have vanished." He gestured to the crates. "I was already planning on leaving. You told me yourself that Barnage was recently taken. That's not even considered part of the Ends! Something is about to happen, but I don't know what. I can't help but feel we have to do whatever we can to try to stop it."

Cade sighed. "You're both crazy as far as I'm concerned." He stood to get up, and the throbbing in his head returned tenfold. He could hear voices. They seemed very far away at first but continually grew louder, throwing him off-balance.

Forever my song will play.

And with you my heart will stay.

Jace rushed over to him. "Cade, are you okay? You don't look well."

"I'm fine. Just a headache," Cade said, rubbing his temple.

Jace looked at Cade's chest and his eyes opened wide. "Cade, that necklace…"

Cade looked down to see the ring around the necklace was stuck to his shirt. Jace leaned in closer to the ring. "It's as if you're—"

"I'm encoding with it?" When Cade focused on it, the ring released itself and the headache dissipated. "I wasn't even trying to."

Jace, fixated, continued to look at it. "May I have it for a moment?"

Cade nodded and handed it to him. "It's the ring passed down from Grandmaster to Grandmaster. It is called the ring of the Traveler, but it's more a symbol than anything else. A simple ring of iron. We stopped encoding with iron once we could forge with tungsten."

"Are you sure about that?" Jace sat down at a well-used workbench of rough-hewn wood. He pulled out a series of bound lenses and peered at the ring. "Ah. Mm-hmm. You see that? There's a scratch right there."

Cade leaned in and saw the scratch. "So?"

"There's something underneath. It's not iron," Jace said, looking up. His eyes grew wide and sparkled once more. He leapt up from the workbench, sat down at an old pedal-driven grinding wheel, and began to pedal, spinning the small wheel at increasing speed.

"Hey! What are you doing? That's priceless!" Cade rushed over to him.

"Don't worry," Jace said nonchalantly. Orange sparks flew from the ring as it ground against the wheel. "I assure you there is nothing I can do to harm this ring."

Cade looked at Ashlyn, who just shrugged.

"Ah-ha!" Jace exclaimed as he stood up, the wheel still spinning. "Look at that," he said triumphantly. He held the ring up to Cade and Ashlyn, who had moved up closer.

The aging iron veneer had been stripped away, and in its place was a metal of gleaming gold, marbled with folded wisps of bright silver.

Cade's jaw dropped. "That's..."

Jace nodded. "Pure Rynthium. The most valuable substance on the planet."

Cade took the ring from Jace, still in shock. Rynthium, named for its initial discovery in Rynth, was an ore that large Ancient-built machines ran on. Even the best modern mining equipment had only managed to mine individual grains of it. And the most skilled metallurgists did not know how to form it into anything of real substance. He took the ring and held it over his finger. The artifacts in the room all activated at once, lights flashing and beeping as if possessed.

"Cade, maybe we should—" That was all he heard as he slipped on the ring, and his vision broke into innumerable motes of light and disappeared, leaving him stranded in darkness.

He had once again returned to the Firmere, but not by using Nocturne. The ring was doing it. He had encoded to it without thinking. It was connecting him here somehow, allowing him to see the Firmere. His vision of the realm seemed to sharpen, and he discovered he was not surrounded by perfect darkness. He looked at his hand, which was now made of blue, shimmering smoke. His heartbeat quickened as he found he could not see his own body. It had been replaced by a churning vortex of the luminescent blue smoke. Wisps of it ebbed and swirled around him in mesmerizing patterns. Watching them was somehow comforting, and he found he could anticipate its movement and flow.

Just breathe, he told himself. Looking down, he saw that both of his casters were also made of the bright smoke, although the smoke's movement was alien to him, its pattern geometric where his own was more unpredictable and organic. The illumination from the bullets across his chest was almost blinding. Each of the bullets had the same smoke compressed within their casings, and when he looked closely, the fine wisps churned, flowing back and forth, like the rolling waves of a miniature sea.

This connection to the Firmere was different than when he had visited with Nocturne. He was more in control, like he still was rooted within the physical reality of the Veris. He looked up and could see another two concentrations of the light. *That's where Jace and Ashlyn stood*, he thought. *Rather, that's where they still stand.*

"Cade," a voice called out. It sounded distant, distorted.

The voice was familiar; the doppelgänger's voice. "You again," said Cade. "Who are you?"

The man's features materialized before him and became sharper. "I am known by some as EonTal, but you can call me Tal. I am glad you have found the ring. I can talk to you here, but my time is short. They will soon discover my transmission."

"What is going on? Why do I see these plumes of light?"

"That is the encoding property of Rynthium. It allows you to see the Firmere as well as the energy of the phantoms and technology that resides within it," Tal responded.

Cade looked down again to see the wisps that radiated where he stood. "This...is my phantom?"

Tal nodded. The face came into focus, and Cade could make out a grave expression upon the man's face. "Cade, you must find Eos. Time is running out."

Cade shook his head in exasperation. "Yes, so you've told me. But I still don't know who or where this Eos is."

"Eos is...a failsafe. She can protect you, protect your world from the Wraiths. But we must find her first."

A failsafe? "But where is she?"

"I have traced a signal to Toltaire, but it is faint, and my location prevents me from pinpointing her location. Her connection to the network is tenuous, but she has been trying to communicate with you through the devices in Toltaire. At least the ones not under Wraith control."

"Where are you? And what are you, exactly? Are you a phantom?"

Tal shook his head. "Those are questions I also seek the answer to. I remember fragments from time to time.

They've secured my memories, my past. Taken them from me. I fight them where I can, from the Firmere."

"Them? You mean the Wraiths?"

Tal nodded before becoming almost unrecognizable, his image degenerating into luminescent dust.

"What are they using the taken for?"

"Find Eos," was all the voice offered.

Cade pleaded to the fading light before him. "But how?" No reply came.

The darkness returned as he released the encoding. His other senses crashed back down like a bucket of cold water. Almost losing his balance, he caught himself and took a deep breath.

As his eyes focused, he could see the concerned faces of Ashlyn and Jace.

He looked at them for a moment and then spoke. "We've got work to do."

13

BURDENS

From the ore of the universe I have fashioned a ring,
   It can see as far as the fallen sing.
   —Excerpt from The Book of the Traveler, Amended
Edition

ASHLYN SHUT the door to the bedroom after she checked on Cade, who was now fast asleep. The use of the ring had seemed to take a toll on both him and his phantoms. Jace had insisted to Cade that with Ashlyn's help they could do the research on Eos without him.

Jace was poring over an old codex of bound notes and diagrams Ashlyn had seen out on the table. Next to him sat the ring of marbled dark gold. It wasn't like any jewelry she had seen before, and she had seen quite a lot. The royalty and aristocracy in Toltaire were nothing if not well deco-rated. Jewelry was the tried and true way to display one's prosperity, or at least to try to convince others of it. Information and disinformation, the keys to survival in Toltaire.

Ashlyn picked up the ring. It seemed familiar, but she could not place why she felt that way.

Jace noticed her looking at the ring. "Beautiful, isn't it? Please be careful with it, though, it is one of a kind."

Ashlyn was intrigued. "There was only one ever made? Why?"

Jace shrugged. "From what we know about the Ancients that mined here, Rynthium was the most important ore. It is exceedingly rare; a single grain of the stuff can fetch a handsome price on the open market. They took the secrets of how to mine the metal with them when they left. Most of the mines the Ancients left behind are completely tapped out. When we do try to mine what few deposits we find, the drill sparks a chain reaction, turning the entire vein to dust. How the Ancients manipulated it is still a mystery to us."

Ashlyn had seen artifacts left behind by the Ancients that had small amounts of Rynthium embedded in them. But an entire ring's worth? She had never seen anything like it.

Jace continued, "I'd imagine we could buy our own kingdom with that ring."

Ashlyn's eyes grew wide, and the ring slipped from her fingers to the floor.

Jace scrambled to catch it and placed it out of her reach, giving her a disapproving look.

"It's worth *that* much?"

Jace nodded. "At least. Between you and I, I believe it is a key to help us fight the Wraiths."

"It's a weapon?"

Jace shrugged. "Maybe. I did find references in the Book of the Traveler that talk about the Bearers and the rings that they wore. Already we have discovered the eight prime Bearer metals mentioned throughout the book. It is said in the book, however, that the Traveler himself wore a ring that was unlike the other Bearers'."

"Do you really think the ring was worn by the Traveler himself?"

He patted a large leather-bound book bursting with loose pages beside him. "That's what my research says. Now if it would only contain a reference to Eos, we'd be getting somewhere."

Ashlyn noticed a thin but colorful book on the table. It read *Tales from the Forgotten Hells*. She grinned as she picked up the book, its cover depicting a group of small children running from a shadowy figure. "Are you hoping to find Eos in old fairy tales?"

Jace shrugged. "I know it's a long shot, but if there is one thing I have learned from my research, it is that you can never dismiss a story outright."

Ashlyn furrowed her brow. "What do you mean?"

"Every story has a truth to it. Even something as fantastical as folklore has a history lurking within."

Ashlyn giggled. "You're saying the Forgotten Hells are real?"

Jace was undeterred. "What I'm saying is that maybe there is more truth to them than we give them credit for. Do you know when these tales were first recorded?"

Ashlyn shook her head.

"They were carried and adapted from a tale that originated in the cradle of civilization itself, long before explorers even knew the land of Chalice existed. Nobody knows who even wrote the tale."

"Really?" Ashlyn asked, cocking her head to the side.

"Yes!" Jace exclaimed. He seemed to grow more animated whenever she showed interest, gesticulating with his eyes growing wider. "Now bear with me, but what if we were to suspend disbelief for a moment and imagine that the Forgotten Hells were a message from the Ancients? What if they were trying to tell us something?"

"That's ridiculous. Why would they make up stories about things like the Nine Doors of Hell?"

Jace's shoulders slumped, and he let out a slow sigh. "I don't know. Cade seems convinced we must find this Eos, whoever or whatever it is. I'm just trying to find any lead I can."

Ashlyn noticed his expression soften when he mentioned Cade. "You said you both came from Gallance. Did you and Cade grow up together?"

Jace, who had already buried his nose back into his notes, looked up. "Yes, he and I have known each other since childhood. Why do you ask?"

"Can you..." She hesitated. She didn't feel she could ask Cade directly, and since they were going to all be working together, she felt she had to know. "Can you tell me what happened to Cade?"

Jace paused and then sighed. "Of course, you don't know. Cade is not really a talkative one, at least not as much as he used to be. Here, let me fetch us something to drink."

Ashlyn took a seat, and Jace put two small glasses on the table and removed the cork from a small decanter of golden brown liquid. He poured a little into each glass, looked at his glass again, and then poured double the original amount.

"The side of the story everyone hears is the happy side: Cade charges into battle against an army led by a Wraith, kills said Wraith, prompting the signing of the Accord that ends the war. Cade is named the 'Protector of the Realm' and everyone lives happily ever after."

Jace downed the entire glass.

"Here's the part no one talks about. Cade, after his service in our good King's Army, headed home. It should have been a hero's welcome. And it would have been, too; the banners were up, the bandstands built, and a huge feast lay prepared and ready. Instead, he was greeted by an empty village."

Just like Barnage. "It was taken."

He nodded. "It was the first time a town had been taken. He went to his house to look for his wife and two children, but they were not there."

Ashlyn reached for her glass and swallowed the contents. It burned her throat, but she kept herself from coughing.

Jace poured more into the glasses. "He formed pacts that day with the phantoms of his children. Ever since then, his sole purpose for living has been to avenge them."

"What about his wife?"

"Serafina? Her phantom did not remain. But even with two phantoms, it is too much for one mind to bear. I just hope the madness doesn't take him."

"Madness? You mean from having too many phantoms?" Ashlyn said as she remembered Karessa and her breakdown during the Taction.

"It's sometimes referred to as 'Bearer's Burden.' Even carrying one pact takes a huge toll on one's mind. The Bearer becomes unable to tell the difference between their thoughts and the thoughts of the phantom. In a way, they begin to lose their identity, and they no longer understand who they really are. The only way to prevent 'Bearer's Burden' is with Nocturne. It became hugely popular among Bearers during the Wraith War, because they could form multiple Pacts that would allow them to perform additional encodings in the field, which meant staying alive. Now that Bearers are all but shunned, there is virtually no market for it anymore. Pretty soon it will be gone."

Ashlyn broke in, "What...what will happen to him?"

"Nothing good. He's addicted, no question, and he needs a lot of it for it to be effective. From what I've heard, some users don't wake up after a dose."

Ashlyn grew quiet for a second. "Jace...back in Barnage, I saw Cade shoot an unarmed man who had surrendered to him."

Jace sighed, taking a sip before speaking again. "Cade is a fiercely protective person—always has been. His entire life has been defined by that one quality. When he was unable to protect his own family, well, he stopped taking any chances with those in his care."

They were both silent for a moment when they heard the bedroom door creak open.

"Well, good morning, sunshine!" Jace said as he gathered up the glasses and put them away, as if the conversation never happened. "Are you sure you should be up so soon?"

Cade nodded. "Good as new. Any luck?"

Jace shook his head.

A knock sounded at the door. A moment later, two short knocks followed. Jace hurried to open the door, but no one was there. As if it were a normal course of his day, Jace grabbed the note that had been pinned to the door and began reading. "Uh-oh."

"What does it say?" asked Cade.

Jace snatched the large leather book he had been reading and stuffed more papers into it. "It says we're leaving right now. Damn. I wish we had more time. I'm going to miss this place." He picked up a length of thin rope, which he began tying around the large grain sacks that littered the great room.

Ashlyn, who stood next to one of the sacks, looked at Cade, but he seemed just as clueless as her. She leaned over and sniffed and stepped away from the bag. She knew that odor well from the game hunts she had attended back at the castle. Gunpowder. "You wired this place to explode? I was sitting next to a bag of gunpowder?"

All Jace managed was a sheepish grin. "Sorry. Like I said, I wasn't expecting you." He fastened a spring-loaded fire starter to the door and tied the rope to it. "I hope they don't come looking for me here. It'd be a shame to lose all this." He looked at Cade and Ashlyn. "I suggest we take the back door."

14

THE BLUEWASH

A Rynth man, Vanter Badgens, after visiting the Bluewash, was arrested for disturbing the peace today. He was observed forcibly grabbing and detaining passersby and raving about the existence of a large, moving island. When asked for a statement about his actions, the man continued his rant. "It's real, I tell you. A floating island! I was there! Why won't you spoony bastards—" He has been incarcerated at the Rynth jail until his hearing next month.

—From the Rynth Security Force Weekly Blotter

"WE'RE LOST," Cade said, looking at the map. They had managed to bribe a local railbus operator in Rynth to drop them just short of their destination. Jace's route had led them to the rocky shores of the Bluewash, one of the Ancient-created lakes just south of Rynth.

"Nonsense," Jace said, snatching the map from Cade.

Ashlyn crouched over the water's edge, peering into its depths. "Look at this!"

Cade looked over and saw the water of the lake was

perfectly clear, allowing a full view all the way to the bottom. "It's not very blue."

Ashlyn stood up and scowled at him.

"You really have never been to the Foundation before?"

Jace tapped his chin as he looked at the map. "No, I only recently had the location revealed to me. The Foundation is very secretive. Hmmm, this is where the coordinates say to go. I'm absolutely positive." He pulled out a paper with the translation he had made. "From the looks of it, we should be near the town of...Krek."

"There wasn't any town on the map," said Cade, seeing no sign of a town. A thick fog that hung like a heavy wool blanket over the lake was not helping with visibility.

"It wouldn't be, now would it? It's a secret," Jace offered, undeterred. Cade just shook his head.

A fishing boat broke free from the fog and eased its way to the small dock nearby.

"Let's go ask that fisherman," Jace said as he marched forward.

The fisherman was tying up the boat when they approached.

"Hello, there!" Jace said, walking up to the man. "We're looking for a town that should be near here." The man eyed them for a moment and shook his head.

Cade could tell the man was not native to Chalice and had some trouble understanding them. By the man's dark olive skin, Cade guessed he was from Hakken.

Jace persisted. "Gentle sir, I have it on good authority—"

"Are you Krek?" Ashlyn cut in.

The man hesitated, looking at the party, and nodded.

"See? Krek is a person, not a town. Simple clerical error," said Jace, turning to Cade. "Not lost."

Cade didn't get a good feeling from the silent man, who refused to look Cade in the eye. He wasn't sure if the years had made him too paranoid, or if he was finally paranoid enough. But for a secret organization trying to stay hidden, who better to use as a guide than someone who most people would never bother to ask? After some crude pantomiming and repetition, the man nodded again and motioned for them to board his vessel.

The ship reeked of fish, but the ride was smooth. Jace and Ashlyn retreated below deck, but Cade needed some air and chose to remain on deck. He still didn't quite feel himself after encoding with the ring. He should have taken more time to recover, but with towns on the interior of the Pathways being taken, time was not on their side.

There was no telling how long it would take for them to arrive, so Cade turned his thoughts to the ring. A ring worth an entire kingdom. He could not believe the ring that had been passed down through the Coda Grandmasters was really the ring worn by the Traveler himself. But how else could you explain a ring made entirely of Rynthium?

The thought of how he had slipped into the Firmere when he put the ring on unsettled him. It was difficult to encode with a new material, yet he had encoded with Rynthium without even thinking about it. If they were going to use the ring to their advantage, he would have to learn how to control it. He slipped on the ring and focused on the material. As he began encoding, the material pressed tight against his hand. The first stage of encoding called the object to the Bearer. The second stage required physical contact, which would allow the Bearer to assume the inherent essence of the material. Every material had an essence. Some were dangerous, like sandstone, which would make the bearer brittle. Others could be very useful, like aluminum, which would make the Bearer lighter. Not every material could be encoded, and some only with great skill, which could exhaust the Bearer's phantom before anything meaningful could be done. Although they weren't sure why, the easiest materials to encode were metals.

This metal, however, was already second nature to him. Cade held back from encoding to the second stage. If he could master that, he could wear the ring on his hand without endangering himself. Cade couldn't help but feel excited about encoding with a new material. He remembered back to when he first learned the core materials from his father at the Coda temple. He could hear his father's voice:

"Good. I can see you focusing on the element. Do you feel the metal pushing on your hand? Remember—you cannot force an encoding. You must know it, understand it. Everything has a purpose. You have a purpose, though you do not know it yet. So does a tree, so does the wind, and so does this ring. You need to understand what that purpose is. Only then will it let you borrow its power."

Cade smiled at the memory. The older he got, the more his memory betrayed him, but some memories were too strong to be smoothed away by the rapids of time.

He turned back to the task at hand. What was the purpose of Rynthium? He, like the rest of the world, knew very little about it. The Ancients didn't leave a lot of it behind, much less any clues about it. Cade thought back to the Book of the Traveler. The ring was mentioned only once. Why was the Traveler the only one with a ring like this? What did he use it for?

He couldn't help but think it was linked to the Wraiths. Why else would the Traveler possess it? He had taught the Ancients how to fight the Wraiths, so perhaps it helped provide a tactical advantage. It had to be a weapon. All the more reason to master its usage.

Cade soon found he could keep himself from fully encoding the ring while wearing it. Maybe the last time was a fluke?

"How are you feeling?" Jace said. He was leaning against the railing of the ship, looking at Cade, eyes wide with interest. "I saw you wearing the ring again. I told you to tell me next time you did so I can take notes. You realize this is a clear disregard of the scientific process."

Cade smiled.

"I'm serious! I think..." He stopped in mid-sentence and raised his hand, pointing to land. "Is that...?" Cade would have missed it if Jace hadn't pointed it out. The island itself was very flat...too flat, and was only a few feet above the water line.

Ashlyn, who had emerged from the cabin, hurried to the railing. "Vanter Island!"

The mysterious floating island of the Bluewash was the subject of many heated debates about whether it existed it all.

"That answers that," Jace said, transfixed as he studied the floating myth.

They thanked the quiet fisherman after he brought them ashore. As Cade disembarked, he was surprised to find that his first step onto the surface of the island was rock solid. With both feet on the island, he didn't feel any rocking or movement of any kind. If he didn't know any better, he would have guessed it wasn't floating at all. The earth felt hard underfoot, and the foliage gave the illusion that it was land like any other.

A narrow path led from the dock and into a large forest of towering trees, which was in stark contrast to the scrubbier plants on the edge of the island. Jace led the way, beaming, even though he had never been here before. Jace had always carried within him the undying spark of an adventurer. Cade couldn't help but feel a pang of jealousy that something like this could bring the man so much joy. Cade had felt that way too, once.

They came to a clearing within the forest and found themselves at the entrance of what looked to be a small village. There were a handful of buildings, and Cade was surprised to see they were in the modern architectural style one might find in a city like Solak or Toltaire.

There were people hurrying between buildings; they didn't seem to notice the new arrivals. Cade looked at Jace, who shrugged. He noticed two women talking in the street near the entrance, and upon noticing them, they waved enthusiastically. A young, athletic woman with long blond hair, who looked to be in her early twenties, bid farewell to the person she was talking with and approached their group.

She offered a hand bearing gold-painted fingernails that shone like polished gems. She seemed genuinely excited to see them, her face beaming with exuberant energy. "Hello! You must be Jace Exile. I have heard so much about you. I'm so excited to finally have a face to put to the name." She turned to Ashlyn. "And you must be the lovely benefactor of the Order, Princess Ashlyn Winshire. It is truly an honor for you to visit our humble city." Seeing Cade, her voice went up another octave. "And you are the Cade Elegy of legend, but everyone knows that. It seems I am meeting the forgers of history itself today! We've been expecting you."

They were all caught off guard by how much the woman already knew. They had sent no notice of their arrival. And they should have just been expecting Jace. *We were sloppy,* Cade thought. He was still not paranoid enough.

Jace spoke first. "Yes, of course, it is our pleasure as well, Miss...?"

"Oh! I forget myself. I am Faye Yooley. And our humble outpost here is the Principality of Carl."

"Carl?" Jace asked.

"Yes! The head of the Foundation. Come, he will be very excited to see you have made it safely. We weren't sure you were all going to make it." She leaned in a bit closer and lowered her voice, even though no one else was around. "Something big is happening. Carl won't talk about it much, but I think that's mostly because we don't know anything yet. Everyone's a bit on edge."

As they walked, Cade noticed the street wasn't really a street at all. It was made of a dull, solid gray metal.

Noticing his gaze, Faye spoke. "I see you've already discovered one of our secrets here on Vanter Island: it's not an island at all."

Jace kneeled and ran his hand along the corrugated metal. "What exactly is it?"

"The best we can tell it was built by the Ancients. It's not really like any of the other structures we have seen, but we believe it is likely a Gen 3 in terms of technology."

Jace rubbed his chin. "But what's its *purpose*? Surely it is more than a floating platform."

Faye nodded. "We've sent divers to investigate, and we discovered there are large intake ports all around the structure. From what we can tell, it's a self-sustaining filtration system for the lake. The water in this lake is exceptionally pure; that's the reason it was given the name Bluewash. Our theory is that it converts what it filters into a power source. And even though the movements of the island seem random, it is quite predictable, because it follows the same path every 1,024 days."

Jace, who looked lost in thought, nodded, still staring at the metal. "I wonder why they felt the need to filter this particular lake."

Faye shrugged. "Another mystery of the Ancients, unfortunately. It would have been nice for them to leave an instruction booklet or something. Let's keep moving, if you don't mind. Carl will be very excited to see all of you."

Faye pointed out details of the island to the group with the ebullient enthusiasm of a camp counselor. "To the right we have the Commons, where we get together and have meetings. To the left we have our intelligence headquarters, where the majority of our strategic planning takes place, and off in the corner there, we have our very own restaurant! I probably don't have to tell you, but the grilled fish there is simply to die for!"

They came upon the largest building of them all, which reminded Cade of the gigantic hangars built near docks to construct large ships. Protruding from its center, a tall cylindrical lighthouse stood watch. Faye stopped and turned to face them. "And here is the pride and joy of our humble operation: Phantom Works." She swung the large door open and ushered them inside.

It looked even bigger than it had from the outside. As far as the eye could see were tables with various artifacts, creations of steel and wood, workstations arrayed with mechanical tools the likes of which Cade had never seen. Men and women in long coats were bustling about, hard at work or locked in heated debate.

A solid-looking man, dressed military-style, with a massive barrel chest and arms that could have been hewn from the trunks of trees, noticed them and beamed as they filed into the room. He strode over to greet them.

Cade's jaw fell open. Before him stood Carlon "The Fist" Stront, Commander General of the Unified Armies of Chalice, heralded as the strategist who had brought about the end of the Wraith War.

He fell in and saluted. Soldier habits die hard. "General Stront. You..."

"No, no, none of that, I am not a general anymore...I'm a prince!" The man threw his head back and roared with laughter. "And please, call me Carl."

The three of them looked at each other, uncertain.

He swept a large arm out toward the hangar. "Welcome, friends, to the resistance!"

15

FOUNDATION

With over one hundred confirmed Skex kills to his credit, General Stront is an anomaly of military leadership. His divergent strategies in dealing with the Wraiths culminated in the battle on Gigan's Hill, which was the inciting incident that led to the Accord.

—From First Contact to First Combat: The One-Month War

"THANKS TO A LOOPHOLE in our wonderfully bureaucratic government, any location that is not considered stationary," he said, stomping his foot on the ground, "...such as Vanter, is not technically considered part of the country. After we signed the Accord, I requested my boon from our dear King Liam, and that was for permission to operate Vanter as a wholly independent principality within Chalice. It buys us political...discretions...we would not have otherwise. We were able to get our operations here up and running quickly, and the location does wonders to keep out unwanted visitors."

A handful of people on a floating island in the middle of nowhere didn't sound like much of a resistance. As if on cue, Carlon continued, "Now, I know it doesn't look like much. I imagine you all were conjuring up grandiose imagery of barrack upon barrack of multi-Pact Bearers encoding with the lost alloys, armed to the teeth with fully loaded casters in each hand." He snorted, his powerful chest threatening to tear the buttons off his shirt. Carlon's uniform happened to be the same type of dark royal blue that high-ranking officers wore in the field. "Truth is it wouldn't make a difference, not how the Wraiths are fighting. Vanter? This is just one cell of many. We have agent cells in every nook and cranny of Chalice, gathering intelligence and capable of running completely autonomously. If our cell falls, the Foundation survives."

He motioned for them to follow and led them down the main drag of the long hangar. The man had a stocky frame but walked more quickly than his bulk would have suggested. He moved with crisp efficiency and purpose, as if he would not tolerate any motion to be wasted. They had to walk fast to keep up with him.

"You see that?" Carlon said, pointing to what looked like a row of guns welded together. "That right there is an anti-siege gun developed by my team here. Skex always swarm in groups, making them easy to take down if you can get the ammo out fast enough. These guns here each have a rotation barrel, capable of delivering three rounds per second once it gets spun up. We've linked them together so we can man the weapon with only one gunner and one loader to feed the belt through. Sure to come in handy once they start sending those damned overgrown bugs at us."

They continued walking. One of the scientists was attacking a man wearing curious dark gray armor. "Ah! And that right there is the new field armor we've been testing. Strong and nearly impervious to Skex claws. We actually got the inspiration from the Skex exoskeletons." He scowled and grunted. "Can't stop bullets...yet. Now this here...this is really something," he said, picking up a small cylinder and tossing it to Jace. "This is a new type of grenade we've been working on." Jace snapped up, startled, and fumbled the cylinder before he caught it and held it to his chest, eyes frantic. The man bellowed with laughter. "Don't worry, it won't do much to us, though it makes a right mess. It's got a goo in it that kills the damned symbiotic moss that grows on Skex. No moss—no energy."

Faye, who had been following close behind, opened a door at the end of the hangar and gestured for them to enter. The room was austere, except for a host of military medals and plaques hanging from the walls.

Carlon sat down in the large command chair behind the solid wood desk at the back of the room and motioned for them to sit down on the plush leather chairs in front of them. The seating seemed uncharacteristic of a remote military installation, considering it must have been transported at great expense. They sat down, eager for answers.

"I was at the helm of the Wraith War from day one. Every operation, every mission was approved by me. Hells, I even fought in some of the engagements myself, as much as that pissed off the king. If it wasn't for Cade here, I probably would have kept doing it until I got killed myself. But you know what I learned at the end of it all? The Wraiths cannot be beaten. They are too advanced, too strong, and they are a hell of a lot smarter than we are."

Carlon leaned back, laced his fingers together, and rested his hands on his stomach. "Sounds a bit defeatist, doesn't it? But that's truth for you. You can put a dress on it, call it pretty and take it to dinner, but that won't change what it is, no matter how bad you want it to. Now here's the part that's really going to get your butts on edge: I think the Wraiths orchestrated the whole Accord from the very beginning. They *wanted* the war to end. Not because they were afraid of us, and definitely not because they thought we might have stood a chance of defeating them, but because they wanted us to *think* they were afraid of us."

This was a radical way of thinking, and not one Cade had considered.

Jace spoke first. "What proof do you have?"

"None, save for common sense. Should I remind everyone that our Wraith friends came to us in a vessel that *flew in from another planet*? I can't fathom the technology required to do such a thing. If they can navigate the stars, chances are their combat capability is far greater than they let on. It is simple hubris that drives the belief we are a match for them."

Cade cut in. "But we had the Bearer Corps. Those are the same abilities that allowed the Ancients to defeat the Wraiths in the first war."

Carlon belted out a laugh. "The same Ancients that could mine Rynthium? And build ships that navigated the depths of the ocean? The same ones that built the casters? The Ancients who had the Traveler in their corner to help them?"

Cade did not offer a reply.

Carlon leaned forward in his chair. "The Wraiths came here for something, right? Maybe they came for retribution after they got beat down in the first Wraith War with the Ancients, or maybe they came for the Rynthium. After they signed the Accord, the war effectively ended. And our intelligence shows they aren't mining any Rynthium. So why are they still here? Likely they are here for whatever they came for back when they were here fighting the Ancients. And we're just whiny pawns to be moved about a board of their own devising. They waged their mock war until they learned how they could get what they needed, and ended it."

"And what do they need?" asked Jace.

Carlon did not skip a beat. "People. Dead ones. But you already knew that. We've all known this, but everyone is too damn afraid to confront the Wraiths again, so we let them have their way. We have no idea what they are doing with the people they take, but we know that all roads lead to the Thread. It's the one place we cannot get near; it's too well-guarded."

Jace nodded. "That is what we've heard as well. But as you said, the place is impenetrable. We can't hope to learn more. Especially if the Wraiths are as powerful as you say."

Carlon raised his index finger. "And that is *precisely* why I have asked you all to come here. I believe we can fight the Wraiths."

Cade spoke, confused. "I thought you just said that we could not hope to beat them?"

"We know their movements have increased lately. Skex have been spotted in both Rynth and Toltaire. Something is about to happen, and they are distracted. This is the opening we've been waiting for."

Cade frowned. "You're not suggesting..."

"I am," Carlon replied.

Horrible images of the assault on Gigan's Hill flashed in Cade's mind. He could feel his muscles tense at the memories that still felt fresh. "You can't be serious. You remember what happened last time, right?"

Carlon's expression darkened. "I don't need any

reminders. The difference this time is we have the under-ground railway that runs concurrently with the Pathways to the Thread."

"You're going to sneak in through an underground train?" Ashlyn asked.

"In a sense, yes. There's a collection of trains under Wraith control that only move between Rynth and the Thread. They are the only trains permitted near the Thread."

"Well, there is the *No Man*," Jace corrected. The *No Man* was an anomaly of the Pathway rail network. It never stopped moving, and as such, no one could board it.

Carlon ignored Jace and continued, "We were able to retrieve a schedule from an Acolyte we rescued. We believe we can commandeer one of these trains."

"But how can we mount an entire assault with only one train of soldiers?" Ashlyn asked.

"Simple," Carlon said, looking at Ashlyn. "We don't put soldiers on the train. We put a bomb on it."

Cade sat back in the chair. "What kind of payload could hope to devastate a structure of the Ancients?"

Carlon smiled. "There is an agent in Toltaire who has not only built an explosive more powerful than anything we've ever used before but has also rigged the explosive with the ability to fire off caster shells, like a frag grenade."

"You're trying to take out the structure and the Wraiths in one go," Cade said.

"Oh no, you're not working with..." said Jace, burying his face in his palm.

"Yes, we are working with Agent Beatrix."

Cade stifled a laugh.

Ashlyn made a face. "I feel like I'm missing something."

"It's nothing," Jace said, dismissing the question. "What

about the Nexus in Rynth? There has to be something there that can help us, I'm sure of it."

Carlon shook his head. "I'm aware of your line of research, Exile. But even if that were true, we are no closer to gaining access to the Nexus in Rynth. And if we get inside and there was something there, how long would it take for us to learn how to use it? We don't have the time."

Carlon turned to Ashlyn. "This leads me to why we need your help, Ashlyn." He met her gaze. "With Rolan gone...we need your Order's help. You can get us access to an underground railbus that can transport the weapon to Rynth from Toltaire."

Ashlyn nodded, expression now solemn at the mention of Rolan. "What about my father? He will help, I'm sure of it. Have you approached him?"

"The king? Princess, our intelligence tells us that he is helping the Wraiths. His meetings with them have increased recently, and with cities on the interior disappearing, well, it's obvious he's turning a blind eye. We can't risk including him in our plans."

Ashlyn sighed, dejected. "I guess I already knew."

Carlon shrugged. "What else can he do? If he opposed them, the Accord would crumble, and we would lose any confrontation we had with them. Your father is backed into a corner." He shook his head. "But we have to assume he cannot be trusted. That is why we worked through Rolan. I know this is hard for you, Princess. But we are so close, and we need your help."

She lifted her head and met Carlon's eyes, face stern. "Tell me what we need to do."

16

TOO LITTLE TO LOSE

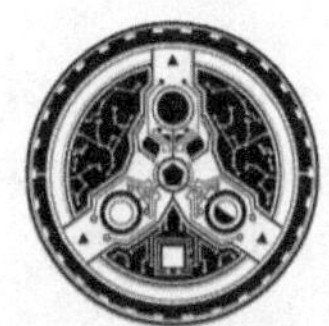

Skex are a cross between a man and a beetle, best we can tell. While their exoskeletons give them a natural armor against most attacks, they are mortal. They can be easily dispatched with traditional firearms using approved LRSX ammunition. If you deplete your ammunition store, they can be attacked with the standard-issue weighted sword. Take care to aim for the joints indicated in Figure 2.1.

—From Bearer Corps Combat Tactics

CADE WOUND his way up the steel spiral staircase of the giant lighthouse, lost in thought. Carlon had pulled him aside after the briefing and left Jace and Ashlyn with Faye.

"We don't ever turn the primary light on, not anymore. The harder we are to find, the better," Carlon chuckled. "Here we are."

They entered a large, circular room with immense curved glass panels all around the perimeter. "Welcome to the Watchtower."

Cade was underwhelmed. The ever-present fog of the Bluewash allowed only a superficial view of the surroundings. Carlon, who was watching his reaction, roared with laughter. "Never gets old! I love doing that to newcomers." He gestured to one of the men sitting at a station near the door. The man nodded and flipped the large switch next to him.

Though no light emerged from the tower, the fog seemed to disappear, allowing them to see far and wide. Everything looked as if they were viewing through green-glasses. Details Cade would only expect to see in daylight were easily visible.

"That's more like it, eh?" The man slapped his thick paw on Cade's back.

"How?" was all Cade could manage.

"Good question! With the Ancients and their technology, there are always more questions than answers. I wish I knew. And I've made it my business to. But for now, I'm focused on the questions I *can* answer." He motioned for Cade to sit on one of the many chairs that punctuated the long table in the center of the room.

Carlon threw a large file filled with loose papers onto the table in front of Cade.

"What's this?"

"An answer."

Cade opened the file and noticed his name on the first page. He flipped through the reports. "You've been watching me?"

Carlon nodded. "For quite some time now. There was a point when we thought to recruit you into our resistance."

"Why didn't you?"

Carlon smiled. "Now you're asking questions you already know the answer to."

"With all due respect, sir—Carl. I don't have time for this. I have to prepare for the mission."

Carlon shook his head. "You're not going."

"What? Why?"

Carlon picked up the file and tossed a report onto the table. "The warehouse explosion in Solak. The blast set nearly the entire block on fire." He pulled the next file. "The broken dam in Hyridge. They had to evacuate the valley." Cade shifted in his seat. "And let's not forget the incident in Kayvant. It goes on."

Carlon put the file down, linked his arms behind his back, and walked to the nearby window. "We thought a man, a Bearer no less, with nothing to lose, could be a powerful ally." Cade remained silent. "Until we realized how dangerous a man with nothing to lose really was."

Cade's expression smoldered like the ashen coals of a great fire. He opened his mouth to speak, but Carlon held up a hand.

"In every one of these cases, you put yourself and others at great risk. It is quite clear you do not value the lives of others, and especially not your own. Mark my words, Elegy: you will fail them. Ashlyn and Jace are crucial to the success of this mission, and it's my job to ensure that they succeed." He fell silent and turned to Cade.

"Raiders."

Carlon watched him with eyes of stone.

"That's what the Endguard told me when I reported the disappearance of my village...the murder of my family. That's what everyone told me. Didn't matter that nothing was looted and the bodies were missing. Raiders. Even when the next village was taken, and the one after that."

He met Carlon's eyes.

Cade said, "What would you have me do? Roll over and

let the Wraiths take whatever they want? They are taking more and more people every month, with nary a footnote in the daily post. Someone must do the work everyone else is too afraid to do. We've become too paralyzed with this farce of freedom to understand the price that we're paying. I don't regret what I've done—and I wouldn't hesitate to do it all again."

The large man shook his head, as if expecting Cade's reply. "That's your justification? Everyone on this island, along with men and women spread throughout Chalice, is fighting the battle against the Wraiths as well. And they are doing it while upholding the safety of those around them." Carlon snorted. "When you shot the man in Barnage...what did you feel?"

Cade raised an eyebrow.

"Oh yes, Malix is an old friend. What did you feel?"

"He was a liability. Even if he was truly unarmed, he could have alerted others or sold the intel."

Carlon nodded. "A fair assumption, and likely correct. But you still haven't answered the question."

Cade looked down at the table. "I didn't feel anything."

"And that is why you cannot go."

Cade shook his head. "I don't understand."

"On the battlefield there is no right or wrong, only orders. You do what you are told and move on. You didn't feel anything in Barnage because *you're still on the battle-field.* You're on your own mission, everyone who gets in your way be damned."

"I want to defeat the Wraiths, same as you."

Carlon pulled out the chair next to Cade and sat down, scratching his chin, the day's stubble already threatening to become a beard. "Let me put it another way: given the choice to avenge your family or save the people of Chalice, which would you choose?"

Cade glared at him.

"I don't expect you to answer—it's not a fair question. But we both know the answer. Your quest for revenge clouds your judgment." The man's tone grew even more serious. "One misstep or deviation from our goal and the Wraiths will crush this pathetic sliver of a chance we're clinging to. It's simple. Your mission isn't our mission. That's why you cannot go."

The man's expression softened, and he smiled as he sat back in his chair. "Don't worry, I'm sending Faye. She might not look it, but she's the best there is. She will take good care of the princess. You are welcome to stay here, since we could use someone to train—"

"Sir!"

Carlon stood up. "What is it?"

"Light spotted up ahead. Krek's boat, by the looks of it."

Carlon peered at the small boat as it trundled toward the island's shore. "He's not scheduled to land tonight."

Cade joined them at the window. "Krek? You mean the Hakken man?"

Carlon turned to him, "Krek isn't from Hakken, he's a native...*Hells*. Sound the alarm!"

"Sir?"

Emerging from the water behind the small boat, a swarm of Skex, unmistakable even at distance, began clambering onto the shores of Vanter.

"Sound the alarm now!" Carlon raced to the stairs, faster than his girth would have suggested. He grabbed the pole that ran through the center and slid down past the surrounding flights of stairs. Cade followed suit, encoding his hands with tungsten to prevent them from burning. A shower of sparks flew from the friction as the ground of the hangar rushed up to greet him. He pushed the tungsten throughout his entire body, touching down on the ground floor with a hard clank.

"Man the battle stations! I want those bugs dead yesterday!" The agents moved quickly at Carlon's command, grabbing long, black rifles, and manned the battlements along the side walls. It appeared they had prepared the hangar for such a contingency.

Carlon grabbed the special gauntlets off the suit of armor he had demonstrated earlier and took the tarp off the experimental crank-powered gun. "Faye! Evasive maneuvers. Get us to land." Faye nodded and ran to the adjoining room.

Jace and Ashlyn, who had been talking with Faye, ran over. "What's happening?"

"Skex," Cade said.

"Here? How is that possible?"

Cade shook his head. They heard a deafening thud as something pounded against the hangar door.

"Here they come!"

Faye emerged from the control room. "Course set, sir!"

Cade looked at Carlon. "Orders, sir?"

The man cursed, face pulled tight. "Damned if she won't need your help to get out of here. Hells take you, Elegy, if you screw this up." He turned to Faye. "Use the escape route. Protect the princess at all costs."

Faye saluted and quickly led them to a hatch at the back of the room as the hangar door blew off its hinges and crashed to the ground.

Faye began turning the locking mechanism, arms refracting with the diamond encoding. She had rings on every finger, which was rare for Bearers—he hadn't noticed earlier. Most Bearers could only manage encodings with a few of the core materials: tungsten, diamond, and aluminum. The subtleties required to manipulate more advanced materials were lost on most Bearers without decades of training. Cade grabbed the other side of the mechanism and helped turn it until the hatch unlocked. Faye ushered them in. "Go, go, go!" Cade looked up to see dozens of Skex pouring in the room, overwhelming the agents unlucky enough to be on the front line. He saw Carlon, teeth gritted, spraying gunfire into the swarm, his massive arm turning the crank as fast as it could go. "Come on, you ugly bastards. Is that all you can do?" Faye shoved Cade through the hatch before pulling herself in and sealing it from within.

The tunnel was dark and damp, and the air was stale. The floor was slick with a thin layer of wet moss that had somehow managed to spread within the tight space. Cade bumped against the wall, and a cool blue glow began to emanate from a device inset into the tunnel. Faye looked at Cade, eyes narrowed. She detached the device from the wall and held it up like a lantern. "This way." She led them down an access tunnel. Cade could see they were not man-made; these tunnels were part of Vanter itself.

"Here." She stopped and reached up to open the hatch. Fresh air rushed in. She pulled herself up in a deft motion and helped Ashlyn and Jace out of the tunnel. Gone was the cheerful hostess they had first met. There was more to her than he had thought upon their first meeting.

They emerged from behind the hangar on the island. They were out in the open, but the darkness provided some concealment as they pressed themselves against the outside wall. Faye peered around the corner and then held up a hand, signaling for them to stop. She pointed to a building on the other end of the main strip and whispered, "*Stables*," then waved them on. Time to move.

They ran across the exposed street as fast as they could, Faye taking point with Cade bringing up the rear. They had almost made it to the building when the Skex spotted them.

Skex were intimidating beasts. Their exoskeleton-covered bodies were inlaid with thin, running lines that resembled watered steel. They could move on two legs with their powerful hindquarters, but they tended to use the hooked claws on their forearms to move at even greater speed. Underneath the overhang of their claws, they possessed long triple-jointed fingers that resembled the segments of a battle gauntlet. Their heads were shielded, not by exoskeleton, but an angular metal helmet with no visor or openings. Cade had no idea how the creatures could navigate.

"Hells," Faye cursed, pulling out her pistols as they skittered toward her. She unloaded an entire cylinder, bringing down the first one. Pistols didn't pack quite the same punch as the rifles.

Cade ducked behind cover and saw Jace and Ashlyn, eyes wide and fearful, pressed against the wall. "It's going to be okay," he said. He pulled a shell from its sheath. Eighth one down. Garren Wall. Died fighting the Skex in the Wraith War during the battle of Kayvant, even after his entire unit deserted. He slipped it into the cylinder and traded places with Faye, who started to reload. The cylinder spun up, and the sparks flew.

He pulled the trigger, and the Skex vanished; only smoke remained. Faye ducked out and fired a round into the next one. It collapsed, legs shuddering and drawing in close.

Skex had very few weak spots. Faye was either incredibly skilled or an incredibly lucky shot.

Ashlyn screamed. He turned around the corner expecting to see a Skex, but there were none to be found. She instead pointed to something behind him.

The shore. He didn't even know the island was moving, but he could see the coast of the lake hurtling toward them fast. Too fast. He grabbed Ashlyn and Jace, encoded diamond, and brought them in close. He performed a secondary encoding, this time with the ground underneath his feet, securing him to the metal floor of the island. Out of the corner of his eye he saw a Skex that had broken free and was racing toward them. It raised its heavy claw high and swung down.

Cade felt his body lurch as Vanter smashed full speed into the shore of the lake. The Skex was gone, likely thrown across the island. His mind raced. *Faye.*

He released his encodings and put down the stunned Jace and Ashlyn. He turned the corner. Faye was gone. He cursed. She must have been thrown, too. "Let's go!" he yelled.

The island, despite the impact, had held its shape. The lakeside was decimated, along with the corpses of Skex that had been ashore during the collision. Cade led them into the small stable he had seen on the island and was shocked not to find horses.

"Kalafir!" Ashlyn exclaimed, breaking from her stupor.

Kalafir were rare beasts. They looked like horses, only larger. Most kalafir breeds were a full head higher than the biggest horses, and their coats were almost always a sleek jet black. Aside from their great size, their most distinguishing feature was their elevated ankle joints, that almost gave the impression they had inverted knees. They could not be bred in captivity, so the only hope of riding one was if they were discovered in the wild and tamed. They had tragically short lives, only around five years, but the beasts were the fastest and most loyal animals one could hope for. These kalafirs had been spooked by the impact, tapping each of their hooves one at a time, as if testing to see if the ground they stood upon was still real. They seemed to settle somewhat upon seeing Cade enter the stable.

"No time to admire." They had already been saddled in preparation for their original mission. Cade hoisted Jace upon the first kalafir and noticed Ashlyn had already mounted the next one. Jace looked at her, annoyed. She shrugged, smiling.

They burst out of the stables at full gallop, turning hard toward the shore, and the great animals bounded over the rubble left behind from the impact.

As they raced away on the open plain, Cade noticed lights flickering to the east. That must be the Skex base camp. He yelled over galloping hooves to Ashlyn, who he could tell was the more experienced rider. "Keep heading due south. I will catch up."

Cade broke away and headed toward the light. In minutes, he was dismayed to find what he had feared. He bore down on the great beast, and it galloped even faster toward the camp. As he neared its edge, Cade encoded diamond for strength, leapt off the creature and sailed through the air. He landed next to a sinister-looking machine with a long barrel. It was still warming up. *I'm not too late.* The strategists called them ballistae, but that was only because they had no other name to use. Hauled by a pack of Skex, the ballistae were used as artillery against fortified structures.

A group of Skex, seeing Cade, scrambled toward him. A

loud, grating tone sounded from the machine, and it began to pulse. It was now or never. He looked around but could find no object to jam the machine. With only seconds remaining, he did the first thing he could think of. Cade wrapped himself around the open barrel of the weapon, torso covering the opening. He encoded to the hard steel of the barrel, effectively locking himself in place and blocking the barrel's exit.

The weapon fired. With nowhere to go, its payload hit Cade's hardened torso, and unable to leave the barrel, exploded. The barrel was torn open by the blast, throwing metal shrapnel across the camp and throughout the army of Skex.

WAKE UP.

He sat up in the darkness and grabbed his stomach, blackened but whole, shirt nothing more than tatters. He turned over and vomited. Wiping his mouth, he looked around. *Where...?*

He heard a snort and felt a wet nose rubbed against his face. He looked up to see his kalafir, waiting for its new master. Amazing creature. Getting his bearings, he hauled himself up onto its back and headed south.

He rode through the clearing and noticed two slender shapes darting quickly like lost shadows through the darkness ahead. *Hells,* he thought, *I should never have left them alone.* A scream—Ashlyn's—sounded in the distance. Cade cursed and dug his heels into his kalafir. Carlon's voice echoed within his head: *Your mission isn't our mission.* The man was right—he took too many chances, put too many people at risk. He drove the beast hard, fur already lathered with sweat, as they raced to catch the dark figures.

Scouts. Not as dangerous as the larger Skex but deadly enough. Built for speed, they were as fast as the kalafir. They must have been watching for anyone who tried to escape the island.

Far ahead, he could make out the silhouettes of Jace and Ashlyn. They must have cut east, trying to dodge the scouts. He made sure his feet were hooked in the saddle as he pulled out his shotcaster. At this speed, a caster pistol would have trouble hitting the darting creatures. He broke it open and loaded a shell. He grabbed the reins with one hand and pulled even with the scout, squinting through the darkness. The large barrel's intricate etchings began to glow a dark red, ready for Cade.

A powerful blast from the direction of the island came from behind him, lighting up the dark night. *Forgive me, Terlok Marr, no time for ceremony.*

He fired, evaporating the scout. He turned his head behind him to see the island engulfed in flames, his earlier effort wasted.

He faced on. Where did the other one go? Cade let go of the reins and reached for another shell when his kalafir lost its footing and he was thrown from the beast.

The scout was upon him before he even stopped tumbling across the rocky plain. It raised a pointed arm, sharp as a spearhead, and struck at Cade. Instinctively, he raised his arm and grunted in pain as it pierced his forearm. He encoded with tungsten, trapping the creature within his arm. He encoded his other arm with lead and pounded upon the hard carapace again and again until it cracked and shattered. He was still punching the wet pulp of meat and broken shell even after it had shuddered and fell still.

Ashlyn's voice. "Cade? Jace, he's bleeding. Grab the pack."

He lowered his fist, heart thundering in his chest.

Your mission isn't our mission.

Perhaps it could be.

"Cade? Are you okay?"

He nodded untruthfully.

CEYWIND

Ceywind's architecture is unique, even by the standards of the Ancients. It is believed that Ceywind served as a launching point for deep-sea mining, while the city itself served as a refinery for the collected minerals.

—From Chalician Archaeologist's Quarterly, *Vol. 4*

ASHLYN WAS quiet for most of the journey from Vanter. The sun had risen, and Jace had laid out a route that would take them to Ceywind, where another agent had arranged passage for them to Toltaire.

Cade brought his kalafir beside Ashlyn's. "You okay?"

Ashlyn let out a small sigh and faked a smile. "Do you think...do you think they're okay?"

Cade shrugged. "Well, you saw the weapons they had in that hangar. If anyone stood a chance, I'd say it was them."

"Don't you think we should have stayed and helped? What about Faye?"

They had been so focused on their exit, Cade had

forgotten about Faye. Carlon's words continued to cut him. "I don't know. The general said she's their most capable agent, so I'm sure she's fine. Carlon ordered me to take you to the city."

Ashlyn sighed again, nodding. "The Skex saw us retreat. Do you think they will follow us here?"

Cade shook his head. "I hope not. If they attack a major city, the king will have no choice but to end the Accord. But we must assume they are following us. We will need to move quickly."

Jace, a few paces ahead, came to a stop as he crested the grassy hill. "I think this is it," he said. Cade and Ashlyn rode to the top of the hill, and the port city of Ceywind spread out before them. They had ridden the kalafirs all night. The poor beasts, bodies lathered from the effort, laid down where they had halted. "It's best for us to leave them here; they would draw too much attention in the city," said Jace.

Ashlyn put her hand on hers and stroked the short fur of its head. "Thank you." She turned to Cade. "Do you think they will be all right?"

"The kalafirs? It'll take more than this to keep them down. They are hardy animals. And to be perfectly honest, you can't truly domesticate them. Their freedom is the best gift we can give them."

They walked down the hill to the entrance of the city, the smell of saltwater strong in the wind.

Cade took in the view of Ceywind from the top of the hill. It was sprawling, composed of innumerable open-air markets filled with peoples from all lands making deals and hawking their wares. Ceywind was the largest port in all of Chalice and served as a central hub for traders. He nodded to himself, thankful they could hide amongst the crowds here.

Row upon row of wide wooden docks, held up by large posts encrusted with barnacles, lined the shore. As many docks as there were, almost every berth was occupied. The city was alive day and night, and the unforgiving dock foremen ran the entire place like clockwork. By Cade's estimation, there were over two hundred ships.

Despite not being connected to the main Pathways, Ceywind housed many Ancient structures, which was a large reason for its settlement in the founding days of the country.

The city itself was bookended by two steep cliffs on either side, a rather strange juxtaposition given how even the terrain was in Ceywind. It was already theorized that Ceywind, like other cities in Chalice, had been terraformed to the Ancients' liking long ago.

"All we need to do is find the contact from the resistance they told us about. Ah, here it is." Jace pulled out a slip of paper from his codex: "Captain Renalt."

The scent in the wind began to change as they approached. Cade wrinkled his nose. Carrion?

"Did they give us a description?"

"Yes. He's tall—about six measures, fair complexion, red hair, muscular build." He frowned, turning over the note. "It doesn't say where we should meet him."

Ashlyn gasped.

"We won't need to look far," Cade said. Jace looked up and dropped his book.

Hanging from the gallows next to the entrance of the city was a fair-skinned man with long red hair. Around his neck a crude sign hung, with only one word painted in red lettering: *Treason.*

Cade motioned for Ashlyn to pull up her hood and ushered her into the city, with Jace trailing behind.

"What now?" asked Ashlyn despondently.

"We stick to General Carlon's plan. First, we must get to Toltaire and secure the weapon. Any number of ships could take us there. We just need to find one that can be discreet," said Cade. "Jace, let's split up and start asking around the docks. Ashlyn, I think it's best if you just keep your head down. We don't want to risk you being recognized here." Ashlyn nodded.

"WE'RE FULL," said the foreman at the dock, eyes unmoving from the clipboard in front of him.

Cade had spent most of the day walking up and down the docks, with no result. Undeterred, he persisted. "We can pay you handsomely."

The man heaved a sigh, put down his clipboard, and looked wearily at Cade. "Listen. The Crossfort Ball is happening in one week. Maybe you've heard of it?"

Cade did not like the man's tone. The Crossfort Ball was the biggest event in Chalice. It was impossible not to know.

"Mine and every ship out here has got a full load of goods for that ball, and we have to get there with time to spare. They'd run me through all nine doors of the Forgotten Hells if I was short a single fork, and I don't even want to think what would happen if we were late." A bell sounded. The man looked back down to his clipboard and hurried away.

Jace walked back from the end of the dock toward Cade.

"Any luck?"

Jace shook his head, deflated.

"Come on, we still have one more option."

They made their way to the Grid, the largest market in Ceywind, built around gigantic pylons of Ancient origin. The pylons were polished steel in appearance and thrust out of the ground over a hundred feet into the sky. They were spaced in columns and rows, a grid of unknown purpose. The most impressive thing about them, however, wasn't their size, but what they could do. The pylons radiated cold air, providing refrigeration on a massive scale.

Fishermen hunched over their ramshackle stalls next to the pylons, busking about the catch of the day wearing long coats and fur-lined hats. Emanating frigid air, the pylons could keep food and other perishables fresh for days. The Grid was a bustling marketplace, with throngs of locals, sailors, and traders feverishly buying and selling around the clock.

As they walked farther from the pylons, the air grew warmer, and the lights of the marketplace grew dimmer. Not that the scant light mattered much—the market outside the pylons was not a pleasant sight. Dilapidated buildings, rotting food that hadn't sold, and refuse illegally dumped by dock crews became more and more prevalent as they pushed their way through the thinning streams of people. Ashlyn broke down first and plugged her nose.

"Here it is—the Breakwater." Cade knew more than a handful of the locals had alternatively christened it the Breakwind, for reasons unsurprising. "If we're going to get to Toltaire, we're going to need to find a captain not helming a transport ship. Not to mention one who won't ask too many questions." He pointed to the strip of taverns along the rough cobblestone road.

"Okay," said Jace, "where should we start first? The

Breakwater Lighter, the Hallowed Harem, or the Siren's Song?"

Cade looked to the Lighter. He saw a few men with too-short necks loitering in the front, talking in hushed voices and looking over their shoulders. He turned his sights to the Harem. True to its name, he saw women in bright red dresses and deep red lipstick hollering to any passerby who looked like they might have a chipcoin to their name. Lastly, he looked to the Siren's Song. There he saw a pile of passed-out men next to the garbage cans and another man doubled over and retching in the alley.

"There," said Cade, pointing to the Siren's Song.

Jace nodded. "All right, I'll do the talking."

"Wait. What?"

"It's nothing personal, Cade. We need to charm them a bit first, right? Naturally, that's me."

"I'm charming. Besides, you look like a tax collector with that giant book tucked under your arm."

Cade looked back at Jace, who met his gaze with narrowed eyes. "I'm doing the talking," they said at once.

Jace put out his fist. Cade looked at him and followed suit. Ashlyn sighed, rolling her eyes.

"One, two, three!" they said in unison.

Cade's hand remained a fist. Jace had made his hand into the shape of a gun.

Cade smiled. "Bomb beats caster."

"I thought that caster beat bomb?"

"What? How do you not know that? We played this in school."

Jace shrugged. "It was a long time ago."

Satisfied, Cade, Ashlyn, and Jace walked into the Siren's Song. Cade studied each of its occupants as they passed, making mental notes.

They were accosted only moments after they had seated themselves at the bar. A dried gourd of a man with a too-large head teetering upon a thin neck leaned against the bar. He stared at Jace, smoking a short pipe, his face only inches away from Jace's.

Jace cleared his throat. "Can I help you?"

The man continued to stare at him, unblinking, and blew dark brown pipe smoke into Jace's face. Cade made to stand up when the man slapped a large coin onto the bar in front of Jace.

A challenge coin. Chalician Navy, by the looks of it. Cade reached in his pocket and placed his own coin on the bar next to the man. Serif letters adorned its edge, which read, "Sons of the Traveler." The man cast his eyes upon Cade. Cade met his gaze. "He's with me."

The man snorted, snapped up his coin, and skulked back to his table.

"What was that all about?" asked Jace.

"If you don't have a coin of your own, you have to fight the challenger in a duel."

"What?"

Cade laughed. "I'm joking. You'd just have to buy him a drink. Though if I hadn't put my coin down, the whole bar would have eventually cleaned you out. There appear to be quite a few veterans here, from the looks of it."

The barmaid approached, a buxom young woman with olive green eyes. "What'll it be, travelers? Rockland Rooter? Wraith's Draught? Grinolt Gassers, perhaps?"

Cade shook his head and slid a large chipcoin toward the girl. "Not here to drink."

In a single deft yet graceful motion, the girl pocketed the coin. Occupational skill, no doubt. Cade did notice a string of small hilts jutting out from behind her leather bodice as she put the coin away. Throwing knives, by the look of them. He had a hunch that working here she knew how to use them. The girl, expression now serious, nodded to Cade.

"We're looking for a captain with a ship to take us to Toltaire. The faster the better."

"Captains we have, aye. Most of these cowards can't even piss straight, much less sail. But there's a few." She pointed to a proud-looking woman, eyes like lit torches. "That there is Tryst Forecall. Best sailor in the joint, by my estimation. Though a word of caution, she's got a temper like a loosed arrow and a mouth to match."

The captain sat with a group of men in blue uniforms. Cade had seen them before. King's Navy. *Hells*.

"Who else?"

She shrugged. "I'm not sure. It's a pretty crowded place."

Cade sighed and slid another chipcoin across the bar. The girl smiled.

"That man with the wide hat there has right solid sea legs. His skiff isn't the fastest one out there, but you'll find none more reliable." Damn. He'd have to do.

Jace cut in. "What about him?" He pointed to the mountain of a man in the corner of the bar. He wore a crisp uniform of dark green and stood as tall as the Thread itself. He had no glass before him, a sentinel amongst the revelers. In contrast, next to him was a shirtless husk of a man with a mess of gray hair and tattoos that ran from his shoulders to the tips of his fingers. Hunched over, the man's chin rested on the bar. His glassy eyes were open and aimless, and finding no purchase, decided to roll into the back of his head.

The girl just rolled her eyes. "Don't bother, sweetheart. He hasn't left port in a month."

Jace leaned in close to the girl and gave her the half-smirk he did whenever he was trying to be charming. "Are you sure there isn't anyone else you're holding back on telling us about?"

The girl just looked at Jace for a moment, annoyed. Then she cocked her head to the side. Her eyes began to sparkle with opportunity as her red lips curled into a clever smile. "Well, there is one other captain..."

Jace perked up. "Really? Who?"

The girl held her chin up high. "Why, only the *greatest* captain the world has ever known, of course: Captain Wraithbane!"

Cade grabbed Jace's shoulder. "Come on, Jace, let's—"

Jace leaned forward, ignoring him. "Who is that? I've never heard of him."

Cade kicked him hard under the bar.

"Ow!" Jace glared at him.

The girl put her hands on her cheeks in feigned surprise. "You don't *know*!" She grabbed an empty stein on the bar and slammed it on the bar three times.

A handful of men throughout the bar let out a roar. Jace's eyes opened wide and he stared at Cade, whose head was already buried in his hands.

The bar began to chant the shanty:

> "Captain Wraithbane he's insane,
> Captain Wraithbane feels no pain."

A man behind them stood up and took the lead, swinging his mug as he sang. Jace just bit his lip, helpless to stop it.

"He cuts through the Skex—one two three,
Leaves 'em dead, now we're free."

Soon the entire bar joined in.

"Captain Wraithbane fears no thane,
Captain Wraithbane strong as a train."

"He steals from the crown, straight from
    the hold,
Gives to the people, all the gold.

"Captain Wraithbane may he reign,
Captain Wraithbane our domain."

The bar cheered and hooted, pounding their wooden mugs against the tables. Cade just shook his head at Jace.

The girl, now beaming, said, "There are some who say he still sails to this day." She turned to Cade. "Just give me wave if you change your mind about that drink." She winked and hurried off.

Jace looked at Cade, confused. Cade sighed. "She was just playing with you, Jace. It's just a legend from the war. Next time, let's stick to me doing the talking." Jace nodded, his face a deep red hue.

But the damage had already been done. A drunken man who reeked of fish and broken dreams, stumbled over to Jace. "So...you're looking for a captain, are ya?"

Cade stood up. "No, thank you."

The man looked at him, eyelids thin slits. "I'm not...not talking to you. Him," he said, poking Jace's chest with pointed finger. The man swayed like a boat on the ocean before leaning closer to Jace. "I'll have you know I'm the finest sailor here."

Damn, we've drawn way too much attention already, thought Cade.

Jace spoke, not making eye contact. "I'm quite certain that superlative is reserved for someone of a more pleasant odor."

Hells.

The man swung at Jace, but not before Cade kicked him across the room, knocking down two tables along the way. In moments, the entire tavern was in an all-out brawl.

A brute of a man swung a chair at Cade. "I thought," he yelled as he ducked the blow and punched the man in the stomach, "...we agreed..." He dodged a bottle that was aimed at his head. "...that I would do the talking!"

The doors to the entrance slammed open as a man yelled, "Skex! Skex have invaded the city!"

Those sober enough to comprehend what was happening dropped their fists and ran out of the bar. It was too late. The Skex had already arrived. *Skex attacking a major city?* Cade thought. *There's no way the king can maintain his silence now.*

Cade caught a glimpse of a Skex skittering toward the door. The barmaid was already there, throwing the door closed and shoving the bar in place.

He felt a gentle tap on his shoulder. He turned to find the tall sentinel they had seen earlier. "This way," the man said, pointing to the back door. They made it outside the bar just as the Skex breached the tavern and began to spill in. Though being outside wasn't much better; more and more Skex had started to swarm from the Grid and into the other streets.

"Follow me." The man ran with surprising speed, his

long legs capable of great strides. It wasn't until then that Cade realized the large man was carrying the drunk with the tattooed arms he had seen at the bar. He urged Ashlyn and Jace on until they came to the steep cliff where the Breakwater's main strip ended.

Cade could hear a cacophony of screams and scraping claws growing louder behind him. They came to a great door inset into the cliff face, which was swung open.

Inside, they descended. When they reached the bottom of the carved stairwell, they were greeted by an enormous room, equal in size to the Stardome. Another underground construction of the Ancients, Cade marveled. Packed within were black market merchants with wares they couldn't sell at the Grid. They scrambled to collect their goods as chaos broke loose. Fools. When the Skex come, you drop everything and run.

He saw medicine dealers fussing and tripping over bottles, smiths throwing cheap replica casters into bags, and even a large shop selling equipment for spies, which was already being looted by the opportunists taking advantage of the distraction. Cade looked at the other end of the underground market and saw a large door. *Of course,* he thought, *that door should lead us straight to the edge of the docks where we were earlier.*

They rushed through the stalls, and the noise in the enclosed space soon became deafening. *They're here.*

Skex began spilling around the sides of the stalls, flanking those still in the center of the market. *Including us,* he thought.

The large captain skidded to a halt and pointed to the door they had been headed to. Skex were now swarming through it.

"Damn it. Head to the far wall!" Cade yelled. It wasn't

much of a plan, but it would buy them a few moments to think before they were flanked.

On the far side of the room, Cade and Jace searched for an opening in the metal wall. He could see strange characters embossed into the metal, but he could not decipher their meaning. The captain just shook his head. He knew there was none. Cade faced the room. They'd have to fight their way out.

Unbidden, something his father once told him echoed in his mind: *There is great power in not knowing what's impossible.* He turned around again and looked at the wall.

"Cade! I can read this!" Jace exclaimed, waving him over. He pointed to one of the small symbols embossed in the metal of the wall.

"What's it say?"

"Exit. I'm sure of it."

Exit? "I don't see any door."

"Over here!" Ashlyn grabbed his wrist and before he could protest pressed his hand against an embossed square in the wall. The metal lit up when his hand made contact, just as other Ancient artifacts had been lighting up whenever he got close.

The large section of the metal wall began to creep up, inch by inch. His mouth fell open. "It's a..."

"Waterfall?" Ashlyn said, stupefied.

Just beyond the metal doorway they had opened, the floor dropped off at least a hundred feet, and water gushed out on all sides of a colossal underground chasm, spilling water into a steaming lake below. The underground chasm easily dwarfed the market behind them. Sequences of immense pillars ran through the chasm and seemed to penetrate through the roof of wet stone. *The pylons. We're underneath the Grid,* he realized.

"Over here!" a voice bellowed behind him. Cade spun and saw the captain in the stall with the spy equipment, his friend still draped over his shoulder like a rag doll. Next to him was a whisperboat.

Whisperboats weren't illegal, but they were only ever used for smuggling operations. The sleek boat was ten feet long and painted matte black. Whisperboats were designed to be able to pack a lot in the water-tight storage just above the two long pontoons. The boats were man-powered, so there was no engine noise to contend with when stealth was required. There was only room for one to sit on the boat itself—the driver. Being used for smuggling, the design optimized for storage over passenger space.

Cade grabbed one side as the man grabbed the other and they dragged it over to the gate.

More screams. The scraping sound came closer.

"Get in! No questions." Cade ushered Jace and Ashlyn into the storage above the first pontoon, which was just big enough for them, and sealed it shut. The large man laid the tattooed man into the other one. "Hurry!"

The large man got in the rowing seat and grabbed the oars as Cade took hold of the boat from behind.

He encoded to diamond, power blazing through his body. He heaved the boat hard, sending the boat hurtling down into the lake at the bottom of the chasm just as the razor-sharp edge of a Skex claw sliced through his back and slammed him into the ground. The diamond encoding gave him strength, but had left his skin vulnerable. The creature yanked him from the ledge, sending him flying back toward the market. He encoded to the metal of the floor in time to feel the sharp end of its claw scrape against him. He rolled, and still holding his diamond encoding, he kicked at the creature, sending it skidding toward the chasm. It stopped short of falling off the ledge. *Lucky bastard.*

He heard advancing claws behind him. *Hells.* Before he could turn to meet his fate, he noticed two small children, his children, run past him and jump into the chasm. *Right.* He took a deep breath and ran at the Skex blocking the gate, pushing lead through his entire body. He grabbed the Skex, pulling it over the edge with him. The Skex, unfazed, scraped and stabbed at him as they fell. Away from the pack, they weren't as smart and didn't notice details.

It didn't notice the blue sparks or hear the spin of the caster chamber.

Yin Neman. Cade flared diamond and forced the Skex underneath him as they fell. Member of the Sons of the Betrayer. Over fifty confirmed Skex kills. Killed on Gigan's Hill.

Cade grabbed the flailing claws, locking them in place.

Yin Neman. Husband.

He aimed.

Friend.

Smoke.

The body of the Skex disintegrated as Cade continued his rapid descent into the underground lake. He could already feel his body flush as the heat emanating from the pylons enveloped him. The water surrounding the pylons boiled and steamed. Was that how the topside stayed cool? The bottom pylons exchanged the heat generated from the topside refrigeration by having the ocean water wash it away?

He splashed into the hot seawater below, making sure to keep distance from the pylons. The water, thick with salt, stung his eyes as he tried to orient himself. The sluice gates must be used for expelling the salt-rich water. He surfaced and tried to rub the salt from his burning eyes. Cade squinted. *There.* The whisperboat was headed toward one of the sluice gates.

He could feel each of his phantoms grow faint as he swam. Cade pulled back on the strength of his encoding. The current was already helping him move through the scorching sea within the chasm.

"Over here!"

Cade surfaced again to see the captain pointing to the far side of the chasm. He turned to see Skex dropping into the water, one after another, attempting to give chase. One Skex, flailing its appendages, squealed as it cooked after contacting a pylon. "You've got to be kidding me. They just don't give up."

He swam up to the captain and saw the boat was unable to fit through the thick metal beams barring the sluice gate while salt water rushed around the boat.

"Let me help." The bars were strong, but a final push from Cade's exhausted phantoms allowed enough space to wedge the boat through.

Cade grabbed the edge of the boat just as the current sent them hurtling at great speed into a darkening tunnel. The large pipe continued to fill with water as more channels fed into it. He could barely make out the captain with something in his hand, a blue light blinking off and on. The man yelled to him, "I've activated the beacon for the ship! Hold on!" Cade took a final breath before the pipe filled completely with water, submerging the entire boat as they were propelled through almost perfect darkness.

Every second felt too long. How long could he hold on to a single breath?

The darkness gave way to a dark blue. They shot out

into the open sea, and the pontoons, still in one piece, did their job as they began to rise.

But instead of the ocean surface, they were greeted by the sleek contours of a metal ship that pulled them in through a small bay door. The water around them was jettisoned by a gust of air from a duct near the bay door, leaving them inside the belly of an Ancient ship. The interior was made of dark brushed metal, with thin lines of blue light running across the sides. Other than the familiar scent of seawater, the air smelled fresh, unlike the strong damp scent most large wooden ships had.

Cade gasped for air, lungs protesting every breath. Ashlyn. Jace. He ran to the storage compartment and threw the latches. Jace shot up, breathing hard, eyes wild. The pontoons were air-tight; they must have been low on air inside. Chest heaving, he pointed to Ashlyn, who lay immobile.

Cade scrambled to pull her free of the compartment and began compressions on her chest. One. Two. Three. One. Two. Three. "Come on."

One. Two. Three.

He looked at her and hesitated when instead of Ashlyn, he saw the face of his wife. "I will not lose you again."

One. Two. Three.

We will solve your uncle's murder. One. Two. Three. *Just come back.* One. Two. Three. One. Two. Three. *I shouldn't have left you and the kids.* One. Two. Three. His thoughts were chaotic, tripping over one another.

"*What do you want from me?*" he yelled, but not at her.

"Cade..." Jace set his hand gently on Cade's shoulder.

He hung his head low as his heart continued to race. He could even feel his heartbeat in his hands.

Heartbeat. Hands. He looked down, his hands still pressed upon Ashlyn's chest. She opened her eyes. "Cade?"

His eyes grew wide, and he felt as if his heart would burst. He sat her up and held her close. She put her arms around him as well, and he felt the warmth of her cheek against his.

"I'm sorry. I'm sorry. This is my fault," he whispered.

Ashlyn pulled herself away and looked into his eyes. "It's okay, Cade. I'm okay." She placed her hand on his cheek and smiled.

"Um, guys?" Jace broke in, pointing at the growing group of crewmen who had now entered the room.

Cade flushed and nodded, regaining his composure. He stood up and helped Ashlyn to her feet.

The large captain had taken out the tattooed drunk and laid him on the floor. "Ice bucket." A sailor dumped the bucket over the unconscious man, who just groaned.

Jace walked over to the captain. "Captain. We owe you a debt of gratitude for what you have done."

He held up his hands. "You're mistaken. I'm not the captain."

The groaning drunk stood, wiping his face. "I suppose someone has to be. Welcome aboard the *Manta*."

Cade looked at Jace, who shrugged.

The tattooed man faced them. "Now get off my boat."

18

STAYING AFLOAT

While rare, the Ancients built a handful of ships that have been discovered throughout Chalice. All of them, despite their age, are known to be seaworthy. Most of them appear to run by somehow harvesting energy from the ocean itself, possibly for extended deep-sea mining operations.
—From Chalician Archaeologist's Quarterly, *Vol. 3*

"SIR..."

"Don't want to hear it," said the captain as he climbed the ladder to the top deck.

"We haven't had a job in over a month."

"You are awful at following orders. I must see to getting a new XO."

Cade, Ashlyn, and Jace followed them through the ship and to a room that appeared to be the captain's office. The room, much like the man, was a mess. Bottles littered the floor, and numerous scraps of paper were scattered across every surface. They hovered just outside the door, as there was no part of the floor not covered with trash. Even the furniture itself was in disarray, with a couple of overturned chairs lying across from a small wooden desk, and the bunk in the corner had been flipped upside down.

The man, unconcerned with the state of the room, walked in and righted one of the fallen chairs. He sat down and began rummaging through the bottles on the floor.

"This isn't difficult. Just send them on their way."

A knocking sounded from outside the ship. Ashlyn looked at Cade, who could only shrug.

"Half of our crew have left already, sir. If we stay docked any longer, the other half will soon follow."

The knocking continued to get louder, accompanied by the sound of scraping.

The captain, finding a bottle with a satisfactory amount of liquid still inside, popped the cork and finished it off. "Great. We'll save a fortune." He opened a drawer in his desk, and finding a new bottle, pulled the top off with his teeth.

The knocking and scraping sound was now above them.

"Captain—"

The captain grabbed his head, wincing. "What, by the first door of the Forgotten Hells themselves, is that blasted noise?"

"Skex, sir."

The captain shot a pointed look at the tall man, who Cade had decided must be the first mate.

"Skex?"

"Skex."

The man, stood up, scowling. He strode to a cabinet and pulled out a blunderbuss, larger than one Cade had ever seen, detailed with gold and ivory filigree. He loaded it with ammunition, hoisted it up on his shoulder, and teetered a bit as he fought to maintain his balance. He took his free hand and slapped himself hard across the face, sighed, and walked out the door.

The first mate shook his head, embarrassed. "This way."

The captain heaved open the topside hatch and threw himself onto the deck without a care as to where the Skex might be. The rest of them, after the first mate scanned the perimeter, were ushered up. They were followed by a handful of crew members, armed with rifles and a motley assortment of weapons.

"I want that sail up yesterday, you lazy sons of bitches."

"Aye, Captain!" the crew belted in unison as a team assembled and began pulling ropes that slowly ratcheted a large man-made mast into place. Though it was an Ancient-made ship, they had added their own modifications to the deck. Wooden railings were lashed to the perimeter of the deck, which was no small feat, given the smooth pointed shape of the ship's hull. Upon the center of the deck they had affixed a man-made mast so that they could sail the ship. They watched as the large sail was unfurled by the bustling crew members while the first mate continued to bark commands.

"And get these bug bastards off my ship." The captain wheeled around, leveled his gun at an advancing group of Skex, and fired. The gun sent a tangle of Skex flying off the ship with fewer limbs for the trouble. The blast had also sent the captain staggering back, but he managed to stay upright. Despite the heavy rocking, the man moved with fluid ease upon the deck.

Within moments, the deck was clear of the Skex. The captain turned to face them. "Why are they still here? Make them walk the plank."

"We don't have a plank, captain."

"I miss my old boat," he said, frowning. "Go swab the decks," he barked at the idling crew.

"But it's a metal ship, sir, we don't—"

"*Now.*"

"Aye, captain," the team chanted in unison.

The captain paced in front of them. "It would stand to reason those foul beasties are after you lot, especially considering they seem to be focused on our ship in particular." He looked at Cade, eyes squinting. "Now why, by the Traveler, would that be?"

Cade opened his mouth to reply, but Ashlyn stepped forward. "We humbly request your assistance in a matter of utmost importance to Chalice. If you can arrange us passage to Toltaire, I can guarantee you will be rewarded handsomely by the king himself."

He walked up to Ashlyn, whose hood was now pulled back. He snorted. "The princess. Perfect."

"Captain! Skex ballista spotted!" shouted a man from atop the crow's nest. Cade looked to see the devastating silhouette of the artillery's massive barrel as the encroaching Skex rotated it into position from the shore.

"*Hells!* Can't be helped now." He looked at them, shaking his head. "The curse continues. You're lucky I hate Skex more than I hate the sea. Get below deck." He spun around to the crew. "Why the hells are you swabbing the deck? Get the sail up!"

The first mate grinned and quickly led them below. They passed men seated at terminals in what appeared to be the bridge of the ship, with screens scrolling alien characters. Cade noted the men were equipped with familiar sidearms. Chalician Navy. These men weren't just crewmates—they had fought together.

The captain strode into the room, barking orders as he

made his way to the command chair on the bridge. The echoing blast of the ballista sounded in the distance. Cade gritted his teeth and braced himself, but the impact never came. A near miss. The captain, unfazed, continued his orders. "Get us out of here."

"Aye, Captain. We will be clear of the port momentarily," the first mate replied.

A man ran into the small bridge. "Three ships spotted leaving port. One brig and two Gen 1 corvettes."

"How many Skex each?" asked the captain.

"About ten each on the 'vettes, maybe forty on the brig."

"How fast?"

"Chip log estimates the 'vettes at thirty-five knots."

The captain nodded, deep in thought.

"The brig will match our speed soon enough at seven knots, but those corvettes will be on us quick. They are only Gen 1 ships, but there ain't much faster," the first mate advised.

"And what do we have on this scrap of tin, an egg beater?"

"Um, no sir. We have a Rynthium drive."

"Then I suggest you get it fired up." The men around the bridge sat straighter in their chairs at this, stealing nervous glances at one another. The first mate hurried to a chest near the command chair and unlocked it. He reached inside and brought out a small wooden box, inlaid with gold lines. He pulled off a key that hung around his neck and turned it before handing the box to the captain. The captain pulled off his own key and inserted it into the second lock, popping the steel latch. The captain cast a glance at Cade. "You better be worth it."

The first mate carefully took out a vial, which looked empty. Cade could just make out the faint glint of the few grains of Rynthium that lay within. The man hurried out of the room.

Jace couldn't help himself. "Where did you get Rynthium from?"

"Stole it," the captain said without turning.

A man near one of the terminals in the front spoke. "Sir, the 'vettes will be on us before the drive spins up."

The captain nodded. "Get someone topside and batten down the mast. Prepare to lower the bridles."

"Aye, Captain."

The first mate, returning, turned to their party. "I would suggest you take a seat and strap in."

They found seats at the unmanned terminals on the bridge. There was a large porthole that allowed them to see into the ocean as the ship cut its way across the waters. As they strapped in, Ashlyn whispered to Cade, "What's happening?"

Cade shook his head and looked to Jace. "I've read about this." He began to flip through his codex. "Yes, here. Ships that can actually submerge." He showed them a sketch of a sleek, flat ship that looked just like the *Manta*.

Ashlyn's jaw fell open as she looked through the porthole. "Ashlyn, are you okay?" Cade asked. She pointed. He looked up to see a long, dark shape undulating toward the ship. Jace froze in place, eyes wide with wonder.

"One Xansian en route to bridle one, Captain."

"Excellent. It would appear the sea hates us less today. Increase vibration on bridle two by three clicks."

A great sea snake, twice the length of the ship, wound its way toward them. Its dark purple and silver scales, which almost looked metallic, glowed as they reflected the scraps of sunlight that penetrated the surface. Its eyes glinted like multifaceted diamonds. Cade felt like he could hear an almost imperceptible groan emanate from the beast as it opened its great jaws, revealing what appeared to be row upon row of flat silver teeth. The massive jaw collapsed on the offered bridle, and the ship shuddered as the beast took hold.

Ashlyn's face was almost touching the glass of the porthole. "I had only ever heard of them in storybooks. I didn't know they really existed," she said in awe.

"Second Xansian almost in position, Captain."

The ship shook again as the second beast took hold.

"Increase vibration to maximum."

Cade felt the ship being pulled underwater, and he made out the ethereal outline of the Xansian as it pulled them deeper into the depths. He had heard stories of ships that could harness Xansians to propel themselves underneath the surface of the water, but he had always believed them to be fantasy. There were no ships even in the Royal Navy that had this capability.

Awed, Cade turned to look at the captain, who had fallen silent. The man kept his head low and eyes closed. Had he fallen asleep?

"Captain, current depth is twelve hundred fathoms. We should..."

The captain raised a hand, silencing the officer. The index finger on his other hand swung back and forth, as if it were conducting an orchestra only he could hear.

The hull of the ship began to creak as they continued their rapid descent. Less and less light filtered through until the porthole revealed nothing but darkness.

"Two thousand fathoms."

The captain's eyes remained closed. The hull let out a long creak, protesting the abuse. Ashlyn jumped at the noise, grabbing Cade's arm. He looked at her and nodded.

"It's going to be fine," he said, though he wasn't sure if he believed it himself. The crew sat quietly.

The captain's eyes snapped open. "Ascend."

The bridge sprang to life as the crew members followed the order and the vessel began to rocket to the surface. Cade clung tight to the seat of his chair under the intense momentum.

They breached the surface at speed, just as the two corvettes sped above them. The force of the rising ship had sheared one of the corvettes in half and sent the other one hurtling through the sky. The airborne corvette soon hit the surface and capsized. The crew let out a cheer, but the captain remained still. "Get me eyes on that brig."

As if on cue, a sailor ran into the bridge, breathless. "'Vettes confirmed disabled. Brig made up ground during our descent and is bringing itself about. Distance five hundred yards."

An officer laughed. "There's no way they can hit us from that far away."

The captain knew better, and so did Cade. Skex in numbers were dangerous. The more Skex in a group, the smarter they became. "With forty bugs on board, they could pick a rat off our bow if they cared to. How long until the drive is warmed up?"

"About three minutes, sir!" a voice yelled from just outside the bridge.

"*Hells*! Prepare for evasive maneuvers."

They were sitting ducks until the drive was online. Cade stood up.

The captain swung around to look at him. "Where do you think you're going?"

"The deck." Cade ran off the bridge and into the corridor.

"Like the hells you are. Stop him!" the captain commanded.

Cade climbed the ladder, and a sailor tried to pull him down as he flung open the hatch. Cade encoded to diamond and freed himself from the man's grasp. He threw down the hatch and made his way to the rear of the ship. No one followed him.

He saw the brig, which had pulled around to fire its cannons. Cade steadied himself. He heard the blast of the cannon from the Skex ship. He could just make out the large ball of iron as it hurtled toward the *Manta* at fantastic speed. Concentrating, Cade encoded to the surface of the ship, hardening his body and locking his feet firmly into position at the same time. Following the cannonball with his eyes, he encoded to the iron projectile. He felt a pull toward the remote encoding, but his stronger encoding to the deck kept him rooted to the ship.

The pull became stronger as the ball sped toward him. Within seconds, he could feel his feet trying to wrench themselves free from the hull of the silver ship. It was close.

Now, a voice told him. Tal was with him again.

Instead of dropping the encoding, Cade reversed it, using his phantom's energy to push out the encoding and send the cannonball in the opposite direction. The projectile careened backward and splashed down short of the brig. Reversing an encoding was clumsy; there was no telling where it could have landed.

He checked his phantoms. Present but tired. The Skex, undeterred, readied another shot. Cade heard the thunder of the cannon.

Cade encoded to the projectile. He could not feel the pull of the encoding. He tried again...nothing. *Hells*. They must have alloyed ammunition. Any battle-ready brig would be prepared for Bearers. It flew fast and true, aimed right at him. He felt panic rise within him.

No choice, and no time for mistakes. Cade released his encoding to the deck of the ship. He encoded tungsten, and the dark silver descended across his entire body, enveloping him as he danced on the brink of overencoding. He also flared diamond, and he felt the strength course through his metal-hardened body. The phantoms would not last long, but he only needed another second. He wound his arm back.

Now, Tal told him again.

What followed was a deafening loud *crack* as Cade's fist, a fusion of tungsten, diamond, and bone, met with solid metal. Cade felt the cold stinging rush of saltwater surge around him as the ship submerged from the force of the impact and the ocean pulled him under.

19

FORGOTTEN, BUT NOT GONE

The Xansian is one of the great beasts of the deep. While no definitive proof has been provided regarding their existence, a great number of Chalician sailors have reported sightings of the creatures. Commonly described as a "sea dragon," these serpentine denizens of the sea have been rumored to haunt only the depths of waters near the major Ancient cities of Chalice.

    —From Bestiary of the Ancients

COLD SALT WATER enveloped him as he submerged. His encoding broken, he was no longer attached to the hull of the ship. The water continued to rush all around him. Cade could not tell which way was up or down. His left arm, the one he had used to hit the cannonball, was numb and unresponsive. He tried to swim with his other arm, but the surface never came. His lungs were burning now. He despaired, and the waters grew ever colder. A dark shape seemed to move just beyond his vision. As it moved closer, he could make out the undulating outline of a great snake. Xansian.

Its faceted eye, like dark mother-of-pearl, studied him as he floated helpless in the suffocating abyss. It swooped underneath him, and he grabbed its scaled back. The scales were the shifting colors of a dying sunset and smooth like polished steel. *Steel*, he thought. The scales were steel—he was sure of it. He encoded to it with his near-exhausted phantom, and his hand stuck to the back. As if waiting for that, the beast took off through the dark abyss. The Xansian seemed to hum with energy, like some impossible device of the Ancients. He held on until thin black tendrils encroached upon his vision and he could see no more.

CADE OPENED HIS EYES. Everything was blurry, out of focus. He was submerged in some type of liquid but could still breathe. A dream?

He was upright, suspended somehow. As his eyes began to focus, he could see he was in a glass tank of some sort. Beyond was a large room. The room reminded him of a structure of the Ancients. It seemed familiar, but he didn't remember seeing it before. There were tables of brushed metal lining the empty room. He tried to make a sound, but nothing escaped his lips. He lifted his arms, which felt like they were moving through wet sand. He started when he noticed his arms were those of a small boy. Panicking, he tried in vain to pound his small fists on the glass, but to no avail.

A woman with long dark hair wearing a long white robe entered the room. She regarded him for a moment and began pressing on a tablet she was holding in front of her.

She placed her hand on a small black panel inset into the tank, and he felt sleep take him.

———

CADE AWOKE ON HIS BACK. He could breathe freely, no longer in the tank. Bright lights passed by overhead as the world around him came into focus. He sat up and could see a group of people in white robes escorting him on a metal cart down a large hallway lined with impressive double doors. He felt cold, exposed, and scared. The hallway was unnaturally silent, save the sound of the wheels of the cart upon the floor, creaking towards an unknown destination. Each of the doors made him uneasy. He thought he knew what was behind those doors, but he could not remember what. He counted the doors. Nine doors. Just like in the Forgotten Hells.

But the Forgotten Hells were not real, just a place from scary stories told around campfires. There were nine doors in the Forgotten Hells, each one a portal into a different kind of hell. The Hell of the Broken Mind. The Hell of the Poisoned Brood. Each door opened was more terrible than the last. He tried to dismiss the association, but it stuck with him.

Cade heard a scream come from one of the doors as they passed. His entire body seized and trembled as they passed, and he shut his eyes tight as the scream degenerated into a low, unnatural wail.

———

WHEN HE OPENED his eyes again, Cade found himself

in a large room filled with strange consoles and panels. Before him was the beam of the Thread. It was so close, he couldn't even see the sides of the beam. He turned around and noticed the people who had transported him there were behind him, cordoned off by a transparent wall and trans-fixed on him.

Cade faced the beam once more, breathing quickly. The beam, as in his Nocturne dream before, seemed to call out to him. He was scared but was not sure why. He approached the beam, as he once had in a dream, and touched the light. Panic set in. It wanted to pull him deeper inside. Cade fought its pull, trying to wrest his small arm free. The light once again stuck to his hand, unyielding. It pulled him closer until he was absorbed by the light.

Inside, the light coursed around him. Cade remembered visiting the giant waterfall behind Toltaire castle, the water rushing down so hard it was deafening yet beautiful. The light of the Thread was the same way. The light flowed, like water. He thought he could hear music playing at the edge of his perception, something far greater than any piece he had heard before. It was at that moment he realized the fear and trepidation he felt was not coming from him. It was coming from the light. He could sense emotions, swirling around like a maelstrom imprisoned within the beam. His heartbeat quickened as those feelings took on a shape, a shadowed form, knocking at the door of his mind.

A voice bled into the prison of light. "...made it, thanks to you..."

The voice sounded distant. He turned, looking for its source, but finding no one. "...know why I'm telling you..." The voice became clearer. Ashlyn.

"...won't listen to me. I know exactly what he'll say, 'Ashlyn, I am much too busy to hear of your flights of fancy.'

He won't even look at me anymore. I know why. I look too much like my mother." A sigh.

"But they sent an army after us. An act of war. My father must listen now. Right?"

"I don't even know my own father. I've spent more of my life afraid of him than anything else. But I can't help but feel he can help us." Silence. "Goodbye, Cade."

As Ashlyn's voice faded, so did the light, until all that was left was perfect darkness.

20

GRAY LIES

Commencing on the date of signing, the Kingdom of Chalice, by decree of King Liam Winshire, hereby annexes the Ancient facility north of Wythlain to the Wraiths. In exchange, the Wraiths agree to provide electrical energy to the populace of Chalice.

—*From* The Accord of the Wraith War

ASHLYN EXITED HER CHAMBERS, shutting the door behind her and taking a deep breath. It felt good to change into clean clothes. It was a necessity, since her father was very particular and would refuse to see her if she wasn't at least somewhat presentable.

She felt bad leaving Cade and Jace behind, but Ashlyn knew they would not want her to seek her father's aid, especially after Carlon told them her father might be helping the Wraiths. But she couldn't believe that. If she could help unite the Chalician military and Carlon's forces, they would not only have a greater chance at making their plan work, but they could stop the Wraiths from taking more cities within the Pathways. She remembered the story Jace had told her about Cade's family. If she had a chance to save lives, she had to take it. Her father was headstrong, but she could count on the only thing the man truly loved: his kingdom.

Ashlyn slowed her pace as she neared his office chambers. He did not spend time in court unless his presence was required. He spent most of his time doing his business in a private office. The office was not as impressive as the court, but her father always said he worked better in silence; she knew that first-hand. When Ashlyn was young, her father always made sure Ashlyn was far away, saying "her antics are a detriment to the rule of this kingdom." If it hadn't been for Rolan, her childhood would have been a stark affair. She sighed, remembering playing hide-and-seek with him in the castle.

"Princess." One of the king's guards nodded to her as she walked up to them. A severe man with short-cropped black hair, dressed in full armor, barred the door. Another man, more aloof, stood guard with him. They were soldiers of the king's elite Royal Guard, ready for battle at a moment's notice, and she saw the grips of what could only be casters holstered within the belts around their specialized armor. At least two members of the Royal Guard were always present at the king's side, the only exception being when a Wraith paid him a visit. The Wraiths would not allow it.

Ashlyn stood up straighter, pulling her shoulders back and holding her head high. Even though she had only been gone a short time, she was already forgetting herself. "I seek an audience with my father."

The more severe man, unblinking, responded, "His Majesty has requested that he not be bothered at this time."

Ashlyn gave the man a pointed look. "Then it is a good thing I am not here to bother him," she replied, pushing past him and opening the door. The guard grabbed her arm and looked as if he was about to pull her back when a voice barked from inside the room. "Ashlyn? What is the meaning of this?"

She looked at the guard, whose expression hardened. His grip was still tight on her arm, but she held his gaze. He let go and nodded, scowling. Ashlyn turned and walked into the room, the guard following close behind. The king sat behind a large desk of black-speckled marble. It was carved from a single monstrous slab, legs and all. Her father believed impressions were everything and spared no expense in the decoration of his rooms. Every one of them held some unique artifact he deemed worthy of his station.

The king was a large man. Not bear-like, however, like General Carlon. Her father was tall, well above six feet. While older, his body was still lean and strong. He had always taken care of himself since she could remember and recalled him telling her, "You can't take care of a kingdom if you can't take care of yourself." He was much stronger than he was before the Wraith War. The war had triggered something in him, and he started practicing combat drills with his Royal Guard every morning. Looking at him now, she could see small cuts and scrapes on his arms, no doubt from this morning's practice. His hair and beard had turned a salty gray, and he kept it trimmed short, military style. His eyes, a dark green, burned at her, impatient.

"Father, I have something important to discuss with you." She shot a look to the guard lurking too close behind her. "In private."

King Liam gave an annoyed sigh and nodded to the guard, who hesitated, then slipped out the door and closed it behind him.

"Make it quick. I have much to do. These are trying times."

"Indeed, they are, Father. I'm sure you've heard the news of Ceywind by now. Attacked by Skex in broad daylight, no less."

The king snorted. "I've heard about it, but that's not what happened."

Ashlyn's brow furrowed. "What do you mean?"

The king shook his head, threw a newspaper across his desk toward her, and looked back down at his work. Confused, she picked it up. The headline read, "Barnage Razed in Raider Attack." She continued reading the article. "Raiders? You can't be serious. I saw Barnage myself. It was not razed. Everyone was taken, Father. What about the Skex? How do they explain that?"

Her father looked up. "We are working closely with the Wraiths. They supplied us with shock troops to track the raiders responsible for the attack. They tracked them to Ceywind, but they escaped." He grabbed a quill from its well, "Now, if you'll excuse me."

Ashlyn was dumbfounded. She stood quiet for a moment, collecting her thoughts. "You know the truth. I know you do," she said.

He looked at her dead-on, which was rare. She knew he avoided looking at her; she resembled her mother. His eyes were cold. He held up a finger. "Careful," he said. He paused, looking back down at his work. "It's time for you to go."

"No," she said. "If you're not going to stop them, I will."

The king rose, his eyes once again meeting hers. The look this time, however, was not one of warning. "Guards," he called. The man from inside rushed in. The king gestured to Ashlyn. "Take her to the dungeon."

21

PROTECTORS

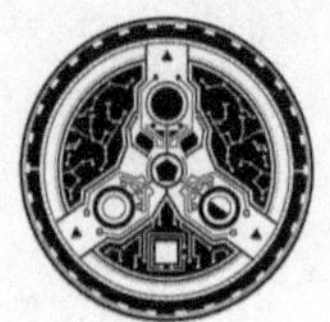

Open discord and disobedience among ex-military personnel continues today in the wake of the Accord signing. The One-Month War took a heavy psychological toll on those that had to face down the legions of Skex commanded by the Wraiths, leaving many soldiers unable to cope in a postwar world.

—From The Toltaire Times

CADE LIFTED heavy eyelids to discover a man staring at him. His long gray and wiry hair fell around his face. The captain of the *Manta*.

"You really opened the ninth door, kid."

Cade tried to speak, but no sound would come.

"Best not to talk, Elegy." The man continued to stare at him. "Name's Hale Clendon, by the way. Don't think we got around to that." He stood up. "What you did back on the ship was dumb. *Real* dumb. Just because they call you a hero doesn't give you the right to act like one." The man shook his head. "That Xansian saved you, you know. Picked you up and just set you right back on the deck when we resurfaced. Just like that. I ain't ever seen the likes of that before."

The man regarded Cade for a moment before continuing. "You can learn a lot about a man from the way he fights. You fight with passion, I'll give you that, but you're reckless. Still, you taught me something today." Hale stood up and paced the room.

"I was the captain of a ship in the Chalician Navy. Joined up to do my part. Sea and I were friends then. We did well in the war. Brought down more than our share of Skex and transported goods to the front lines." He stopped at the window, looking out into the rainy streets of Toltaire. "Time came for a short leave. I passed. Our next mission was too important to leave to chance." His voice became strained. "My family...the town, was burned to the ground. I could have been there. I could have saved them."

Cade tried to speak, but his chest hurt too much. His eyes were all that obeyed him.

"The king signed the Accord," Hale said, snorting. "Never been so mad. They're monsters. We all knew it, and here we were, giving them a chance to take our freedom *and* our dignity." He shook his head. "I went rogue, my men and I; for us the war never ended. We started raiding the government banks, taking what we could. We would give it to the people in the Ends, give them a fighting chance to survive."

The man sighed. "Until the king's own navy found us. Burned our ship while we were still on it. Only a handful of my men and I survived the attack, and our boat was lost. Until we discovered the *Manta* and started over again." The man walked back over to Cade and sat down in the chair next to the four-poster bed. "The sea has taken everything from me, one way or another, no matter how hard I fought."

He stared intently at Cade once more. "Your heroics

bought us time, but you know what saved us? The captains of the other ships in port. They blew those bugs right out of the water. I thought everyone had given up; I know I had." The man smiled. "You and I, we're protectors. Maybe we try to protect more than we can. But that's not what counts. People saw what you did. Turns out they didn't need protection. They needed a reminder. A reminder that we can fight back." The man stood up, and Cade heard the clink of a coin as it was set on the table beside him. "I owe you one."

Cade closed his eyes and slept.

"WAKE UP, CADE. PLEASE WAKE UP."

Cade opened his eyes and was surprised to see Jace hovering anxiously above him. With some difficulty, Cade sat up. His throat was dry, but he managed a hoarse whisper. "Jace?"

"Thank goodness you're finally awake. Ashlyn still hasn't returned."

Cade rubbed his eyes. His hand ached. He looked at it, and a dark purple bruise ran from his fist to his chest. He stretched it out and made a fist. It still worked.

"Where did she go?"

"She went to the castle to talk to her father about the Skex and see if he can help us fight."

Cade shook his head. "Bad idea."

"That's what I told her, but she seemed convinced she could talk to her father."

Cade sighed. "What about her agents? Can we find one of them?"

Jace shook his head. "I wouldn't even know where to begin."

"Could we sneak into the castle?"

"No, I've spent hours trying to think of a plan. Here." Jace opened his codex and flipped to the back, where he kept his maps. He unfolded a large piece of paper that detailed the plans of the castle. "Here is Toltaire Castle. There is only one primary entrance here. It's guarded around the clock. It's impenetrable."

Cade got to his feet. He noticed a challenge coin on the bedside table. In bold, intricate lettering was the name "Wraithbane." Cade smiled grimly and pocketed the coin.

"Where do you think you're going?" asked Jace.

"To the castle," replied Cade.

"I just told you it is impenetrable."

"I guess we just have to walk in the front door, then."

22

EOS

Toltaire is the city that sprouted from the overwrought fortress known as Toltaire Castle, which remains the seat of power for the Royal family of Chalice. The fortress itself was constructed upon the edge of a sheer cliff, which falls hundreds of feet into the ocean. It is said there are passages within the castle that extend into the interior of the cliff itself.

    —*From* The History of Chalice

"I AM HERE to request an audience with the princess," Cade said as he approached the gatehouse of Toltaire Castle. Jace had told him the idea was too risky, that if Ashlyn really was detained, requesting a meeting would only end up with him getting thrown in the dungeon.

Toltaire Castle was the first and strongest fortress of Chalice. Just outside the main Pathway network, the castle backed onto a cliff that protected it from direct attack by sea. A narrow river, the Eremin, flowed just outside the castle's main gate, serving as natural defensive perimeter before cutting into the cliff and cascading into the sea. The castle itself was enormous, with sixteen towers lining the outer wall and another eight towers lining the inner wall. Inside the inner wall, the towering stone cut an imposing silhouette against the afternoon sun.

The gate guard looked at him through his helmet's thin visor. "Bearer Elegy? We were not informed of your arrival. Please, we will have a guide escort you to the receiving room."

Cade nodded and stood until a butler greeted him at the gate. The older gentlemen cast a disapproving glance at Cade's attire. Cade knew his traveling clothes were not suitable for a royal visit, but he did not have time to waste at a tailor. "This way," was all the man said, voice dripping with disdain. He led Cade down the inner ward in the grand entrance of the keep.

Where the outside of the castle was utilitarian and cold, the lavish and ornate appointment of the grand entry rivaled the great chapels of Hakken. Countless ornate fili-greed sconces lined the room, holding thick, cream-colored candles that cast a warm welcoming glow upon the walls, as well as lighting the facets of the gemstones inset within the central chandelier. Lush red carpets lined the walkways between the other rooms on the floor. Sprawling tapestries hung from the walls, and Cade was surprised to note that some even depicted the battle of the Traveler and the Betrayers. He had assumed those would have been taken down after the *Book of the Traveler* was banned.

Even more amazing were the decorations and displays a flurry of servants were attending to. They were busy running gilded streamers and putting the finishing touches of fine art exhibitions from Toltaire's elite artisans.

"Please pardon the mess. I'm sure you are aware of the

Crossfort Ball coming up. As a titled member of Chalice, you are welcome to attend as well, of course," said the butler.

Cade hadn't really heard what the man said. He was watching a handful of servants busily arranging a display of Ancient artifacts near the front of the room. The presentation case was encrusted with large diamonds and sapphires, but he couldn't quite see what it held. He held his breath as they neared. Please, please, don't turn on, he begged as they walked closer.

His prayer was not answered. Once they were within a few feet, the devices sprang to life. A few of them lit up, spilling out blue and green lights throughout the great room. Others begin to whir and emit a series of tones. One servant who had been trying to set up an artifact for decoration fell off his ladder with the artifact itself after it startled him.

The butler rushed over to help the man, but Cade's attention had turned to an artifact that was being set up as the centerpiece of the exhibit. It was a sword, but unlike any he had ever seen before. It emanated a soft blue light that possessed almost imperceptible movement. Its iridescent surface shifted with the light like liquefied pearls. The blade itself was sleek and long, its tip revealing a shattered edge. The handle and hilt broke the aesthetic, since they were the design of a Chalician artisan. As Cade moved closer, he felt the Traveler's ring pull tight against his finger. A split-second later, the world fell away, and he was once again thrust into the Firmere. In a room filled with people and artifacts, he found himself surrounded by the bright, swirling smoke of life and machine. But greater than all of it was the incredible blue vortex swirling around the blue shard.

Cade Elegy. He stopped, hearing the voice in his mind.

The voice was not one he had heard before. *Confirmed phantom match. Exiting sleep and entering pairing mode. Please stand by.*

Cade continued walking forward, reaching for the vortex before him. *Hello, Cade. I am Eos.*

Two entities moved before him, and another whisked to his side. "This exhibit is off limits," a gruff voice said.

Cade snapped out of his trance, and the encoding with the Traveler's ring broke. He found himself looking at the strange sword but was barred by two guards in front of him who were eyeing him suspiciously. He turned to see the butler had returned to his side. "Sir, I'm afraid I cannot permit you to touch it. It is the grand prize for the Crossfort Tournament. Please excuse the artifacts...we're not quite sure what is happening. This way, please."

What was that? Cade thought as the butler led him out of the room and down a wide hallway. The man stopped just outside a small sitting room. "The princess will be notified of your arrival. I must tell you the princess has fallen ill, and will not be receiving anyone in person. However, a court—"

"That's fine. I'll wait," Cade cut in. *At least I know that if she can't meet me, she's being held against her will.*

The butler raised an eyebrow. "Very well. An attendant will be by shortly with refreshments," he said as he pivoted and left the receiving room.

Cade sat and waited until the butler's footsteps could no longer be heard from down the hall. *Eos,* he thought. That was who...or what...Tal had asked him to find. What was it doing at the castle? Cade shook his head. Focus, Cade. I must help the princess.

He stood up, poked his head out, and confirmed the old man was no longer in sight. He spied a noble walking through the entryway with another man who might have also been a noble. There were still many servants bustling about the area. The extra activity would allow him to move about without rousing too much suspicion.

He pulled out the map Jace had made for him. Cade remembered the story Ashlyn had told him when they first met. Her father had locked his own young daughter in the castle dungeon. What was to stop him from doing it again? He took a left out the room, trying his best to appear nonchalant as the workers busied by.

He found the servant's hall that connected to the grand entry and slipped inside. From there, he made his way past the servant quarters and found a door that led to a trash chute.

"Hey!" a voice sounded from behind. Cade froze.

A man rushed up to him. The dark silver color of tungsten began to spread across Cade's arm as he made a fist.

"Are you Cade Elegy?"

Cade nodded, keeping his hand behind his back.

"Oh, wow! I'm not...supposed to ask, but can I have your autograph?"

Cade nodded again, feeling dumb. He released his encoding, signed the man's ledger, and shook his hand. He breathed a sigh of relief as the guard marched away. He would have to be more careful. His face was too recognizable within the castle.

He took a right and found himself in the hallway that should lead to the back entrance to the dungeon. It would be guarded, of course, but being less traveled, it would buy him precious moments. As predicted, two guards were stationed in front of the entrance he needed. He made as if to walk by them when he lunged at the first guard and hit the base of the man's neck to knock him out. The other guard, scrambling to ready his weapon, started to yell, but Cade was already upon him and put the man into a headlock until he passed out. They would both live. So far, so good. He slipped into the entrance and descended the spiral staircase into the dungeon.

In the dungeon corridor, he heard the groans of the imprisoned denizens. There was also a persistent hissing that he couldn't quite place. As his eyes began to adjust to the meager torchlight, he saw rows and rows of locked doors with small, barred windows, perhaps fifty in all. He cursed under his breath. *This is going to take a while*, he thought. The dungeon was damp and smelled of mildew. The subterranean veins of the Eremin river must run close to the dungeon.

There was also something else in the air, a smell like burning sulfur. It was familiar, but he didn't remember where he had smelled it before. He checked door after door, but most of the cells were empty. He was hurrying from cell to cell. By now, the attendant would have noticed his disappearance. And if he couldn't find Ashlyn before the guards he dispatched were discovered, they wouldn't make it out in time.

The smell started to get to him. It was becoming stronger. He stopped running, but not because he wanted to. His feet became heavy, too heavy. Everything seemed delayed. He turned his head, and the images his eyes sent back seemed more like pages from a children's animated flip book. Even his thoughts seemed to slow down. But his brain did manage to finish one full thought before he collapsed, choking for air: it smells like nerve gas.

Figures wearing masks were upon him as his muscles seized. He tried to encode, but his body failed him. They grabbed Cade and threw him into a cell at the end of the hall. He only caught flashes of the strange, padded room as he struggled to breathe. A blindfold was wrapped tight around his head, and he could feel his wrists, legs, and neck bound with some type of fabric. He heard the masked guards shuffle out of the room as the door slammed shut. Cade tried to encode to his bonds, but doing so only caused his restraints to tighten around his wrists and neck.

I'm going to die here, Cade thought as the restraints choked him. He released the encoding on his bonds, but they stayed taut. His phantoms were present, but they were of no use to him here. He was swaying ever so slightly and sensed that his body had been suspended from the ceiling, facing the ground.

The blindfold was thick and cut into his temples. He couldn't look to see if there was anything around worth encoding with. His hands and legs were tied, and they had taken all his rings, even his wedding ring. He had not taken the ring off since the war. He felt...lesser, somehow, without it.

The room was quiet save for muffled scratching of rats in the distance.

He had been in prisons before—misunderstandings happen when you are a Bearer—but this was nothing like those times. He continued to struggle, gasping for the air that could not enter his constricted throat. He began to feel the edge of his consciousness crumble until cold water splashed across his face.

"Did you think you were the first Bearer to break in here?" The man's tone was contemptuous, and he spat on Cade. The man loosened the restraint on his neck. "Don't want you dying before we have what we need."

He could hear the man crouch down next to him. "Like your restraints? Our trapmaster helped design this prison, special for your blasphemous lot. The more you encode with them, the tighter the restraints become. Ingenious, really."

Cade remained silent.

"Why don't you make this easy and tell me what you, the supposed Protector the Realm, think you were up to trying to sneak in here?"

"Just trying to get to the ball." His voice was strained and weak.

The man kicked him square in the ribs. Cade grunted.

"I'm impressed you made it this far, I really am." He heard the man pacing. "I know you were helping the princess. What I don't know is what you're after. Tell me, and I will ask the king to consider a lighter sentence for you."

A lie. They had no intention of granting mercy to a rogue Bearer, Protector of the Realm or no.

"Won't talk?" The man sighed. He grabbed Cade's bruised arm and began to twist it. Cade encoded to the straps.

The man cursed as Cade's arm became impossibly pliable and he fell backward. Cade reversed the encoding, forcing the energy outward and knocking the confused man over.

After a few moments, Cade felt the man's foot once again meet his ribs, sending agonizing pain shooting through his chest. He coughed and tasted blood in his mouth. Cade's old refrain surfaced within his mind.

One more day.

23

THE BEARER'S CHOICE

The burden of the Pact does not rest solely on the Bearer. The phantom defies its calling...the constant pull to ascend to a greater state of being. The reasons a phantom chooses to remain are many. Finding that reason rests upon the Bearer.

 —*From* The Book of the Traveler

"I HOPE MY THEORY IS RIGHT," Ashlyn said as she continued to scratch and scrape at the wall. The utensil was ill-suited to the task, leaving her hands blistered and raw. She fought the urge to curse; it was unbecoming of a princess. Besides, she didn't want to draw attention. She wasn't sure when they would come back again. She was just happy they had not noticed the spoon missing from her plate.

Of course, they hadn't treated her as they would a "real" prisoner. She got nice meals and all the comforts befitting royalty. It did not lessen her fury that her own *father* had once again locked her down here. She had been stupid. She wasn't convinced of his involvement with the Wraiths before, but she was certain now.

Ashlyn had clung to the far-flung hope that everything was a big misunderstanding. That it was all orchestrated by the Wraiths, and her father was just trying to run his kingdom as best he could. She didn't know why she continued to defend him; he had done nothing to earn her affection. But he was still her father, and that bond was tough to break.

She continued to chip away at the mortar in the wall. She *was* getting somewhere, but it was taking longer than she imagined. A bigger chunk broke loose, and she nearly yelped with excitement before catching herself. She redoubled her efforts.

Her father was keeping her away for a reason. Maybe he thought she would get in the way of whatever was going on and didn't care for the rumors this type of behavior would stir up. She was glad she had not revealed any details about the Foundation.

Another piece broke off. She grinned. Ashlyn took the other end of the spoon, inserted it into the hole, and pounded the spoon with her shoe as if it were a hammer. It was lucky that she was wearing her heavier traveling shoes when they had put her in the cell. The last piece broke free.

Ashlyn put her eye up to the hole, but the cell was dark, and it was hard to see anything.

"Cade?" she whispered.

Silence.

"Cade, it's Ashlyn," she said, louder now.

"Ashlyn?" A raspy voice answered back. It was very weak, but she recognized it.

"Cade!" Her theory had been right. "How's that rescue coming along?"

"Part...of the plan." She heard him cough. He did not sound well.

Ashlyn let out a sigh of relief and slumped down upon the stone bench. When she heard the commotion outside earlier, she had a feeling it might be him.

After his coughing stopped, she heard him swallow and speak once more. "What kind of cell are you in?"

She looked around. "Uh, looks pretty standard, I guess. It's about as big as a bedroom."

"Anything metal?"

She wasn't sure why that would make a difference, but she played along. "The bars are some kind of metal...iron maybe? Oh, and my trusty spoon."

"We can work with that." She was on the ground now, with her ear as close to the hole as possible to try to hear him.

"Cade, what's this about?"

"I'm trying to find us a way out of here. Tell me, do you remember where Rolan was killed?"

She furrowed her brow, and her mouth went dry. "In... in my receiving room." The castle was immense. Each member of the household had their own sitting room. There were enough guests to warrant it, too. It still bothered her that Rolan had been killed in *her* sitting room, of all places.

"How far away from where we are now?"

Another strange question. "Um...the room isn't too far removed from this one, just three floors up."

"Okay. The good news is that we can get out of here."

Ashlyn grimaced as she prepared for the bad news.

"You're just not going to like how."

All the questions finally made sense.

"No. Absolutely not."

"Ashlyn, it's the only way. You must become a Bearer."

Her heart sank deep within her chest. After the war, she had grown to believe Bearers were bad, opportunistically using the dead for their own means. Even those who meant to do good succumbed to the corrupting power granted to them. Bearing a phantom was for other people, not her.

"I can't. It's immoral."

"Do you think I am immoral?" A fair question.

Silence.

She sighed. "It's different, though. You're the Protector of the Realm. You had to do what was needed to protect us all."

"But you still think *how* I achieved that wasn't right."

Ashlyn gave no reply.

He cleared his throat. "There was a girl in a small town I was passing through once. She had taken ill and passed away from the illness in mere days. Her mother begged and pleaded with me to see if her phantom was still with us, to make sure that her daughter had Ascended." He coughed again.

"Cade, what does this have to do—"

"At first, I was thankful that I didn't find any sign of her, but just when I was about to stop looking, I heard music playing, ever so softly. That's how it works, finding phantoms. You hear their Songs. I had never seen one so young stay behind before, so I formed a pact with her to find a way to put her to rest."

"But why would a little girl stay behind?" she asked.

"Children don't often stay behind; it's exceedingly rare. I did everything I could think of to find out how to free the girl's phantom. Nothing worked. I made sure her mother was looked after, and I made sure her little doll was buried with her during the funeral. I even delivered her final home-work assignment at school. Nothing worked. One day, a group of men came to the village. I observed the farmers giving these men their harvest crops. When I pressed them, I discovered that the farmers were paying these men to not raze their fields. They were hostages in their own town. It was destroying them, and it was obvious the token peace-keeping force in the town was not equipped to handle these men. As I spent more time there, I couldn't help but get caught up in their plight. Since I had not been able to help the girl, I had an important choice to make. Either keep trying to help the little girl or use the power this girl had entrusted me with to help the town."

"You fought the men?"

"I tracked them to their encampment, and I made sure they would not bother the town any longer."

"I can't imagine for a second that the girl would have wanted that. Did you feel guilty at all?"

"That's the thing. As I was fighting the last one—I reached affinity with the phantom."

"Affinity?"

"When you form a pact with a phantom, their Song, as we refer to it in Coda, blends itself with your own Song. Your actions and the choices you make can increase your affinity with a phantom, making the times when you use the phantom's power more effective. When you reach affinity, it is the phantom's way of telling you that you are on the precipice of fulfilling the Pact."

"The girl *wanted* you to defeat the men? That was why she formed the Pact with you?"

"Exactly. It started to make more and more sense when I thought about it. These men had been bothering them for a long time. The girl's mother was one of the women who continuously toiled in the fields, so her share was reduced every time the payments were taken."

Ashlyn grew quiet. Stories like this were generally not shared as a manner of respect for the dead, so it was fascinating to hear a real account.

"Isn't that selfish, though?"

"Yes, it is. But just because someone passes on doesn't mean they become selfless. Sometimes it is toward an end that is pure, and sometimes it is not. That is where the Bearers come in. We decide with whom to form a Pact, and we choose to help them ascend. Without any Bearers, more and more phantoms would gather in the Firmere, caught in the space between planes."

"But how do you know? That you're doing something good?"

She heard a sigh. "You don't. As a Bearer, you have to work in the margins of right and wrong."

Ashlyn nodded, even though she knew he could not see her. She was using Cade as a tool because she did not want to get her own hands dirty. Just like...just like her father would do. She had believed herself to be different; she believed she could be better than him. She was more like him than she thought.

"You wanted me to help you find out who killed Rolan. Now you can, and Rolan can help you."

Rolan had always been there for her. He would console her when she had a bad dream, read her stories about faraway lands, and even take the fall for her when she stole treats from the kitchens. He was more of a father than her real father had ever been. Didn't she owe it to Rolan to be the one to help him? He had died trying to get information to her; information that very well could save the world. Wasn't that worth some sacrifice?

Ashlyn took a deep breath. "Okay. Let's get started."

24

TRIAL BY PHANTOM

Pacts are my gift to you. This gift has been given to everyone. Cherish it, study it, and use its power to improve the world around you.

—From The Book of the Traveler

SAYING she'd do it had been the easy part.

"Try again," Cade instructed. His voice was only a hoarse whisper now. He needed to take breaks between fits of coughing.

Cade had spent the last hour teaching her the fundamentals of phantom bonding through the Pact. It was a subject on which you could spend a lifetime and never master. She only had hours.

As luck would have it, the parts she needed to use were the easiest to learn. There was a lot of subtlety with Bearing, Cade told her. For example, anyone given a knife could cut a tomato. A skilled chef, however, could cut one into perfect slices and do it in a few deft motions. The same rules held true with Bearers. An unskilled Bearer could form a Pact and encode with a simple material. A skilled Bearer could encode with higher efficiency, needing less material, and maximize the energy of the phantom.

"This is nothing like cutting a tomato," she said, frustrated.

"Close your eyes. Remember when you last saw Rolan."

Sighing, she closed her eyes. She took herself back to that day, crouched down next to Rolan, remembering the secret pocket sewn into the inside of his vest he had taught her to look for. She remembered the warmth leaving his body as she held his hand. Tears welled up. She fought them back.

Music began playing. Faint, distant. It was a melody she was certain she had never heard before, but it was still familiar. She couldn't explain it, but it had a shape to it, a form, as if the music itself was corporeal. Each note evoked a memory, as if someone were playing a piano where every key contained a piece of herself within it.

Her heartbeat quickened, and she wiped her eyes. "I...I hear it."

"Say the words."

She cleared her throat. "Song that lingers unfinished; the one whose Sigh has escaped to the stars. Allow me to sing your final verse." Cade had told her the words helped bond the intention of the Bearer to the phantom. The words she spoke were what followers of Coda would say to form a Pact. She figured it was as good as anything else. If she was going to break one belief today, she might as well go all-in.

Nothing happened. "It's not working, Cade."

"Remember. The words themselves are not important. You must open yourself up for the phantom to join with you."

Ashlyn took a deep breath and listened once more. She

heard the music, far away. She continued to listen to it and imagined drawing the music closer to her. The music became louder. She pulled it even closer and imagined wrapping herself in it, until the sounds of the outside world faded away and only the music could be heard.

She felt a surge of warmth, as if steam was pushing through her veins. The feeling radiated and pulsed through her. She took a sharp breath inward, as if she had been holding her breath underwater and had finally came up for air. The feeling subsided, and she felt...different.

Cade said he really couldn't explain the sensation, but he did tell her not to fight it. She understood now.

"Ashlyn? Can you hear me? Are you okay?" Cade's voice was quiet, careful not to disturb the guards, but it carried fierce concern. Her senses felt sharper than normal. Was she just imagining things?

"Yeah, I'm...fine, I think. My head..." Her thoughts felt crowded in her own mind, as if they were being squeezed tight. It almost felt like when she had too much to do and didn't know where to start. But this was more extreme; the thoughts she was having were pulling her different directions. She began to panic. Was she losing her mind? Would she even know if she was? *No*, she thought. She took another breath and tried to quiet her mind. *I can do this. I need to think about something else. Cade. How is Cade?*

She could somehow sense that Cade was relieved. She could feel something else—guilt? *Can you feel someone else's guilt?*

Her thoughts aside, she felt stronger, and more confident. Was it all in her head? *I could get used to this*, she thought. She shuddered at how quickly she was being seduced by the phantom's power.

Cade's voice sounded through the door. "We need to

practice encoding. Try the bars on the door. Remember their core property."

"Right," she said, almost forgetting their objective.

"Grab the bar and focus the phantom. Let it fuse with the metal."

She grabbed the bar with one hand and closed her eyes. She didn't need to close her eyes, but she figured it would help her concentrate. She imagined the new force within, swirling around her, and she *pushed* it into the bar. This is what Cade had called "encoding." She felt her grip tighten around the bar. Not of her own doing, but the encoding itself was closing the gaps between the material and her skin. Fusing the material to oneself was called a first-stage encoding. She tried to pull her hand away and found that it was stuck to the bar, like it had been glued there. This alarmed her at first, but she had been warned already of the effect. She took a deep breath, relaxed, and let the second-stage encoding take hold. She began to feel...heavier.

Ashlyn opened her eyes. "Cade, I'm doing it! How... how is this possible?" she marveled.

Cade's voice, even weaker now, spoke to her from the other cell. "The phantoms from the Firmere can encode the essence of an object in the Veris into another object. They twist reality, if only for a few moments. The Veris rejects the distortion of reality, fighting to restore itself. This is why phantoms can become exhausted. The more rules you try break in the Veris, the physical world, the more difficult it is for the phantom."

She looked at her hand and noticed that it was starting to turn a deep silver. She started to panic. "My hand...it's turning silver...it's not stopping!"

"Your encoding is too strong. Pull back your phantom

before you overencode. You are in control. Nice and slow." Cade's voice, though weak, was calm and reassuring.

Ashlyn took a deep breath and closed her eyes again. The feeling didn't abate. She felt her body get colder and more rigid, like she was turning into a statue. Her heart quickened. I am in control, she repeated, taking a slow breath. I will not die here.

She *pulled* the phantom back to her, somehow, and felt herself get lighter. She opened her eyes and saw her hand was back to normal. She trembled, remembering what her body had done only moments before. That was close.

She wasn't sure if she was delirious from the near-death experience, but she smiled to herself. She knew she *should* feel bad for becoming a Bearer. But instead, for once in her life, she felt like she really was in control. Rolan, you and I are going places.

She set out to try once more when she heard footsteps coming down the hall.

"Cade, someone is coming. I haven't had any time to practice!"

Cade did not reply.

She knew if she didn't take this opportunity, they might not get another one.

Ashlyn, emboldened by her new abilities, calmed herself. I can do this.

As the footsteps neared, she grew increasingly nervous. She hoped the guard on duty was anyone but Gregory. She really liked Gregory, and he wasn't hard to look at, either. He was always so kind to her. Not just polite because she was the princess, but he seemed genuinely nice and sincere. That was a rare trait in Toltaire. She brightened just thinking about sweet Gregory.

Her heart fell to the floor and shattered into tiny pieces

when Gregory appeared around the corner. She felt an alien chuckle rise within her. *Rolan, this is not funny*, she thought. *You be quiet*. Now she was talking to herself. How did Bearers stay sane?

Cade was still quiet. The guard was close now, and he must not want to alert him.

Ashlyn, who had moved to the bars, took a deep breath and called over to Gregory. "Oh, hello, Gregory! I'm so glad to see you. I dropped my earring just outside the door there. Can you please fetch it for me?"

Gregory smiled, which made her hate herself even more. He stooped over to pick up the earring Ashlyn had placed just outside the bars.

Ashlyn, holding onto the bar, encoded with the iron. She made a fist, raised it over her head, and brought it down on the back of Gregory's head. He fell to the floor, unconscious.

"I am a terrible person," she muttered and slumped to the floor of the dusty cell. She had tried not to hit him too hard. She hoped he would be okay.

Ashlyn reached through the bars and grabbed the keys from the loop on Gregory's belt. She saw a knife tucked into a small scabbard, which she also took. She unlocked her door and made her way to Cade's cell. His door was solid, not like the bars of Ashlyn's cell.

As she opened the door, she couldn't help but gasp. Cade was suspended in the air, splayed by straps that cut into his arms and legs. A thinner strap was secured around his neck and was attached to the ceiling. Underneath him, a pool of blood had accumulated.

Ashlyn hurried inside and began to cut the strap around his neck with the knife she had taken from Gregory. "Hang on, Cade."

She finished cutting the last strap, and he fell to the floor with a dull thud. She rolled him over and looked at his face. His eyes were open but unfocused and distant. She held her hand over his mouth. She felt his breath, though it was light. Too light.

Tears welled up in her eyes, but she fought them back. "Cade...I'm so sorry."

Move, a voice seemed to say.

She stood up. They couldn't stay here. She grabbed Cade's arms and managed to drag him out of the gruesome cell. She looked down the hall to a wide stairwell that led to the next floor up. She began to drag him toward the stairwell when she heard footsteps hurrying down the stairs. She tried to drag Cade back into the cell to hide, but before she made it back to the door a dozen guards rushed into the corridor. Seeing Ashlyn, they charged.

Ashlyn dropped Cade, raising her arms to show them she had no weapons. The guards did not slow down. The lead guard, at full sprint, unsheathed the sword at his side and raised it high. *Did my father give this order?*

She cowered and covered her head with her hands.

He wouldn't do this, would he? The footsteps continued to get louder. She heard the man yell and braced herself for the attack.

Why?

Silence. She looked up and saw a look of terror upon her attacker's face. The other guards had skidded to a halt and gaped at her.

Ashlyn looked at her arm and saw she had grabbed the blade less than an inch above her head. Her hand looked as if it were wearing a sleek silver evening glove.

The guard's eyes grew wide. "She's a Bearer!"

The other guards, breaking from their trance, hurried

forward. Ashlyn cowered down with the blade still held in her hand, teeth gritted, and eyes closed. She could feel swords and bullets bouncing off her hardened skin. She wasn't a fighter. What was she doing here? This was all a big mistake. How could her father allow this?

Fight, said a voice within her.

The voice pulled her out of her thoughts. Rolan?

The swords continued to clash upon hardened skin. She looked up and saw a soldier with a large war hammer approaching. Her father was responsible and had ordered this. She felt alone. Except she wasn't alone, not anymore. She had Cade, Jace, and now Rolan. The Ashlyn she had been was gone; she was someone else now.

She cleared her mind. Rolan would help her. The swords and spears continued to rain down upon her, and she felt anger well up and grow hot.

She stood and adjusted the sword with the grip clasped firmly in her palm. "I...am...your...princess."

The soldier with the hammer moved in to strike, and Ashlyn effortlessly sidestepped the massive weapon. She hit the man from behind with the flat of the blade as hard as she could. No time to think. *Move to the next one*, an alien thought instructed. The man swung, and she swatted the attack away and stuck the man square in the gut with an encoded fist.

Within moments, the soldiers lay fallen around her. She stood, breathing hard yet not tired. She held up her hands in front of her and looked at them as if they were somehow not her own.

Ashlyn hurried to Cade, put his arm across her shoulders, and began to move back toward the stairs. The man was heavy, too heavy. How will I get him out of here?

Earrings, said the voice.

She absently touched her ear and felt the remaining diamond earring she had put on before she had gone to talk to father. The core property of diamond: strength. That would do the trick.

She took a deep breath and focused on an earring. She felt it press uncomfortably against her ear as her muscles became stronger, and she felt lighter. A drop of blood fell from her ear as she walked over to Cade. She moved to sling him over her shoulder, but she misjudged and instead sent him hurtling into the wall behind her.

"Cade! I'm so sorry," she gasped, hurrying over to him, and more careful this time, placed him over her shoulder. She felt a laugh rise within her. "Rolan, this is not funny," she found herself saying aloud. *Ugh*, she thought, *I have to stop doing that.*

The rush of footsteps sounded from the stairwell above. More guards. She wheeled around, finding only a single staircase leading downward.

"Hold on, Cade," she said, as she descended into the castle's dungeons.

25

ESCAPE

A Bearer must take care when accepting a phantom. A phantom's knowledge is passed to the Bearer, albeit imperfectly. What that means is thoughts may surface that are unlike your own. And you may find you know how to do certain tasks, where no prior knowledge existed before.
—From Introduction to Bearer Psychology

ASHLYN RAN down the hall as fast as she could, careful not to hurt Cade more than she already had. He still hadn't spoken, and his eyes remained closed. She wanted to check on him, but the guards would be upon them if she didn't keep moving.

They came upon a simple steel door in the dungeon that looked out of place. *A storeroom?* Perhaps they could hide there until the guards passed by. She set Cade down to the side and pushed on the door. It would not budge.

Snorting, she dug her heels in and braced her hands against the door. She felt her ear sting sharply as she encoded to the diamond.

Pushing hard upon the riveted steel door, she could feel the lock begin to creak and buckle. A little more...

The door's protestations ceased, and it swung open wide. She dragged Cade inside and shut the door. She sat down next to him as her eyes adjusted to the dimness. It looked like an old storeroom, but it had a stronger smell of mildew than even the dungeons above them. She could hear the trickle of water from the other end of the room.

We can't stay here forever, she thought. The guards would sweep the whole area until they were found. She gathered herself, stood up, and walked to the end of the room.

The trickle of water was more of a fountain, with the water pooling a bit before it drained through a large crack in the stone floor. *The Eremin river*, she thought. It ran alongside the foundation of the castle, and veins of it flowed underground. All the veins emptied into a great waterfall on the backside of the cliff upon which the castle was built.

Ashlyn bit her lip, surveying the stone bricks. They were large, but she thought she could move them if she used her diamond earring. She placed her hands upon the stone. It did not budge when she tested it with a light push. She began encoding, feeling the power surge into her hands as they shimmered. She pushed again, but it would still not move. She stayed focused and pulled the encoding even farther, her arms nearly becoming translucent. Panic welled up in the back of her mind, but she ignored it. Overencoding or not, this had to be done. The stone skidded an inch and then flew into a powerful jet of water from the Eremin. The underground stream was strong, its current taking the massive brick with it.

She sighed, looking at the imposing rush of water as it

began to pour into the room. *Well,* she thought, *at least no one will follow us.*

Ashlyn, encoding once more, slung Cade over her shoulder and held tight as she ducked through the hole in the wall and let the current grab them. They rushed forward at incredible speed, surrounded by darkness as they descended deeper underground. She flailed with her free hand, trying to find a handhold among the passing rocks. Her hand just slipped across the wet surface of the underground riverbed. Her lungs began to burn. *Hold on, Cade.*

Encode, a voice urged.

She flared the diamond encoding and reached a hand toward a passing stone outcropping. She felt her nails tear as her fingers dug in. Her grip was true, and she managed to pull herself and Cade onto the small ledge. She looked at him and saw the color in his face had drained away. Horrified, she took her hands and compressed them into his chest. She heard a strangled noise as Cade coughed up the water that had accumulated in his lungs. She sighed in relief as she rested against the stones.

Ashlyn rubbed her injured hand. The river raged beside them, leading to the ocean outside the cliffs, which afforded them some light.

Her hand brushed the floor of the ledge when she noticed something odd. Upon inspection, she discovered their perch was not a natural formation. It was made of carefully carved stone bricks. She looked to the wall behind her and discovered the same bricks traveling as far up as her eyes could see.

"Cade, I've got good news. I think we're right next to the old granary silo." She looked down the length of the wall. "Though I'm not sure how we're going to get inside. Any ideas?"

She laughed, partly from exhaustion and partly because of her tenuous grip on her own sanity.

He would know what to do. *Think, Ashlyn*, she told herself. What would Cade do?

Looking at the wall before her, she laughed again. He would probably fight his way out. She placed one hand on the warm stone and *pulled* it into her fist. Wheeling back, she brought it crashing into the wall. The wall held fast.

She brought her fist back again and sent it as hard as she could into the wall. Encoded or not, it *hurt*.

A small crack took root in the stone. Her hand ached, but she pulled it back once more. Ashlyn yelled as she punched her fist through the stone and felt the rock shudder and crumble.

"Good idea, Cade," she said, pulling out the broken bits of stone.

Her senses dulled and her earring released its tight grip against her ear as the phantom within her grew quiet.

Pushing Cade through the opening she had made, she pulled herself through and was submerged in the dim light of the silo. She felt around the opening and discovered steps that appeared to spiral upward.

The silo itself was no longer used for grain storage, but the staircase was still used by the castle's staff to transport goods between floors. She slung Cade's arm around her shoulder and began her slow ascent.

She had only made it a couple flights of steps before her protesting muscles began to tire, no longer aided by diamond-assisted strength. She set Cade down before slumping against the inside of the smooth stone wall.

A door farther up the stairs creaked open and torchlight flooded into the silo. Ashlyn froze, holding her breath and pressing herself firm against the wall.

A thin man, hunched with age, emerged from the doorway and spotted her.

A look of recognition flashed in his eyes. It took a few moments, but Ashlyn realized she knew the man. Gilliam, the seal-carrier she had saved years before from near certain death. The man glanced down, saw Cade, and nodded. He walked over to Cade and pulled an arm over his shoulder. Looking at Ashlyn, he cocked his head upward.

Wordlessly, he began climbing the stairs with Ashlyn following close behind.

After climbing for what felt like hours, they came to another door. He opened the door and ushered her inside.

Ashlyn recognized the floor. Her brother Elon's chambers were just up ahead. The man must have known that with the guards patrolling the entrance, there was no way they could escape. Elon was rarely home, usually on an assignment from her father. They could rest here.

She turned to the old man. "Thank you, Gilliam."

The man nodded with a faint smile. He turned, hearing footsteps descending from the silo steps above, and pulled the door closed behind him.

Ashlyn dragged Cade into the servant entrance of Elon's closet room and secured the door behind her. She laid him onto the floor and took a hold of his wrist, checking his pulse. Faint but present. She let out a wavering breath and sat, unsure of what to do next.

"How are we going to get out of here?" she whispered.

She heard the tumblers on the lock in the front chamber fall into place, followed by the sound of a door swinging open. Ashlyn scrambled up and cracked the door to the main chamber.

Peeking through the crack, Ashlyn saw Elon addressing the guards at his door.

"No, I do not need you in my personal chambers. I am quite capable of taking care of myself.

"Yes, I am well aware that my sister has escaped. I will do my best to protect myself against an unarmed woman," he said with more than a hint of sarcasm.

Her father had gone to great lengths to keep them separated. He had always wanted a boy, and when Elon was born, he directed all of his attentions to Elon. Even though Ashlyn was the firstborn, her father did not deem her worthy of inheriting the kingdom.

Elon locked the door, pocketed the key, pivoted his wheelchair away from the door, and rolled to the dresser. Elon was very slight for a boy, and due to complications during childbirth, he was unable to walk on his own. Ashlyn noticed, the few times she had met with him, his handicap never seemed to dampen his spirits. While he generally wore a solemn expression, his eyes were always bright and penetrating.

Even seated, his presence commanded respect. He was handsome and regal, and his ornate wheelchair looked as if he were perpetually sitting upon a throne. She could understand why her father had placed so much faith in him. He had the disposition of a born leader, and he commanded the complete respect of everyone he worked with.

Ashlyn considered telling Elon what had happened to her. Would he listen? Or would he side with her father?

Looking into the full-length mirror across from the dresser, Elon pulled off his traveling hat. He reached back and pulled out a small pin, and long, thick locks of hair came tumbling around his shoulders. He unbuttoned his collared shirt, revealing a cinched corset around his chest.

Ashlyn's eyes grew wide, and she stumbled trying to get a closer look, knocking down a suit that hung near the door.

"Who's there?" Elon demanded, wheeling around.

Ashlyn, unsure what to do, opened the door slowly and met her brother's eyes.

"Ashlyn?"

She nodded.

"You're hurt. What happened? Why are the guards looking for you?"

Ashlyn could only stare at him, dumbfounded.

Elon's eyes grew wide as he touched his hair. "Right." He sighed. "As I'm sure you are aware, father always wanted a male heir to become his protégé."

Ashlyn just stared at him.

Elon broke his gaze and cast his eyes to the floor. "He never got one."

"Sister?" was all Ashlyn could say.

Elon nodded. "After I was born, the doctors knew Mother was not going to be able to birth another child. From what I could piece together, Father was beyond distraught at not having a male heir. In what I can only describe as a fit of madness, he decided from that point on that he would masquerade me as a boy."

The slight frame, the soft voice. The separation from Ashlyn. The pieces fell into place.

Anticipating a question Ashlyn did not ask, Elon shook her head. "I don't know what advantage he sought by maintaining this farce. Perhaps it was a brief madness that overtook him during my birth. And perhaps he did not want to appear weak or insane by having to come clean once he regained his senses."

Elon paused, gathering herself. "I know something is coming. We have been visited again by the Wraith ambassador, which hasn't happened since the treaty was first signed. I fear the worst, but I cannot get Father to tell me what's happening. Do you know?"

Ashlyn opened her mouth to speak when she heard Cade cough, slumped on his side.

Elon, startled, rolled to the closet to investigate. "Is that...?"

Ashlyn nodded.

Elon crossed her arms and tapped a finger on her chin. She turned and grabbed the suit that had fallen. "Put this on."

"What?" Ashlyn said, brow furrowed.

"If I can do it for my whole life, you can manage an afternoon. We're getting you out of here."

26

ELON

Toltaire was the first major city established by the early settlers. The city continues to be a popular destination and has begun to infill previously undeveloped parts of the city. This has given rise to numerous tall buildings and a feeling of claustrophobia for those new to the bustling city.
—*From* The History of Chalice

ELON AND HER AGENTS, members of Rolan's network, escorted them to the side entrance of the castle. Thanks to the endless stream of couriers with deliveries for the Crossfort Ball, they managed to carry out the wardrobe trunk that held Cade without arousing suspicion.

They rode down a circuitous back street, taking care to make extra turns to ensure they were not followed. Ashlyn told Elon of General Carlon and about the weapon they must collect in Toltaire.

They stopped before a well-concealed townhouse crammed into the bustling commercial district of Toltaire. Property was so prized that every last square inch of the city had been purchased and built upon or backfilled. The entire cityscape was now a teetering jungle of wood and brick. Gone was the architectural beauty she remembered growing up. While it was terrible for the people who yearned for the wide-open spaces of old Toltaire, it was wonderful for people who did not want to be found.

"We'll be safe here for a while," remarked Elon. "The Order has quite a few of these houses, and they take care to cycle them regularly." Ashlyn knew her uncle Rolan had arranged for safe houses to be available for the Order of the Phantom, but she had never visited one herself. Paranoid measures for a city that couldn't keep a secret.

Ashlyn afforded herself a moment to relax and found herself struck by the novelty of being in the same room with Elon. She had seen so little of him...her...as she grew up that Elon didn't really feel like family at all—just another person who lived at the castle.

There was a knock at the door, startling her. Elon nodded to one of the guards. "It looks like they were able to find your friend."

The door opened, revealing a worried-looking Jace. When he saw Ashlyn, his face lit up. "You're all right!"

He ran up to her and hugged her, much to her surprise. "When I heard you both had been captured, I had lost all hope." His gaze turned to Cade, who had been laid on the bed nearby.

"Cade...what did they do to you?" He hovered over his friend, brow heavy with concern.

"Let him rest," Elon commanded and turned to Ashlyn. "You mentioned a weapon that could destroy the Wraith ship. Where are you going to take it?"

Before Ashlyn could speak, Jace cut in. "We need to transport the weapon to Rynth."

Elon raised an eyebrow. "Why Rynth?"

Jace glanced at Ashlyn, who nodded. Jace pulled out his leather-bound book and held it up. "We will rendezvous with a Foundation team that will secure a railbus to the Thread."

Elon grimaced. "The Wraiths control all trains to the Thread, even in Rynth. That is a dangerous plan."

Jace nodded. "It's all we've got right now."

Elon shook her head. "Well, if General Carlon believes in the plan, so do I. We must see you to this weapons-maker straight away."

A cough sounded from the bed. Cade, sitting up, rubbed his eyes. "I must go back to the castle," he said, his voice hoarse.

Ashlyn balked. "You can't be serious. We were lucky to make it out of there. If it wasn't for Elon..."

"That voice...Eos. The machines," stammered Cade.

"Cade, what are you talking about?" asked Ashlyn, sitting on the bed next to him.

"A sword. A broken sword of glass...It spoke to me."

Jace cut in, eyes wide. "Broken sword? You mean the Shard of Rynth?" He laughed. "The Shard is one of the most prized artifacts discovered in Rynth. It's made of a mysterious color-shifting material that has never been seen before. How do you not know that?"

Cade just looked at Jace, expression blank.

Jace sighed. "Never mind. You're saying it *spoke* to you?"

Cade nodded. "I have to go back. I had...a dream about it."

Ashlyn looked at Jace. "You aren't considering this, are you? I almost cost us this mission already."

"Hmmm," said Jace, tapping his chin. "Cade's been activating artifacts left and right these days, so I imagine this is no different. And we already admitted the plan we have is a long shot. If Cade can speak to the Ancients though that device—"

"He didn't say he was speaking to the Ancients," said Ashlyn.

Jace shrugged. "I don't know who else would talk to him through an artifact, do you? But I can tell you that this artifact may be the missing piece to our plan."

Ashlyn just shook her head. "How are we going to get back there and get it? It's impossible."

Elon turned to Ashlyn and grinned. "There is one way."

Ashlyn's eyes grew wide. Of course.

"The Crossfort Ball," they said in unison.

After the war ended, a grand ball was held at the castle to honor the military who guarded the key fortresses of Chalice and helped maintain the sovereignty of the young nation. It became devout tradition and served as an opportunity for military leaders who longed to rub shoulders with Toltaire's elite. An invitation to the party could mean big things for a career, and in peacetime there was plenty of time to play politics.

"I'm not following; why would a ball help us get the Shard? Will security not be as tight?" asked Jace.

"No, if anything, security will be doubled. But we could end up walking out the door with the Shard without even having to steal it," Ashlyn said.

Jace cocked his head. "I'm listening."

She continued, "The ball is held once a year. And the aristocrats love to gamble, so they started using it as an excuse to gamble for the most sought-after treasure in Chalice."

"The Shard?" Jace said, incredulous. "You're telling me

they just give away the most prized artifact in all of Chalice?"

"Not exactly," Elon said. "In order to win the Shard for the year, you have to win a card tournament. It just so happens that no one has ever beaten our dear father."

Jace rubbed his temples. "Okay, let's assume for a moment we can do that. How will they both not be arrested on the spot? Aren't they both wanted?"

"That is true," said Elon, "...but if there is one thing my father hates, it's scandal. He cares too much about appearances. If he arrests his own daughter and Protector of the Realm in public...well, that would be a scandal of epic proportions. No one outside the guardsmen know they are fugitives."

"I've seen the papers calling the Skex invasion in Ceywind an act of cooperation with the Wraiths to track down raiders," said Jace. "From what I've heard, a lot of people aren't buying it. If the king were to lose any more credibility, it could be a tipping point."

Both Ashlyn and Elon nodded, smiling.

"What's the dress code?" asked Cade.

THE CROSSFORT BALL

The Crossfort Ball, while a military event, possesses none of the austere trappings most military organized events are known for. No expense is spared on any detail, from the magnificent displays of Ancient artifacts to the custom hand-woven towels in the castle washrooms. It is an event of excess, meant to symbolize both the might and prosperity of Chalice.

—*From* The Toltaire Times

CADE LOOKED into the mirror at the suit he was wearing. It was in the traditional military style, but it had been altered to his exact measurements and was made of a much higher-grade cloth than was typically afforded to soldiers. The collar was shortened to match modern tastes, and the jacket with Bearer-grade tungsten buttons gave him an imposing silhouette. He hardly recognized himself.

"Perfect fit, if I do say," the tailor said, admiring her work. As a veteran, Cade was permitted to wear formal military attire, replete with the markings and awards earned during his tour of duty.

"You cut a striking figure, if I do say so. Even if the scenery is a bit ravaged," the woman remarked. Cade noticed the cuts and scrapes on his hands and face. They couldn't be helped.

He was assured the tailor could be trusted, but he kept a close eye on her nonetheless. Still, he couldn't argue her skill with a needle. The old suit he had been issued after service fit like a used grain sack, and it felt like wearing one, too. This new suit was both stylish and comfortable.

"How do I look?" he heard Ashlyn say as she entered the room.

Cade turned around and thought for a moment he had reached Affinity with a phantom, because time stopped. Ashlyn was adorned in a long, flowing gown of gold, as if spun by the rays of the sun itself. The color complemented her auburn hair, which had been pinned up, save for a single long, stray lock that framed the side of her face.

He thought to say something, but the words failed him. He knew she was a princess, but tonight she looked the part, as if she had stepped right off the page of a childhood storybook.

"Hello? Cade?" She looked at him, concerned.

"I...uh...you look wonderful." He cleared his throat and a knock came at the door.

"Are you decent?" Jace poked his head in. "Wow, you guys are quite a lovely couple."

Cade could feel himself turning red. He glanced at Ashlyn and was surprised to see her doing the same.

He realized that up until now, he hadn't really seen her as a princess at all. She wasn't the carefree and entitled noble he had assumed when he first met her. She had a weight to her. Though she may never rule, she still carried the burden of an entire kingdom on her shoulders.

She smiled at him, and he couldn't help but smile back. Tonight, they both would be someone else. They would play the part of the storybook princess and her knight, going to the ball.

Elon rolled into the room. "The carriages are here. Ready?"

Cade and Ashlyn nodded to each other.

They took their train of assembled carriages to the ball, each one with special instructions to facilitate their departure. With so many of Toltaire's elite en route to the ball with their own processions of carriages, they arrived unnoticed.

Cade slipped on his rings, which Elon's guards had procured from the dungeon's locker. The Rynthium ring was there as well; his captors must have had no idea what it really was.

The courtyard of the castle was bursting with people. Journalists shouted from behind cordoned holding areas as attendees strode toward the crowded entrance with raised chins and expressions of feigned indifference. Others negotiated with the guards, trying to find a way inside.

"You okay, Cade?" Ashlyn said, glancing at him as they walked, her arm linked around his.

His muscles were tensed. He was growing uncomfortable within the mass of people. His mind, tempered for battle, could not help but try to calculate optimal battle tactics in any situation. In crowds, however, there were too many variables.

"I'm fine. Let's stay focused."

As they approached the golden walkway to the entrance arch, the gathered crowd gasped. Seeing the princess with

Cade was headline news. Shouts rang out from the crowd, calling their names. It was good to be noticed—their plan counted on it.

At the door, they were stopped by the guards, and Cade could see their eyes grow wide with recognition. They knew better than to risk a scene here, especially one that involved the princess.

As they entered the castle, a sweeping view of the main ballroom greeted them. It was lavishly decorated, with helixed streamers of small crystals running from each end of the room, and ice sculptures chiseled into scale models of the military forts that served Chalice. And of course, rare artifacts of the Ancients were on display. The Shard of Rynth itself had been hoisted high in the room, tonight's prize for the victor. The ballroom floor was bustling with nobles in fine black suits and ladies wearing intricate gowns that spilled onto the floor like colorful paint.

Cade started to sweat. The opulence made him uncomfortable, but even more worrisome was their plan. He didn't even like the word "plan." Using the word inferred complexity. He didn't like complexity.

"Are you sure your man is reliable?" he asked.

Ashlyn nodded. "He's the best there is. He's been my father's exclusive card dealer for years, but he's loyal to my Order. Now hush."

The center of the ballroom was awash with colorful dancers, and skilled performers wowed the crowd with acrobatic feats as they hung from silk ropes suspended from high above.

The caller recognized them but gave no indication he was aware of their recent outlaw status. The man bellowed, "Miss Ashlyn Winshire, Princess of Chalice, attending with Cade Elegy, Protector of the Realm."

Clusters of people within the ballroom stopped talking and looked to the entrance. The room was so quiet, Cade could hear music he hadn't heard before being played from a stage in the back of the room. It was beautiful, and Cade guessed that more than one of the performers had practiced Coda.

The shocked guests turned back to their conversations, gossiping about this exciting new development.

More fanfare, exactly what they needed. The king would be hard-pressed to make a move now, though their appearance was sure to make him livid.

As if on cue, the king himself strode up to them. The man's presence was intimidating. Following close behind him was a sizable entourage of guards and lackeys, but the king towered over them like they were schoolchildren.

"Elegy. I was not informed of your attendance. What, may I ask, brings you here?" The king's voice was calm and even; he knew there would be many ears around them tonight.

Cade seized the opportunity. He projected his voice so those around him would hear his reply. "I have come to request my boon, Your Highness."

Gasps rippled through the ballroom.

The king's eyes narrowed for a split second and then relaxed when he caught himself. "I'm not sure I follow. To what boon are you referring?"

Ashlyn took the opportunity to speak. "Every person granted a title in Chalice is entitled to either property or a boon of their request. Cade was not granted property when he was named the Protector of the Realm, so he is here to request his boon, if you will it, Father."

The king eyed her, his jaw set. He was not sure where they were headed with this, but he had no desire to make any more of a scene. Political power was his favored currency, and he was very careful how he spent it.

"Very well. Let me hear your request. I will grant it, if within reason."

"I have only a small request of you, Your Highness," Cade continued. "I wish to play in the tournament."

The crowd erupted with a flurry of excited whispers.

The king raised an eyebrow and grinned. "Your boon is granted. You are welcome at the table this evening, Protector."

Cade looked over at Ashlyn, who nodded. He could tell she was nervous. After her father threw her in prison, she didn't know what to expect.

The crowd grew quiet, and Cade could hear the music once again. He knew this song.

Ashlyn grabbed his arm. "The 'Vermilion Waltz!' We *have* to dance."

It still eluded him how she could be so wrapped up in one moment and completely forget herself in another. As mad as she seemed to him, a part of him wished he could do that. Unfortunately, he had never taken the time to learn the waltz. Or any dance, for that matter. He shook his head.

"Come on, I'll help you. Just follow my lead!" She pulled him to an open space on the floor, took one of his hands in her own, and placed his other hand on the side of her hip. She stepped back and he stumbled a bit, not anticipating the motion. She smiled, and he tried again to follow. He stepped on her foot, causing her to wince. She took a deep breath, squared herself with him one more time, and began once more.

She whispered in his ear, "Don't try to think too much. Just follow the music."

Don't think too much. The same advice he had given

Ashlyn when she agreed to become a Bearer. Cade took a deep breath, and, much to his surprise, started to dance.

It was a bit awkward at first, since he was staring right at his feet. But his feet seemed to know what to do, and he looked up, meeting Ashlyn's eyes. She was beaming at him, and he couldn't help but smile back.

They continued to glide across the ballroom, but soon he was no longer following Ashlyn's lead; she was following his. She looked confused for a moment but allowed him to take the lead, and their dancing began to flow with the notes of the music, their steps in harmony.

The ballroom guests around them began to give them room. More and more people from the party had dropped their conversations and began watching their perfect dance.

The realization hit him. Etan, his son, had known how to dance. And by bearing his phantom, now Cade could, too. Much to Cade's dismay, Etan had not been interested in learning Coda from him, though Cade never gave up trying to teach him. He *did* enjoy dancing with his mother, though. Serafina loved to dance.

When Etan was old enough to walk, Cade could remember Sera laughing and dancing around the house with the boy. As his son grew older, he took a liking to dance, and Serafina taught him everything she knew.

And here he was, dancing as his son once had with his mother. Looking at Ashlyn, and seeing the joy on her face, it reminded him of Sera. He closed his eyes and moved with the music as it wafted through the grand hall. He imagined he was dancing with Serafina now, as he never had before.

Cade opened his eyes, holding back tears. *Fool*, he told himself. *You are on a mission.* His eyes met Ashlyn's, and his heart skipped a beat. She was so beautiful, the way her bright green eyes sparkled, how the long stray lock of reddish-brown hair framed her face, and the way she seemed to smile just a bit more on the right side than on the left. He returned her gaze and then glanced at the wedding ring he still wore. *I am a monster*, he thought, breaking out of his reverie.

Ashlyn, who looked at him with concern, was about to say something when guards cut through the crowd, dragging a man with his hands clasped in irons.

Cade glanced at Ashlyn, whose face had paled. He didn't need her to tell him that was their inside man.

He bit his tongue. *I hate plans.*

After the excitement died down, the caller quieted the room to make an announcement.

"Esteemed ladies and gentlemen of the Crossfort Ball, it is now time for the tournament!"

Cade took a deep breath.

"We should go," Ashlyn said, grabbing his arm.

Cade stood his ground and shook his head. "Not until we get what we came for."

She tried to protest, but he had already made up his mind. He weaved his way through the crowd to the Grand Table. The table was a masterpiece. Hewn from a solid block of wood of an ancient tree, the ivory grain of its surface was carved into a detailed rendition of the 128 songs from the *Book of the Traveler*. Cade snorted, doubting anyone in the room was a follower of the Traveler.

He looked at the men and women who had gathered at the table. He didn't recognize any of them, save for one: General Tsori.

Tsori had the distinction of being stationed in the least desirable of all the forts in Chalice. Multiple days' ride from the Pathways, the fort was ill-supplied and all but forgotten as a point of military significance. But the mines nearby were plentiful in ore, and the defense was needed to deter foreign pirates.

It was a dead-end career, yet Cade had heard rumors of servicemen who requested transfers just to work under Tsori's leadership. Cade himself, having drafted in the Ends, served briefly under Tsori before being transferred to the front lines. The general noticed Cade approaching and nodded.

The rest of the participants took their seats, the king last of all. The king locked eyes with Cade from across the table. "Do you like the new dealer, Elegy? I figured we'd change it up for the big game."

Cade looked at the dealer, who gave no indication she had heard the conversation. He needed to figure out how the king would cheat if he were to have a chance at winning.

"All right, everyone," the dealer began, deftly shuffling her cards. "We're playing the modified card format, 'Wraith's Rite.' Everyone starts with ten thousand chips, and the first one to win them all wins the Shard until the next tournament. Ready to begin?"

Everyone at the table nodded, but the dealer was only looking at the king when she asked the question. The dealer started to deal the cards to the ten players at the table. When she had finished, Cade looked down at his cards. A red phantom, a blue phantom, and a wraith. A bad starting hand. He did his best to remain dispassionate. Time to do some reconnaissance.

Cade encoded with the Rynthium ring on his finger, and it took all the composure he had not to make it obvious as the transition swept him into the Firmere. He kept his hand on his knee so the ring's movement wouldn't catch any unwanted attention. Cade saw the world burst into thousands upon thousands of small pieces and dissolve into nothingness. He concentrated only on the group before him. Around him he saw ten wisps of the bright smoke, one of which was his own.

When it was the king's turn to bet, he noticed the smoke flicker. A bluff?

Sure enough, another participant called his bluff and found that the hand was, in fact, weak. Now he just needed to figure out how he was cheating.

Cade played conservatively, taking time to monitor each player's habits and how their Songs reacted as they played. If the king was cheating, he was showing no signs of it.

Getting nowhere, his chip pile began to dwindle.

"What's the matter, Elegy?" the king said, grinning. "Not ready to play at the big table?" The king raised by pushing his stack to the center, challenging one of the men at the table. Cade encoded to the Rynthium.

Watching the dealer carefully, he noticed her Song swirl when she dealt the next card to the king. She was feeding him cards.

During the next phase, Cade encoded to a card in the deck, calling it to him, and broke the encoding a split second after, causing the pile to topple and require a reshuffle.

To the observers, it looked like the dealer had slipped. A look of horror washed across her face as she glanced at the king, who just glared at Cade.

After learning the tells of the other players with his Rynthium sight, Cade started to win more hands. Though unaided, the king was still a strong player, and his earlier aggressive playing style vanished in lieu of a more defensive strategy. Whenever he noticed the dealer reshuffling the cards, Cade made sure to pull again and force them to recut the entire deck.

The king flashed him another angry look as if to say, *I know what you're doing.*

Cade remained impassive until all that remained were the king, the general, and himself.

By Cade's estimation, Tsori was the strongest player of the three. Cade hadn't targeted him the entire game, and now that he was paying closer attention, he noticed the general's Song didn't have a very strong tell. Cade struggled to guess at the man's strategy.

The king backed out of the hand but was not heavily invested. Cade could tell that the king's game was off now that the deck was no longer stacked in his favor. That left Cade and the general.

The general spent some time silently regarding Cade, studying him for any clue that might give him an advantage. Then he spoke. "Now what's a soldier like you want with the Shard?"

Cade, without hesitation, said, "To finish what we started."

The man paused and looked Cade in the eye. He snorted a laugh. "I'm all in."

The general at this point had amassed a great deal of money, almost as much as Cade. And they hadn't even seen the borrower card yet. It was a bold move.

Cade had a great starting hand—three gold phantoms. It was the best starting hand in the game. "I'll call," he said, taking care to keep his voice steady.

The dealer turned over their cards. The general had three wraiths—the worst starting hand in the game. Why would he choose to bluff with such a bad hand? Even before the borrower card was flipped over, everyone knew that Cade had won the hand.

The general stood up and bowed to the king. Before he

left, he leaned over to Cade and said, "Nice job with that shuffle. You got balls, son, I'll give you that. Just be sure you don't go and lose them. Good luck." He clapped his hand on Cade's shoulder and left the table.

Only the king and Cade remained. The king had spent the last hand studying Cade. The king suspected Cade was using some advantage, but Cade took care not to reveal anything. Nobody could really know what he was doing, because as far as he knew, no one since the Ancients had encoded with Rynthium.

As they played hand after hand, Cade could see the king's Song begin to change. The smoke gradually became denser, more tumultuous. Cade interpreted it as the king becoming increasingly angrier, though the king concealed it well. It was apparent he was not used to losing. Cade made sure to lose a hand here and there, but it didn't seem to affect the king's darkening mood much.

Once the next hand was dealt, Cade encoded to the Rynthium ring. Except this time, nothing happened. *Damn,* he thought, *my phantoms are quiet.* He had been so absorbed in the game that he had not been paying attention. Rynthium seemed to use a lot of a phantom's energy; much more than the materials he was accustomed to encoding with.

Cade tried not to give away his initial alarm. He looked at his cards. Two wraith cards and a blue phantom. Not a great starting hand. After glancing at his cards, Cade put his bet on the table. The king seemed to sense that something had changed. "My, that's a bit conservative," the king said, raising the bet.

Cade paid him no mind and called the raise.

The dealer put the field cards on the table. Cade tried to hide his displeasure. With these cards, there was almost no chance of winning the hand. *I can still bluff him*, he thought.

The king, his dark green eyes fixated on Cade, raised the bet. Cade tried to remain stone-faced but could feel a bead of sweat on his forehead as he matched it.

I can still win this. All I need is another blue phantom card. The dealer placed the last card on the field: a gold phantom. Cade's heart sank.

The king smiled, as if he could sense Cade's predicament. The king raised the bet again, still staring at him.

Hells, Cade thought. He folded.

The deal swept the accumulated chips to the king's pile. The king bellowed out a laugh. "It appears your luck has turned. I can see right through you, boy."

Cade ignored the comment. *I can do this. Just have to calm down.* He remembered a lesson his father had given him long ago.

"Who do you think you are fighting?" his dad had said, side-stepping one of Cade's strikes. Cade, breathing hard, didn't answer and twisted around with a heel kick. It met with nothing but air. His father pushed Cade in the opposite direction of his momentum, knocking him down. Cade grunted, angry now, and lunged again with a flurry of strikes, each of which his father blocked.

"You're not fighting me, I can tell you that much," his father said. Cade pushed forward, but his father raised his hand. "Enough. Your effort will only continue to exhaust you."

Cade paused and caught his breath. "You're too fast. I can't land anything."

His father grinned. "You can't land a strike because I am not your opponent. You are fighting yourself."

Cade furrowed his brow. "I don't understand."

"You're letting your emotions control you. Timing, precision, coordination, and strategy all go out the window when you allow fear or anger to dominate you. Losing these key abilities weakens your ability to fight."

"But don't our emotions also give us strength?"

"Yes, the right ones do. But you must choose how to shape and channel them. Use an emotion that opens your eyes, not one that closes them. Use it as an anchor against fear and against anger. Once you can master this, you will become a true martial artist."

Cade nodded.

His father fell into Bearer stance. "Now, let's try again."

Cade took a deep breath, clearing his mind. He thought of Ashlyn, who had already risked so much for her kingdom, to the extent that she went against her own beliefs. He latched on to the emotion that invoked within him. There was a purity in doing the right thing, no matter the price. His anchor in place, he looked at the next hand the dealer had dealt him. Two gold phantoms. Not bad. He raised the king's bet, but not by much. He wanted to goad the king into thinking Cade's hand was weak.

"Very interesting," the king said, still grinning.

Cade continued to think of Ashlyn and her sacrifice. He met the king's gaze, Cade's eyes now guarding his thoughts. The dealer placed the field cards down now. Two more gold phantoms. A very strong hand now for Cade. He kept his anchor feeling at the forefront of his mind, using it as a shield.

The next card landed on the table. A gold phantom. Cade would win this hand. He looked up and saw Ashlyn in the crowd, worry etched on her face. His eyes met hers. *She is so beautiful*, he thought. But it wasn't her autumn-brown hair, her bright green eyes, or how she looked in the shimmering gown of gold. It was the beauty of the Song that played within her, each note perfect and whole. He turned back to the king, meeting his eyes once more. Cade smiled.

The king furrowed his brow and studied Cade for a full minute. The entire ballroom had fallen silent. Not even a hushed whisper could be heard as everyone waited for the king's next move. The king laughed. "I'm all in." He threw down his cards, two silver phantoms. A very good hand.

But not good enough. Cade set his cards down on the table, and the audience roared to life with yells and applause. The dealer nodded to Cade and held her hand toward Cade. "The winner of the Crossfort Ball Tournament is Cade Elegy, Protector of the Realm."

The blood looked as if it had drained from the king's face, and Cade could tell the man was straining to contain his gathering fury. Cade had to be careful. He had won. If he pushed his luck too far, the king might decide to risk the scandal of arresting him now.

The Master Treasurer made a show of bestowing the Shard to Cade. It was presented within an intricate pressed leather sheath, replete with royal embossing. The Treasurer pulled the Shard out and hoisted it high in the air for all to see. The Shard emanated a faint blue light, and its iridescent surface shifted with the light. It was sleek and long, the tip revealing its distinctive shattered edge. The base was affixed to a man-made handle and hilt, giving it the appearance of a broken sword.

The ceremony itself felt awkward and not well rehearsed, but Cade figured this was the first time they'd ever had to do it. The audience roared its approval as Cade took ownership of the Shard. The event would be the talk of Toltaire for quite some time.

The king watched the ceremony in silence. Afterward,

he strode over to Cade. He feigned a friendly look and shook Cade's hand in front of the crowd. He leaned in to Cade's ear, and over the din of the crowd, said, "You won't live the night." He leaned back, his smile genuine and sinister, and applauded along with the crowd.

A woman's voice sounded within his mind.

Connection established.

28

RENDEZVOUS

*While publicly disavowed by the Royal Guard, the Intercep-
tors in Toltaire are nevertheless a very real counterintelligence force in the capital city. The fact that so little is known
about them is a testament to the Interceptors' efficacy.*

—From Seats of Power: Toltaire

THE MOMENT THE CEREMONY ENDED, Ashlyn's
tenuous smile retreated, and she grabbed Cade's arm. "We
have to hurry."

Cade nodded. She could not believe he had done it. She
hastened him through the crowd, leaving behind a wake of
stares and whispers. They collected his casters and their
coats from the storekeeper and headed out through the busy
courtyard.

Outside were Elon's carriages. They would most
certainly be followed by Interceptors, the elite royal military
unit integrated into the city's expansive spy networks.

The goal was to throw their pursuers off course by
winding different carriages through the labyrinth of streets

that littered Toltaire. The city streets over the past decade had devolved from a well-manicured and organized layout to a sprawling cacophony of lanes, boulevards, streets, and highways. The sprawl would work to their advantage. Elon had placed her other carriages in strategic locations across the city to aid in confusing their pursuers.

"See you at the rendezvous, Cade." Ashlyn smiled at him, and he nodded back. She entered the first carriage, and Cade entered the second carriage, following Elon's earlier instructions. The idea was to make it hard for their pursuers to focus on one target. Plus, if Cade didn't have to worry about Ashlyn, he could escape if they cornered his carriage.

She ducked inside, and the carriage took off. She glanced out the window behind her and was relieved to see that no other carriages seemed to give chase.

A bundle of clothes lay neatly packaged on the seat, so she began changing out of her evening gown. She looked at the gown one last time as she finished buttoning up her shirt, remembering her dance with Cade in the great ballroom, twirling and gliding across the dance floor. As princess, she had danced at many balls like this one, but this time felt different. Before, the suitors that had been arranged for her seemed disinterested. They were more interested in garnering status and favor with her father than with her. Though she was perpetually pursued, she had always felt alone. But that dance with Cade...she had felt connected to him. She shook her head. No, thoughts like that would have to wait. There was work to be done.

As they weaved through the city, they came to an abrupt stop. She slipped out under the hidden hatch in the bottom, dusted herself off, and made her way to the rendezvous point.

The old steel factory came into view. It was still in

service, but Elon knew the owner, and they planned to all meet up once they could each assure they were not followed.

She ducked into the alleyway, casting a quick glance behind her. She knocked on the back door four times and waited.

The door creaked open, and she was overjoyed to see Jace.

"You made it!"

"Yes, I did, and not a tail in sight."

"And the Shard?" Elon asked, turning her chair toward Ashlyn.

Ashlyn nodded.

Elon shook her head in disbelief. "I can't believe it worked. When I heard that Devin was captured..." Ashlyn's smile faded as she remembered the agent who had been discovered by Father's men. Elon regained her composure and held up her chin. "He was a good man. We will avenge him through our deeds."

A knock sounded at the door. Ashlyn grinned, eager to see Cade, and moved toward it.

Elon whispered, "Wait."

Ashlyn paused, glancing at Elon.

Only three knocks.

Elon beckoned Ashlyn toward her. "Move!"

They heard a loud bang as someone tried to kick in the door.

"Over here!" Elon led them down a ramp to the lower level of the mill. "Get inside and bar the door."

Above them, he heard a loud commotion as men began streaming into the room. "Down there!" one of them shouted. They disappeared into the room, and with Jace's help, Ashlyn hoisted a thick metal beam across the large door.

"That should hold them for a while," Elon panted. "Of course, we're trapped down here, so I don't know what good it will do us." She shook her head. "Someone sold us out."

Ashlyn remembered what had happened to Rolan. The city couldn't keep a secret. Not for long. They heard pounding on the door, which was made of solid steel. It would hold.

Jace paced about the room. "Is this the forge?"

"Yes," Elon said, pivoting toward him.

"This is an older forge, by the looks of it," he said as he walked up to a massive domed chamber that stood in the center of the large room.

Jace opened the door, and Ashlyn saw his face light up. Inside was a device the size of a wine barrel, with thick tubular wires crisscrossing its surface. It had the telltale geometry of a first-generation Ancient device.

"Ashlyn, come here and give me a hand."

"Why, what do you want to do?"

"Science."

29

PRESSING ON

While a variety of artifacts are still being uncovered, none have yet matched the unique beauty of the Shard of Rynth. The Shard's purpose, like most Ancient artifacts, is still unknown. But another big question haunts archaeologists: where is its other half?

—*From* Chipcoins to Levitating Trains: Artifacts of the Ancients

A MEMBER of the Order was waiting inside the carriage. "Master Elegy," the man said. "Permission to depart?"

Something felt off to Cade, but he couldn't place it. He still was shaken by the strange voice he had heard earlier.

"Sir?" The man looked at Cade.

"Yes. Let's go."

The man rapped on the side of the carriage, and they were off at full gallop down the streets of Toltaire.

Cade had just settled into his seat when the world around him began to disintegrate. Pieces of it shattered, swirled, and faded into the void. Soon, Cade was all that remained, standing upon the infinite plain of the Firmere. He saw a pinpoint of light off in the distance. The light rushed to meet him, stopping only a few feet from him. He realized it was the Shard before him, without its handle, vertical and suspended motionless in the air. A bright glow emanated and pulsed around it.

"Hello, Cade. I am EosFor, but you may call me Eos. I have been waiting for you."

The voice was a woman's, strong but calm, with an almost lyrical quality. Cade took a step forward. "What...or who...are you?"

"I am of The Seven, created to combat the Wraiths. When the people you call the Ancients left this world, they predicted the return of the Wraiths. I was left behind to protect you."

"Are you a phantom?"

"No. I am a machine. My components and circuitry exist in the Firmere. Like the casters you possess."

He recalled the light that had emanated from his sidearms when he encoded to Rynthium. *Like the casters?*

"The same," the voice said.

Cade looked up. "You can read my thoughts."

"If you and I are in direct contact, yes. I took the liberty of pairing us earlier. It will allow for enhanced communications."

"Enhanced communications?" He recalled the artifacts that had activated whenever he was nearby. "You've been trying to contact me, haven't you?"

The Shard...Eos, pulsed at that. "Yes, I have been trying to reach you for some time. My access is restricted, however."

"Why find me?"

"Predictive analysis. I observed citizens through the

networks still available to me. I weighted selection based on the following criteria: phantom affinity, combat ability, morality, courage, wisdom, and expendability."

He cocked an eyebrow. "Expendability?"

"You have no significant ties or relationships. There is nothing to make you hesitate when confronted with a dangerous scenario," said Eos. "You have nothing to lose."

Cade fell silent.

Eos continued, "There is much at stake, and we are running out of time. The Wraiths are working to activate an Ascension gate. We must work together to ensure that does not happen."

"Listen—"

"Detecting a rapid body heat fluctuation from the man sitting next to you. Exercise extreme caution."

Cade found himself wrenched out of the plain even faster than he had entered. He looked at the man next to him, who now held a gun to Cade's head.

"Hells," Cade cursed as the man pulled the trigger. Cade had encoded to tungsten, and the bullet glanced off his hardened skull. He swung at the man, but his fist just clanged against the man's own encoding.

Eos's voice rang in his mind. *A Bearer. Only one phantom detected*, she advised.

It would have been nice to know that before he tried to shoot me, thought Cade.

Sensors had not yet calibrated, said Eos.

The man kicked at Cade, switching his encoding to diamond to force Cade out of the carriage. Cade encoded to lead and held his ground. The man howled in pain as the bones in his foot were crushed by the strength-assisted kick.

Cade threw his weight into the man and sent him flying from the carriage. The carriage nearly tipped over as they sped through the streets. Cade ducked his head back inside as the edge of the carriage scraped along the wall of a narrow alley.

Unable to get the door open in the tight space, he smashed an encoded fist into the roof of the carriage, splintering the wood. He hoisted himself out of the new hatch and looked down to see the driver had jumped from the carriage. Straight ahead, a blockade of Interceptors had been constructed. He reached down and pulled the pin that held the two carriage horses in place, freeing them.

Cade leapt from the carriage as it crashed into the blockade at full speed, sending a shower of twisted wood and debris across the entire street. Cade's gunmetal skin reflected the warm glow of the street lamps as a rain of focus-fired bullets bounced off him.

He approached the man at the front of the group when he heard a deafening explosion erupt from behind him. Wheeling around, he turned to see a building erupt into a maelstrom of fire. Though he could not see the building, he already knew which one it was.

The rendezvous.

He dropped to his knees as he watched the flames consume the remains of the building. Bullets continued to ricochet off him as they waited for his phantom to tire out.

Carlon's voice once again echoed in his mind: *You will fail them.*

Cade, we need to keep moving, said Eos.

He stood and turned, eyes blazing with anger.

He leapt at the closest Interceptor as the man scrambled to reload his sidearm. Cade hooked him with an assisted punch, shattering the man's skull.

Cade.

An officer tried to approach him from behind, so Cade

kicked back, snapping the man's leg and sending him to the ground before smashing the man's ribcage under his boot.

Cade!

Cade spun around and wheeled his fist at the next attacker. His fist glanced off the man's face, which had turned a dark silver.

This made him even angrier. He launched himself at the man, flaring lead and pinning him under his crushing weight. He encoded with diamond and proceed to hammer him with a flurry of powerful blows. The man's skin became darker as he tried to encode more deeply, until his panic got the best of him. The man had overencoded, his face a permanent mask of terror.

Cade rose, scanning for his next target.

The world around him shattered, transporting him back to the plain. Eos pulsed red before him.

"Take me back," Cade growled under gritted teeth.

"Your friends may be gone, but you can make sure their sacrifice was not wasted."

Cade lunged at Eos, but he succeeded only in dissipating the apparition.

"Pick someone else," he whispered.

"There is no time. It must be you."

He sighed, his senses returning. He blinked and was on the street, as if not a moment had passed. He encoded to aluminum and bounded away into an alley as the Interceptors regrouped.

Where are we headed? he thought as he afforded one last glance at the flaming wreckage down the road.

The Thread, said Eos.

30

NO MAN

Brought in another wacko—sorry—"individual" raving on the streets and such about the Firmere. Says he just blacked out and was standing on some sort of plain of darkness. Went on and on about these moving points of light. A lot of people come in here saying they saw the Firmere. The thing that I always find interesting is that a lot of the stories are the same.

—*From* Toltaire Security Force Report, Sgt. Bront Cogmire

EONTAS WAS one of the first casters forged and as such was almost entirely handmade. The key to its effectiveness is—

You will fail them. Carlon's prophecy had come true.

Cade, I need you to pay attention, said Eos, interrupting him.

Cade sat on the train as it sailed north, his head buried in his hands. He kept Eos in its sheath, which he hid beneath his jacket to hide its subtle glow. Sensing his lack of interest, Eos fell silent. They had only been paired for a handful of hours, but Cade already missed being alone with his thoughts.

He *had* failed them. He never should have allowed them to split up. He could have protected them.

A tight cluster of worn buildings came into view. The "Old City" was what the affluent called the slums of Toltaire. Peppered between the ramshackle houses stood a handful of gleaming metal behemoths, permanent vestiges of the Ancients.

The buildings were a boon to those who could not afford their own housing. They were towering structures, some able to house hundreds of families. When the Wraiths activated the Thread, the buildings began regulating their own temperatures, which helped keep the inhabitants alive during the colder winters.

The aristocracy had long ago relinquished the Old City to the working class, opting for the newer and better-maintained buildings of the city outside the castle.

Cade stepped off the train, careful to keep his head down as the people filed out of the car. *You'll want to travel due east fifty yards and take a left from there,* Eos instructed.

Cade nodded and then thought better of it. Eos couldn't see his reaction...or could she? It was probably better not to make too many assumptions.

Can you see me? Cade practiced talking to Eos using his thoughts. He had addressed her a few times out loud on the train, which garnered him a host of suspicious stares from the passengers.

It depends on your definition. I have sensors that monitor you. I know your heart rate, where you are looking, what you are thinking, and even what you last ate. As far as actually seeing you, if you pass in front of any camera emplacements that are still active, I can see your physical form as you see it, yes.

Sorry I asked, he thought. Cade still had much to learn from Eos, but time was not on their side. Once an enchanting bauble for nobles to squabble over, it was now their last hope against the Wraiths. What other secrets lay within this faux sword?

Cade pushed those thoughts aside. Their mission was clear: deactivate the Thread using any means necessary.

I am still not clear why we must attack the Thread, he thought.

It's hard to explain. The technology present there...it is not their own. It is what is allowing them to collect the phantoms.

But there is a missile the Foundation has built, he thought to Eos. *We can help them take out the Thread.*

You underestimate the Wraiths. The Wraith's movements are increasing, and any large transports to the Thread would be obliterated from orbit.

Cade sighed. He knew the Thread would be well-guarded; getting in was not going to be easy. They would need more firepower. That meant caster shells, but those were in limited supply.

Take a right down this alleyway, look for this symbol, said Eos.

A symbol flashed in his mind. "Got it." He cursed at himself, having said that last bit out loud.

Ancient text was rare to see, the *Book of the Traveler* being the largest known source of it. But there remained buildings that used the script to designate purpose. The script Eos now shared with him called out hidden military caches with equipment to fight the Wraiths. They soon found the symbol they were looking for, a small black triple chevron about two inches across. It was so worn and faded that Cade would have mistaken it for graffiti had he not known what he was looking for.

What are we supposed to do with it? I don't see any entrance, he thought.

I'm unlocking it now, said Eos. After she spoke, Cade stumbled as the ground underneath him started to move. He stepped off what appeared to be a metal porthole, just large enough for a man. It slid out of sight, revealing a narrow ladder that led down below, and a light flickered on illuminating the way.

Move. We won't have much time inside, Eos warned.

Why not?

Power in this area is routed from the Thread. The Wraiths will be able to detect that we have activated it. They will send proxies to investigate.

Proxies? Cade thought.

Skex. Pockets of them are installed in each city so they can be remotely activated and controlled.

Remotely controlled? Eos offered no reply as Cade made his way below using the ladder secured to the side of the tunnel. Once he cleared the entrance, the opening slid back into place and sealed them inside.

He followed the passageway to a large clearing. It was clean, immaculate even, considering how long it must have been sealed off from the world. Hundreds of shelves were lined up, two by two, filled with round metal canisters.

Take a canister from row one. I would recommend also taking a canister from row 82, for EonCull.

Cade scratched his chin. "EonCull?" *You mean one of the casters, right? Is that what the Ancients named it?*

Correct. EonCull is the larger of your two casters, as we previously reviewed. It is a shotcaster. Though it can fire standard caster shells, specialized ammunition can make it effective in short-range crowd control.

Cade walked over to the first row and opened a canister. Packed inside were more caster shells than he had ever seen in one place. Hundreds of them. A single caster shell had enormous worth, and here they had found a room filled with them.

Cade shook his head and started to speak aloud. "How is this possible? Each one of these have been imprinted by someone?"

Imprinted?

"Imprinting is what we call it when a person passes and imprints their Song upon an object. Imprinting forged bullets is how we make caster shells."

Ah, I see. There are other ways to make a caster shell, however, said Eos.

Cade remembered the strange shell casing he had found in Barnage. He began loading the shells from the canister into a brown leather rucksack.

To understand how caster shells work, it is imperative you understand how casters work. Casters are mechanically simple.

"How so?" he accidentally said aloud.

In the Veris, the physical plane you now inhabit, a caster has no mechanisms or processors. It is, for all intents and purposes, a chunk of metal.

That much Cade already knew. No scientist had been able to find out what made casters special, despite years of research. Copies were attempted, even still. The intricate etchings were also studied and painstakingly replicated, in case they played a role. Despite all these efforts, all Chalician-forged casters were nothing more than intricate paperweights.

Cade noticed another symbol at the far end of the underground cache and began making his way toward it to get a better look.

The truth of the caster lies within the Firmere, Eos continued.

Cade nodded, remembering the light of his casters when he had seen them in the Firmere.

As advanced as those who created me were, the Firmere was not always accessible to them. Not until the Traveler showed us the way.

He stopped loading the backpack. Who was the Traveler? he asked.

That is classified. I can tell you that the Traveler taught them how to use Rynthium, not as a fuel source, but as a way to manipulate the Firmere itself. Through his teaching, they bonded the technology of the Veris with the Firmere.

Cade hurried his way to the row with the shotcaster shells. "Why were casters needed?"

To kill Wraiths.

"So the casters were designed solely to kill the Wraiths," he said. He had figured as much.

Yes, though they can be lethal to other beings. The shells, like the casters, have a counterpart forged in the Firmere. It is a machine designed to destroy entities within the Firmere.

Cade nodded, though he had even more questions.

Looking up, he noticed a symbol at the end of the warehouse. It was a circle, with three dots equidistant from each other in the center.

"Eos, what is this symbol?"

I do not have clearance to divulge that with my current security level. A pause. *I am detecting Skex that are en route We must leave immediately.*

She didn't have to tell him twice. Cade rushed to the

ladder and pulled himself out of the opened hatch. He was happy to be out. Even in the sizable warehouse, being underground with no natural light made him claustrophobic.

As they turned the corner out of the alleyway, Cade overheard the irregular scraping march of Skex nearby. He ran down the alley, careful not to make any more noise than necessary.

With Eos navigating, he retraced his steps to the railway station. All the railbuses operating out of Toltaire steered clear of the Thread, as part of the Accord. Fortunately, there was one railbus that still took the northern route, close to the Thread.

It was, however, no ordinary railbus. When the Wraiths turned on the Thread, all the railbuses the Ancients had built powered up and could be run by an operator. But one third-generation train, which earned itself the name *No Man*, ran entirely autonomously, never stopping at any of the stations in Chalice.

Can't you stop the railbus? he asked.

Even if I could, it would arouse suspicion. It will be arriving on platform two, said Eos.

Cade cursed under his breath, wringing his hands as he walked up to the platform. He positioned himself near the track, trying to appear nonchalant. He failed at that as the other passengers looked at him.

So much for trying to keep a low profile, he thought. It couldn't be helped. This was the only railbus to the Thread not controlled by the Wraiths, and it was by far the fastest way to travel.

He saw it as it crested the hill. The *No Man* hurtled toward the station at maximum speed and the cars began to flash by him one after another.

Cade inhaled deeply, counting the cars as they passed. *Twenty...twenty-one...twenty-two...*

Now, instructed Eos.

He encoded to the railing on the last train car as it sped past. The encoding held, and Cade glided through the air to the car itself. Just as he had a hand on the rail, the phantom gave out. Encoding to anything you weren't already touching would exhaust a phantom quickly.

Cade anticipated this and had already prepared a second encoding with his remaining phantom. He caught the edge of the railing, and his body slammed into the rear of the car. He felt his foot brush the ground, kicking up the gravel between the tracks, and he pulled up before it could catch on anything. Using the last bit of energy from his phantom, he was able to hoist himself up and onto the car's platform.

He dusted himself off and couldn't help but turn around to see people at the station pointing and talking with the other travelers.

News of his hitchhiking would surely get to the wrong people. They would have to move fast.

31

THE BAKER

'Arti-hacking' is now coming into its own, helping revolutionize industries within Chalice. With the power supplied by the Wraiths through the Thread, arti-hackers take artifacts and adapt them to work within existing industries, from metalworking to even food preparation.
—From The Toltaire Times

ASHLYN COVERED her mouth and nose with a scrap of clothing and tried to squint through the dark smoke that now poured through the thick lead door Jace had opened.

Jace turned to her and Elon. "It worked! Taking the combustion generator outside of the reaction chamber does create a compounded explosion!"

The chamber was small, but it had been big enough to hold all three of them. It happened to also be strong enough to shield against the blast from the Ancient device Jace had rigged.

Elon wasted no time. "Let's move. There will be more."

They pushed through the bits of charred wreckage. The

superstructure of the building burned bright, making the remains of the interior unbearably hot.

A beam cracked overhead and hurtled toward them. "Watch out!" Jace screamed. Ashlyn could see it was going to hit Elon. She dashed forward, but she knew she could not cover the distance in time. "No!" Ashlyn screamed, horrified.

Through the smoke, Ashlyn continued forward, clawing through the wreckage. "No...no..." she said, not accepting what had just happened. She pulled back a scrap of sheet metal and gasped.

Standing tall, arms holding back the massive steel beam, was Elon. The young woman was straining, and Ashlyn could just make out the unmistakable color of dark silver upon her skin. "A little...help?" was all Elon said.

Ashlyn encoded to diamond and shoved the great beam off to the side. Elon collapsed back onto her chair, out of breath. Ashlyn stared at her sister, not knowing what to say.

Jace broke the silence. "Sorry to interrupt, princesses, but we have to move!"

They exited through the service bay of the lower level, which deposited them in the back alley of the factory as the massive smokestack toppled over, crushing the remains of the building.

They escaped through the backstreets of Toltaire, trying to put as much distance as they could between them and the smoldering factory. They ducked into an alleyway untouched by the light of the streetlamps. Ashlyn and Jace sat and tried to catch their breath. She looked at Elon again.

Elon sighed, not meeting her eyes. "When Mother died, Father got worse, if you can imagine that. He was never good to begin with. I don't think he was meant to lead, despite what he thinks. I could see the pressure on him, the persistent burden that wore on him every moment of the day. I believe it changed him somehow, broke his mind. His insistence on me being a boy was evidence of that. He needed someone to share his burden, someone who could free him. He made me into what he needed. But by the time I could help him, he was too far gone. He still managed to show tenderness at times. But once Mother was gone, so was he."

Ashlyn could see Elon fighting to hold back tears. "How...?"

"I felt Father's burden, the one he was forcing upon me. Without Mother, I feared I would become just like him. Despite Father's growing madness, Mother was always strong. You remember, don't you? I wanted to be strong, like her. I started reading books about phantoms."

Ashlyn's eyes grew even wider. "Mother?"

Elon looked at Ashlyn, expression somber, and nodded. "I've been bearing mother's phantom for a few months now. I practiced in my room, in secret, because it was the only place I could do it and not be seen. With her phantom...I can walk." She held up her hand, and Ashlyn noticed for the first time her sister wore more rings than would be considered fashionable in Toltaire. She had been blind not to notice.

"I found out if I encoded to tungsten, my body could support my weight, making me tougher. The diamond was even better, because it gave my legs the strength to run. You wouldn't believe how many circles I ran around in my chamber." She chuckled. "I can only encode one substance at a time, but having Mother to help me is the only way I made it this far. I wish I could have told you earlier, but Father went to great pains to keep us apart. I think he saw you as a threat to his whole charade. That, and you look just like her. I can only imagine seeing you is a constant reminder of what he has lost."

How could she not have known?

Jace interrupted, "We shouldn't stay here long. We need to get to a safe house. Is there one nearby?"

Elon shook her head. "We have to assume they are all compromised. We need to move."

"What about Cade? We need to wait for him," Ashlyn said.

Elon positioned herself next to Ashlyn and put her hand on her shoulder. "Ashlyn, they would have sent a much larger force after him... We have to assume they got to him, too."

"You're not suggesting..."

Elon bit her lip. "I can't say for sure. If he's still alive, you have to trust he'll find us."

Tears welled up in Ashlyn's eyes, but she shook off the encroaching despair. "Yes, he will find us."

Elon looked at her as if she wanted to say something but seemed to think better of it.

Jace broke the silence. "We stick to the plan. Let's meet up with Beatrix."

"ARE you sure this is the place?" Ashlyn asked, eyeing the building suspiciously. They were in the merchant district of Toltaire. The streets were not crowded, given the hour of the night. They traveled at a relaxed pace, careful not to arouse unwanted suspicion. Elon's elaborate wheelchair did not help in keeping attention at bay.

The district exuded charm with its restored classic Chalician architecture, shops and buildings packed in neat rows. The storefront they arrived at was a townhouse-style dwelling with a shop on the bottom and a room on the top for the owner to live. The sign above the shop bore the name Toltaire Tortes & Tasties in brightly colored pastel letters.

"This can't be it," said Jace as he double-checked the address scrawled on the paper before him.

"What were you expecting?" Ashlyn asked.

"A weapons shop of some sort. Not...this."

Ashlyn looked at him impatiently. "It's no use just standing out here and scratching our heads. Let's at least go in and ask if they know where the previous owner relocated to." She marched up to the door, which had a sign written in friendly lettering: "SOLD OUT—WE'LL BAKE MORE CAKE TO TAKE TOMORROW!" Ashlyn knocked once on the door. After a moment, she heard some footsteps coming down the stairs.

The door cracked open. An elderly woman with long, graying black hair and a kind face juxtaposed with fierce blue eyes poked her head out of the door. "Sorry, I'm afraid we're all sold out for today."

Jace stepped up to the door. The woman's expression hardened, and she retreated back behind the door as it snapped shut.

Ashlyn looked at Jace, eyes narrowed. "Well, you made quite an impression."

Jace ignored her and rapped on the door.

A voice sounded through the door, "Go away! That's something I know you're good at doing!"

"I think it's time you told me what's going on," said Ashlyn.

"It's a long story." He sighed. Jace turned back to the door. "I'm sorry, you know I am. I had to go. You and I both know we were at the end of the road. I need your help."

The door opened, though her expression was none the softer. "With what could I possibly help you? I'm just a simple baker now."

"Mother...please," he implored, meeting her eyes.

"*Mother?* That's what you wouldn't tell me?" Ashlyn said incredulously.

"Of course he wouldn't tell you about his own mother," the woman said, rolling her eyes. "He just does what he pleases. Always has." She sighed, letting the door fall open as she retreated into the shop.

Ashlyn entered with Jace and Elon. The shop was beautiful. Rich colored tablecloths were draped over wide wooden tables, with small pails filled with an assortment of fresh-cut flowers. She could smell bread baking in the ovens around the back.

She stole a glance toward the kitchen and was surprised to see a very sophisticated setup with graduated cylinders, beakers, and tubing. Not quite the baking paraphernalia she had expected to see.

Jace approached the woman. "Beatrix..."

The woman raised her hand as if to silence him. "No, you don't. You won't sweet-talk me into accepting any apology you have to offer. Instead, tell me who your friends are," she said, nodding toward Ashlyn and Elon.

Jace cleared his throat. "Of course, I had completely forgotten. It is my pleasure to introduce you to their royal highnesses, Elon and Ashlyn Winshire."

Beatrix's brow furrowed, and then her eyes grew wide. "Prince...and Princess Winshire?" The woman glanced around furtively, as if unsure what to do next. "Oh my, where are my manners? Something to drink, yes, something to drink. Tea! Yes, tea. Oh, would you like tea? Please, please, sit down!"

Beatrix shot Jace a dark look. "Why didn't you tell me sooner? Honestly, Jace." The old woman shook her head and disappeared into the kitchen.

"She seems nice," said Ashlyn.

Jace shrugged.

"We need to send word to Carlon and let him know what happened," said Ashlyn.

"If Carlon's still alive," Jace said, shaking his head. "And if he is alive, I doubt he's on Vanter."

"Where would he go?" asked Elon.

Jace shrugged again. "Given the activity in Rynth, that would be as good a guess as any."

Elon tapped her chin. "Rynth is going to be taken, isn't it?"

Jace just looked at the ground. Ashlyn understood. Exiled from his home once more, this time it wasn't by choice.

"Do you really think we can stop them?" Ashlyn said, expression hopeful. "If the Foundation has fallen, are we just kidding ourselves?"

Jace nodded, still looking at the ground. "You're right. We're three people wanted by the king himself, no less. What kind of resistance could we hope to mount?"

"You're wrong."

Ashlyn looked up to see Beatrix in the doorway, holding a tea tray with small porcelain cups arranged neatly upon it.

"I'm sorry?" asked Ashlyn.

"You're wrong. You're not just three people. There's more. Many more," stated Beatrix. "The Foundation fights on, from here to the Ends."

"Lady Beatrix, I'm afraid—" Elon started.

"Bah! I am no lady. I lost that right years ago. I may be old now, but I'm not out of the fight."

Ashlyn looked at the woman, confused. "I don't think we've had a proper introduction. Who are you, exactly?"

The woman stood up straight and held her chin up high. "I am Beatrix Bestforger, former Chief Technologist of the Chalice Military Force and master castforger." She looked at each one of them in turn. "And I can help you teach those bastards a lesson."

BEATRIX LED them down a short hallway and stopped in front of a painting of a woman holding a pink parasol.

"During the war, it was obvious we were going to need technology far superior to what we already had. The Chalice Military Force, by order of the king, was empowered to create research strike teams with the charter of building experimental weaponry based on Ancient technology," said Beatrix as she pulled off the painting.

Beatrix took off the necklace she was wearing, and Ashlyn noticed it held an ornate skeleton key. Beatrix inserted it into a small keyhole within the wall. She twisted the key clockwise one turn and then counterclockwise three turns. On the last turn, Ashlyn heard a barely audible *click* when the final tumbler fell into place.

"I was a castforger, so I made caster shells, of course. But deep down, I had always wanted something more. Our team had two primary objectives: caster replication and what we called the caster missile. Caster replication you are no doubt already familiar with. Jace, as luck would have it, was on my team and was dedicated to that objective, though we knew even then it was futile."

Jace shrugged. "We archaeologists take what we can get."

Beatrix ignored him. "That meant most of the team was focused on building what was a very, very large bomb." The old woman leaned hard into the wall, and a section of it swung inward, revealing a small empty room. After a moment, a light flickered on, illuminating the interior.

Powered lights? There is much more to this woman than meets the eye, thought Ashlyn.

"But how could you set off a bomb of that size? Even caster shells won't fire without a caster," asked Ashlyn.

The woman ushered them inside, smiling. "Clever girl—you're absolutely right." She closed the door and pushed a red button on the wall. The room began to descend.

Ashlyn reached out and braced herself against the walls of the small room.

The woman looked at her, still smiling. "No need for that, sweetie. You're perfectly safe. There is still so much we do not understand about the technology of the Ancients, the casters most of all. Our group had the privilege to dissect one, you know."

Ashlyn's mouth dropped. "But they're worth a fortune!" Destroying one would be unthinkable.

The woman laughed at Ashlyn's reaction. "I know, I felt the same way. But we were desperate to learn more about how they operated." She sighed. "We didn't learn much, to be honest. At least nothing that would aid in the replication project."

The room ground to an abrupt halt, and Ashlyn fought the urge to reach out again. The doors opened, revealing a laboratory that would have made any scientist in Chalice envious.

An entire array of unique artifacts lined the towering

bookcases that surrounded the lab. A few emanated light that filled the room with a cool white glow.

Ammo canisters overflowed with blank caster shells, and a portion of the far wall was dedicated to a wide array of casters. Some barrels were long and elegant, with ornate markings the entire length. Others were short, with glyphs etched upon each side. It must have taken considerable effort to get enough time with the originals to create such detailed copies. Even though it was a small section of the lab, it spoke of a lifetime of work.

Beatrix noticed Ashlyn's reaction. "Beautiful, aren't they? They don't fire, of course, but I don't have the heart to get rid of them. Perhaps I can make them work one day. I haven't given up all hope, yet."

Jace looked at Beatrix. "Just a baker, huh?"

The woman shrugged. "A girl's got to have a hobby."

Jace shook his head in disbelief. "You've recreated the laboratory, brick for brick!"

Beatrix was beaming but trying her best to appear nonchalant. "I wouldn't say 'brick for brick,' but I was able to salvage most of it. After the war, they assigned the equipment to storage."

Jace smirked at Beatrix.

"What? It is still technically in storage. Just in storage here, is all," Beatrix retorted.

Jace turned his gaze to what Ashlyn figured could only have been the caster bomb. "You never gave up."

"I couldn't. I have a debt to pay."

Jace nodded solemnly.

Beatrix motioned for them to follow. "This way."

Ashlyn had been so fixated on the caster collection she had overlooked the large metal device in the center of the room. It looked like an elongated tube of brushed steel.

Rivets held it together at every angle. The top panel was swung open, revealing its interior. It rested on a thick steel platform, and tools were strewn around it, as though it had been recently tinkered with.

"Here is my opus. Made up of 1,332 inlaid caster shells hand-crafted with love by yours truly. The shells themselves are grouped and oriented in alternating directions, providing for a full 360-degree spherical shrapnel radius once it hits its target."

Elon rubbed her chin thoughtfully. "I've never seen caster shells quite like those. They're enormous."

The old woman smiled. "I forged these myself. The base design was taken from an explosive variety we discovered from our research of the original caster cache discovered in Rynth."

Ashlyn pointed to an array of what looked like wine barrels made of steel inside the missile. "Are those...?"

Beatrix nodded and motioned for them to come closer. "There are six first-generation combustion reactors wired in sequence. Enough to blow a city block sky-high. I don't know where the Wraiths came from, but I do know this will send them back."

"Does it work?" asked Elon as she rolled closer to peer inside.

Beatrix sighed. "I don't know. But it should, in theory. I never had a chance to find out for sure, thanks to Jace leaving the team."

Ashlyn looked at Jace, who rolled his eyes. "Not this again. The war ended. They would never let us continue development with the Accord in place. Don't make this my fault."

Beatrix ignored him, continuing. "As you noted earlier, Princess, caster bullets won't fire unless shot from a caster."

She led them to a workbench and opened a box that held the components of a caster. "When I dissected this gun, I noticed this component here," she said, tapping on a tiny cylinder of light silver.

"While seemingly innocuous, my experiments with live caster shells revealed that contact with this piece of the gun is what triggers a caster shell to fire, minus the auto-aiming functionality, of course. And with pieces I reclaimed from third-generation artifacts, I can rig multiple shells to fire from a single cylinder."

Jace, sensing Ashlyn was lost, elaborated. "She can use the triggering mechanism from a functioning caster to set off a chain reaction, which will cause these custom caster shells to fire and explode in a blaze of glory."

Beatrix beamed like a proud parent showing off her newborn. "But that's not the best part," she said, pointing to a bundle of packed metal spheres that lined the interior of the bomb. "I finally had a breakthrough that allows for the ignition of the blast powder the Ancients used for mining. With this starter mechanism, I can ignite all the blast cells within here. One of these cells can level a building."

Ashlyn took a step back from the device. "Oh."

"Don't worry, it's perfectly safe," she laughed, "unless you press this button here. In which case, we'd all see the stars again." Beatrix held up what must be the detonator for the device. Ashlyn was not comforted.

Jace turned to look at the missile. "Now all we need to do is figure out how to get this thing to the underground rail lines."

Beatrix grinned. "How do you think I got it here in the first place?"

32

A KING'S BURDEN

Citizens of Chalice, I have a promise to make. Today marks a turning point in our fledgling nation. Do not for a moment think that I will sit upon this throne and idle my days until we all wither from age and regret. Right now, we stand upon an overabundance of opportunity. The very secrets of our planet's past and future are within our borders. We will stand on the shoulders of our ancient forefathers, and we will rise, as they once had, to the stars themselves. This I promise you.

—From King Liam's Inauguration Speech

"THE WRAITH HAS RETURNED?" King Liam was not pleased. For years he had clawed and scratched to craft an empire in Chalice, and now it was all falling apart. *Even the largest stone can become a grain of sand upon the shore,* he thought. He just hadn't expected it to happen so quickly. Chalice was dying, and it was his fault.

It did not seem like very long ago when things were going well for him. His company controlled all the mines of note, and his investments were growing at an alarming rate. Securing the throne from the previous ruler was the ultimate validation for his ambition. He had other plans, of course, but the arrival of the abominable Wraiths ruined all of that.

Liam snorted. He once had the hubris to believe they could fight the Wraiths. Beings who traveled among the stars! What real hope did they have? But hope he gave them, his people. And they had some semblance of peace for a time. It was an illusion of peace, but that's nearly as good as the real thing. His treachery was his greatest secret and his greatest gift to his kingdom.

Liam did not know why *it* had decided to return. His dialog with the Wraith had become more and more strained with every visit. The Wraith seemed annoyed at having to talk with Liam.

"Any sign of Elon?" he demanded.

"They're scouring the city as we speak, Your Highness," the older man said breathlessly, trying to keep pace with the king's stride.

Where *had* that boy gone to? The betrayal was more than he could take right now. It should have been impossible for them to escape with the amount of manpower Liam had at his disposal. But if Elon was helping them...well, Elon was a quick study, and Liam had been grooming him for years to be his replacement. If anyone could have escaped his grasp, he took some comfort that it was his protégé.

He slowed his pace as he came to the grand hallway. *Best not to make a scene,* he told himself. *You still hold some power here.* He convinced himself he could cover up this unannounced visit, or figure out a good way to spin it to the papers. Perhaps an amendment to the Accord? More promises to cooperate with the Wraiths?

He knew that was unlikely; the Wraiths did not respect them. *But they do need us. I just don't know why.*

Liam had been playing a dangerous game by spying on the Wraiths. It was against the Accord, but he needed answers. But aside from the reports of erratic energy patterns emanating from the Thread whenever a village vanished, he had nothing to show for the effort. At first he could blame an illness or point a finger at a pirate attack from a nearby country on a seaside town. But when multiple towns were wiped out in a single month, there was very little he could do to stop the rumors.

The rumors were all true, of course, which made them harder to stop. *Time reveals all truths*, he thought. What you did with the time you bought was most important.

Liam kept his expression complacent, with just a hint of resolve. The people looked up to their king. He was *the* example, a paragon of what one should strive to be. The man who could carry the weight of the kingdom on his shoulders. It was his burden, and his burden alone.

He entered his receiving room and saw the Wraith sitting there on *his* throne. No doubt intentional, to drive home how little they thought of him and his people.

The creature was grotesque. It was somewhat humanoid, but its skin was like tumbled obsidian. Its eyes were impassive yet calculating, with pupils like fine pinpricks. Liam did not detect any cruelty in its expression, but there was contempt, though he could not place why.

A human adorned in the red robes of an Acolyte stood beside the Wraith. Liam tried his best to conceal his annoyance. How the Wraiths managed to secure so many former soldiers after wreaking havoc on Chalice, he could not guess.

The Acolytes made him almost as uncomfortable as the Wraiths. There was something unnatural, something forced that he could not put his finger on. This one was different, however. He wasn't as passive as the others he had encountered and did not avoid eye contact as most tended to do. There was a fierce intensity to him.

"Hello, Zeleroth," Liam said and bowed deep in an exaggerated sweeping motion. It was best to overplay subservience when dealing with Wraiths. It was not something that came easy to him. "You honor us greatly by visiting us in person. To what do we owe this momentous occasion?"

"No need for pleasantries, human." Its voice was methodical but heavy, as if every word was a tremendous burden to utter. "Our time on this planet is almost at an end. You have held up your end of the Accord by giving us the people we needed."

The king, who stood now, nodded. "Yes, but it has been difficult. You have taken far more people than we agreed. I cannot hold this kingdom together if there is no kingdom left when you are done."

The Wraith's expression remained unchanged. "You know what we are capable of. This Accord is for your benefit—not ours."

The king bit his tongue. What he would have given to have his caster in his hand right now. *Calm yourself,* he thought. *You are the only hope for salvaging what is left of this country.*

"Why are you here?" the king asked.

"We have one more city to take, but for this one I will need your help."

The king's brow furrowed. "How dare you..."

"We are taking Rynth. There is a resistance forming, however. I require your army to work with our Skex and help contain the threat and prevent any attempts to evacuate the populace."

Liam's face fell. "That was not part of the Accord. That is too high a price."

"Obliteration of your planet is too high of a price. Or would you prefer that?"

Liam could see the Wraith was growing impatient. He couldn't help but be distracted by a strange grinding coming from the Acolyte, whose jaw was locked shut and scraping back and forth. The man's otherworldly gray eyes were locked on Liam.

The king cleared his throat and continued. "It will be done." Time would reveal what he had agreed to, and he knew he would not be remembered kindly. Liam did not care; he did not do what he did to be portrayed as a fair and benevolent ruler in some history book. The best leaders, the ones who had to make a real sacrifice, they were the ones who were often derided as failed monarchs.

Liam loved the people of Chalice, despite what his numerous detractors thought. He was driven not by wealth or by power—he already had plenty of both. He was consumed by the need to do what was right for his subjects. They relied on him to do what was best for them. They could not care for themselves, not without him to guide them.

And as much as Liam loved them, he hated them, too. Hated them for being too stupid to understand what he had given up for them. Too stupid to understand the pain he felt for having to sacrifice his own people for the greater good. His wife hadn't understood, either.

Elon would be the one who was well-remembered. The one who erased the horrors of the war. He had groomed Elon himself for such a role, and now it was time.

Liam kept his eyes focused on the Wraith. He was a lot of things, a failed father and a failed husband most of all. But he would be the king he needed to be to help his people survive.

33

TWO SIDES

Who was the Traveler? This is one of the greatest questions that has eluded researchers since the Book of the Traveler's *discovery. Originally thought to be a work of fiction, the book outlined the teachings and techniques that brought about the discovery and communication with phantoms.*
—*From* The History of Chalice

CADE REACHED for the door at the rear of the railbus, but as his hand neared it, it opened itself by sliding to one side. He stepped inside the cabin of the car, and the door slid shut behind him. The roar of the wind ceased, and Cade found himself in complete silence.

The inside of the car was immaculate. Nothing looked worn or out of place. Cade had expected to find some trash or wear from the years of adventurous hitchhikers he had heard stories about, but there was no evidence to suggest anyone had ever stepped foot into the car. Cade wondered for a moment if all the stories were just that, fabrications of someone's imagination.

He was glad he did not have to make the trip by horse. The ride on the train was almost too smooth. The cars were the latest generation technology, and they somehow hovered a few inches above of the tracks. Cade shifted in his seat. It didn't matter how many times he rode on trains like these, he always felt uneasy. He didn't know how something so massive could float; it didn't seem natural or safe.

To make sure there was no one else on board, Cade continued to travel from car to car. No surprises; each car was just as clean and perfect as the last. By the time he made it to the front of the train, he was convinced he was the first man to ride in the train since the Ancients left Chalice.

It occurred to Cade that Eos had not spoken to him since they boarded. "Eos, are you there?"

Yes, I am currently analyzing the ship's data store and log files.

"Anything of interest?"

I am still running queries, but there hasn't been anyone on this train in a long time. Unfortunately, some of the records have been tampered with, so I can't verify what the data believes to be true.

The implications of tampered records aboard a runaway railbus intrigued Cade. Was it the Wraiths? If so, why would they bother to tamper with records on a malfunctioning railbus?

Cade took a seat next to the window in the first car. The windows ran seamlessly the entire length of the car. As Cade sat looking at the countryside rocketing by, the cleanliness of the windows struck him as odd. He could not see a single spot or piece of dirt, neither inside nor outside. And the train felt so still; if he closed his eyes, he could have been convinced he was sitting still. This railbus was much more advanced than the one Malix conducted, that much was a given. The progression of Ancient technology fascinated him.

Cade, there is a technique I am permitted to teach you. I do not have much time to train you, so we must make efficient use of the time we have before we arrive.

"Technique?"

Please take out your chipcoin pouch.

He took out his money pouch and emptied its contents onto the small glass table in front of him. It was mostly metal-based lower-denomination coins, but he had a few glass hexes as well.

The Ancients called these coins netcores. Though they are small, they played a key role in the first war with the Wraiths.

Cade picked up a chipcoin and looked at it closely. The coin itself was round, no bigger than a coat button, and was clear as glass. Inset within it was a tiny chip with six different sides. Each side of the chip had nearly imperceptible markings dotting the edge.

The netcores possess two primary components: a microreactor for power generation and a processing unit for amplification. Every netcore is capable of establishing and maintaining a connection with any other netcores within its proximity. The more you have near you, the more you can connect to.

"Connect to what?"

Each of these netcores can amplify your Bearer encodings. The more you are connected with, the more amplification you have access to. And because each one can dynamically connect to those nearest them, you can chain together a large quantity at the same time.

"Does it make my encodings stronger?"

Precisely. It also offloads work your phantom must do to maintain the link between the Veris and the Firmere. This greatly prolongs the stamina of the phantom, allowing you to do more than you would normally be able to do with your pact link.

"Incredible," Cade said, still holding the coin. "All this time...we had no idea. How does it work?"

You must form a connection with it through the Firmere, using your phantom.

"So I encode with the chipcoin, like I would any other material?"

You don't encode with it. You activate it via the phantom. Once activated, it will attune itself to you and provide you with its amplification.

Cade frowned. "What do you mean by 'activate'?"

I'm afraid I can't describe it in detail, since I cannot do it myself. I have only the instructions embedded in my memory.

"Great."

I estimate our arrival time within one hour. I would recommend you start practicing now.

Cade sighed. "Wait a minute. I've listened to you and taken you this far. But you haven't explained to me what is really happening here."

What questions do you have?

"For starters, why are the Wraiths here? Didn't the Ancients defeat them?"

That is true. The Ancients, with the help of the Traveler, defeated the Wraiths long ago. As you know, this was a mining settlement. The Ancients were not prepared for conflict. The breakthrough of Firmere technology is what helped them advance to defeat the Wraiths' superior combat ability. We did not expect them to find us again.

"But what do the Wraiths want with us?"

They are building a device.

Cade remembered what Karessa had told him back at the temple. "Are you talking about the Ascension Drive? What is it?"

Correct. We never learned its full purpose. What we did learn is that they wish to open a gate between the Firmere and the Ascent. One they can activate at will.

Cade rubbed his chin. "But why do they need us?"

We had one theory. When you die, you are given a choice.

"To remain in the Firmere or to go to the Ascent. They are using the phantoms that can travel to the Ascent."

That is the theory.

Cade was quiet for a moment. They need our phantoms. That's why they are here.

"Okay, next question. Who are you?"

As I told you before, my name—

Cade cut her off. "I remember what you told me. But why do you *exist*? Are you a weapon?"

Eos appeared to hesitate. *In a sense, I suppose I am. But that was not my original purpose.*

"What was your original purpose?"

I'm afraid that information is classified.

Cade shook his head.

"Why did the Ancients leave?"

That is also classified.

"The way I see it, the Wraiths came back for whatever was in the Thread. My family died because of it. Don't I deserve answers...don't they?"

Eos offered nothing more. *I must recharge using the train's energy access port before we arrive. I will be unavail-*

able for some time, depending on the remaining strength of the core.

"Fine," Cade said, frustrated.

Eos said she was a machine, but Cade had seen many machines built by the Ancients. He had never seen anything like Eos. Machines were precise, exact, and one-dimensional. Eos acted like he would expect a human to, albeit a very smart one. Cade knew there was more to Eos than he could understand. He hoped to live long enough to learn more, but for now it would have to wait.

Cade took a chipcoin from the table and placed it in front of him. He took a deep breath and focused on the chipcoin, much like he would when he would focus on a material he was encoding with. *I need to activate it. How?*

He spent the better part of the hour trying every idea that he could think of, but to no avail. There was too much about the Firmere he still did not understand. Eos had to know more. Frustrated, he placed the coins back in his pouch and leaned back in his seat. The chair was surprisingly comfortable, and the cushion seemed to conform to his body.

He closed his eyes and hoped he could try to sleep to pass the time. As a rule, Cade did not like to have time to think. Thinking meant facing memories he did not want to deal with.

Cade heard a noise, and his eyes snapped open. He looked and saw a young boy sitting in the seat a few rows from the front the cabin. He did not need to see the boy's face to know it was his son, Etan.

How long had it been since his last Nocturne dose? There hadn't been time to find any dealers in Toltaire. Dealers weren't exactly the reputable type, either, and talking to them would mean risking capture.

Cade closed his eyes again and could hear the faint murmur of voices. They were too quiet to hear what was being said, but they were present. It was only a matter of time before thoughts that were not his own would come.

It was the most difficult part of being a Bearer, losing your identity.

When you had other people's thoughts running through your head, and could do things you never remembered learning, it made you question who you really were. What if you liked who you had become better? What then? When the phantoms moved on, did they really ever leave, or was a piece of them left behind? Cade had helped hundreds of people Ascend. Did that mean he was no longer the man he once was? Was he a man built of a hundred other pieces, all vying for dominance within him? If he was nothing more than a patchwork of phantoms, would he even know?

Cade pushed the thought out of his mind. It was pointless to think like that. He looked down at his right hand, at the rings he wore. He was happy to have his wedding ring back after escaping the prison. He did not like being without it; it was the only thing he owned of any real value to him. He brushed the etchings on the outside of the white gold ring with his fingertip.

"Hello, Cade."

Cade nearly leapt from his seat when he looked up and saw a man sitting just opposite him. When had he sat down there? *How did I not hear him?* He would have noticed.

Cade recognized the man as the doppelgänger from his Nocturne veilings. Tal. This was the clearest he had seen the man before. The other times he had seen him, Cade had been in the Firmere. But this...Tal looked real. Even though he looked like Cade, Cade could see he was older, and the man's mannerisms and movements were nothing like

Cade's. Tal was looking at him with a newspaper held in both hands. Tal smiled when he saw Cade start. He folded the paper and tucked it under his arm as he relaxed back in his seat.

Eos, are you there? No answer.

"Tal?"

Tal nodded toward Cade, who still had his hand outstretched. "Beautiful ring. It looks like it has a quite a story."

Cade couldn't help but stare at the man, unsure if he could believe his eyes. According to his own observations and Eos's data, no one had been aboard this train in a long while. Unless...Tal was editing the train's log.

Cade glanced once more at his wedding ring. "Yes...it has been in my family for some time."

Tal gestured toward the window. "The sights are beautiful, but the ride can be long at times. Would you mind telling me more about your ring?"

"It's been in my family for ten generations. Passed down to the firstborn when they get married. It is given to the spouse so they can make their own mark on the ring."

Tal nodded, smiling. "Truly an impressive piece of history. May I see it?"

Cade hesitated and looked at his hand. The ring was gone.

"This is really something. Generations of meaning," Tal said.

Cade looked up, panicking, and saw the man holding his ring.

Tal held the ring close and read the inscription on the inside, the marking his wife had added for Cade. "'Reach.' What do you suppose that means?"

Cade's heart pounded. "Who are you, really?"

"A protector. Like you."

"Give me back my ring."

Tal closed his hand around the ring, making a fist. His eyes sparkled as he leaned forward, smiling broadly. "Take it from me."

Cade encoded tungsten and swung his fist at the man's head. The man just batted it away, never breaking eye contact with Cade.

He swung his other hand at Tal, who caught it and shook his head.

"If at first you don't succeed...try the same thing again?"

Cade tried to wrench his arm from the man's grasp, but the man held firm and hurled Cade against the back of the car.

He hit with a loud *clang* as his encoding absorbed the brunt of the impact.

The man stood, took off his suit jacket, and folded it neatly over his chair.

"Reach. That's from the *Book of the Traveler*, isn't it?" Tal unbuttoned the cuffs of his shirt and began rolling up his sleeves. "I've heard many translations and interpretations of the Book, and there are exactly none that I'm happy with."

Cade stood up, encoded to aluminum, making him lighter, and charged the man. He leapt, and switching to lead, leaned his shoulder into where the man stood.

The man, feet still rooted firmly on the ground, leaned backward impossibly far. He smiled as Cade sailed past him. Dropping his encoding, Cade landed, bracing himself against the floor, and skidded to a halt.

This guy can't be human. Is he a Wraith? Cade thought.

The man had already turned to face him. "Try again."

Cade approached the man cautiously this time. He

planted his back foot and shifted his weight between his legs. He brought his leading arm up, fist pointing forward, while his back fist hovered near the middle of his chest.

"Half-moon stance. So you *do* know some Coda," the man said, raising an eyebrow. "You almost had me fooled into thinking otherwise."

Cade's eyes narrowed. This guy was getting on his nerves.

He encoded tungsten and jabbed with his leading hand, careful not to commit his full weight. Tal let the blow glance off his hardened body. Adding an encoding of diamond, Cade followed with an uppercut.

The man, grabbing the fist and stopping it from connecting with his chin, looked at Cade's hand, and then at Cade.

"Multiple encodings? Two phantoms are a lot for one man. How long have you been Bearing them?"

Cade flared his diamond encoding and managed to wrench his arm free.

The man's smile faded. "Long enough, it would appear. Ready?"

Tal threw a punch at Cade, which he narrowly managed to block.

"It's the eyes, you see."

Another punch. Cade deflected it as he sidestepped to deter a follow-up strike.

"Their color is the first to go."

Tal kicked at Cade, his foot flat, as if to push Cade back. Cade blocked the attack using both arms as a shield in front of him.

"Much like your mind, it's like the eyes are also unsure what they should be."

Pushing his advantage, Tal continued to advance upon Cade.

"But you see, it's the phantom. The phantom, like with encoding, can alter the Veris. The phantom can change your eyes and more."

Cade blocked the man's next blow, but his attacker barred the arm and used his forward momentum to throw Cade to the floor.

"To do this, the phantom, from the Firmere, *reaches* into our world."

He picked Cade up off the floor, suspending him in the air as Cade struggled to free himself.

"Which begs the question—" Tal said, tossing Cade through the window of the train.

Cade managed to grab the lip of the window's edge and slammed into the side of the car's exterior. He encoded his hand to tungsten, but the bits of broken glass had already cut into his hand.

He scrambled up as the man approached the shattered window.

"—if the phantoms can reach into *our* world, can't we reach into *theirs?*"

Cade, balancing from the edge of the window, grabbed the top of the train car and pulled himself onto the roof. The train hurtled forward on its track through the Chalician countryside, the wind threatening to push him off. He turned around and found Tal already standing on top of the car.

Tal held up a single chipcoin between his middle and index fingers. The coin started to glow, giving off an orange light. The man turned, placed his hand on the car connected behind him, and wrenched it from the tracks as he hoisted it high above his head.

Impossible.

"Don't think of the Veris and Firmere as two separate places; they're not. Instead, think of them as they really are —two sides of the same coin."

Tal threw it at Cade, who fell backward, dodging the flying car as it hurtled an inch from his nose.

On his back, he looked up to see the man had relieved Cade of one of his casters. He placed his foot on Cade's chest, pinning him to the roof of the car. Tal slid the wedding ring over the barrel of the gun and pointed the gun at Cade's head. In the man's other hand, he held the chip-coin, no longer lit.

"You say you want to protect others, but you are ignorant to the gifts before you."

Cade roared as he struggled to move under the man's enhanced strength.

The chip, briefly, flashed orange.

Tal nodded his approval, smiling once again. "There's hope for you yet," he said, pulling the trigger.

CADE LURCHED FROM HIS SEAT, gasping for air. Wild-eyed, he looked around the silent cabin, but he was alone. He looked behind him and saw the car was still intact. The window next to him was also untouched and whole.

Eos broke the silence, her voice echoing in his mind. *Charging complete. I estimate our arrival time within ten minutes.*

"Did you see that man?"

Who? Eos asked.

"What about the data-log-thing? Did it pick up

anything?" Cade was starting to wonder if his Nocturne withdrawal was causing more serious hallucinations.

There is no record of anyone else other than you on the train.

Cade rubbed his temples.

However...the last ten minutes of the train's log data are missing.

He looked down at his hand, which was balled up into a fist, knuckles white. He relaxed it and opened his palm.

In it lay his wedding ring.

34

HELLS

If we compare the major cities of the Pathways, it is easy to see that each city had a very distinct purpose, primarily around the mining of different raw materials. The only Pathway location that does not fit that purpose is the Thread. There is only one record of someone gaining access to the Thread, if the account is to be believed. That excepted, no one has ever seen the interior of the facility.

—*From* The History of Chalice

CADE SHIELDED his eyes as the blinding light of the Thread enveloped the interior of the train car. The windows dimmed as the light hit it, and he could see again.

The Thread was in full view, its enormous column of surging energy reaching through the clouds. Cade had never seen it up close, and he was in awe of it. He was used to seeing it at a great distance as a thin gossamer strand of light.

Here, it may well have been the surface of the sun.

Cade guessed few had seen the Thread this close. The

facility was far north of Rynth. The ruins of Wythlain, the city the Wraiths leveled to the ground when they first came to Chalice, were just south of the Thread. And Gigan's Hill, where the last battle with the Skex took place, lay before them. The area was patrolled regularly, and the only trains in and out were manned by Skex. The *No Man* was the only exception to that. But getting near the Thread could be a challenge.

"How do we get off the train?" he asked Eos.

We're coming up to the main station. Short-range sensors indicate signs of life, but I don't have the resolution to say more than that. We'll need to overshoot the station to avoid detection, replied Eos.

As the station came into view, Cade's heart sank. Swarming the station was the largest army of Skex he had ever seen. He ducked low behind the window.

The windows are shielded from the outside. They cannot see you.

Cade remained crouched, not wanting to test if what she said was true. As the railbus sailed by the station, he could see the Skex boarding a variety of old and newer generation railbuses.

"Where are they headed?"

Based on earlier activity, Rynth. This is a good sign. It means we still have time. Let's get ready.

Cade made his way to the rear of the train.

One mile from here, there is an access tunnel for a disused waste drainage system we can utilize.

"Nothing like crawling around in the sewage of the Ancients."

Eos did not respond. She seemed almost human most of the time, but she didn't seem to possess a sense of humor. "Can you laugh?" he asked.

Yes. If the jokes are funny.

Cade sighed.

He stepped out of the last car and onto the balcony. The wind cut past his face, and he braced himself against the railing.

Now, said Eos.

Cade encoded tungsten and jumped. He hit the ground hard, rolling across the dry, rocky terrain—the tungsten preventing him from sustaining any notable injuries. He dusted himself off, thankful that getting off had been easier than getting on.

They had landed in the shadow on the far side of Gigan's Hill, which was shielded from the blinding light of the Thread. Only a few yards in front of them lay the mouth of a tunnel, half-buried in sand.

Once inside, Cade could see the access tunnel was large enough for him to stand without crouching. Cade took Eos from her sheath to help illuminate the dark tunnel. The tunnel was deep enough that even the light emanating from Eos could not penetrate the darkness at the end of it.

"These were drainage tunnels? What exactly were they draining?"

The Thread contains an antiquated first-generation power converter. The river you call Sepia can be rerouted to run straight into the Thread itself to cool the power core in case of an emergency.

"Eos, what is the purpose of the beam? It's not just an energy source, is it?"

I do not know. We can only assume it is a component of the Ascension Drive.

A chill ran through Cade as he remembered his recent visions of the Thread.

We must keep moving. Our time is limited.

"How close are we to the entrance?"

It's just up ahead. Once we get to the auxiliary entrance, there is a port I can interface with. My clearance allows access to the main system, so we will be able to deactivate the primary protocols and escape before we are detected.

Cade continued down the tunnel, taking care to be quiet, though Eos informed him that it would not make a difference.

They came to a large clearing with scaffolding to the side of what must have been the main tunnel, given its size. At the top of the scaffolding was a small door. Cade climbed to the door and noticed a glossy black panel mounted on the side.

"Where is this access port?" Cade moved Eos toward the door to get a better look when an invisible force pulled Eos from his hands and stuck the shard to the black panel with a dull clunk.

Acquiring access now. Just a moment.

"Okay, then," he said, shaking his head.

Remote systems have been granted restricted access only, even with my credentials. It appears the Wraiths have reprogrammed most of the backdoor entry systems to prevent us from doing any damage remotely.

"So what do we do now?"

We will need a port with access to the main system. I have local access here, but they have changed all the entry codes.

Cade heard a click as the door in front of them slid open. *Time to go.*

They made their way inside, with Eos navigating him through the serpentine halls.

Take a right here. Wait.

"What is it?"

I'm getting a signal. It is faint.

"A signal? For what?"

I can't be sure, exactly. The signal is not clear, though its header indicates a distress call.

"Sounds like a trap."

Perhaps. It is encoded with a private key only I have access to, however. Whoever it is, they might be able to help us. The signature of the distress call is Ancient-derived.

"You're kidding."

I am not. Take a left here.

He turned the corner and was confronted by a large steel door.

One moment. The door clicked and swung open wide. Next to the door, a black glass panel had been mounted.

The signal is getting stronger. Place me on the panel.

Cade moved Eos next to the panel, and she snapped into place.

He looked down wide hall and had the feeling that he had been there before. The architecture reminded him of the expansive housing structures left behind by the Ancients, but there was more to it than that. On each side of the hall there were four deep red doors. On the far side of a hall, a larger door stood sealed, also a deep red.

"Nine doors...I don't like this." He recalled the dream he had back in Toltaire. In it, he had seen these doors. Nine doors was a bad omen in Chalice—a reference to the scary old tales that were told about the nine doors of the Forgotten Hells.

Eos pulsed blue, and Cade retrieved her from the panel.

"Eos, where are we?"

Main laboratory access hall.

"Where does that door lead?" he asked, pointing to the first door on the right.

Schematic record lists it as "Acolyte Reconditioning."

Cade's eyes grew wide. The First Door of the Forgotten Hells. Hell of the Broken Mind.

"And that one?"

"Skex Incubation."

The Second Door. Hell of the Poisoned Brood. Were the tales of the Forgotten Hells true? No, nothing more than a coincidence. "*Where* do we need to go?"

The signal is originating beyond the far door.

The Ninth Door. Hell of the Slave Army.

He took a deep breath and let it out slowly. "A coincidence. Nothing more."

Cade placed Eos back in the sheath, which he secured to his back. "Do your sensors pick up anything on the other side?"

Sensor effectiveness is dampened by the door's shielding, but I do not detect any measurable signs of life.

The door clicked and swung open.

In the room was a full battalion of armored Skex.

"Damn it, Eos."

35

THE NINTH DOOR

Nine doors, none to hide. Nine doors, sanity tried. The last door, claws scrape. The last chance, you must escape.
—*From* Tales from the Forgotten Hells

CADE ROLLED HARD, avoiding a barrage of energy weapon fire. The lights of the great hall flickered as countless pulses of ionized energy poured from the room.

"No measurable signs of life?" he said.

I recommend we focus on the task at hand.

He wheeled his head toward the door they had entered. A caged red light flashed above it, and the door sealed shut.

Great, he thought to himself, *I'm trapped in hell.*

Cade threw himself behind a large pylon to the right of the door, narrowly avoiding another volley of energy projectiles as the Skex streamed into the hall.

Most Skex carried a type of energy weapon. Their hands were made up of small segments, with articulated claws and an opposable talon that allowed them to operate the rifles, though with much less dexterity than a human.

The energy blasts were nearly useless against a Bearer who was using the appropriate encoding. The energy could be absorbed and deflected by encoding with diamond, which had the useful side effect of making the body non-conductive.

Eos's voice. *My sensors have indicated there are 104 Skex troops in this hall. Five have been dispatched to apprehend you. No Wraiths appear to be present, though the one controlling these will have been alerted to our presence. If you can dispatch the Skex, I can override the emergency lockdown.*

"Five? No problem." Cade pulled his casters from their holsters and prepared his ritual.

Ton Efret. Family Taken from Holten. Served as a soldier in the King's Army before joining Coda. Died protecting Chalice from the Skex.

Jesen Galled. Coda Master, 4th Degree. Died protecting Chalice from the Skex.

Skricko Mazpar. Refugee from Byzar. Coda Master, 1st Degree. Died protecting Chalice on Gigan's Hill.

They would protect one last time. Cade breathed a word of thanks. It was all he could do.

He placed the dummy caster shells from the cache in the remaining chambers. He loaded them after the other shells, just in case. He hadn't had a chance to use one yet in a fight and wasn't about to take any chances.

Cade leaned out from the cover of the pylon and fired off three bursts in rapid succession before ducking back. He wanted to ration the use of his phantoms until he really needed them.

He continued his ritual. The casters, with aiming assisted by the technology of the Ancients, ensured that every shot counted.

Cade was relieved to discover the dummy shells worked just as well as the imprinted ones. The only notable difference was the dummy shells didn't auto-aim toward his targets. Cade wasn't used to missing, so when one of his bullets flew past a charging Skex, he was caught off-guard. *I'll have to make a note of that*, he thought.

Cluster from the east is repositioning. Fallback to south pylon, Eos's voice instructed. Eos's sensors, combined with her knowledge of tactical positioning, gave them a distinct advantage over the Skex.

More Skex are being allocated to us. Be on your guard.

When Cade's ammo ran low in his caster pistol, he would use his shotcaster to blast a hole through any Skex that were clustered together. That forced them to regroup, giving him time to reload. But despite their dwindling numbers, the Skex seemed to improve as the battle wore on.

"Talk to me, Eos, what's going on?"

The Wraith commanding this battalion is diverting more of their focus to this melee. It seems that they now perceive us as a formidable threat.

"I liked it better when they were underestimating us."

Relocate to right pylon on my mark. Three... two...one...now.

He encoded with diamond and aluminum. This allowed him to sprint quickly between the pylons without taking fire. The Skex had strength of numbers, but one thing they did not possess was quick reflexes. As he sprinted to the next pylon, he squeezed off two dummy rounds, both of which found their mark.

Cade nodded in satisfaction as he checked the strength of his phantoms. "We might actually have a chance here."

Another round of energy blasts rocked the pylon to which he had relocated. He placed his hand on the pylon and attempted to encode with it. Steel. He grinned. Complex alloys were beyond his capabilities, but simple ones, like steel, he could do.

Encoding with the solid steel pylon would use far less of his phantom's power than his small ring. It wouldn't make him as durable as tungsten, but he could walk away with only a few bruises if he was careful.

Leaning out from cover, hand tightly encoded to the steel, Cade surveyed the battlefield. There were still a sizable number of Skex remaining; he estimated about fifty.

Fifty-two, Eos corrected.

Cade took out the Skex closest to him with a caster shot. He noticed there was a group of Skex assembling something in the back of the room, resembling a large gun with multiple barrels. He ducked back into cover, avoiding another barrage of fire.

They are assembling a Bearer-Class autocannon, Cade. Exercise caution.

Cade heard the barrels begin to grind and whir. "Hells," he said under his breath, his curse now being a statement of fact. Skex could build things impossibly fast, since they could work together as a single mind.

He leaned out, leveled his shotcaster, and eliminated the group that had set up the weapon with a focused blast. Cade ducked back into cover to reload. He would only have moments before the next group got into position.

The Skex reminded Cade of ants. It didn't matter how many you took out; the others would fill the holes as if nothing had happened.

The grinding sound began again, and a hail of bullets tore through the room. They kept the machine running, erring on the side of wasted ammunition. If they couldn't match his reflexes, they would overwhelm him with brute force.

"You have to run out of ammo sometime." He heard a familiar clink that made his heart sink.

Cade, encode—

He didn't need the warning. He knew a Bearer-Class frag grenade when he saw it. Cade remembered what had happened to Commander Jord during the final battle.

He felt his tungsten ring pull tight against his hand. A second grenade rolled into view, along with a third, and a fourth. He pushed his phantoms to their breaking point and rushed out from behind the pylon.

They were ready for him. He was hit full-on with the blast of the autocannon, which sent him crashing against the wall. He tried to move, but the constant fire kept him pinned.

Bearer-Class weapons served two distinct purposes. Their primary purpose, of course, was to kill Bearers. Failing that, they worked to ensure the Bearer exhausted their phantoms. It was working. He groaned as he turned over, pain radiating through his body. He wouldn't be able to survive another one.

Focus. He knew there would be another grenade coming in to finish him off. He had to keep moving so he would not be outflanked.

Cade could detect a marked change in the Skex's behavior. They were far more aggressive now, and not just with the weaponry. They were favoring losses to catch him off balance, as evidenced by the bodies of the Skex that lay dead from their own grenades.

Cade encoded with lead and used the increased weight to move out of the autocannon's line of fire. He fired a shot into the next group that rushed him. More poured forth, this time from the opposite direction, not giving him an opportunity to reload. There were too many, and their tactics continued to improve faster than he would have expected.

His casters out of ammo, he swung open a nearby door. Cade flared diamond just as he took three energy blasts to the chest. The shot propelled him back into the interior of the room. Still on his back, he managed to kick the door shut.

The panel, Eos instructed.

Cade threw Eos toward the panel, and Eos snapped tight against it. He heard a mechanism engage, securing the door.

I'm afraid it will buy us little time.

Out of breath, Cade turned and reeled back.

"What...what is this place?"

Seraph Analysis.

Seraph? He had not heard that name before.

Metal tables lined the room. Bodies, human bodies, lay atop each one, most mutilated beyond recognition. The smell was almost unbearable. He covered his nose with his palm and fought back the urge to gag. *So this is where it all ends*, he thought.

Cade's face fell as he stepped away from the grisly scene. "What do they want with us?"

The Wraith is drawing closer. Be on your guard.

His face twisted into a sneer as he cracked open the barrel of his shotcaster. "Doesn't matter." He heard a high-pitched whine sounding from the door. Cade wheeled around, caster leveled.

The door exploded, sending Cade skidding across the floor and broken glass and twisted metal spraying through the room like a shotgun blast. The wind knocked out of him, he dragged himself over to the wall. His hands shook from the concussive force of the blast, and he struggled with bloodied fingers to put a shell into his caster.

Encoding with his tungsten ring again, he fired a shell into the Skex pouring through the entrance. More filed in, scrambling over their fallen. *The chipcoins*, Cade thought. He tried to use them, but nothing happened. What had he done on the train earlier to get them to work?

This is it, he thought as he crawled behind an upturned table.

He reloaded his casters with his dwindling supply of shells and waited for them to come to him. He laughed, delirious. It was not nearly enough for what was to come. He had failed.

Even so, he would still fight.

They came. He fired a barrage of bullets into the horde as they flanked him from both sides. There were more left than he remembered. *Reinforcements? Not fair*.

His casters emptied, he encoded diamond, opting for strength over armor in close combat. He moved with the discipline of a trained soldier and the tenacity of a man possessed.

He didn't remember how many Skex he took down in the room. He did remember how hard it became for his feet to find solid purchase as the fallen Skex piled up around him. The slits of light inset into the steel helmets bolted on over their heads died out when they fell. One helmet had been torn from the head of one the Skex. Cade could not make out the features of the elongated head, because it was covered in dark red blood. He could, however, see two large black eyes staring at him. He had never seen the face of a Skex. It held no malice or emotion, but instead it seemed curious, as if it had just been awakened.

The Skex continued to fight better and with more

tenacity than he had ever witnessed in the Corps. One Skex clawed at his back, ripping Eos from her sheath and silencing the voice within his mind.

When the last of his phantoms fell quiet, he turned to face the next wave of attackers, ready to accept his fate. Behind the gathering Skex, a solitary Wraith entered the room. The Wraith appeared to glide through the room, despite the carnage. The Wraiths he had seen moved with an eerie smoothness, as though their bodies were not grounded to the world around them. He seemed wholly unconcerned with Cade's presence as he opened a metal cabinet in the back of the room. A steam-like gas tumbled out of the cabinet as the Wraith pulled out a large glass vial of black liquid.

Nocturne. Even at a distance, Cade knew what it was. He hated how much he wanted it. Every cell in his body seemed to scream for it. The Wraith began filling a syringe with the pitch-black liquid. There was more Nocturne there than he had ever taken before. That dose would surely kill him. But why would they do it this way?

The Skex had now flanked him and grabbed his arms and legs, pinning him down. The Wraith hovered over Cade for a moment before plunging the large syringe into his chest.

A failed father, a failed husband, a failed brother, and a failed friend.

The familiar black tendrils clutched at his vision until the veil of darkness fell upon him.

36

WRAITH

The use of Nocturne was a boon to the war effort for the Bearer Corps. Many Bearers' minds were ill-suited to hosting phantoms, but Nocturne eliminated those problems with no short-term side-effects. Its ingredients and manufacture have remained a closely guarded military secret.

—From First Contact to First Combat: The One-Month War

A MAN SCREAMED as a blast of energy hit him square in the chest.

Cade was on the front lines. It was a sight he had seen countless times. He relived this memory every night that sleep had been merciful enough to take him.

The Skex were surrounding their position. His unit was deep within enemy territory, and they were outnumbered. This was *the* day. The day the Wraith War ended on Gigan's Hill.

One more day, he thought. That was what he had told himself on that last day of the war. He believed that day would end it. But it hadn't ended there, not really. So Cade had made the same promise every day since. Live for one more day. Put one foot in front of the other. As long as it takes to make whoever killed my family pay.

He watched once again as the Skex flanked their position.

"What are you waiting around for? *Move!*" His leader, Commander Jord Black told him. Cade nodded again, as he had on that day, and rushed toward the enemy line.

He watched as Jord took the grenade to protect his team. No matter how many times Cade was forced to witness it, it was still horrifying.

Cade sealed the Pact with Jord's phantom, which had stayed behind.

"Incoming!" a corporal wailed.

"Hells," the dream Cade spat.

He felt his phantoms tire as he fought the massive Skex on the battlefield, the type they now referred to as a Skex brigandine. The creature lunged at Cade, who tried to block the attack, but it connected and knocked Cade to the ground.

He remembered nothing more after that, and this was where the nightmare would end.

Except this time.

Cade's body rose, but it was not Cade who was in control. Catching the brigandine off-guard, he rolled to the side of the brigandine and shot a caster shell into the unarmored spot behind its head. Brigandine bodies were tough, and for some reason even caster shells couldn't penetrate through their irregular armored exoskeletons.

The brigandine's body disintegrated on impact of the shell. It was then Cade noticed the Wraith.

It was smiling as it leveled its weapon. Cade was the

faster of the two, and he fired a shell that struck the Wraith right between its eyes. The Wraith crumpled to the ground.

The sound of a horn trumpeted from the distance. Cade looked to see the banner of the King's Guard. *Reinforcements.*

The Wraith was dead. They had won the day.

Cade felt his body sag, and all went dark once more.

"He's awake?" a voice said, surprised.

Footsteps.

Cade's head was in splitting pain, his vision fuzzy, but he could just make out a form hovering over him.

"Curious." The voice was uneven and laborious.

Reality came crashing down upon him, and he found himself lying on a long metal table. His arms felt heavy, as if they had just carried a tremendous weight to exhaustion. With some difficulty, he pulled himself up. He could taste blood in his mouth. The thought of standing felt beyond him, so he remained seated as the figure approached.

His eyes focused on his surroundings, and he noticed the man before him was not a man at all. It had a sickly skin of dark glass. It was a simulacrum of a man. A Wraith. Behind the Wraith stood two men, guards, robed in red. Acolytes.

He looked down to see that not only were his arms not bound but his rings were still on his hands. His phantoms were still worn out from the fight, but he could sense some time had passed, and they would be rested soon. He had to buy some more time.

The Wraith smiled at him, though the effort was unnatural. Why bother to pantomime a semblance of humanity? Cade had seen enough to know the Wraiths had none.

"The dose of Nocturne we gave you should have put you into a coma," the Wraith continued, unblinking.

"Increase the dosage and accelerate the reconditioning. I will not be interrupted again."

"Who are you?" Cade demanded, though his voice was only a whisper.

The Wraith picked up Eos, examining the unique artifact, and set her lengthwise on the table beside Cade, nodding. The Wraith smiled once more, his lips curling like the string of a bow strung too tight. "You don't remember?"

Cade shook his head.

"You are quite famous...for killing me."

His heart sank as another piece of the puzzle fell into place. "You're not dead."

The Wraith laughed, though it sounded more like a guttural hiss. Though the Wraith did not smile again, Cade could tell it was enjoying his discomfort.

"Why haven't you killed me yet?"

"You will be more useful to me alive. Besides, you and I have a...bond. While misplaced, you are heralded as a hero among your kind. Myself, I am also seen as a hero by my people."

"We are nothing alike."

The Wraith slowly shook its head. "It is appalling to me how you don't recognize the gifts you have been given."

Cade furrowed his brow, but even that took more effort than he would have imagined.

"Can you comprehend immortality? What if you were destined to spend eternity trapped between the Veris and the Firmere?"

Cade sat silent as the Wraith took another step and hovered over Cade. "No. You don't have to. But we do. I am of the greatest species that has ever lived in this universe, but I am trapped here, with no possibility of ascension."

The Wraith headed toward the door. "Your entire existence is a failed experiment. But you hold a potential within you, Seraph. You will realize that power with my help."

Seraph. That word again.

Cade shook his head.

The Wraith motioned to one of the men guarding the door, and the man brought out what looked like a dark gray river stone and set it next to Cade. He could see that it wasn't stone, however, but metal. Its shape was irregular. Was this what Wraith technology looked like? It was in stark contrast to the clean lines and angular shapes of the Ancients. "Don't mistake me. I am not asking your permission." The Wraith leaned forward and pressed a small indentation on the front of the device. The box slowly pulsed with a harsh yellow light.

Cade reached for the box, but he could not move. No matter how he tried, he was frozen into place. "Nocturne is a fascinating substance. We cannot really take credit for it, of course; the ones you call the Ancients were the ones who first began synthesizing it."

Cade tried to speak, but his body ignored him. Panic set in. He tried encoding with his rings, but they would not respond.

"Use of Nocturne weakens the connection between the Veris and the Firmere; stretches it...thin...like a thread. This machine cuts the thread. It greatly simplifies reconditioning." The Wraith flashed its hollow smile.

"Goodbye, Elegy." It picked up Eos, muttered something to one of the guards, and left.

The guards walked up to the table, hoisted Cade up, and placed him on a metal gurney, along with the strange glowing box.

Cade struggled against his invisible bonds. He focused

his phantoms into his hands, to the point at which they should have overencoded.

Move, damn you! he screamed to himself.

They wheeled him out of the room and into the main hall. He remembered his dream once more. He had been here before. He felt the dread he had felt during the dream. He was helpless as they wheeled him down the hall. *Reconditioning,* he thought. This must be how they made Acolytes. What they had done to Karessa, to Rast, and to the other soldiers who had fought alongside him.

What had the Wraith said earlier? Nocturne weakens the connection between the Veris and the Firmere. He needed to amplify the connection somehow. *Amplify. The chipcoins.*

The pouch he had carried was still on his body as they rolled into a small room. Could he activate them in his current state?

Cade tried to encode with them, but again, nothing happened. *Dammit, what do I need to do?*

If the phantoms can reach into our world, can't we reach into theirs? The words of his doppelgänger echoed in his mind. Cade cleared his mind. He *reached.* He didn't try to encode this time. Instead, he imagined he had hands that existed within the Firmere itself. The hands were infinite, reaching on forever and holding everything within their grasp. He *reached* to his coin pouch; he could feel the power within them. He could sense the latent energy, asking to be freed. He held them in his hands, and he let its energy bind with his own.

Nothing happened, but he continued to reach and hold onto the coins. *Connection established,* an unfamiliar voice sounded within his mind.

The pouch on his belt began to smoke, drawing the attention of the guards. They started to argue about what to do, and within moments the pouch erupted into flame. The guard pushing the gurney tripped, and the gurney fell over. The room filled with a bright orange light from the coins that had spilled across the ground.

Cade blinked and found himself kneeling. He moved his hand to look at it. He was in control again. The guards turned their attention to him, having been distracted by the burning pouch.

Cade rose, smashed the device next to him with an encoded fist, and turned to face his opponents.

"Let's try this again."

The first guard rushed him, encoding diamond. Diamond encoders tended to overcommit their bodies with the additional strength, making it easy for them to fall off balance. Cade guided the man into the wall beside him, flared tungsten and elbowed the back of his head. But instead of knocking him out, the strike shattered the man's skull and sent him careening into the metal wall, leaving a crater where he had impacted.

The other man, incredulous, looked at Cade but rushed him anyway. The Acolyte threw a well-placed jab, and Cade noticed the man had overencoded his fist with the steel on the floor. Cade, with his own encoding, punched the man's fist, smashing it despite the encoding, and then struck the man's neck, incapacitating him.

Cade looked at the coins scattered on the floor. He would have to be cautious of the amplification. He touched the coins, which were still hot to the touch, and put them away.

He looked across the room and saw a row of what looked like silver coffins with rectangular view ports. He was relieved to see that there appeared to be no one inside them. Still, the sight of them made him uncomfortable.

I've got to find Eos, he thought as he ran out of the room and into the depths of the Forgotten Hells.

37
<hr>

TRANSPORT

The Nexus, a great metal tower that reaches high above the Rynth skyline, has no known entrance on the surface. But underground, more and more passages are being uncovered by intrepid archaeologists. It is believed one of these routes will lead to the base of the Nexus and to the greatest treasure of the Ancients.

    —*From* Chipcoins to Levitating Trains: Artifacts of the Ancients

ASHLYN DIDN'T like being underground. Most of the underground sites around Ancient cities were off-limits, and for good reason. They were difficult to police and as such were a fertile breeding ground for smugglers. Of course, she was now technically a smuggler herself.

"Okay, this is the place," said Ashlyn.

"Has anyone thought about how we are going to actually get this thing on the train?" asked Jace.

"It's not that hard. I've done it many times!" Beatrix exclaimed.

"Really? How many times?" he asked.

"Okay, I haven't actually done it yet. But it's simple. The supply trains that run along this track go straight to Rynth. You'll see," she said as they continued to push the large steel cart down the dark tunnel.

"I don't like this. The whole point was for us to use your Order of the Phantom to charter a railbus for us," said Jace.

"After the factory, we must assume anyone could be a double-agent," Elon said.

Like Rynth, Toltaire had its share of underground tunnels the Ancients had created for their mining operations. Beatrix had purchased a home above the tunnels to aid in the recreation of her lab.

They guided the bomb from the system of ropes and pulleys Beatrix had rigged and onto a rusted steel cart. Ashlyn found herself holding her breath as she helped unhook the bomb from the ropes. Working together, they managed to push the heavy cart down the short tunnel until they came to a large clearing. Ashlyn saw the unmistakable silver tracks of a railbus waystation crisscrossing throughout the large underground room. A long railbus, one without windows, was already stopped at the interchange. It was the type of bus that was used to help move goods rapidly between cities. A low pulsing sound echoed inside the chamber, indicating to them that the railbus was charging.

"This Pathway line leads to Rynth. Let's hurry," Beatrix told them,

With an encoded push, Ashlyn helped move the cart's wheels onto the tracks. They hitched the cart to the end of the railbus, and the cart snapped into place.

"That thing is heavier than it looks," Jace panted.

Beatrix looked around. "Good. I don't think anyone saw us. Transport trains like these only keep one or two conductors onboard, and they're usually sleeping." She peeked into the last car. "This is the supply car. You should be able to find a place to hide inside. Hurry before it finishes charging!"

"It's locked," Jace said, trying the handle.

"No problem," Beatrix said, pulling a crowbar out of her bag and handing it to Jace.

"Ashlyn, a word?" Beatrix pulled Ashlyn aside as Jace set upon the door with the crowbar. "I know my son acts like he knows everything, but his, ah, optimism, if you want to call it that, gets him into trouble a lot. Can you promise me to look after him?"

Ashlyn smiled. "I will."

Beatrix nodded at this and took a deep breath. She pulled Ashlyn in for a hug. "Thank you."

Jace popped open the door, the three filed into the cramped storage car, and the train started to move.

Ashlyn pressed a button in the front of the car, which opened the door to the next car.

The commuter car was darker than what Ashlyn was accustomed to. It had an earthy smell, like wet mud. She wrinkled her nose.

She heard Elon whisper behind her, "Why is it so quiet in here?"

Ashlyn squinted as she reached the first row of passengers. When she saw them, she gasped.

"Hells," she heard Elon mutter.

"What's going on? Why are we whispering?" Jace said as he walked up. "Whoa!"

Rows of Skex, standing at attention, filled the car, their metallic heads reflecting the lights from the tunnel. If the Skex had noticed them, they made no show of it.

"I've never seen anything like this," said Elon as she

rolled in next to Ashlyn. She approached the closest one and waved her hand in front of its metal face. It continued to stand, motionless.

"Fascinating," Jace said, getting a closer look. "I've never seen one up close before."

"Why aren't they moving?" Ashlyn asked, walking down the aisle.

"No idea," Jace said.

"I don't like this. Let's keep moving," said Elon as she wheeled down the aisle.

They walked in silence, moving from car to car, each filled with unresponsive Skex. In the first car one Skex sat at the front of the car, clutching some sort of metal chest.

"What do you suppose that is?" asked Ashlyn.

"Why don't you open it?" said Elon.

"Me? I'm not touching that. *You* open it," replied Ashlyn.

"Settle down, settle down. I'll open it," said Jace. He made his way to the chest, and keeping one eye on the Skex, opened the lid. Inside lay a smooth dark purple orb. "I've never seen an artifact quite like this. I can't tell if it is Ancient-made or not." He reached out to touch it.

The Skex snapped to attention.

"Jace..." Ashlyn said, worried.

The Skex started looking around frantically, as if confused. Others began chittering and screeching.

"Jace, what did you do?"

Jace's face went slack as he stared into the orb, which began to glow.

38

ENSLAVED

Why do the Skex wear those helmets that cover their heads? They have no discernible way to see, yet collectively they move like water through the bed of a stream. What gifts do they possess that allow for such graceful coordination?

—From First Contact to First Combat: The One-Month War

THE WORLD AROUND JACE DEMATERIALIZED, like reality had been nothing more than a drawing, an exquisite false rendering. He stood before a plane of darkness, but he was surrounded by wisps of lights, shifting like sand in a storm.

Before him he saw one such light. He understood that it was the orb. It seemed to swirl and then stop, as if it were regarding him.

He could hear a voice, but it was faint, as if from far away. He strained to hear it.

What you?

The voice was raspy and labored. *Are the Skex talking to me?* he wondered. "I, um, I am Jace Exile. I am a human."

Not Wraith.

"No, I am not a Wraith."

Help us.

"Help you? What do you mean?"

Skex slave. Stop Wraith.

"You want me to stop the Wraiths? How?"

Need...champion. Good control.

"You need someone to control you...a champion?"

Yes. The vortex of smoke seemed to swirl at this. *Will you?*

Jace was taken aback. These creatures, the ones they had fought for so long, were reaching out for help. What else could he say?

"I will."

JACE GASPED and whirled around the carriage of the train car, disoriented. Ashlyn grabbed his hand. "Jace, it's okay. What happened?" He looked at her, eyes wild. She could see his nose was starting to bleed. He turned around, breaking from her grasp, and retched.

Ashlyn bent down next to him, face riddled with worry. "Jace, are you okay? What happened?"

"I talked with them," Jace said.

"What did they say?" asked Ashlyn.

"They...want to help us."

39

EONTAL

There are those, while publicly decried by the scientific community, that have taken to the dissection of Ancient artifacts. As not all artifacts are protected by the crown, this is not illegal. But it is a waste. All dissection methods have revealed little as to the workings of the artifacts.

—From Chipcoins to Levitating Trains: Artifacts of the Ancients

"DAMMIT," Cade growled as he found himself back in the same hallway he had been in only minutes before. The passageways in the Thread wound about in many different directions, and he was struggling to navigate. *I'd never thought I'd say it, but I'm starting to miss Eos.* He didn't like having his mind read, but saving the world was a bit easier when you had an all-knowing machine to help you.

Cade turned down a hallway and noted that he hadn't seen a single Skex since escaping from the reconditioning room. It was more evidence that something big was happening. Cade hoped the Wraith was still nearby; he knew he needed to get Eos back. And where the Wraith was, Eos would be as well.

Cade stepped through the hall when he noticed the ninth door where he and Eos had encountered the army of Skex. It was where she had told him the distress signal was originating from. If there was an Ancient imprisoned there, perhaps they could help.

He walked up to the door and took a deep breath, bracing himself for anything. He pushed the button and the door opened. Inside, not a single Skex remained. He surveyed the room and found no other signs of life.

In the back of the room a metal arm projected a white sheet of energy across an odd-looking artifact. The artifact's markings were like the other Ancient-built artifacts Cade had seen before. As he drew closer, the artifact began to hum, and the lights that dotted its surface pulsed with a bright green light.

Eos? he thought. He wondered if Eos was trying to communicate to him through the artifact, as she had done before. Intrigued, he reached out to touch the artifact.

"Ah!" he yelled as an arc of electricity jumped from the shield of energy, coursing through his hand. He rubbed his hand, which felt like it had been stabbed with a thousand tiny needles.

Looking at the metal arm, he encoded diamond and twisted it, which sent sparks flying before dematerializing.

Cade turned to the artifact and reached out his hand.

Hello, Cade, a voice said.

Cade jumped and spun around, leveling his caster at the entrance, but the door was still closed.

A man's voice. "...Tal?"

I see you are still alive. Without the energy shielding you have destroyed, we can now speak freely.

"You're not a rogue phantom after all."

Tal laughed. *No.*

"So you're a machine...like Eos?"

It is difficult to explain. I am a consciousness within a machine.

"How were you able to communicate with me from so far away?"

Before the Wraiths locked down my access to this facility, I could transmit myself over great distances using the communications tower here. I knew Eos was trying to reach you, so I did what I could to help you.

"What have the Wraiths done to you?"

When they discovered me in the system, they managed to isolate parts of my consciousness within this device.

"Why? What do they hope to find out?"

The Wraiths have stolen every piece of Ancient computing they can find. The walls you see here are evidence of that. They repurposed all of these machines to solve one problem.

"The Ascension Drive."

Correct. The Wraiths...they are suffering from the madness of immortality.

Cade remembered his conversation with the Wraith. "Is that why they are using us? To help them escape from immortality? That's the purpose of the Ascension Drive?"

Yes. The Wraiths have figured out how to use the phantoms to open a gateway to the Ascent itself. A shortcut to the final plane of existence. But they will need a lot of phantoms to engage it.

"Tal, I need your help to stop them. They took Eos."

I know. I took the liberty of locating her while we are

talking. Without the shielding, I can access the internal network, including the surveillance systems.

"Where is she?"

I will tell you where, but I need you to patch that cable in front of you to the port on that wall.

"You mean this one?" Cade plugged the tapered metal spike on the end of the cable into the opening on the wall. Above it, a square on the wall lit up.

"Is this...a map?"

Yes, that will lead you to where Eos is. I will buy you some time, but not much. But before you go, I have one more request.

Cade raised an eyebrow.

I need you to destroy this machine.

"But...won't that kill you?"

Quite the opposite. This device restrains me, chains parts of me to this system. If you destroy the machine, you will free me.

Cade nodded. "What do I need to do?"

The central core is based within the Firmere, so you'll need a caster shell to eliminate it.

Cade drew his caster. He loaded a dummy bullet into the chamber and leveled his caster at the machine.

Until we meet again, Bearer.

Cade pulled the trigger. He turned to leave the room, casting one last look at the remains of the strange machine.

He was thankful to leave the Forgotten Hells behind. He committed the route Tal gave him to memory, which led him by the containment room he had been held in earlier.

As he passed the room, Cade heard the gentle notes of music, as faint as an old memory. He paused, hovering at the threshold. The Second Door, he recalled from an old scary story, the Hell of the Broken Mind. *Acolyte Recondi-*

tioning, Eos had called it. They were all men and women once. Good ones.

He closed his eyes. The music became louder as he focused upon it, breathing it within him.

He spoke the words, sealing the Pacts of the wayward Acolytes.

40

THE NEXUS

What lies within the belly of the Nexus? It towers above Rynth, an ever-present reminder that the greatest mystery of Rynth still waits to be discovered. With no entrance or explosive powerful enough to penetrate its walls, one can only surmise the entrance lies hidden underground. Perhaps within our lifetime, its elusive seal will be revealed, and we can finally claim the greatest glory of the Ancients.

—*From* Secrets of the Ancients

"THIS A BAD IDEA," Ashlyn said as they pressed forward. They had been able to ride the train all the way to Rynth from the underground station in Toltaire. The Skex that had occupied their car seemed to somehow be controlled by Jace via a strange purple orb.

"We have no better options," Elon stated. "Unless you would like to push the cart yourself."

They were surrounded by a cluster of Skex in Rynth's underground station. A phalanx of the armored brutes, under Jace's control, pushed the heavy cart with the missile in front of them. Occasionally, one would stumble and fall as if it were still learning how to walk. But the longer they pushed forward, the more in sync they seemed to become. Jace now sat upon the cart with glassy eyes, his hands glued to the dark purple orb as it pulsed its mysterious light. Ashlyn did not like the color, or lack thereof, of his face. *What is it doing to him?*

All around them, more Skex continued to file in from the arriving railbuses. The new arrivals were controlled by a power other than Jace, and Ashlyn noticed dozens of Skex which held chests like the one they had opened earlier. *Those orbs must be how the Wraiths can communicate with and control so many Skex at one time*, she postulated.

"I wonder what happened to the Foundation agents. You don't think..." Ashlyn said, not wanting to finish the sentence.

"I don't know. We may be too late," Elon said with concern. "Let's keep moving. Do you remember where you were told to meet the Foundation's team?"

Ashlyn nodded. "They should be at the north end of the station, but we'll have to wind through the side tunnels to reach it." She caught herself holding her breath each time one of the insect-like brutes walked past her. "Why do you suppose the other Skex are not attacking?" Ashlyn asked, fighting the urge to hold her nose. She did not like the way the Skex smelled. They reeked of an unkempt horse stable.

Elon shrugged. "Tough to say. Perhaps Jace is telling the others to ignore us. I'm just happy we're being left alone."

They followed the endless stream of Skex through the twisting underground labyrinth until they came to a clearing the size of a large stadium. On the opposite end towered a curved metal wall. It wasn't the normal brushed steel Ashlyn had grown accustomed to seeing. Instead, it was marbled with black lines, like the rings around the trunk of a tree stump.

"Invelium," said Elon.

Thousands upon thousands of Skex congregated inside the underground tunnels. Ashlyn thought, *How long have they been hoarding them here?* She looked at the cart behind her. The bomb, which had once seemed so impressive, looked inadequate given the sheer immensity of the army. Was the explosive on the cart big enough to take out the Thread itself?

Jace's group of Skex came to an abrupt halt in the clearing. Ashlyn looked around to see why they had stopped and noticed a group of human bodies strewn across the floor. They bore the deep telltale gashes of Skex claws. She recognized the face of one as the team leader Carlon had introduced her to. Ashlyn's eyes grew wide with both horror and revulsion. She covered her mouth to keep in the scream that had stuck in her throat. Their plan had failed.

The wall in front of them began to shift by some unseen force. A deafening rumble shook the underground room as the wall rotated in place, revealing an opening.

"I don't believe it," Elon said, eyes narrowed and alert.

The other Skex began to march once more, streaming through the opening.

Jace's Skex remained unmoved. Ashlyn, still trying to gather herself, heard coughing and turned to find it was Jace. He had set the orb down and was staring at the entrance that had appeared. She rushed over to him.

"Jace. Are you okay?" she asked. His face was pale.

He nodded. He looked at Ashlyn with a faint smile. He

pointed at the doorway the Skex had opened. "Welcome to the Nexus."

"Impossible," Elon said, shaking her head.

Jace, regaining his composure, pulled out the codex from his coat pocket. "If you look at the diagram of the underground tunnels, this is the location that would lead to the base of the Nexus tower," said Jace, tapping a page in his codex.

"It doesn't matter what it is. We need to leave immediately. We have to abort the mission," said Elon.

"But we can't. We've come so far," pleaded Jace.

Elon shook her head. "Don't you get it? The Foundation team is dead. There's no way we can take out the Thread now. We need to leave and warn—"

"Warn who?" Jace cut in. "Carlon is probably dead, and we already know what side the king is on. We're all that's left."

"What do you propose we do then?" asked Elon.

Jace paused a moment, watching the Skex as they filed into the entrance of the Nexus. "I say we find out what these Skex are up to. I would be surprised if there aren't more inside. My guess is the Wraiths are hoarding them here for something big."

"You don't think they are going to take Rynth, do you?" said Ashlyn.

Jace nodded. "What else could it be?"

Ashlyn just shook her head. How could her father let this happen?

Elon rubbed her chin, considering the theory. "Assuming that's correct, if we were to move this bomb into the center of the Nexus, where they are stockpiling these creatures..."

Ashlyn finished her sentence. "We could take them all out in one go."

Jace frowned. "What about the Thread?"

"Jace, the Wraiths have the railbuses locked down. We may not be able to attack the Thread, but we may be able to save Rynth," said Elon.

Jace looked at the orb he had set down near his feet.

Of course, thought Ashlyn. She put her hand on his shoulder. "We can't save them all, Jace. I'm sorry."

"I know," Jace said, nodding slowly. He sighed, picking up the orb and returning to the cart. The Skex clustered around them and began to move once more.

They crossed the threshold and marched into the heart of the Nexus. They stayed close to its outer perimeter, which, she discovered, spiraled upward, revealing floor after floor of inert Skex.

They came to an abrupt stop as the ramp ended. Ashlyn, exhausted, was thankful that they had the Skex to move the heavy cart, or they may not have made it to the top. On the last floor, strangely, there were no Skex present. Instead there sat what looked like an oversized railbus in the center of the room. It didn't quite look like any Ashlyn had ever seen. It had sleek flanges on each side, like the wings of a bird. On its rear was a large copper-colored cylinder with four smaller flanges mounted around it.

Jace bounded from the cart. "It's really here."

"A railbus?" asked Ashlyn, confused. "But where's the track?"

Jace began feeling along the side of the railbus, as if searching for something. His hand met a small black strip, and a door swung up in a vertical arc, revealing the interior.

Jace shook his head, smiling. He pulled out his codex and flipped to a page near the end. He held it up, tapping on a drawing that looked just like the railbus before them. "Not a railbus. It's a starship."

"Wait. A what?" Ashlyn pulled the book toward her. The sketch in the book looked almost identical to the machine before her. Jace grinned, snapping the book shut and tucking it back under his arm as the hurried to the door of the ship. The ship resembled the Ancient-made train cars, including the smooth metal-plated door. She watched as Jace took a deep breath, held it, and pulled the handle. The door slid open, and he hurried inside.

Ashlyn looked to Elon, who shrugged. Ashlyn pushed Elon into the ship. The inside was quiet, and the air was musty from years of lying derelict. The ship was spacious, possessing what looked like a front bridge, crew quarters, and a sizable loading bay in the back. They could see Jace darting from room to room, scribbling down notes and diagrams in his codex.

"Jace, we're supposed to blow this place up," Elon reminded him.

"I know, I know. But! But maybe we don't," he said, continuing his exploration of the ship's interior.

"What are you looking for?" Ashlyn asked.

"I don't know. An artifact, a record of some sort. They had to have left us *something*."

Ashlyn set her hand on his shoulder. "Jace, I know you've spent your life looking for this. But the entire city is at stake here. If we detonate now, we can take out this army. We can't miss this chance."

Jace slumped against the wall, dejected.

Elon wheeled toward him. "Let's get the cart into position."

The ship clicked, and the lights sprang to life. Alien characters scrolled across the panels before them.

"What did you do?" asked Ashlyn.

Jace shook his head.

A large panel flickered and lit up, revealing a familiar face.

Ashlyn stumbled back and gasped. "I don't believe it."

41

MISSION

The war we waged with the Wraiths...I take no joy in our victory. The Wraiths, they are like me in many ways. But they cherish themselves above all. And I...I cherish you.
—*From* The Book of the Traveler

CADE BEGAN his descent into the Thread's core, his new burden already settling upon him.

He came to a doorway and heard activity within the room. He pressed up close against the wall and peered into the doorway. Within, Skex scurried about, hauling metal chests from the transport car of a railbus.

A hulking Skex came lumbering down the hall next to him. Cade encoded to tungsten and raised his fist. The Skex ignored him and continued into the room, joining the others who were unloading the car. Not even one gave any indication they were aware of or cared about his presence.

He took a cautious step forward, but the Skex remained unconcerned, instead focused on their work. Cade, still on guard, made his way to one of the chests stacked against the far wall. Opening it, he saw hundreds of large packaged rolls of chipcoins.

They must somehow be using them for the Ascension Drive. That explained why the Chalician banks were so anxious to cycle out the old currency.

Cade placed as many of the rolls as he could carry into his pack. He slung it onto his back, the added weight already straining against his shoulder. He hoped he didn't have far to go.

Cade left the room, keeping a wary eye on the workers until they were out of sight. He hurried down the adjacent passageway, where he discovered a large door. To the right was a smooth black panel, identical to the ones Eos had used to enter the other rooms.

Cade checked the ammunition cylinder on his caster. *Empty.* He checked his bandolier. All that remained was the newly forged shell Jalek had given him back in Solak. Cade pulled the shell from the belt. He hesitated, turning the shell over in his fingers, and slid it into the cylinder.

One shot left.

He chuckled, shaking his head. It was like a scene from the pulp novels he read as a kid.

He snapped the cylinder into place and opened the door.

Deep in the center of the large room was the beam of the Thread itself, surging into the earth. It was contained by a dark shield that dulled the overpowering light emanating from the beam. The whole room vibrated from the immense power flowing through it.

All was not well in the room. There were Acolytes, shouting and running back and forth between the different consoles around the room. Circled around the outer perimeter of the room, Cade saw over a dozen Wraiths suspended in strange pods. He watched them rocket skyward, one after the other.

Leaning over one of the consoles was the Wraith Cade had talked to earlier.

Despite all the commotion and the hum of the Thread, the Wraith wheeled around when Cade entered, as if sensing his arrival.

"I should have given you more credit." His face looked different than it had earlier. Annoyance? He turned and gestured to the group of Acolytes, who had stopped what they were doing.

"Take care of him," he barked as he turned away, taking out Eos as he approached the Thread.

The Acolytes obeyed without hesitation. Cade could tell these Acolytes were not trained for combat. But they were not timid. The first one rushed him and encoded with what Cade figured was lead and diamond. The man threw himself on Cade, hoping to pin him. Cade noted these Acolytes, like the Skex, were prone to self-sacrifice. He could only guess that it was part of the reconditioning.

Cade encoded to aluminum and sidestepped the leaping man, who crashed onto the floor with a loud thud. Cade triple encoded with diamond, tungsten, and lead and stomped on the man as he moved to get up. Not an honorable counterattack, but honor required more time than he had.

He looked up and saw an Acolyte now had a caster leveled at him. A distraction. He had been overconfident.

He heard the familiar *crack* of the caster.

He flared aluminum for speed, sidestepped, and charged the gunman. He plowed into him at full sprint and crushed him with a metal fist. The bullet did not change its course. They were using the dummy rounds.

Cade ducked behind a column just as another round whizzed by. Even in the bedlam unfolding around him, he could hear music playing. It only took a split second for him to understand it came from the Acolytes he had dispatched. He spoke the words, sealing even more Pacts. It was too many, but he needed their power, and he didn't plan on living much longer anyway.

He was now encoding to almost every ring on his finger. Cade became a blur of destruction. The remaining Acolytes were cut down one after another until only the last Acolyte remained. The man stood his ground. He could see the man's jaw set, his teeth grinding in the same way he had seen the other Acolytes do. There was something in his eyes...resolve? Pity? Cade couldn't tell.

Cade picked up the strange caster from the incapacitated Acolyte that lay before him. He fired, and the man disintegrated into nothing.

Disintegrated.

Of course. Why didn't I notice it earlier?

He spoke the words once more, sealing another Pact. He would need all the help he could get.

The Wraith finished with its work at the console. "That's enough," it said, its lips twisted and curled into an unnatural sneer. "Everything is ready to begin. But for you it ends."

Cade leveled his caster, but the Wraith was on him faster than should have been possible. Cade had started encoding tungsten when a blow to his midsection sent him hurtling across the room.

He hit the far wall, winded but alive. Before he could gather his bearings, the Wraith was there, this time smashing his fist into Cade's face. Cade had fully encoded tungsten, but his phantoms were struggling to maintain the encoding with this much abuse.

"This is not hard for me...Elegy." Another strike, the force of which sent him flying once again, denting the solid metal wall behind him. "I can keep doing this." Before Cade could recover, the Wraith grabbed Cade and slammed him into the ground. "But can you? Your precious phantoms will fail you."

It was right. He couldn't keep this up for long. Even with phantoms of the Acolytes, this type of sustained punishment would drain him within minutes. He had to do something.

The pack.

He *reached.* A monotone voice sounded in his head: *Connection established.*

The Wraith took a step back, hesitating, as if it could sense what he was doing. It was brief, but the reprieve gave him precious moments to recover.

Another strike followed, but Cade was ready. His lead encoding was strong, and Cade didn't budge. Instead he sent his own diamond-assisted fist to the Wraith, sending it skidding backward across the metal floor, sparks flying from the friction.

The Wraith stood, smiling. "You can't stop the collection of Rynth. It's already begun."

Rynth. *Hells.*

Cade encoded diamond and aluminum and dashed over to his caster, snatching it up and turned to level it at the Wraith.

Cade remembered the battlefield from his dream. The Wraith had crumpled onto the ground. Caster shells always disintegrated their target.

He encoded to the marbled gold ring of Rynthium, and

the Veris scattered. In the void before him, he saw a smoky white light directly before him. His caster. It was pointed at...nothing. But above where the Wraith should have been hovered an intricate creature, woven from twisted wisps of fine silver light.

The creature of living light, the Wraith, sensed its detection, and shrieked as it lunged at him.

He did not hesitate. He raised the white light in his hand, the caster Eos had called EonCull, which bore his last shell. He prepared his ritual for the sacred shell that had been forged.

Dol Requiem. Coda Grandmaster. Brother.

He pulled the trigger.

Light poured out of the creature as the wisps unraveled into a thousand strands of knotted light. It became so bright Cade had to break the encoding.

Before him, the Wraith lay on the ground. Parts of it began to grow black, like it had been dipped in tar, and the floor around it seemed to disappear into darkness.

It looked at Cade with its dark eyes and spoke. "When we kill you...we know...you will make it to the Ascent." The Wraith's degeneration continued, and his voice came slowly. "But when we are killed...there is no salvation for us." The encroaching darkness consumed the Wraith, and it was no more.

"You don't deserve salvation," Cade said, rising. He bent down and picked up a caster one of the Acolytes had dropped, tucking into his belt. He collected the shells from the robes of the other Acolytes. He wasn't sure how many he'd need, but it would have to be enough. He saw Eos propped up against the console the Wraith had been at and picked her up.

Cade, we must hurry.

"Eos, we're taking down the Wraith ship."

That is not advisable. You are ill-equipped to take on a Wraith warship.

"Sorry, Eos. You can read my thoughts. You know I have to do this."

Cade... Eos fell silent.

Scanning the perimeter of the room, he saw one pod that remained, hatch still open.

Time to finish the job, he thought.

Cade strode over to the pod and crawled inside. He pulled the hatch closed, and the lights of the pod sprang to life. The control panel lit up, revealing words in an alien tongue. Without him pressing anything, the pod shot up through the facility, and he found himself launched straight into the night sky, the beam of the Thread mere feet away.

They will pay for taking my family. For Rynth. Was there still time to save Rynth? *No. The Wraith was right. I can't save them.*

He knew how to kill the Wraiths. If he didn't act, he would lose his chance. *I will avenge my family.* He clenched his fists hard, his nails biting into his palms.

Your mission isn't our mission. Carlon's voice. His hands started to shake as a trickle of blood flowed from them. Ashlyn. Jace. They would have saved Rynth, if they had lived. He screamed, slamming his fists into the hatch.

Protector of the Realm. A farce. He slammed his fists against the glass, harder now. Dark silver fell like a shadow over his arms.

Ashlyn had believed in him. Jace had believed in him. His children had believed in him.

Maybe he could, too.

He pulled his arms back and crashed encoded fists into the hatch, sending it hurtling below.

He took a breath and leapt into the Thread.

It enveloped him whole, a blanket of golden light wrapped itself around him. Music, an entire ethereal orchestra, filled his ears. The mysterious energy of the Thread, which he once feared, seemed to encourage him.

He opened his eyes but was not blinded. He could see a vortex of light in the distance below him. He encoded lead, his body becoming heavier.

The vortex rushed to greet him as he slammed into the iris of the Thread. The Thread itself seemed to flicker from his impact. He could see a crack form where he stood.

Cade. Eos's voice. *The phantoms contained in the beam are activating a cross-plane reaction to my physical state. If you can wedge me into the iris of the beam, we might be able to damage the focusing lens.*

Cade pulled out Eos and noticed the shard was glowing bright blue. He plunged the shard into the crack that had formed.

Blue arcs of energy flew from the breach in response. Jets of crystals shot out from the shard like roots from a germinated seed. Within moments, the shard was held in place by dozens of the crystal outcroppings. The shard's decorative handle did not survive, and all that remained was the jagged edge of crystal. Cade reached out and grabbed it with both hands.

A blast of blue energy shot out. His encoding of diamond deflected it. He pulled, but it would not give. He strengthened his encoding and wrenched harder, shattering the bolts of crystal from the blade. Still, the shard would not move.

He wrapped his hands around Eos once more, breathing hard. The beam seemed to surge, and Cade felt as if a thousand hands had been laid upon his own, urging him on. He encoded diamond and pulled.

It shot from the iris like a caster shell, but he held firm. The light of the Thread erupted forth. Strands of light sprung forth, unleashed from their prison, before evaporating into complete darkness. For the first time since the Wraiths destroyed Wythlain, the beam of the Thread was gone.

"Eos?" he said, panting.

Eos's blue light was gone.

"No..."

The shard flickered and began to glow.

We must act quickly. I'll need you to interface me with the main console the Wraith was using.

"Nice to see you, too, Eos," he said as he walked over and placed Eos on the interface panel.

Okay, preparations have been made. We must leave now. It won't be long before the facility is recaptured.

"Recaptured?"

They will need to repair the Thread to finish the collection. Without it, they cannot complete the Drive.

"Eos, the Wraith said they were going to collect Rynth. We need to stop them."

Agreed. Gathering sensor data in Rynth now. Interesting...

"What's interesting?"

The square panel from the console in front of him lit up. It was like the screens of the Ancient artifacts, except this one showed a moving picture. Within it, he saw a familiar face.

"Ashlyn?"

"Cade? You're alive!" she exclaimed.

He hesitated for a moment as he looked at her. "I thought I had lost...never mind. Where are you?"

"We're in Rynth. There are Skex here. Thousands of them. We're going to stop them."

Cade furrowed his brow. "How?"

"We have the bomb," Jace cut in.

A voice, a female's, sounded from inside the ship, startling Ashlyn. *Any damage we do to them in Rynth will only be temporary. There are still thousands of Skex headed to Rynth.*

Ashlyn frowned. "Who is that?"

"Eos. She's a, ah, a machine. It's a long story. But chances are she's probably right."

"If this is a waste of time, then what do you recommend?" asked Elon.

"Why don't we take the fight to them?" said Jace.

"What do you mean?" asked Cade.

Jace grinned. "Cade, *I found it.*"

"Found what?"

"The *Exilia!*"

"The what?" Cade asked, confused.

"Oh, sorry. That's what I named her. It's the starship inside the Nexus!"

"You're kidding me," Cade said.

The female voice spoke. *My diagnostics report the primary power cells for this ship have almost been depleted. It has insufficient power for launch.*

Jace frowned. "Maybe we could route power from the Thread?"

Cade shook his head. "Yeah, about that...we turned it off."

"You did *what?*" Jace exclaimed.

"Another long story," Cade said. "We'll have to think of something along the way."

Cade felt the uncomfortable heat from the chipcoins in his pants pocket. He moved them to his jacket pocket. He was still in awe at how much power the coins had given him. "Too bad we don't have access to a cache of chipcoins."

"Why would that help?" asked Jace.

"The coins can generate a tremendous amount of power, like a small reactor. If we had enough of them..."

Eos stepped in. *It would be difficult, but it is not impossible. However, you would need tens of thousands of chipcoins to make it work.*

"Is that all?" asked Elon.

Cade looked up at the screen and raised an eyebrow.

"The Royal Bank is not far from here. I just don't know how we'd move them," Elon offered.

You don't need to, said Eos. *If you can create a trail of coins to the main vault, we can chain them together to reach the cache.*

Elon smiled. "I think it's time we made a withdrawal."

Before Cade could reply, an alarm sounded within the Thread control room. *Cade. We must leave now,* said Eos.

Cade looked at the faces of his friends on the screen. "Good luck."

"Don't worry about us, just get over here!" Jace replied.

Cade grabbed Eos from the panel and backtracked to the room where the underground rail station had been located. It was an older train, first-generation by the looks of it. It was surrounded by Skex who looked to be frozen in place.

"What's going on?" he asked Eos.

The Wraith you killed was likely the one controlling

these Skex. Without a master, Skex go inert.

Cade sidestepped around the group and boarded the train. "Okay, Eos, do your thing."

I cannot. We deactivated the power when we shut down the Thread.

"But you just said we have to take the train."

I cannot activate it. But you can move it.

"Eos, we don't have time for this. What are you talking about?"

Encode with the track.

While a Bearer could summon an object they were not touching by encoding with it; they could conversely move themselves by trying to summon an object that was heavier than they were.

"That's impossible. The amount of energy required do to that would drain the phantom immediately."

Unless you amplified the phantom.

The coins. By his estimation, there were at least thirty cars on the train. The majority of them were still packed with one thing: crates of chipcoins.

"You're not suggesting..."

It will be good practice.

Cade shook his head and moved to the front of the train so he could see the track. He encoded to the floor of the train car, rooting him in place. He'd shoot right through the glass otherwise.

He closed his eyes and *reached*. He visualized his hands, reaching into the infinite expanse of the Firmere. There. He felt the presence of the chipcoins.

Connection established, a monotone voice echoed in his mind. With it, he felt his phantoms grow stronger. He put his arm out and encoded to the section of track before him.

Nothing happened.

He closed his eyes again. He reached farther, holding more of the chipcoins through the Firmere. He felt his phantoms begin to strain and pull on him, like wild dogs on a leash.

He opened his eyes and held out his arm once more, encoding to the track.

He almost jumped when the entire train began to creak and groan as the wheels struggled to turn. *Steady*, he told himself. The wheels began to turn and yielded a bit more with every second he maintained the encoding.

Eos remained silent. Cade wondered if this was something that happened during the time of the Ancients? Perhaps the Ancients, at the pinnacle of their phantom-based technology, flew around from place to place using a similar concept?

The wheels were gaining momentum. They were moving, and the phantoms were holding. It could work.

He just hoped he wouldn't be too late.

42

WITHDRAWAL

Engage Phase 2 of Chalician currency exchange program, by order of King Liam. Ensure that all outstanding chipcoins are enumerated according to the provided instructions and prepared for shipment from the Bank of Rynth to the Thread.
—Top Security Clearance Order

ASHLYN'S PALMS were sweaty as they entered the Royal Bank of Chalice in Rynth. It was the largest bank in Chalice, and it housed more of the country's wealth in its vaults than all other banks combined. The exterior of the building was the most impressive piece of Ancient architecture in Rynth. Adjacent to it was the Nexus, the tallest structure in all of Chalice.

The interior of the bank was breathtaking, albeit manmade. The polished white marble was inlaid with bronze filigree, weaving and curling around the floor like a vine wrought of polished metal. To either side of the entry, a grand stairway swept upward to private banking rooms.

Elon eyed her as they walked in. "Relax, will you?"

Ashlyn glared at Elon. "There is an entire army of Skex literally right underneath us! How can I be relaxed?" Elon just held a finger to her lips and rolled forward into the main foyer.

Ashlyn took a deep breath. All she had to do was make sure there was a trail of coins linking to the main vault so Cade could use the chipcoins there. No problem.

A thin yet very tall man dressed in a fine charcoal-gray suit was barking orders at scurrying workers. "I want those backup power cells up yesterday, people! And turn off the lights in the auxiliary vaults. I don't want to waste what little power we've stored up. There's no telling when the power will be back on."

The man turned and glided up to them as they entered the foyer. "Welcome to the Roy...oh my. Your Highness... er...*Highness-es!* My apologies for not recognizing you sooner. I had not received any notice of your arrival, or I would have prepared you a more fitting reception! Please, please, right this way." Ashlyn was surprised he recognized them until she realized that Elon was likely a regular visitor. He signaled to one of the tellers behind the counter before escorting them onward.

He led them to a lavishly decorated sitting room off to the side of the main foyer. This particular room was where the biggest account holders were able to do their business discreetly. He nodded to one of the young scribes in the room. She looked at Elon, and her eyes grew wide before she hurried off.

"This is hopefully more to your liking. Apologies for the power outage. We're still trying to remedy the situation. No doubt you are here to check on the status of the current audit?"

Elon showed no hesitation. "Precisely. The king is always telling us to be more hands-on with the state of affairs in Chalice, so we thought it best to personally see to the progress. I hope our spontaneity hasn't inconvenienced you terribly."

"No, of course not, please don't mention it. Flexibility is a cornerstone to our success, and besides, it is rather an honor to be visited by two members of the royal family in one day. I have already arranged for your account manager to come show you our progress within the vault. Refreshments will be arriving soon, but please do not hesitate to let any of us know if you desire anything else."

Elon glanced briefly at Ashlyn. "That sounds lovely. Thank you."

The man paused. Does he suspect something? Ashlyn tried to shrug it off; she was being too paranoid. The man spoke to one of the tellers in the room and then left.

Elon looked at Ashlyn triumphantly. "You see? Nothing to it."

"I'll feel better once we've made it out of here."

Elon frowned.

"Do you think Father knows about the Skex in Rynth?" Ashlyn asked.

Elon sighed. "I don't know. He is very secretive about his dealings with the Wraiths. I can't help but think he has some leverage he is unwilling to share with me. Let's try to stay optimistic. We're not out of the game yet."

A short old man, dressed in a fine but old-fashioned tan suit, entered the room. Through his manicured white beard he flashed a warm smile. "I hear today is my lucky day! I get to guide not one but two of the royal family in the same day. You two should know better than to get an old man too excited."

Ashlyn couldn't help but smile. Elon was right; this would be easy.

He led them down to the entrance of the vaults, guarded by a host of armed soldiers the bank kept on watch at all hours. The bank had too much money to risk anything less than maximum security.

"You'll notice this large door here to the vault. I wish we could say *we* built this beauty, but this is a remnant of the Ancients' unparalleled skill in metallurgy. This door is the only way in and out of the vault, and the door itself is built out of an indestructible alloy known as invelium. It is, without a doubt, perfectly impenetrable."

Saying the round metal vault door was large was an understatement. It was as tall as a house and looked to be at least ten feet thick. Ashlyn realized the smaller vault doors she had seen in Toltaire were likely modeled after this design. Six large metal hinges along its edge held it in place. The vault door was already wide open. They conducted so much business during the peak hours, it was more efficient to leave it open throughout most of the day.

"This large room here with all the cabinets, which we call Prime, is where we do the majority of our work," the man said, gesturing to the bank workers hurrying about. Steel cabinets, inlaid with rich dark wood accents ran from the floor to the top of the vaulted ceiling, which was twice the height of the vault door. Rolling ladders were used by the workers to reach the higher cabinets. There were even harnesses attached to the ladders for the workers to secure themselves should they fall from the ladders.

Ashlyn heard a deep rumble that seemed to reverberate from the floor beneath them, almost like an earthquake. Their guide raised an eyebrow for a moment, and the noise seemed to stop as suddenly as it started. Ashlyn shot a concerned look at Elon, her lips pursed.

The man cleared his throat. "Ahem. Let's continue, shall we?"

As the old man bustled about on the tour, Ashlyn, following behind Elon, slipped a chipcoin from her pocket and slid it between two cabinets they were standing against. They had agreed Ashlyn would have to be the one to place the chipcoins in the bank. Elon was insistent that being in a wheelchair made her an unwilling spectacle.

"Just beyond this point is the great warehouse. Soon to be empty, sadly. Now that chipcoins are being taken out of circulation, we are shipping out crates of them daily. There are so many, we estimate it will still take about four months to empty them all."

As he recounted the fate of the chipcoins and why the royal notes were being utilized, Ashlyn pulled out another chipcoin and tucked it into a groove next to the main doorway. She hoped she had spaced them well enough.

Just as she was wedging it into place, a man who looked like a security officer, ran up to them at full sprint, eyes wild. He stopped just short of them, breathing heavily. *We've been discovered*, Ashlyn thought, fighting down panic. The man hunched over, hands on his knees as he caught his breath. "Your Highnesses! Skex have...have breached the bank. We must get you out of here!"

Ashlyn's heart sank. She looked to Elon, who looked equally grim. They had run out of time.

The four of them hurried uphill as best they could back through the passage from which they had come. When they reached Prime, they were horrified by the gruesome scene. The motionless bodies of bank employees who had been hard at work only moments before littered the room. A small security team had fallen back into Prime, trying to protect what remained of the workers.

The room itself was in ruins as surviving employees managed to pull down the large cabinets that had lined the walls to form a crude barricade. They huddled behind it, terrified and defenseless against the sudden onslaught.

A deafening boom sounded from the front of the building, causing Ashlyn to instinctively duck down. Her ears rang while the din of chaos continued to rattle in the background. She turned to see what had caused the explosion and to her horror saw the guards who had attempted to defend the entrance were no more.

Elon. Ashlyn turned to Elon to see if she was okay. Elon nodded to her, her lips drawn into a hard line. She stood.

The first few steps were shaky, but she found purchase on the smooth metal floor. Standing tall, Elon's body belied its intended masculinity, showing hints of curves not seen from her chair. Others might have noticed, too, were it not for the sounds of battle coming from the bank's lobby. Stray energy blasts knocked down cabinets and sent the frightened workers to seek shelter deeper within the vault.

Elon, stance now firm, grabbed a hold of the massive vault door. "Guard! Ashlyn! Give me a hand!"

Pushing aside her shock, Ashlyn ran to the door and pulled as hard as she could. Despite the door's incredible weight, the hinges were well taken care of, and the door began to move.

Just as the door was almost sealed, an energy blast ricocheted into the room. It missed Ashlyn but caught the guard next to her. She fought the urge to scream and held her position.

Elon and Ashlyn closed the remaining gap and rotated the manual lock into place. Once secured, they fell to the floor, winded and out of breath. "That should hold them," said Elon.

They could feel the vault door vibrate as energy rounds pounded into it. Invelium was indestructible. They were safe. Even if they didn't survive, their part to play was over.

Elon grinned at Ashlyn. "Guess my secret's out."

Ashlyn laughed, which settled her nerves somewhat.

Another large explosion sounded, and the door shook. A loud humming sound spun up, becoming louder and louder. The vault door became hot to the touch.

"That can't be good. We should get back," said Elon. They retreated farther into Prime, opting for cover behind a fallen cabinet far from the door.

Elon shook her head. "So much for invelium. Looks like the Wraiths came prepared." Elon, who had sat back into her chair, pressed a button, and the intricate machined arms on both sides of the chair separated with an audible click, revealing the unmistakable grips of casters. "So did I," she said, drawing one out.

"This one has a bit of a spread to it. Just point and shoot." She handed the caster to Ashlyn, who took it, awed. Elon pulled out the other caster and double-checked the ammunition in the barrel. "You've got seven shots there. Make them count." Ashlyn nodded.

Elon reached into the pack secured in the chair's secret compartment and pulled out an immense diamond the size of a grapefruit.

"What is *that?*"

"It's the Vissera Diamond, the largest diamond in the world." She grinned at Ashlyn. "I borrowed it."

"You *borrowed* it?" Ashlyn was floored Elon had managed to sneak it out of the castle. Though with a wheelchair with concealed storage, maybe it wasn't that unreasonable.

Elon shrugged. "I like to be prepared."

The door was changing color now, first turning to orange and red and then to white as molten invelium began to pour into the room. In moments, the door was gone.

"Elon?"

"Yeah?"

"I know we've only really been sisters for a couple days now, but...I..."

Elon touched Ashlyn's shoulder and looked her in the eye. "We're going to survive this. We'll catch up after we squash these bucket-heads."

Ashlyn laughed, despite her nerves, and nodded.

The Skex came, flooding into the room like ants. Five... eight...twelve...too many. Ashlyn's grip tightened on her caster, face flushed from the oppressive heat of the now cooling metal. *This is it*, she thought. They couldn't win against these numbers, but she would do her best. The thought calmed her somehow.

After them, a tall, muscular man strode into the room, resplendent in traditional body armor. The markings were those of the royal house. "Father?" both Ashlyn and Elon said at the same time.

"Elon? Ashlyn? What is the meaning of this?"

Ashlyn stepped forward, disgusted. "Father? You are with *them*? How could you?"

The king's eyes were hard, and his jaw was set. "I don't expect you to understand."

"You never do, do you? You think this is how you help our kingdom? By killing your own people?"

"What else would be done? Allow for our entire country, our entire planet to be wiped out by the Wraiths? I have only acted out of love for this kingdom and saving the people within it. But love comes at a price."

"But the price...is too great," said Ashlyn.

The king shook his head. "Your mother said the same thing before she died. You two are so alike."

"Mother knew about this?" asked Ashlyn.

Liam nodded, meeting her eyes. "She threatened to tell of my deal with the Wraiths. That I allowed them to take the cities of Chalice."

"You didn't..."

"Love comes at a price," he said, expression cold.

Ashlyn felt numb. All this time, she had no idea. She looked at Elon, her face smoldering with rage.

A Skex approached Ashlyn from the entrance and raised its energy rifle.

The king frowned. "Wait. That is not part of the arrangement. I am granting these two passage back home."

A rifle blast sounded from a Skex that stood behind him. Ashlyn's eyes met her father's. His eyes were wide with shock as he fell to his knees. He looked one last time at her, helpless, and collapsed upon the floor of the bank.

"Move!" yelled Elon, who was once again out of her wheelchair, pushing Ashlyn out of the way of another blast from an advancing Skex.

Ashlyn snapped out of her stupor and encoded with the tungsten ring she had been given. Elon had been able to procure her a full complement of rings from the armory, though hers were more fashionable than the utilitarian ones she had seen Cade wear.

The ring, pressed tight against her hand, did the trick. It dissipated the energy upon impact. Warmth coursed through her body, and even though she felt a little shaken, she was no worse for wear. She did find the ring's tight grip on her unsettling, but Cade mentioned she would get used to it in time. "Think of the material as an extension of your body. It is becoming a part of you," he had said. It still didn't make her feel any better.

Rolan's instincts flooded into her mind, and she let them take over. It dawned on her why she had become so good at Bearing. Rolan must have been a Bearer himself, and she was benefiting from his experience.

After the first wave was shot down by Ashlyn and Elon, the Skex began to adapt to a new strategy. They discarded the energy weapons and switched to melee tactics.

The sisters continued fighting, back-to-back, turning away every Skex that descended upon them. They conserved their ammunition, only resorting to casters when they were in danger of being overwhelmed.

Ashlyn sidestepped an incoming Skex claw and dropped a diamond-assisted elbow onto the claw, shattering it. She grimaced. Even encoded, that had *hurt*. She wished she could encode more than one ring at a time. Cade had told her multiple encodings needed multiple phantoms, and even then required many years of training to be proficient at it. She wondered if Rolan knew how to do it. She wound up with a diamond-assisted punch and flared tungsten before connecting, puncturing the Skex's armor and catching her arm inside the creature. It fell to the ground and took Ashlyn with down it. She struggled under its weight but managed to wriggle free. She stood, panting. She looked around and was surprised to see no more challengers. She turned to Elon, who was grinning. Somehow, they had done it.

The room trembled as a hulking creature at least twenty feet tall, stooped down to squeeze into Prime from the vault entrance. A Skex brigandine. Ashlyn had heard of these rare Skex but had never seen them in person. It stepped upon the puddle of cooling molten metal on the floor but did not seem bothered by it. The other Skex had avoided the liquid metal. Ashlyn checked her caster. One shot left. She leveled her caster at the beast.

"Brigandine armor can deflect caster bullets!" Elon yelled to her. "They can only be shot in the back of their skulls!"

"Hells," cursed Ashlyn. Rolan didn't seem to have known that, either.

Prime, while a large room, felt small with the massive Skex brigandine filling a substantial portion of it. It was nearly as tall as the room itself, and its gunmetal skin was somehow fused with what appeared to be a patchwork of thick metal plates. And like other Skex, its head was encased by an odd-shaped metal mask. There was no visor for the creature to see, yet it did not seem to need eyes. The brigandine swept its trunk of an arm toward Ashlyn. The corner she was trapped in didn't have enough space for her to dodge, so she encoded tungsten hard as the arm crashed into her. It sent her flying to the back of the room, slamming her into the inner wall of the vault. She shook her head, her vision blurry. *Any ideas, Rolan?*

Elon took the opportunity to position herself behind the brigandine with an assisted jump and raised her caster toward it. It turned, anticipating her move, and brought its other hand down in an overhead smash. Elon must have still been encoding diamond, because she rolled off to the side, dodging the blow by inches. Using the momentum from its last swing, it followed up with another. It found its mark and sent Elon sailing into the wall near Ashlyn.

Ashlyn ran to Elon, who rolled over and groaned. Ashlyn looked up to see the brigandine almost upon them.

She heard an energy blast contact with the back of the great beast, which caused it to stumble forward. It turned around, looking for its new target.

Her father, who had propped himself up on the wall, gripped a Skex rifle in his bloodied hands.

The brigandine turned around, lumbered over to him, and raised its fist high above the wounded man. The creature brought its arm down with tremendous force. Ashlyn felt a strange sensation and noticed Elon was no longer beside her. She looked up and saw Elon had moved clear across the enormous room, and was now in front of the brigandine, blocking the strike that had been intended for her father. Elon was straining against the brigandine's strength, but her eyes blazed with determination. Gripped in Elon's other hand was the Vissera diamond. The brigandine roared in anger but could not escape Elon's phantom-assisted grasp.

Ashlyn didn't waste the opportunity. With the brigandine's back turned to her, she raised her caster and fired a shell into the back of its head. The brigandine disintegrated without a trace.

Elon fell to the floor, her legs no longer stable. Ashlyn had heard of teleportation like this. When a Bearer reaches Affinity with a phantom, time stands still for everyone but the Bearer. Affinity meant the phantom's purpose is fulfilled, and the phantom travels to the Ascent. "Mother..."

She hurried over to her father, still sitting propped against the wall of the room. His chest rose and fell in short breaths. There was so much blood, she was amazed he was still conscious. He looked at her affectionately.

"I have missed you so much, my dear Sashion," he said.

Sashion...her mother's name. "Father?" she said, unsure.

"I'm sorry, I'm sorry. You were right all along."

Her father clung tightly to her. "It's okay. It's over now," she said, trying to calm him.

"I thought I could be more. That I could protect the people. Make a sacrifice...for the greater good."

Ashlyn just sat in silence, her eyes welling up in tears.

"In time...I hope you will forgive me, my queen," were her father's last words. He slumped down onto the cold floor. Elon had pulled herself next to Ashlyn. Elon put her arm around Ashlyn, who rested her head upon Elon's shoulder and cried.

43

SACRIFICE

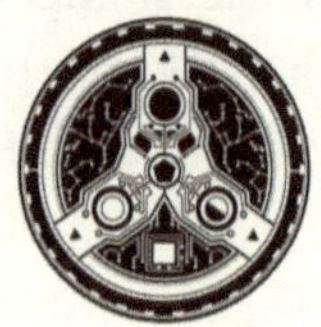

The nature of the Skex has led to many theories on how the creatures function. While they do not seem to possess verbal communication, their advanced coordination demonstrates communication is happening, albeit nonverbally. More fascinating is that the more of them there are together, the better the coordination, which is opposite of what common sense would suggest.

—From First Contact to First Combat: The One-Month War

"THEY'VE BEEN GONE A LONG TIME," Jace said to himself, wringing his hands as he paced outside the ship. Ashlyn and Elon had left him to go to the bank, and his small army of Skex gave him little comfort. The wait was agonizing. He had finally done it. He had found the Nexus, and the ship. If it weren't for being surrounded by tens of thousands of Skex about to be unleashed upon the city, he'd have been giddy with joy.

Jace rubbed his temples. His head ached. He touched

his fingertips to his lip and noticed his nose was bleeding again. He heard a low, rumbling sound, and he turned to see Skex pouring in from the bay doors and toward the *Exilia*.

The purple orb he had set down on the cart began to glow, and the inert Skex he had positioned lurched to life. "No. No, no," he said, reaching for the orb.

A voice leapt to life in his mind. *You have returned.* His Skex froze once more. *The slavers are trying to take us back.*

What would you have us do? the orb queried.

Jace, through the eyes of his Skex battalion, watched as the hordes of mobilized Skex from below marched toward the ship.

"We need to buy some time."

Jace clutched the orb in his hands and commanded the Skex to pull the caster bomb off the cart and haul it into the rear bay of the ship. They were at the pinnacle of the Nexus, the great tower of Rynth, and he already had to leave. He had a Skex carry him inside the ship itself. He had a difficult time trying to use the orb and do something else at the same time. He could only really do one or the other.

The orb was a remarkable find. He'd never experienced anything quite like it. He could make them move, jump, and, he hoped, fight. But he didn't have to tell them *how* to walk. They just knew. And when he made an order, they all fell into place, exactly as he would expect them to. He began to understand how the Wraiths had been able to coordinate the Skex during the war.

Once he was inside, he heard Eos's voice inside the ship. *Opening bay doors.* He looked at the main screen and could see the tip of the great obelisk that was the Nexus begin to unfurl like the petals of a flower. All this time, he had been right. The Nexus wasn't just some monument of the Ancient civilization. It was a gift. A gift that would take them to the stars.

All they needed now was power, and they'd be ready for takeoff.

He took a deep breath and held the orb once more. "I'm sorry, guys. We have to hold them back as long as we can." He shook his head. He was asking them to fight their own. Their own who were under the control of the Wraiths.

Understand. A voice echoed in his mind. *We fight.*

He braced his Skex as the streaming mass of enemy Skex converged upon the ship. Jace's team obeyed his command and rushed headlong into the fray.

44

EXPRESS TRAIN

It is apparent the Ancients had a great need for the small devices we know as chipcoins. An archaeologist cannot explore a region of Chalice without discovering a cache tucked away, with thousands of the coins stacked high. I can assure you they had some greater purpose than currency, though we possess no evidence yet as to their true purpose.
—*From* Chalician Archaeologist's Quarterly, *Vol. 1*

THE TRAIN WAS GAINING MOMENTUM. Cade was starting to get the hang of it. He pulled to one section of track, then to the next, propelling him forward.

Too slow. I need more, he thought. He closed his eyes and reached for more of the netcores. He visualized the connections in his mind. *More.* The strength of his phantoms surged with every connection.

The wheels of the old train were turning so fast they began to slip, screeching across the surface of the track as hot sparks showered their path. He urged them on, adding even more netcores. Every second mattered.

His head ached. So many phantoms. Too many. They picked at the scab of his wounded psyche, vying for control. Cade shook his head. He needed to hold on. It wasn't much farther now.

The wheel slip started getting worse, slowing his progress. The wheels were wearing fast, and they were starting to tear up the track. Cade cursed under his breath. Even at full speed, it was too slow. He closed his eyes. He encoded out through the train. He could feel it, every car, every wall, every rivet. Rooted with the encoding, he became part of the train itself.

Faster. His eyes snapped open as he pulled the engine and its cars off the tracks, eliminating the drag from the tracks. The engine car had grown hot, though Cade could not fathom why. They began picking up speed, and the wind from outside beat against the window on the front of the train until it shattered. Bits of glass shot by and glanced off his face. Unflinching, he bounded forward as Rynth hurtled into view.

Just outside the city's perimeter, Cade saw long trails of railbuses crowding Rynth's central station. Skex were already swarming the area, chasing the citizens of Rynth who hadn't yet taken refuge.

The cars of his train were no longer in a line; instead they swirled behind him as if caught in the grip of a powerful tornado. He didn't turn around to look, but he could feel their movement. Some of cars had started to buckle under the force of the encoding.

The heat in the engine room was nearly unbearable. He felt more and more chipcoins he had connected to slip from his reach. He felt their power leave him, bit by bit, but he was unsure why. It was the end of the line; he would have to leave the train behind to make it to the bank.

He pulled against the train as hard has he could one last time, sending them hurtling into the other railbuses littering the grand station. He severed his encoding and launched himself from the engine car.

The maelstrom of hot steel behind him crashed into the station, sending bits of twisted metal and Skex flying.

45

HOLDING FAST

General Stront, the top general of the Chalician military, had never lost a battle until the One-Month War. When questioned about his earlier victories, he stated, "It is foolishness to start a fight unless you already know what the outcome will be. To do otherwise requires either great foolishness or a lack of any other option."

—From First Contact to First Combat: The One-Month War

"ASHLYN," said Elon. "Ashlyn, we need to keep moving." They both sat in the wake of the battle that had taken place within the bank. Ashlyn, drying her eyes, nodded. She picked up her sister and put her on her wheelchair. She cast one last look at her father before turning and pushing her sister out to the main door of the bank.

They peered out the door and saw even more Skex flooding the streets. Even though the underground access ladder they needed to get back to Jace was just across the street, it may as well have been in another city.

"There's no way we're getting out of here, is there?" Ashlyn asked.

Elon face was grim, and she shook her head.

A bright light flashed, followed by the roar of an explosion. Debris and bits of Skex flew toward the bank, shattering the windows in front as Ashlyn and Elon took cover behind the door.

They looked at each other, dazed, and braved another look out the door. Squinting though the fog of smoke, they made out the outline of a masked young woman armed with an odd-looking weapon. The woman scanned the street, raised her arm, and motioned a group of armed men forward.

"Who is that?" asked Ashlyn.

The woman turned to them and halted. She shouldered her weapon and clapped as she rushed over to the bank's entrance.

"I have no idea," said Elon.

The woman pulled off her mask, revealing long blond hair and striking silver eyes.

"Faye!" Ashlyn exclaimed as she hugged Carlon's agent. "We thought you were dead."

"Going to take more than a few Skex to take me down. Besides, if I get killed by one of those bugs, Carl would never let me let me hear the end of it."

As if on cue, a strange armored cart wheeled down the street. An artifact, not unlike the one Jace had overloaded in the forge, seemed to propel it forward. The main platform of the machine bristled with all manner of mounted weaponry. Manning the barrel of what looked to be a large cannon was none other than General Carlon Stront.

The man smiled broadly and leapt down to them.

"I see we have another recruit," he said as he looked at

Elon, grinning. His smile faded as he turned to Ashlyn. "I hear the underground team didn't make it."

Ashlyn shook her head. "We were too late. I'm sorry."

The large man sighed. "None of this is anyone's fault. All we can do now is stop the bugs and the Acolytes here from taking the city." He looked around. "Where's Cade?"

"He is...was at the Thread. He's on his way."

Carlon frowned. "That would take a day, even by train. And I don't know if you've noticed," he said, gesturing to the dark street, "...but the power has been cut off. No trains are getting here anytime soon."

"He'll be here," Ashlyn said, holding her ground. "We just need to wait a little longer."

More Skex began pouring onto the street before them. The clamor of their claws scraping the gravel streets made Ashlyn's skin crawl. Carlon climbed back atop the armored metal carriage, a chimera of Ancient artifacts, old and new. He barked orders at his men as they loaded another artillery shell into the barrel of the main cannon. "Fire!"

A cluster of Skex scattered from the blast, but they were soon reinforced as more spilled into the street. "We can't hold much longer. There's too many of them. We have to fall back!" Carlon yelled to his fighters.

The Skex swarming their position hesitated, turned, and skittered away.

"What's happening? Are they giving up?" Faye asked, confused.

Ashlyn looked at the retreating Skex. They were headed in the direction of the train station. She held fast to a glimmer of hope.

"He's here."

46

ARRIVAL

Most people don't realize that we're all Bearers. We all bear our own phantom. In Coda, we call that part of yourself the Song. Your Song is your imprint upon the world, familiar yet unique. Its power stretches through the plains of existence, and I believe we are only scratching the surface of its potential.

—Dol Requiem, Grandmaster of Coda

CADE FLEW past the buckling cars of the train. There were still a few chipcoins within his reach. He encoded to the street, pulling himself down fast. He flared tungsten as he crashed down, the stones of the street spraying like shrapnel through the station.

He stood, seeing the bodies of Skex scattered around the impact crater from his landing. The power the chipcoins had lent him was immense and proved difficult for him to control. A sharp pain stabbed at his mind, and he grabbed his head, wincing. *Too many voices. Focus.*

Cade stepped past the cars that had crashed into the

station. They were no longer recognizable; their metal shells had melted like candles. Hot slag still oozed from the edges.

The coins expend heat when they are utilized. If you push them too hard, especially in large quantities, they will overheat, Eos told him.

That explained the escalating heat in the engine room. He was still connected to more than a few surviving chip-coins, though it was a far cry from what he had access to earlier. And once they were clear of the station, the chip-coins that still worked would be of no use. His phantoms remained strong, which gave him some comfort.

Cade, I am sensing a tremendous power fluctuation building near the atmosphere.

"What does that mean, Eos?"

The Wraiths are likely charging their beam cannon from their ship. You are their likely target. I suggest we exit the station.

"Wait, they are firing a weapon at us from *space?*" Cade said as he ran from the station. He could feel his hair stand on end. The rings on his hands began to vibrate.

It would appear that way, yes.

A blast of energy struck the station with overwhelming force, obliterating the entire building. The concussive force of the blast sent Cade skidding across the ground, his metal-encoded skin shooting out sparks. When he turned around, nothing remained but a smoking crater.

"Hells," Cade said.

They won't be able to do it again for a while. It takes time to charge. They will likely send fighter drones in the meantime.

"This just keeps getting better. How far to the bank from here?"

Take the route north from here. It will be at the end of the street.

Cade looked north and saw not a street, but Skex. More than he had ever seen in one place. They rushed like a river through the streets, flooding forward. His heart sank. Chip-coins or no, his odds were not good.

"If you have any ideas on how to get there, now is the time to share."

Eos was silent.

He heard voices. But this time they weren't coming from his mind.

"Is that...singing?"

"Captain Wraithbane he's insane

Captain Wraithbane feels no pain."

Cade saw a flaming barrel arc through the air, detonating upon impact into the encroaching Skex. Cheers erupted behind him.

"He cuts through the Skex—one two three

Leaves 'em dead, now we're free!"

Cade turned to find faces he recognized. The crew of the *Manta*. "Hale?" said Cade in disbelief.

"You'd think we sit by and let Carl have all the fun? I'm cracked, not broken," the lanky captain replied.

Cade grinned. "I need to get to the bank."

"Hardly the time to be managing finances," Hale remarked, signaling for another gunpowder barrel. "But lucky for you, we were already headed that way. We need to join with Carl's main force. Let's go."

They cut through the waves of Skex. Hale's force was small, but many were seasoned veterans. Bearers lined the group, protecting the demolitions team.

Cade tore a Skex's claw off as it swung at his head. He

threw the claw into the next Skex, sending a handful toppling over.

Hale came up from behind and blasted the disoriented group with his blunderbuss. "Is that all ya got, ya filthy bastards?" the man yelled.

A shadow fell over them. In front of them towered not one, but two brigandines.

"Hells, I'm sorry I asked," said Hale.

Cade reached for his casters, when a commotion rose up behind him.

"Captain, they've breached our back line. We're wide open!"

Cade looked down the street. They were so close.

"Cade!" A woman's voice. Ashlyn.

He saw her running toward him, trying to weave her way through the army of Skex.

"Ashlyn—no!"

A Skex swung at her, and her body jerked forward and twisting like a ragdoll.

Cade watched in disbelief as Ashlyn stood, grinning, her face a dark silver. She wound her arm back.

"Cade, *catch!*"

A single chipcoin flew through the air, end over end, toward him. He heard Ashlyn cry out and watched, helpless, as a Skex claw pierced her through the chest.

"*No!*" Cade flared diamond and rushed between the brigandines. He leapt, reaching for the coin as it fell.

He hit the ground. The brigandines turned to face him.

Cade rose, orange light pouring from his fist.

Connection established.

Cade clutched his head with his hands, teeth clenched. He doubled over onto the street. The relentless rush of power overwhelmed him, tore at him, angry for having been awakened. He forced it down and rushed over to Ashlyn, brushing Skex aside like they were toys. She lay on the ground, blood seeping from the wound. He shielded her with his body. The energy in him flared all of his rings simultaneously, causing his body to ripple with waves of metallic color.

Breathing quick, she opened her eyes. "Did you...get it?"

Cade nodded.

She smiled, nodding faintly, and closed her eyes.

"No. No, you can't go," he pleaded. His body continued to ripple through encodings, the frequency increasing, until they blended into a single state. Blasts of energy, razor-sharp claws, and brigandines continued to beat upon him as he crouched over Ashlyn. Rynthium sight overlaid itself upon reality, allowing him to see the Veris and the Firmere at the same time. From Ashlyn's wound, he could see the light within her pouring out in thin wisps.

"No," he whispered, placing his hand over the wound. The wisps paid no heed to the effort and slipped past his fingers as if they did not exist.

Cade, there is nothing you can do. We must go. Eos's voice.

Cade ignored her. What use was seeing the Firmere if he couldn't change it? He looked at the glowing orange coin in his hand, considering.

Cade, Eos pleaded, *don't.*

Cade reached into the expanse of the Firmere. He used his hands, but they weren't his actual hands. They were something more. Something impossible. He reached to Ashlyn, catching the strands of escaping light and pushing them back into her. In the Veris, his eyes began to glow with silver light.

You need to stop. You have too many phantoms. You'll lose control, said Eos, voice concerned.

His hands began to shake, his body convulsed, but he held himself in place. Strands of light escaped from his lips and flowed into Ashlyn. Her wound healed, almost as if the injury was being played back in reverse until it looked as if it never happened. All that remained was a thin silver scar where it had once been.

Ashlyn's eyes snapped open as she awakened, gasping for breath.

She coughed and looked at him, confused. "Cade?"

His body continued to shake, and his face trembled under the strain.

"Run."

Ashlyn's eyes grew wide as she realized they were surrounded by attacking Skex.

"Cade?"

"*Run!*" he screamed through gritted teeth. Blood trickled from his mouth.

Ashlyn, still in shock, was frozen in place.

A brigandine raised its meaty fist up high and brought it crashing down upon Cade.

Cade, who had stood up, grabbed the arm, stopping it in midair. The brigandine, confused, tried to pull it back, but Cade held firm. His eyes were wild, and his body continued to shake from the unseen force.

He glared at the brigandine, growling, and ripped the brigandine's arm from its body. The brigandine fell as black blood, thick as tar, gushed from its shoulder.

How...? Cade started to panic. Just like at the Thread, he had once again become an observer in his own body.

He turned to the other brigandine, who was already preparing its attack. Cade moved first, imperceptibly fast, and struck the brigandine with his fist. He felt the hardened bones of his fist connect with the beast's exoskeleton. The impact of the strike reverberated through its entire skeleton, shattering it from the outside in. The brigandine's eyes dulled, and it crashed to the ground.

Ashlyn, taking advantage of the cleared path, cast one last bewildered and frightened glance at Cade. She could do nothing. She ran back toward Carlon's fighters.

Cade's body started to spasm even more violently than before. "Eos..."

Your phantoms have taken over, said Eos.

"Can't..." When he tried to pull back his reach on the chipcoins, other hands, not his own, just added more. Tremendous power surged through him. He could feel it, but it was disconnected from him; like an echo without sound. The frustration, the hatred, it burned within, though it was not his own.

His phantoms ran wild, and he could do nothing but watch.

INCOMING

Jace collapsed to the floor of the ship as the light from the purple orb extinguished. Cold sweat covered his entire body, and he held a handkerchief up to his nose to wipe the blood that had accumulated.

He had done what he could with his Skex. They were only Skex, but he thought he could feel them in their final moments as they protected his ship. There was so much more to those creatures than he ever knew. He noticed movement on the screen above him.

"What are those?" he said as two bright dots flew by on the large screen on the bridge of the ship. As if in reply, the screen showed a close-up of the dots. "Are those...starships?"

Two incoming Wraith fighters, Eos's projected voice warned from inside the ship.

48

FOREVER

Cade held up a hand, and the Skex that surrounded him hesitated for a moment. The bodies of the Skex appeared to shudder and then move toward him, though they were not advancing under their own power. They were being *pulled* toward him by some unseen force.

The collecting Skex built up momentum and began to fly toward Cade. As the first Skex reached him, his free hand struck out at incredible speed, disintegrating it. He pivoted and spun to kick the next one, sending its lifeless body careening into the distance.

The possessed Cade laughed, eyes wide and hungry, and he shredded the helpless fodder one after another.

Eos's voice cut through the cacophony of the battle. *Cade, you must regain control.*

Cade would have laughed if he could have. What could he do now? Who was he really? For all he knew, maybe this version of him was more Cade than the tired scrap of consciousness from before. Even with the slurry of Nocturne administered back at the Thread still racing through his veins, he wasn't sure.

The questions.

His body looked up as a shiny metal object streaked overhead, and a giant ball of white fire struck him in the chest. He careened through the crush of Skex and slammed into a nearby building.

What is my name?

Cade...Cade something. Hells. He tried to look at the tattoo underneath his arm, but his body continued to ignore him.

His body sprang to its feet. His head flung back and an unnatural howl roared from him. He leapt to the top of the building he had struck, encoding to its steel. He crouched and bounded for the small flying ship that was now streaking toward him.

The ship swerved, and Cade missed it by inches. He fell to the ground and sent a group of Skex scattering like bowling pins. He swung his fists in rage, destroying a corner of the nearby building like it was nothing more than plaster. The man-made building, freed of crucial support, began to crumble and fall, burying Cade in its rubble.

Where was I born?

Names of cities raced through his mind. Kayvant, Toltaire, Grinolt. They all sounded familiar, yet alien. *Are any of these mine?*

Cade's body punched at the wreckage, sending it flying in all directions. He heaved a beam from the building, revealing a woman. Lying amongst the rubble, her eyes were vacant, and the last of her light escaped skyward.

*No...*he wanted to scream, to make it all stop, but he could do nothing. Was this really what he wanted? He didn't remember.

His body once again rocketed backward as white fire engulfed him. He felt a cold rush all around him, swallowing him whole. Everything was dark and silent. His body emerged from a pool of water, and it gasped for air.

What color are my eyes?

His face was reflected in the pool in which he stood. Silver. Silver eyes. Is that right? He couldn't remember.

What is my promise?

Elegy, I need you to encode with me, Eos said, her voice faint among the other voices. *I can help you control the phantoms.*

That name, he thought. *Elegy.* It was important. He reached for it, like a man clinging on to the hope that the next dune would reveal the oasis.

Elegy. A song for the dead.

Fragments of memories flashed by him. Faces and names of phantoms he had borne. All of them had left an impression on him in some way. Pieces of him. That was why he had so much trouble putting himself together. Who he once had been was no longer recognizable to him.

Faces began to surround him. He knew them all. He knew their names, their stories. Etched into him.

Pieces of me. Part of me.

He walked past the people in his mind, the familiar faces. He reached a young boy and a young girl. He knew them from somewhere. He couldn't remember their names, but his heart was filled with an unspeakable joy just by seeing their faces. They each grabbed one of his hands, and the world around him seemed to fade and reconstruct itself. He knew this place.

He recognized the brick pathway leading to the small house. He was just outside the house. The day was sunny and clear. *Home,* he thought. Cade was on one knee, looking into the eyes of his small daughter. Jessa, he remembered. Next to her was his son, Etan. He knew exactly what day it was. The day he left to join the war.

"Daddy, why do you have to leave?" the girl asked.

"There are some bad people out there, sweetheart. I need to help stop them so you'll be safe."

"But why can't someone else do it?"

"If we all let others fight our battles, there would be no one left to fight for us."

She bit her lip and then nodded. "One day, Daddy, I will fight to protect you, too."

He hugged her close. He pulled back and looked at her one last time.

"Daddy...Etan and I are going to help you one last time," the girl said, her voice sad. This was not part of the memory of that day.

Etan walked up and put a hand on his dad's shoulder. "Will you be okay without us?"

"No," was all he could offer.

The girl put her small hand on his cheek. "You can do it, Daddy. We believe in you."

Etan nodded. "And we will never really be far, remember?"

Cade shut his eyes and whispered, "Forever my song will play."

"And with you my heart will stay," his children said.

Time stood still as the Affinity froze time around him. It weakened the control of the phantoms of the Acolytes that had usurped control of his body. He remembered that he needed to encode to Eos. That she could somehow help him keep control.

He tried encoding to Eos. Small bits of crystal shot out from Eos, skittering across the ground. It reminded him of Eos's reaction to the energy beam of the Thread.

That's it, said Eos.

Something deep within him stirred. His skin was a whorled and shifting mixture of tungsten, diamond, aluminum, and lead. The encodings were too strong, and his body was already rigid from the stress of it. He battled against the stalemate with the phantoms, and he felt his hand begin to tremble and then shake as it moved under his command.

He focused everything he could into the control of his arm as he pulled Eos from her sheath. He gripped the shattered edge of the iridescent blade with white knuckles. *Encode*, Cade commanded. He pulled at it with his mind, and larger splinters of crystals grew and fell from Eos. *I need more power*, he thought.

Connection established.

He reached for more chipcoins.

Connection established.

More.

Connection established.

The flying metal object once again appeared on the horizon and hurtled toward him at an alarming speed. He gripped Eos in front of him as a scream, his scream, erupted from his lungs. It echoed through the streets with concussive force, shattering lamps and windows as it swept past.

Encoded to Eos, he felt himself becoming one with the ancient machine. Jets of crystals, like bolts of lightning, shot out from Eos, rooting themselves into the ground around him.

He could not explain what happened to him at that moment. His mind...woke up. Whatever he had been before seemed a cruel joke: clumsy, ignorant, crude. Colors around him grew richer, sounds became clearer, his vision grew sharper.

Cade looked around, awed, as if seeing the world for the first time. Not a single detail escaped him. He knew the Skex before him would step forward with its right claw and attack using its left hand in a sweeping motion. He knew there was a fly two feet from him and that one of its wings was injured. He knew the names of the phantoms that still haunted the world around him. He could feel their sorrow, their loneliness, their longing. He could see even himself with more clarity than he could ever remember.

The questions.

"My name is Cade Elegy."

"I hail from the city of Gallance."

"I was born with brown eyes."

"I sing the songs of the dead."

He did not need to look at his tattoo to know that he was right.

He was in control.

49

LIFT-OFF

Jace sat on the bridge of the ship, or at least the part that he thought was the bridge. Outside, he heard barrages of pulse blasts raining on the ship. He shook his head. He was helpless.

An explosion sounded outside, and he turned to the screen, trying to peer through the billowing cloud of smoke. The door of the ship opened, much to his surprise. *This is it,* he thought. *It's over.*

Elon rolled into view, followed closely behind by Ashlyn, who was coughing. The door shut behind them. Jace could no longer hear the Skex beating upon the hull of the ship.

"How in the...?"

Ashlyn collapsed onto the chair next to Jace. She looked shaken. Her eyes were wide and distant. Neither she nor Elon spoke. Jace looked at the main screen before him that flickered to life. Near the ship, he could see Carlon and his men. "I see you had an escort," he said. But the Skex continued to come, undeterred by the pyrotechnics of Carlon's fighters.

Wraith energy cannon charge detected. Activating primary launch thruster, Eos's voice sounded within the ship.

"Wait, what? We can't leave. We don't have enough power. You said so yourself!"

If we don't leave, we will be disintegrated, replied Eos.

"Yes, but that doesn't solve our power issue. Unless you have a lightning bolt or two you can send our way."

We don't have enough power to exit the atmosphere, but we can remove ourselves as a target for the time being, said Eos. Jace didn't even know why he bothered talking with it. The engine was already spooling up, and he could feel the vessel's hull creak and groan as it freed itself from its long slumber.

"What about those small ships we saw earlier? Are those yours?" asked Jace.

They are Wraith drone ships, Eos answered.

"Wraith ships? What can we do about them? They will shoot us right out of the sky!"

Cade will take care of it, replied Eos.

50

RECHARGE

I'm overloading my power core to assist you, said Eos. Before Cade could question this further, the blade began to shimmer and glow white-hot. He formed an encoding to diamond so he could keep it from burning him. It hummed softly in his hands.

Time to move, Eos. He twisted the blade, shattering the bolts of crystals that had formed around them. He rolled, dodging another ball of fire, and jumped to meet the ship head-on as it flew by him. He wielded the crystal blade in front of him and sheared the ship cleanly in half, laid to waste by the humming blade. Each half skidded and crashed into the building behind him, sending equal parts bricks and fire raining across the street.

I see, Cade thought.

Ninety-five percent power remaining. Eos's voice cut through the chaos around him. The point was taken; he would have to move quickly.

He pushed forward, dodging pulse rifle fire as if the motion had been choreographed. Whatever he saw, he knew. A group of Skex charged him, and he sidestepped their blows, cutting effortlessly through them. Their bodies, still steaming, slid to the ground. He did not try to maintain a safe perimeter around himself. He didn't have to. He knew where every strike would land and played their own attacks off each other.

Sixty-four percent power remaining.

Encoding to Eos, he felt invincible. For the first time since before the Wraiths came, he was not afraid. His fear was what had pushed him into the service and drove him to protect those around him.

Is this how the Wraiths feel? he thought. *Are we just bugs to them, no greater than a Skex?*

Do they fear us? He knew the answer.

Eos's power level was dropping rapidly. Another metal object came hurtling above him, firing off a volley of charged blasts. He encoded to the object, and his body lurched forward, the force of which would have snapped him in half had he not been encoding tungsten.

He hurtled through the sky, and his mind felt clear. He knew what he had to do and how to do it. He struck hard against the small ship, which was no bigger than a railbus car. The vessel dipped low as he stuck to the side. *The buildings.* The ship skimmed the top of the bank, dragging him across the roof, trying to scrape him off. Sparks ricocheted off him as his metal-encoded body started to grow hotter and hotter. He loosened his hand and slid to the rear of the ship, allowing him to grip the rim of what looked to be the engine. The opening glowed with bright yellow light.

He raised Eos in his other hand and severed the engine, sending the ship careening toward the ground. He looked at the fast-approaching ground and could make out Carlon's team fighting the Skex. *Hells.*

Cade repositioned himself to the sleek, pointed nose

cone of the craft and gripped the sides. He felt his feet contact the ground, and he encoded to it, locking himself in place while his hands continued to grip the ship. The metal of the ship groaned and buckled, the abrupt force crumpling it like a tin can.

Fifteen percent power remaining.

He turned to see the astonished faces of Carlon and his team.

"Hell of a way to make an entrance, Elegy," the large man said.

"Where's the ship?" asked Cade.

Carlon pointed skyward.

Cade could feel Eos's power waning, the vibration of the shard diminishing by the second. His hair once again began to stand on end. "Get your men back, now!" Cade yelled as a massive energy beam cut into the opening at the top of the Nexus, sending the opened bay doors crashing down to the ground around them.

Cade dodged a piece of debris and took off for the small starship. He rocketed through the sky, using an encoding to the ship to propel him through the clouds.

Cade managed to grab hold near the rear of the ship, crashing against the superheated metal. *The panel,* Eos's voice instructed.

Connection lost, a monotone voice informed him.

I must be too far from the chipcoins, he thought.

The panel, Eos instructed. He glanced at Eos and saw the light of the makeshift sword was weak. He felt his gut lurch, and his gaze snapped to the ground below. The ship, which had been thrusting toward space only moments before, began to fall.

Cade tore off the panel Eos had indicated. At least he hoped it was the right panel. The interior of the opened compartment contained clusters of black, segmented cells inside, separated by silver bars.

He stared at the components. Eos said he needed to charge the ship. The ship continued to fall, the wind rushing past him, threatening to pull him free. Even though he was trying not to, he looked down. Cade felt the knot in his stomach tighten. He fought the urge to throw up. *Focus, dammit*, he told himself.

He grabbed one of the vertical bars between the cells and pulled on it. It did not budge. Cade closed his eyes and reached into the Firmere, scrambling for anything that could help him. Nothing in the barren expanse made itself known to him. The ship continued is rapid descent to the city.

One percent power remaining.

Eos, I can't reach the chipcoins. They are too far away. Cade felt the power from Eos give out and a wave of force radiated from the shard, like the ripples from a rock thrown into an ethereal pond.

The world became dull as he felt Eos's power drain from him. Even with the roar of the wind and sensation of flying through the sky, everything felt...dim, drained of life. The pain in his head returned, threatening to split and fracture as the phantoms gnawed at the periphery of his mind. He managed to stay in control, hands steady.

He held on, frantic and searching, until he noticed a faint mote of light in the Firmere come into view and become larger as the ship fell. A coin, somewhere on the ground below. Eos had managed to amplify the connection range with the last of her power. The orange light became clearer, and he grasped it within the Firmere and held it tight.

Connection established.

The familiar rush of power surged through him as the network of coins linked together under his command. He opened his eyes and could see the energy of the coins being absorbed by the bar he held within his hand. He grabbed another bar and encoded to them. Electrical energy arced through him, flowing into the cells of the ship.

The repulsion of the powerful electric force threatened to throw him from the ship, but he held, reaching for all the chipcoins Ashlyn had placed for him to the bank's vault. Almost as fast as he could grab more connections, others left, reduced to slag from overload.

Every muscle in his body contracted as the energy filled the power cell. The phantoms within him grew quiet, their voices hardly a whisper now. *Just a bit longer...*

51

INTRUDER

"Eos, talk to me!" Jace sat at the control panel, feeling helpless. Eos had been able to assume remote access earlier but had fallen silent. And now they just sat there while the ship fell from the sky. None of the systems were responding. Only a few lights remained, red ones, which blinked menacingly at them.

"I wish Cade were here," he said, fighting the instinct to panic. Even though he knew it would not do him much good, he stayed strapped into his seat.

Ashlyn, who hadn't said a word the entire time, spoke. "He is here. I...I can feel him."

Jace bit his tongue. He did not press her. *Poor girl*, he thought. Unless Cade had sprouted wings, there was no way he was on the ship.

The city came into full view on the screen in front of them. It was getting larger, fast. Only seconds now. Were they foolish to think this would work? Who were they to challenge gods that could travel the stars as easily as one would take a carriage to town? *At least I'll die knowing I tried*, he thought. He glanced over at Elon, who held her sister's hand, eyes closed.

Jace kept his eyes open as the ground rose to meet them. "C'mon, *Exilia*, you can do it, girl."

Auxiliary power charge nominal, a voice said as the ship's systems sprang to life. Lights rippled on throughout the ship, different screens reporting status and beeping information.

The ship lurched and rocketed skyward, pinning him down. Jace gripped his seat, eyes wide with alarm. His stomach felt like it was in his feet, but he was too scared to be sick. The sky flew past them: first the clouds, then the atmosphere, and finally the blackness of space enveloped them. Almost as abruptly as it occurred, the force pinning him abated.

Gravity force normalization complete. All systems check. Estimated arrival to target in twenty minutes, Eos informed them.

Jace looked out the window in awe at the planet that lay below them. He glanced at Ashlyn and Elon, who were buckled into the seats next to him. They seemed not to notice they were the first Chalicians in space. Whatever had happened at the bank had taken its toll.

A red light flashed on the panels in the bridge. *Threat detected. Foreign entity attempting access.*

Jace turned back to the screen in front of him. "A *what?*"

Entity identified. Male human. Clothing indicates Wraith Acolyte. Attempting entry through service entrance five.

"Well, don't let it him in!"

Intruder has forced open entrance five.

"Don't we have weapons on this thing? Shoot him!"

This is a waste disposal vessel. It has no active weaponry, said Eos.

Jace buried his face in his palm. "Perfect. I finally get a starship, and it's a flying garbage can."

Elon cut in. "Can we lock him into a room?"

I am trying. He is a Bearer, stronger than a normal one. He is forcing open the secured doors.

Jace had expected Skex, but he would have never imagined they'd have to contend with Acolytes. "Eos, where is..."

Intruder forced entry to main concourse. Estimated arrival to bridge in one minute. Preparation for combat recommended.

Jace turned to Ashlyn, her expression calm. She placed her hands on her knees, stood, and lifted her head up high. "Let him come." Elon, solemn, nodded and pivoted her wheelchair toward the door.

The door shuddered as something slammed into it with tremendous force. The intruder forced his hands though the crack between the doors. He pried them open as if they were nothing more than sheets of paper. Jace could hear the mechanics behind the door whir and grind in protest before falling silent.

The intruder stood, surveying them. Ashlyn gasped when she saw the man and took a step back.

52

FREEDOM

Cade still felt light-headed as he sprinted through the main concourse of the ship, but it was no time to rest. He saw a tall man in the doorway in front of him. He wasn't too late.

The man who had killed his brother stood before him.

"Your fight is with me, Acolyte."

The man turned around, glaring at him. His eyes were wild and hungry. He wore a twisted smile, the same one Cade had seen at the Taction. His movement seemed unnaturally controlled and calculated. Cade could tell this Acolyte was different from the others he had faced in the Thread. Where the eyes of the Acolytes at the Thread were blank and distant, this man's eyes were present and filled with blind rage. Meeting Cade's gaze, his eyes glimmered.

"For my brother." Cade leveled Justice at the man and pulled the trigger.

The dummy shell missed as the man dodged by, encoding to the side of the wall. Cade cursed, wishing he had his imprinted caster shells.

The Acolyte moved fast, faster than he should have been able to. He encoded his fist and swung it at Cade's head. Cade managed to deflect the blow before it contacted but dropped his caster.

"I can help you," he told the Acolyte.

The man ignored him and followed through with another punch. Cade ducked underneath it and rolled to the side. Again, the man moved with unexpected speed, not allowing Cade a moment's respite. The man raised his fist and to Cade's surprise stopped.

"Lies. No one can help me."

"I can. And you can help us. We can get back at them. You can get your revenge; pay them back for what they did to you."

The man stood silent for a moment. He shook his head. "I do not want revenge."

Before Cade could react, the man grabbed him by the neck and lifted him off the ground. "They were wrong about you, Protector. You are not strong. You are like the rest." The man held him there for a moment, and Cade could hear the man's teeth grinding back and forth as Cade's legs struggled to find purchase.

The Acolyte seethed as his face twisted into a sneer, the perverse glee having faded away. "*Why are you not strong?*"

Elon tried to pick up Cade's caster but was no match for the battle-tempered skills of the Acolyte. Even with his focus on Cade, the man batted Elon away as if she were nothing more than a small child. Good as the Acolyte was, however, he didn't see Ashlyn attacking from the other side. Ashlyn's blow landed true, and she brushed up next to Cade and managed to break the man's grip. The man, angrier now, swatted her across the room.

Cade felt a weight in his pocket he hadn't noticed before. He cast his eyes downward and noticed the largest diamond he'd ever seen within it. *Clever.*

The man recovered and lifted Cade back off the ground. Cade's vision began to blur. His phantoms were weak; he'd have only one shot. The lights of the ship reflected off the Acolyte's hands. The man, in his zeal, had overencoded his hands into solid metal.

Cade didn't waste another moment. He grabbed the Acolyte's neck with both hands, strangling him, and encoded as hard as he could with the diamond in his pocket. The Acolyte encoded tungsten to counteract the move. Cade had, however, overencoded his own hands with diamond, forcing the Acolyte to counter in kind. The Acolyte's arms dropped to his sides, limp, and he collapsed to the floor.

Cade fell to the ground, coughing and gasping for air. He sat up and looked over at the fallen Acolyte. The man's head was a statue of tungsten, the expression fixed forever upon his face. The expression was not one of anger or hatred, as he would have expected. Instead the man's expression was calm, his eyes soft, and Cade could swear there was the hint of a smile upon his lips.

53

HOPE

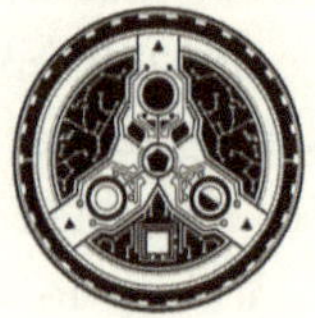

Once you've heard someone's Song, it is difficult not to love them.
—*From* The Book of the Traveler

CADE LOOKED down at his hands. They were now solid diamond and useless. The others stayed silent, too shocked to speak.

He moved his arms up and down. It felt strange to him, because he could still *feel* his hands. Coda masters he had trained with taught him about this. Once overencoded, a limb would feel as if it was still there, like a ghost. The sensation, he was told, never quite went away.

But the Acolyte...he could do it at will, he thought.

He tried opening and closing one of them, but it felt like it was trapped in hardened cement. He turned his hands over, trying to see if anything had changed. He looked at them, thoughtful.

Ashlyn walked up to him, expression somber, and rested an arm on his shoulder. "Cade..."

Eos broke the silence. *Based on my telemetry, the Wraith cannon will be charged in another five minutes. Once they detect our presence, we are the next likely target. We will need to strike first.*

"All right, to the loading bay," urged Jace.

Cade, who had been staring at his hands, turned his gaze to the fallen Acolyte. "Please give me a moment."

Jace looked at him, brow furrowed.

Cade faced the Acolyte. "Song that lingers unfinished..."

"No, no, no. Cade, he was a madman, he doesn't deserve—"

"The one whose Sigh has escaped to the stars," Cade continued. He could already feel the energy of the phantom gather around him as he spoke the words.

Jace just shook his head.

"Allow me to sing your final verse." Cade looked up at Jace. "I will be the hope for those who have none," he said, remembering his promise. "Let's get to the bay."

JACE CURSED. "What do you mean we have no way to fire it?" he said, shaking his head.

This ship is not equipped to launch ordnance of any kind, it is...

"...a garbage can, I heard," said Jace, frowning.

"Eos, can we ram the laboratory with the ship?" asked Ashlyn. The group stared at her.

The vessel possesses insufficient velocity to escape their passive protection systems, Eos replied.

"Eos, you wouldn't have brought us this far if there wasn't a way for us to use this bomb," said Elon.

Cade spoke. "You're right, she wouldn't. There is one way."

He walked over to the bomb. "I can use a phantom to propel it to their station."

"But..." Ashlyn protested. "Your arms..."

"I'll be fine," Cade cut in. "Just tell me how to activate it and point me in the right direction. I'll detach myself once it is on course."

The screens in the loading bay came to life, showing the picture of a large, almost spherical structure floating in space. *The Wraith ship is almost within sensor range,* Eos interjected. *The Ascension Drive is located on the bottom hemisphere of the ship. I would recommend piloting the bomb toward that side of the station to achieve the maximum effect, since it is very likely more Wraiths will be congregated there, trying to reactivate the drive.*

"Understood," acknowledged Cade.

"There has to be another way," pleaded Ashlyn.

"We're out of time, Princess." Cade lifted his arm to put it on her shoulder, forgetting for a moment it had turned to diamond. She brushed it aside and moved in to hug him.

"Damn you, Cade Elegy," she said, tears rolling down her face.

He laughed. "I get that a lot." He hugged her back. He hadn't done that to anyone since...since he had left for the war. It felt good.

"He does," Jace offered. "It's a wonder he has any friends at all."

Cade broke the embrace, and Jace put his hand on Cade's shoulder. "Good luck, old friend. See you soon."

"Luck is for archaeologists. I'll be back before you know it."

Elon, turned to him. "You are truly worthy of the title of

Protector," she said. "May the phantoms you watch over watch over you as well."

"Thank you, Princess."

With that, Eos had everyone but Cade evacuate the bay. Eos instructed Cade on the operation of a suit and helmet, which would allow him to survive the exposure to space for a time. With the available cords he found in the bay, he secured himself to the bomb. He didn't have enough energy to double encode, so he had to make sure he wasn't going anywhere.

He chuckled.

This seems an inappropriate time to be laughing, said Eos.

"It's been a long day." He took a deep breath. "Goodbye, Eos."

Goodbye, Protector.

The bay doors opened, and tethered to the missile, he became weightless. It was an odd sensation. He felt like he should be falling, but instead he just floated there, suspended by an unseen force.

Eos had oriented the ship so Cade could see the station. Up and down had little meaning, suspended like this. He reached, activating the chipcoins he had collected from his friends. He encoded to the point Eos had indicated earlier, where the Ascension Drive was located. With little effort, he was moving.

He had lied to them. He would not make it back. He would be lucky if he could make it to the station.

Eos had known. She knew all along. *Expendability,* she had once said. One of the criteria for selection. Someone who had nothing to lose.

He pulled harder toward the point. The impact would trigger the caster firing pin and set off the explosives in the warhead, Jace had told him. He wished he knew the names of those who had imprinted themselves upon the caster shells. He spoke a word of thanks to the unknown warriors as they traveled through space. It would have to do.

Eos's voice sounded from inside the helmet. *Right on target. One minute to touchdown.*

They were moving fast now with no air to slow the gathering momentum. He unbuckled the strap that held him in place, broke the encoding to counter his own momentum, and let the bomb carry itself the rest of the way. It was the last thing he would ever see, and he would have a front-row seat.

He noticed something break away from the other hemisphere of the Wraith ship. More fighter drones, he thought. They rocketed past him and toward the *Exilia*, unaware of the bomb now hurtling toward the lower hemisphere of the Wraith ship.

Cade watched as the bomb touched down, and an explosion tore through the large ship. It triggered a chain reaction of explosions that bubbled throughout the structure, until the entire ship shook and erupted, casting pieces of itself throughout the vastness of space.

It was one of the most beautiful things he had ever seen.

He felt his phantoms, the unwilling Acolytes, leave him, their purpose fulfilled.

And for the first time since before the Wraith War, he was completely alone.

"I'm coming home, Serafina."

A warning of flashing yellow popped up on the display in his helmet. Low oxygen. Not much longer now.

He floated there in silence for what felt like an eternity. Moments of his life, the ones that really mattered, pushed their way to the surface of his mind. The day he made his

Promise. The day he met Serafina. The birth of Etan. The birth of Jessa. The days they took their first steps. The sound of their laughter as he chased them around the house.

Music started to play...or had it been there all along? He listened and heard not one Song, but many, thousands upon thousands, though it was not a cacophony of ill-fitting arrangements. They were woven together, an ornate tapestry of instruments. Listening carefully, in the vacuum of space, he recognized it as the "Lament of the Traveler." Not just one part, but the full orchestra, as it was meant to be played.

The alert was red now, but his eyes couldn't focus enough to read it. No matter. He closed them, straining to hear the last strands of music that played within him. The music was so familiar, it made his heart ache. "Serafina?" He felt a presence, but he couldn't be sure if he was delirious or not.

"Song...that lingers..." was all he managed with his last breath.

In the darkness, as he drifted off, he heard a faint voice pierce the veil of the Firmere.

"Pact accepted."

UNFINISHED SONG

Cade rolled over in bed. Lifting heavy eyelids, he noticed Serafina looking at him. He smiled. "Are you watching me sleep?"

"Maybe," she said, grinning.

"Creepy," he said, rubbing his eyes. He looked at her. "I missed you so much."

She brushed her hand across his cheek. "Ditto."

He laughed. "I love it when you get all romantic."

"Says the man who punches things for a living."

He ran his hand through her light brown hair. "How are the kids? I should go check on them."

"You're always worrying over everyone else. Who worries after you?"

"I believe that's your job."

She giggled. "Someone has to do it."

He yawned. "I'm so tired."

"It's time to go back to sleep, my love."

"Do I have to?"

She nodded. "Your Song isn't finished yet," she said and kissed him on the cheek.

His eyes became heavy, and he drifted off to sleep.

CADE BLINKED AND SQUINTED, trying to adjust to the light above him. Figures hovered over him, voices muffled. His eyes focused, and he saw he was back on the ship. Ashlyn was leaning over him, a look of grave concern etched upon her face.

"He's coming to!" she said.

Jace came into focus above him. "Hells, Cade, you had us really worried there. We didn't think you were coming back when you stopped moving. Then you just took off like a bullet toward the ship. When we grabbed you, you were unconscious."

Cade sat up, rubbing his eyes. They still hurt.

"Wait. Cade...your arms..." Jace said, eyes wide and tone incredulous. Cade looked at his hands. They were no longer diamond. He opened and closed them. He shook his head, confused.

Cade recalled the memory from Gigan's Hill. His commander had taken over Cade's body after Cade fell unconscious. *Did Serafina...?* he wondered.

Ashlyn leaned over Cade, searching his eyes. "Don't ever scare me like that again, okay?"

"Don't worry—" he started when she leaned in closer and kissed him. To his surprise, he did not pull away. He felt free, almost weightless now. He let her lips linger on his own and surprised himself by pulling her closer.

Eos's voice sounded over the ship's speaker. *Target confirmed destroyed. The Ascension Drive has been neutralized.*

Ashlyn stood up, blushing. "Sorry. I...thank you. For earlier," she said, and turned to the screen.

The main display showed the remains of the station, which was now nothing more than a field of floating debris.

Something flickered in the distance. "What's that?" asked Cade as he got to his feet.

A projection of light from the debris of the station flickered and died. Soon, a point just beyond the projection began to ignite and shimmer. Other points shimmered, like lit paper burning away to ash. The effect gathered momentum and spread quickly, cascading through space.

Ashlyn gasped. "Stars!"

She was right. Cade saw countless points of light blink into view, the cosmos once again laid bare. No more starless nights would haunt him. He stood in awe, watching as the sea of infinite possibilities spread before him.

Father. Husband. Brother. Friend.

He smiled.

One more day.

"You want to go to Jenava? What're you, one of those religious tourist types? Tryin' to catch a glimpse of where it all started?" The old sailor chuckled and waved Cade on board without even waiting for a reply.

Cade went below deck and found an unoccupied bunk aboard the transport ship. The bed reeked of mildew but looked serviceable enough. It would have to do. Most vessels out of Ceywind didn't make trips out to Jenava, so one couldn't be too choosy. The country was mocked by other nations as a place untouched by time, not to mention any other type of advancement. The people were regarded as only a small step above savages.

Cade unshouldered his pack and pulled out a hand-sketched map Jace had helped make. It illustrated the major geographic features of Jenava, but what Cade cared about most was a place called Selar, the home of the oldest known civilization. All other civilizations could be traced back to it.

Jace had pointed out to Cade that it wasn't always called Selar. Once upon a time it had been called Seraphar, which roughly translated to "The City of the Seraph."

Cade folded the map, tucked it into his pocket, and lay upon the threadbare sheets of the thin mattress. He wished he still had Eos. She had deactivated after they defeated the Wraiths. But he knew she had kept information from him. She had always been careful not to reveal too much. The Wraiths knew something about them, about the true purpose of the Thread and the Ancients. He had to learn more. He couldn't help but think one day the Wraiths, or something even worse, would come.

But next time he would be ready.

Thank you so much for taking the time to read my book. Please consider leaving a review wherever you bought the book, or tell your friends about it to help me spread the word.

To receive special updates and content, including ***The Makers of Music,* a free exclusive interactive adventure** which blends the real world with the world of *Phantom Pact*, sign up for our newsletters at:

chadqueen.com/newsletter

Or visit me online at:

chadqueen.com

Chad Queen lives in Washington State with his wife and two children and has been a video game developer for over twenty years. He has worked on role-playing games like Dungeon Siege and real-time strategy games like Supreme Commander and Age of Empires Online. Phantom Pact: The Bearer's Burden is his first book.

For behind-the-scenes information on upcoming work and to play an exclusive alternate reality game (ARG) that incorporates the world of Phantom Pact, please visit chadqueen.com/newsletter and sign up for our newsletter.

9 780999 847435